SEVEN
BLACK
DIAMONDS

SEVEN
BLACK
DIAMONDS

melissa marr

HARPER
An Imprint of HarperCollinsPublishers

Library of Congress Control Number: 2015940707
ISBN 978-0-06-201117-6

Typography by Jenna Stempel
15 16 17 18 19   PC/RRDH   10 9 8 7 6 5 4 3 2 1

First Edition

To Asia, my beloved daughter *and* absolute dearest friend in the universe, who gave me harsh, frequent, and brilliant notes on more drafts than either of us should count—all while working an archaeological dig in Scotland, finishing university, and getting into multiple top-tier PhD programs. You are a total badass woman and an inspiration.

A dead baby. A score of slaughtered sailors. The truth of what started the war was a matter of which side you were on and how you spun the story. In her grief, the queen wept seven tears into the sea, one for each of her brightest diamonds, and then she waited.

—Iana Abernathy, The Cost of Secrets

one

EILIDH

"You were created to serve." The Queen of Blood and Rage sat on a throne inside her small throne room. The throne in this room was nothing more than wood and vine. It flowered at her will, but the blooms were absent today. The queen herself needed no ornamentation to evoke terror. Her eyes did that without any seeming effort from her. Today, she was worse than usual as she'd been preparing to spar when the Sleepers were brought before her. Her hair was bound back in a tight braid. Her hands were gloved, and she wore armor the color of battle-blackened blood.

Behind her on the wall were an assortment of sharpened blades, swords as well as axes and daggers. In front of her, kneeling on the bone-white floor, were five of her Sleepers, half-fae, half-humans who were created to serve as soldiers in her war on humanity. At the queen's either side were her two living children, her Unseelie son Rhys and Eilidh, the queen's daughter with the king of Seelie Court.

No one else was in the room. The usually crowded chamber seemed almost cavernous with so few people present. Unlike many meetings, this one was secret. Neither of the courts knew of the queen's Sleepers.

Eilidh wished she didn't know either—especially when the girl kneeling in front of her mother said, "I'm not a murderer."

"Truly," the queen murmured.

Anyone who lived in the Hidden Lands would recognize *that* tone. Eilidh suppressed a wince. She was the queen's heir, and whether or not she wanted to be the next in line to the Hidden Throne, Eilidh had a duty. She would stand in this small room with her mother and brother. She would witness the proceedings with an emotionless mien.

"I understand that we were born to serve your cause," the girl said. "We *all* do."

The five Sleepers behind her said nothing.

"We will *not* kill for you though," the girl said. She was still on her knees, but her voice was strong, echoing slightly in the queen's private throne room, despite the obvious danger in disobeying the Queen of Blood and Rage. The other five Sleepers remained silent. At least one of them looked as foolishly brave as this half-fae girl who was facing the queen.

Their silence condemned them.

Endellion ruled both the Seelie and Unseelie Courts,

and even those fae-blood who lived outside the Hidden Lands. Possession of *any* fae blood was enough to be declared her subject—by decree of both fae and human law.

"Stand," the queen commanded.

"You need to understand . . . I was *raised* as a human. We all were. You can't expect us just to *murder* them. It's—"

"Them or us." The queen spoke over her as she descended from her throne.

"I'm *both*," the girl argued as she came to her feet. "My mother is human. There is no them or us for the Sleepers. Can't you see that?"

The queen glanced at Rhys, her gaze conveying the order.

When Rhys walked toward the girl, Eilidh stayed beside the queen's throne. Protocol was a part of life in the Hidden Lands, even in the tiny private room where there would be no living witnesses beyond the royal family. Eilidh's role as heir was to observe the proceedings, to learn, to see what a queen must do for her subjects.

The girl stood, but she did not move.

Rhys could've made her. He was the queen's most trusted guard and truest servant. If the queen wanted him to move the young half-fae, half-human girl, he would do so, but the queen held up her hand.

She stepped down and walked over to face the girl. "Do you speak for your whole team?"

Eilidh wanted to tell the girl, to tell *all* of them, to stop what was about to happen. Instead, she forced herself to watch, knowing that these moments were what defined a future queen. She didn't ever want to take the Hidden Throne, but as she had so many times already, Eilidh swore to herself that she would be a different sort of ruler than her mother.

The girl lifted her head to meet the queen's eyes. "I do. We are a unit, but not the terrorists you've tried to make us become."

None of the other five people dissented when the queen's gaze drifted over them. "So you all choose to be human rather than fae? So be it."

In the next moment, a scream began and ended. One of the queen's various blades sliced across the girl's throat. Between one breath and the next, she was dead.

Eilidh didn't let her wince show on her face. Showing her feelings was not something she was allowed to do, even when the witnesses would be soon dead. Weakness wasn't ever acceptable.

Looking up from the body at her feet, the queen ordered, "Mind Eilidh's safety."

Rhys stepped closer to the heir of the Hidden Throne, as their mother glanced at the rest of the group.

In mere minutes, they were dead. They stood no chance against the queen. She had held the Unseelie throne for centuries and had bloodied her blade with every fighter who came close to being her equal. Even the Seelie King himself wasn't so foolish as to raise a blade to her. Centuries ago, when she'd walked into his court, dripping with the blood of his best fighters, and had announced that they would mate and unify their courts, he simply acquiesced.

Standing in the room with her children, the floor strewn with bodies, Endellion sighed. "I need to speak to the other handlers. Most of the Sleeper cells are not performing as they need to be." Her longsword was pointed at the floor; blood dripped from the fae-wrought steel to the stone floor. The queen herself wasn't even winded. She sighed and said, "My *jewels* are the only Sleepers that haven't needed to be eliminated . . . yet."

"Why?" Eilidh asked before she could stop herself.

Her mother smiled. "Because they were created with a different level of attention."

Eilidh had questions, but she didn't bother asking. The queen shared only what she thought necessary. That was the privilege of ruling. Eilidh bowed her head and held her silence.

Rhys drew their mother's attention then. "Shall I clean this or do you still want to spar?"

Endellion looked briefly at him and then back to her heir. "Eilidh will tend to this. You will spar with me. Come."

And then she walked away with no other word, leaving Eilidh with five dead bodies.

two

LILY

"You need to stop hiding and go downstairs." Shayla stood in the doorway to Lily's bedroom. Her long graying hair fell neatly over her shoulders instead of being bound into some kind of twist or held captive under one of her innumerable scarves. An elegant dress, no doubt by a runway designer, made her look like the lady of the house rather than Lily's caretaker, assistant, governess, whatever-her-title-was-now.

"I know. I just don't *want* to. Daidí knows I don't like parties."

Shayla's entire attitude switched from sweet to stern. "You're being *honored*. Act like it."

Lily couldn't meet Shayla's eyes.

"You will put a smile on that pretty little face of yours and march yourself down there," Shayla continued. "You'll go thank your father for the party, and you'll smile at the guests, and make a point to say hello to that Morris boy that's going to sing."

Despite herself, Lily smiled. Creed Morrison was in every tabloid, toured worldwide, and was even in a movie. As if being a rock star wasn't enough, he had to add acting. He had been her fantasy since she'd seen her first photo of him—and now he was here in her home.

"Morrison," she said. "His name is *Creed Morrison*, Shayla."

Shayla waved her hand dismissively. "Whatever. Creed. Morris. Unless he is in one of those musicals your father gets me tickets to see, I don't care." She came over to stand in front of Lily and fussed with her hair, pulling at the curls, unpinning and re-pinning it in several places as she spoke. "What matters, Lilywhite, is that Nicolas brought the boy here to sing for *you*. So go be charming."

"Yes, ma'am." Lily leaned in and kissed Shayla's cheek before heading toward the door. Once she was sure she was out of reach, she teased, "Maybe you ought to come down too and check on Daidí. Make sure he's not under siege from one of the fripperies."

"Your father can handle himself just fine with those girls," Shayla said.

"Come on. For me?"

"Hmph." Shayla didn't bother arguing further. She went on in front of Lily, effectively buying her a few minutes of peace.

Shayla was the closest thing to a mother that Lily had.

Shayla and Daidí both swore that there was nothing romantic between them, but Lily kept hoping. Her mother had been gone for twelve years, and Shayla had filled her vacant place. They certainly functioned like a family. Shayla raised Lily when Daidí was off on business trips, and she looked after both of them when he was home.

Slowly, Lily walked through the hall, hating that she had to wear shoes, even though the tiny sandals were nothing more than a few strips of leather. She'd learned to tolerate shoes, but heels still made her feel wrong. Feet were meant to touch the earth, the floor, the sea. They weren't to be locked away in prisons of leather or fabric. Sandals were the closest to normal that Lily had found, and tonight—surrounded by people—she needed the comfort of nearly bare feet.

At the top of the great staircase, just out of sight, Lily paused to smooth down the skirt of the dress she'd been given to wear. It wasn't as fancy as Shayla would like, but the pale-green dress made especially for her was as flattering as any dress could be. An asymmetrical neckline and fitted bodice topped a skirt made up of layers of some sort of delicate material. Tiny stones sewn into the layers caught the light and shimmered as she moved. Lily didn't have the heart to ask if they were real gems or not. It was easier to avoid an argument if she didn't know. She'd already lost the fights about her bracelets. Obscenely expensive diamonds and emeralds dangled from her wrists and ears.

The short blade that Lily had sheathed in a hand-sewn

leather holster under her ephemeral dress was real too though. Its weight made her feel secure despite the glittering facade. Lilywhite's blade was a double-edged dagger that had been handcrafted for her. She wasn't eager to use it, preferring the tidiness of her longer blades, but she could never be truly unarmed.

For all of her father's protections, he'd also taught her that she was ultimately responsible for her own safety. The party was at her home, and the guests had all entered through a metal detector *and* been patted down, but she was the daughter of the head of one of the most successful criminal organizations in the world. That meant that, even here, she was armed.

Lily rounded the corner and started down the stairs. Her father looked up at her, and the pride in his face made her feel guilty for delaying. He smiled at her, and she knew that she'd been wrong to stall. Mingling at the over-the-top birthday party that Daidí insisted on this year was a little bit beyond terrifying, but he wanted to celebrate her birthday, so celebrate they would. These events layered civility and elegance onto their often violent world, and Lily knew well that the layer of softness was important—not just for how others saw the underworld, but for how the demimonde saw itself.

As she walked down the stairs, she could hear soft music in the ballroom. Soon, Creed Morrison would sing, but right now, a chamber orchestra played classical music that wove around the spaces between conversations. Servers circulated with finger foods and drinks. Usually, Lily stayed at her father's side when she had to attend these sorts of things. Tonight, though, Daidí insisted that she talk to people her own age—other than just her friend Erik.

Erik was there, of course, but for Lily's seventeenth birthday celebration, Daidí had invited all of his associates' children, and he'd hired her favorite singer. It was perfect on paper, but Lily didn't mingle with people her own age. She could escort Daidí to parties, play hostess of the manor as needed, make small talk with the leaders of the underworld, but around other teenagers—even those groomed in the odd etiquette of their society—she felt awkward.

And Creed Morrison? How, or even *why*, her father hired him for her birthday party was a mystery. He was only a year older than her, but he was already an international phenomenon. If he wanted to, Creed could have dropped out of school entirely. He'd never need the things that were taught in the classroom—any more than she would. Her curriculum consisted of drug routes, interrogation methods, and old family hierarchies.

Those lessons left her ill equipped for casual conversations, but they would be essential if she took over the family business. The social part didn't come naturally to her. It never had, but she'd never be much of an asset to Daidí if she couldn't handle her peers.

Smile firmly affixed, she descended the stairs until she reached the landing. Daidí stayed where he was, talking to one of the growers from the South Continent. As she walked through the black-tie crowd, Daidí's associates smiled and wished her a happy birthday. Their children were a little less practiced in their false magnanimity, but they were far more polished than they'd been the last time Daidí had to insist on their socializing. Being Nicolas Abernathy's heir apparent *and a daughter* meant that people her own age weren't sure what to do with her.

Several boys nodded at her. The girls, however, kept their eyes carefully averted. Lily wasn't like them. She wasn't a bartering chip that would be used to strengthen ties to other organizations, nor was she sheltered from the ugliness of her father's job. The boys acknowledged her, even though they weren't sure if they should approach her as a potential date or as a future colleague. The one exception was her friend Erik. They'd shared a few kisses now and again, but under threat of retribution if any word of it was spoken.

Daidí knew, of course, as did Shayla, but they also understood that Erik didn't occupy her heart. Instead, she fantasized about Creed Morrison and Zephyr Waters— celebrity darlings she suspected of sharing her same hidden, and illegal, heritage. She'd studied them in the magazines, but she'd had no intention of ever meeting them. That was part of their appeal. Having one of *them* here was not something she knew how to address.

Daidí didn't mean to upset me. As she did with everything confusing in life, Lily thought through the Abernathy Commandments until she found her answer: *Commandment*

#9: Be kind to those who deserve it. Her father deserved her kindness.

As she walked toward her father, her step was measured, and her smile was convincing. She might be filled with anxiety, but no one would know.

The crowd was manageable. Everything was okay. She could succeed at this if she thought of it like a regular business gathering.

She straightened her shoulders and sailed through the crowd—until Creed Morrison stepped into her path, stopping her advance, leaving her uneasy in a way no one ever had.

Creed had the beautiful dark complexion of the Seelie fae. The fae long thought to be both *kinder* and *better* were those whose skin was sun-burnished. Creed's skin had the telltale signs of fae heritage, but Creed's human father was African American, so Creed had a human excuse he could use to explain his Seelie-dark skin. Lily shared his heritage, but she'd inherited her father's pale skin instead of her mother's dark skin. Not all of the fae-blood were able to pass as human, not like Lily was.

"Lilywhite," he said. She'd heard his speaking voice, listened to interviews for hours actually, but hearing her name from his lips made her unable to reply.

She nodded. *Abernathy Commandment #2: Be yourself.*

"I looked for you before the crowd arrived," he said, as if they were friends.

In the tuxedo- and gown-filled room, Creed's jeans,

T-shirt, and boots were very out of place. The art etched on his skin stood out, more because it was visible than because it existed. He was far from the only person in the room with tattoos, but his weren't hidden under sleeves or jackets. Creed Morrison demanded attention. It was a well-documented—and oft-photographed—fact. She'd read every article on him, clipped pictures from magazines and filed them away. It wasn't an obsession; actually *speaking* to him was the last thing she wanted. She had suspected that he was fae-blood and wanted to understand how other fae-bloods lived. Now, seeing him in person for the first time, she *knew*. Now, he was here, and he was *exactly* what she suspected—and she wanted to flee.

She fidgeted with one of her bracelets, twisting it around her wrist, staring at the glittering green stones. "Had you needed something, Mr. Morrison?"

"Creed," he stressed.

"Creed," she repeated quietly.

He smiled and said, "I wanted to wish you happy birthday before I sing."

Again, she nodded. This time, though, she looked up—and wished she hadn't.

Creed was watching her with an utterly inappropriate intensity. If her father saw, he'd toss Creed out the door, despite the obscene sum he'd probably paid for his presence. Lily felt like her skin was electrified everywhere his gaze fell. She'd felt a tingle of recognition a few times when she'd seen other fae-bloods, but not like this.

Nothing had ever felt like this.

"I didn't know you did these sort of things," she finally managed to say.

"Talk to beautiful girls at parties?"

"No. Sing for hire at parties," she corrected him.

"I don't." He smiled, and she wondered how anyone ever thought he was anything other than fae-blood. He radiated energy. Maybe it was harder for people without fae ancestry to see it, but she'd glimpsed it even in photographs.

Lily resisted the urge to match his smile with one of her own and added, "Incidentally, flattering me is pointless. The sons of Daidí's associates all try it to curry favor with him. I'm immune to praise." She met his eyes, reminding herself who she was, reminding them both that she was not the shy creature she felt like in that moment when she'd first seen him. "The no-one-else-matters gaze is a nice touch, but Daidí hired you to perform. Tonight will be the beginning and the end of your contact with the notorious Mr. Abernathy, no matter what you do or say."

"What if I want *your* favor?" Creed asked as he took a drink from a tray that a waiter held out to both of them.

Lily gave him a derisive smile, but said nothing.

Once the waiter was gone, and they were again alone in the crowd, Creed continued in a low voice, "You're a hard girl to get to meet, Lilywhite. I took this job specifically to meet you. No publicity. No one outside of the guests here right now even knows I'm doing this."

"Fantasies of the crime lord's daughter on your arm to add to your image?"

Creed laughed. "Not quite."

"I might not believe everything I read, but I've seen enough photos of you with different girls to know that you have two types: ones who add to your reputation and ones who are simply . . . unusual. I'm guessing your interest in Nick Abernathy's daughter is about a fifty-fifty split between intrigue and business."

Creed shook his head. "What if it isn't Nicolas Abernathy's daughter I wanted to meet, but *Iana*'s?"

Lily stilled. No one talked about her mother. It simply wasn't done. Daidí's considerable reputation for cold vengeance prevented it. "Those are dangerous words."

"For people of *our* heritage, there are a lot of dangerous words," Creed murmured as he leaned close and brushed a kiss on her cheek.

The feel of his skin on hers resonated through her body like she was a vessel for nature itself. If Creed Morrison's words hadn't confirmed that he was a fae-blood, his touch would have.

When he leaned back, he paused as if the contact had jolted him like it had her, but then a heartbeat later he was kissing her other cheek and saying, "If you want to talk privately later, I'd like that."

Lily realized that he was pressing a small card into her hand. She curled her fingers around it so it wasn't visible to anyone when he stepped back.

Whatever angle Creed Morrison had, Lily couldn't risk honesty with him. The world was divided: humans made up most of the population, fae-bloods—those with any degree of fae ancestry—existed in secret in the human world, and true fae lived in the Hidden Lands. Possessing a drop of fae blood was enough to result in imprisonment within the human world, but the alternative was to to seek entrance to the Hidden Lands, to turn away from humanity. For many fae-bloods, it was safest to simply pass as human. The war carried out by the Queen of Blood and Rage meant that *any* of her subjects were considered war criminals by the human courts, even those who had not sworn fealty to the faery queen—or even met her.

"My only heritage is as Nick Abernathy's heir," Lily said levelly, suppressing the wince from the physical pain of the lie.

She was, in fact, more fae than human. She'd known that for years. Being so fae meant that the words *hurt* to utter, but admitting her ancestry to the wrong person could mean the kind of imprisonment that would try even the considerable limits of Daidí's power. Lily wasn't foolish enough to risk that with someone she'd just met.

"Liar," Creed whispered.

"Fae-blood can't be liars," she said, twisting the truth just enough to ease the pain of a *complete* falsehood.

Creed's expression went carefully blank and he said, "I'm not fae-blood either. Not a drop." He paused, watching her study him, and then added, "You can learn to hide the physical pain of lying, Lilywhite; surely you know that as well as I do. I know what you are, what *we* are."

There was nothing she could say to that, no retort that would disprove his blatant truth.

Creed glanced briefly at her hand, which was curled around his card so tightly that the edges of it were pressed into her skin. Casually, he reached out and trailed his fingers over the knuckles of her closed fist.

She concentrated on not reacting.

"Tonight," he said. "Later. *Anytime*. I want to talk to you."

"I don't . . ." She looked down at her hand. "I don't know why you think I'm . . . what you say I am."

He stared so intently that she could swear she felt his gaze like a physical thing, but she refused to look at him as he said, "Impure water burns your throat. The wrong soap makes your skin blister . . . and alcohol, cigarettes, drugs, they all affect you so much more than they do other people, non-fae people."

Lily kept her lips firmly closed. She still wasn't admitting a thing, but she obviously didn't need to. Creed wasn't guessing. He *knew*. He'd known before he'd met her—as she had about him.

"You don't need much sleep at all unless you have their toxic food," he continued. "When you *do*, you feel weak and need to sleep for hours."

She looked up finally.

"And I'd bet that you have a bit of yard that is

meticulously upkept, no pesticides, no gardener allowed in it. You feel it there without needing to hide. Soil or air, water trickling under the earth, or stone humming secrets. You know what you are when you are connected to nature. You know what *we* are." His voice grew soft, lulling her into a peace that she only ever felt outside. Suddenly, all Lily wanted was to sit and listen to him forever. There was magic in the way words slid from his lips, magic in the truth of them and in the boy speaking them.

She took a step closer to him.

"You like to stand on the bare ground, burrow your toes into the soil when you're tired, feel the earth and its pulse beating to match your own. Nature calls to us, Lilywhite."

Lily reached out and touched his wrist. She wanted to deny everything, but she couldn't lie again. Not to him, not right now. Creed reached out and covered her hand with his.

She wasn't sure how long they stood like that—or how long they would've stayed that way, but Daidí walked over and held out his hand to her. "Lilywhite."

She moved to him obediently, grateful for the familiarity of being at his side at a party, grateful to have a routine to fall into instead of whatever was happening with Creed.

Daidí extended a hand to the boy, who accepted it easily.

"Mr. Abernathy," he greeted, shaking Daidí's hand briefly. "I'm glad I made an exception to my manager's rules to be here to sing for Lilywhite."

Daidí's stiff expression flickered briefly to amusement

at the reminder that Creed was there as a favor and a very expensive one no doubt. "My daughter likes your music, and there is nothing in this world I wouldn't do for her happiness—or for her safety."

Creed nodded, acknowledging the warning implicit in Daidí's voice, and glanced at her again. "Any particular songs you want to hear, Miss Abernathy?"

The titles of Creed's songs, some of which she'd listened to until she could pick them out after only a few notes, all fled her mind. "Surprise me."

"Haven't I already?"

Her eyes widened just enough that Lily was glad Daidí was frowning at Creed instead of scrutinizing her.

Creed smiled, a genuine soul-searing smile that she'd rarely glimpsed in the hundreds of photos she'd seen in magazines, and then with a nod to them both he walked toward the stage that had been set up for him.

At her side, Daidí was silent as they walked to the table at the front of the ballroom where she was to sit like a regent holding court. For all of her father's suggestions that she mingle with those her own age, he still set her apart. Soon, his colleagues would come and give her gifts. Shayla would arrive and catalogue them, and Daidí would nod approvingly. Everyone would pretend that the people her own age who did approach her did so by their own choice. All the while, she would watch Creed sing for her as if private concerts from global celebrities were her due.

"He's like you," Daidí whispered as he seated her at the

birthday table. It was a question as much as a statement.

Lily nodded.

On stage, Creed inserted a little earpiece into his ear and nodded at the man who was stationed to the side at a complex-looking control board. Creed seemed less intimidating now, like the unapproachable rock star in her fantasies. He was safer now that he was at a distance.

"I thought as much from the way you studied him in those journals," Daidí said with a satisfied tone that made her glance his way.

She caught her father's hand as he started to turn away. When she tugged him down beside her, he didn't resist. She kissed his cheek as an excited daughter should and assured him, "I admitted nothing. I *never* have to anyone."

"You can with him," he said.

Daidí straightened again, saying no more, but she knew that her father had had his people thoroughly investigate Creed. No one was admitted to Abernathy Estates without thorough background searches.

As Creed started the opening chords to "Deadly Girl," his eyes were fixed steadfastly on her and her father. She could feel his words like a lure.

Air. Creed Morrison's affinity was air.

The articles she'd read all explained that fae-blood were typically associated with one element. Those of purer fae lines had a second. True fae had two or sometimes three. *Nothing* explained why she had four, and she'd never met another fae-blood she could ask.

Here, though, was one in her home.

The music covered Daidí's words as he told her, "I want you to talk to him. If he doesn't give you his contact information, I'll have Shayla get it for you. You need to know more of your people. That's why I brought him here."

Lily glanced from her father to Creed and back again.

"Happy birthday, Lilywhite," Daidí said.

The real present wasn't the party, or the jewelry, or even the concert. Her father had delivered Creed Morrison to her like a gift. All he needed was a bow.

three

LILY

After Creed's second song, Shayla arrived at the table, and Daidí stepped away, signaling to the guests that they could begin their procession of offerings. Nothing in the gifts they carried could be quite as shocking as the gift her father gave her. She watched Creed as he continued to sing to her, wishing that she could be so bold as to end the party for everyone but the two of them. She couldn't. She wouldn't. Instead, she smiled politely at the head of the Gaviria family and his sons as they all bowed their heads to her.

The Gaviria cartel was Daidí's strongest ally, and as such, they were always first in line to offer felicitations. Their cartel was not a new organization like so many today. They had a history stretching back before the early 2000s, before the war, before the guerrilla attacks by the Queen of Blood and Rage's terrorists, back when this continent was called North America.

"*Feliz cumpleaños*, Lilywhite," Señor Gaviria greeted as he lifted her hand to his lips and kissed the air just above the skin.

"*Gracias.*" She smiled and repaid it in kind by saying, "It's no wonder your sons attract so many beautiful women with you as an influence."

"*Gracias.*" He sighed, keeping her hand in his. "*Pero*"— he shrugged and looked at Erik, his eldest son and her closest friend—"*Erik necesita una buena esposa.*"

Erik met her eyes during his father's oft-repeated comment, but he said nothing. Like Lily, Erik was being raised with the necessary skills to take over the family business. Unlike her, there was no doubt that he would do so.

Studiously not glancing at Erik, Lily said, "I'm sure all of your sons will find good wives."

"*Espero que sí.*" Señor Gaviria half sighed the words.

Dutifully, Erik held out a beautifully wrapped jeweler's box. It was too big to hold something dangerous like a ring, but whether it was a necklace or bracelet, it was clearly meant to be a reminder that he was wealthy and had impeccable taste. She didn't need those reminders. She'd known for years that their fathers had hopes of a marriage. Erik was four years older than her, and while they'd kissed a few times, they both knew that Erik would require a wife meeker than Lily could ever be.

"Exquisite as always," Erik said with a bit too much familiarity for a casual friend. He lifted her hand to his lips, echoing his father's words and actions.

"Too kind as always," she replied lightly.

"We will dance," Erik said, not asking as most boys would. His assertiveness was part of his appeal, but it was the sort of appeal that only worked because he had no actual authority over her.

"I always enjoy dancing with *mi amigo de confianza*." She switched to Señor Gaviria's preferred language and hoped that his father heard the word *friend* clearly enough.

Erik didn't have her heart—any more than she held his—but tonight, she needed a safe, *human* touch. She needed her friend to be nearer to her because of what he wasn't. Being in his arms for a dance would help remind her of who she was—and what she was pretending not to be.

She laid her hand on Erik's arm. "Soon. We will dance soon."

Señor Gaviria beamed approvingly; his youngest two sons said nothing. They were not expected to do more tonight than be seen showing their respects. The Gavirias moved on so Lily could talk to the rest of her well-wishers and approval-seekers. She liked most of them well enough, but after the seventh polite exchange, Lily was already feeling the strain of politic answers that bordered a bit too closely on lies.

When Creed switched to a calmer song, "Belladonna Dreams," she felt her skin tighten and knew *he* was watching her. There was something about Creed Morrison; he was temptation incarnate. She glanced his way, and in that moment, she couldn't see anyone but him. The world vanished.

Then Shayla's voice interrupted her longing: "Lorenz Calvacante. His son, Vincenzo, and his daughters, Maria and Angela."

And Lily returned to her dutiful acceptance of gifts and birthday greetings.

Vincenzo bowed his head. "When the presentation is done, I would be honored to lead you in a dance."

She nodded. All of their generation had been forced by their families to learn the very formal dances of the past. The waltz (Viennese and English), the tango, the foxtrot . . . Someone had unearthed a series of old television shows from just after the turn of the century, and a weird craze for formal dancing had begun. Most of them were horrible at it; only Erik took to dance gracefully.

The Calvacantes left, and Lily's gaze drifted back to Creed yet again as she tried to decide whether or not it was better that they couldn't speak privately.

"In the desert, I bartered my soul," he sang as she glanced his way. "In the darkness . . . please keep me from surrendering to these belladonna dreams."

It was a song he'd written far before tonight, one that rode charts on every continent, but as he sang, he stared only at her, and Lily couldn't help the foolish feeling that his words were just for her. It was impossible, but in that instant, she believed he was begging *her* to save him.

This was part of why the fae-blood were imprisoned. History taught that the fae were manipulative and cruel. Reality proved that they could manipulate people with their affinities and their innate beauty.

Although Creed Morrison wasn't using his gifts to hurt people, he obviously could twist emotions with his voice— or maybe Lily was more susceptible to him. Either way, she felt the magic of a fae affinity in his voice, and it made her struggle not to respond. The question was whether that response was to go to him or to lash out at him with her own affinities. Neither would be wise.

By the time Lily had finished the gifts, Erik was waiting. Gently, he pulled her out of her chair. No one was on the dance floor yet. Her feet made next to no sound as she followed him.

"Tango?" he asked.

The music Creed was playing was all wrong, but they could make it work.

"Don't expose my thigh," she warned.

"I thought this was a weapon-free event."

Lily rolled her eyes. "Am I to believe that neither you nor your father are armed?"

"I only have what I was permitted by my host," Erik said, reminding her in his usual way that he was in a separate class from the rest of the guests. Daidí trusted no one as much as he trusted the Gaviria family, and the idea of any of them being unarmed was as likely as Lily leaving her room without a blade of some sort.

When Erik stepped back, he stared at her, and a prickle of nervousness slid over her, but then he nodded. They both took several steps toward the other. Erik lifted his left hand and simultaneously curled his right arm around her body. His hand rested on her back with a familiarity that the dance allowed.

She took his hand and wrapped her free arm around him as well.

"The rock star can't take his eyes off of you," Erik said as he pulled her closer to him.

She rolled her eyes. "Daidí *hired* him."

Erik walked her backward, hip to hip. "I know you, Lily. You're looking back at him."

Lily followed Erik's lead, the hardest part of the Argentine tango for her. Being passive, even in a dance, didn't come easily. Her skirt brushed against him, and she felt the material swish as they moved, reminding her how close they were.

"He's not one of us."

Lily stiffened in his arms. If Erik knew that Creed was more like her than *he* was, it would be dangerous. Still, she refused to lie to Erik—or to admit things that could lead to trouble.

For a few moments, they danced in tense silence until Erik said, "I like you being in my arms like this, Lily. We *could* be more than this."

She frowned. "I thought you were seeing that girl, Amalie or whatever."

"She's temporary." Erik twisted his hips in a move a touch too familiar for in front of an audience. The speed of the music, Erik's unexpected possessiveness, and the dance itself made for a display that revealed more about their relationship than she wanted. At least they weren't alone on the dance floor now. People began to join them. It offered some degree of cover for the statement that Erik was apparently making.

"We were wrong to think we *shouldn't* unify our organizations," he murmured. "I think we should reconsider."

"I haven't even decided if I'm going on to university after I finish school or—"

"You could still do that," he interrupted. "Get a business degree or pursue law. Father and I discussed it. I would handle the businesses for both families if you choose to go to school."

"We wouldn't suit that way, Erik," she said softly.

"We *could* suit." He dipped her backward, and when he brought her up, his lips were all but touching the skin of her throat.

"I can't be like Señora Gaviria was. Your mother was lovely, but I'm not passive, Erik. Even if I loved you, I wouldn't be able to be a silent partner. Daidí raised me to be in charge."

"I know," Erik said. "I've discussed it with Father. For you, I would write new rules. *We* would. Together."

She stared at him as he removed her only logical objection. She wasn't sure if she should be pleased or angry. Just then, she felt both in equal parts.

"Say you'll be my wife someday, Lily."

They danced for another few moments, and still she couldn't speak. Finally, she managed to reply, "I can't. I'm too young to think about this, and I'm not sure . . . of anything right now. I'm sorry."

"Then say you'll at least consider it," he insisted as the song ended.

Lily wasn't ready for the sort of decisions she was being asked to make. She wasn't sure of where she wanted to be in the next year, much less forever. "I can't even say maybe."

"I can wait a little longer if you're at least willing to think about it, Lily."

The music switched to something that would be entirely wrong for a tango, even with Erik's skill. Lily glanced toward the stage. Creed stared back at her, worry plain in his eyes, and she knew that the tempo change wasn't an accident.

Before she got caught looking at the fae-blood singer, she rested her cheek against Erik's shoulder and said, "Nothing fancy, Erik. Just dance with me for a minute like we're normal people."

Mutely, he complied, and they continued the next, much tamer, dance in silence. At the end of their second song, Erik leaned in and kissed the corner of her mouth, then he led her to her father's side. No one—including their fathers or the fae-blood on stage—could have missed the possessive air of Erik's actions tonight.

As she reached her father, Daidí gave her a curious look,

but she merely smiled at him in reply.

Erik walked away, and she was left alone for a moment. There were guests to mingle with, smiles to wear, and myriad conversations she could join.

As Lily scanned the ballroom, she saw Shayla. She was almost to her when Creed's speaking voice drew her attention. "I'm going to take a break, but the orchestra will keep you entertained during my pause."

He hopped down from the stage with the sort of ease that made clear that ceremony wasn't his habit. He looked graceful, but very much out of place in her father's ballroom. It wasn't that he didn't have the wealth to wear what the most ostentatious of them did. It was that he didn't seem to *care*—not about wealth or status or any of the trappings of it.

And right now, he was watching her with what looked like challenge in his eyes.

Lily, however, wasn't going to change her path, despite the fact that he was now standing beside Shayla. She kept her smile in place and walked toward them.

"You were as wonderful live as on your albums," Lily said as she reached him.

"I try."

Shayla met Lily's eyes and said, "He has one more set after his break."

Then she abandoned Lily to her fate.

Once she was gone, Creed said, "I'd ask you to dance, but I couldn't compete with your . . . what is he?"

Lily laughed. "You have a different girl with you in every picture. How can you possibly sound jealous?"

Creed shrugged. "None of those girls are my girlfriend." He paused before offering, "I want to sing for you. *Just* you. Take me to your garden, and let me."

Her back was to the rest of the guests, but Lily still needed the tension in the air between them to vanish. Erik had already noticed. So had her father, and undoubtedly, so had Shayla. She could see them all watching her, as were a lot of the guests.

Abernathy Commandment #14: Blending in helps you seem less memorable should you need an alibi at some point.

In a light voice, Lily said, "Is that what you say to girls to lure them away?"

His laugh was self-deprecating. "Most of them need no bribes. Only *you* have needed convincing." He reached out for her hand.

"No gardens." She took his hand and started toward the dance floor. "No private concert, but you could dance with me, Creed. That's allowed."

Getting involved with a fae-blood was too risky. She couldn't do it, but for the next several minutes, Lily let herself be held by the boy who had been her fantasy before she'd even known he was a fae-blood like her. After this, she'd return to the life she knew and understood. For a few moments, though, she was going to enjoy herself.

four

ROAN

Roan waited in the alley behind the Paragon hotel for his closest friend and ally. If anyone asked, he was her date. It was a convenient cover for their meetings—and for the fact that he had about as much interest in girls as he had in joining a country club. Roan had given his heart away several years ago, and the only people who believed otherwise were the ones who didn't know him at all. Violet Lamb knew him as well as anyone in either world could.

He shivered a little. The filthy water pooled in gutters behind the hotel made him feel vaguely queasy. There was no way around it though: meeting Violet in the lobby was sure to lead to other problems. She was here filming some sort of action film, and the photographers and fans were all but camped out in the lobby. The hotel allowed it tonight, which gave her a better shot at slipping out through the service elevator without being seen.

It was a familiar routine. Roan waited until he spied her sidling along the building. Her flame-red hair was tightly bound in a braid, and she had a long leather coat with an oversized hood pulled up to further hide the spill of red curls that everyone thought came from a salon. Like him, Violet was fae—specifically, born of the Seelie. Those of the so-called "better" fae court were what was tradition-ally called "sun-burnished." For centuries, the descendants of the Seelie fae had been mistaken for African Americans, Latin Americans, or people with Middle Eastern ancestry. Violet's mother was from the Southern Continent, so she played up the illusion of Hispanic blood whereas Roan and Creed both had human families who were visibly African American. Being even slightly fae-blood would result in imprisonment, so they all had been raised to encourage not only the misconception that they were simply darker-skinned humans, but also that they made themselves appear more attractive by way of cosmetics or other chemicals.

All fae or fae-blood—those who were descendants of the fae, but not true fae—had to simply pretend to be shal-low enough to care about appearance. Some, like Violet, had an easier time of it because of the role they took in this world. Vi was an actress, one who loved her job and the primping that came with it. Tonight, though, she was dressed to hide in the shadows: over-large black sunglasses, her standard tall leather boots, black jeans, and her black leather coat. He teased her once about the leather, but she pointed out that everything else held the scent of smoke too easily.

He took her hand when she was in reach and led her toward the car he'd left in the next street over. No words were spoken until they were both inside the nondescript dark sedan he'd borrowed for the weekend.

"Are you okay?" she said once they were safely out of range of any possible listeners.

"Is there another choice?" he asked. If he were to tell her he couldn't handle the job, she'd do it for him. She *had* done so, more than a few times, but there was a limit to how much he was willing to let her take on for him. The fact that they were cheating by doing his mission together was enough risk.

"You know there is." Her tiny hand landed on his, and he could feel the heat even though she was containing it. Violet's affinity was fire, the precise opposite of his. She had great control over it—at least she did when there was a crisis—so he wouldn't want anyone else at his back.

He turned his hand over and squeezed hers briefly. "Not this time. You've done more than enough for me . . . and for Will."

She shrugged. "Family, right?"

"Always." With Violet or Will, Roan could let his guard down. He could admit that he wasn't as laissez-faire as everyone believed. With them, he could admit that he hated what they were tasked with doing, hated the way it made him feel, and sometimes in words never spoken *too* overtly, he admitted that he hated the Queen of Blood and Rage. With Violet or Will, Roan didn't need to be anything but honest.

"I'm glad Will isn't here," he murmured.

"One of these days . . ." Violet let the words die before she spoke them. Some of the Sleepers had been tasked with easier things, but both Violet and Roan had gone on several missions that ended with human deaths. Will, Creed, and Alkamy had all been spared that awful experience so far.

Both Roan and Violet lapsed into silence as he drove them to the train station. There were times when he'd been able to pretend, to try to keep up some sort of banter as they set out to commit murder. After two years of such missions, his ability to feign indifference was no longer worth the energy it stole—and Vi didn't require it of him.

Once they arrived at the station, Roan pulled into the lot and cut the engine. They sat in continued silence for several more moments.

"Let me do this," she urged.

"No. Smoke only," he stressed. "That's what we agreed. If they're unconscious, maybe the water won't . . ." His words faded. He didn't know whether it would hurt less to die of drowning or smoke inhalation. Being burned sounded like the worst option. That much he was fairly sure of.

Violet said nothing as she opened her door and stepped into the lot. The upside of her career was that it provided cover and alibis. The downside was that she was far too recognizable. Alkamy, who was just as beautiful, coped with the issue of recognition by only releasing one album—and avoiding tour. It gave her *some* ability to hide.

Creed simply didn't care if he was killed or caught; he was all but taunting death these days. Violet, on the other hand, genuinely loved acting and didn't *want* to get caught—but she couldn't refuse orders. None of them could.

Roan closed the car door softly. The order wasn't *hers*. This was his mission, his responsibility.

"Maybe you should stay here," he blurted when he reached her side.

"As if." Violet bumped into him lightly. "Come on. We've got this."

The walk toward the metro station was silent, but when they started descending, she looked over her shoulder and reminded him, "I need electrical shortages. No video footage, just in case it's live feed."

They were halfway down the escalator when he started pulling droplets of water from the air and dowsing electronics. The escalator shuddered to a stop when they were two-thirds of the way to the bottom. Violet didn't miss a beat. She continued walking forward as if the escalator had always been mere steps.

He followed, barely pausing when the escalator erupted in flames behind him. It was necessary, if cruel. There would be no retreat that way, not for any of the people in the tunnel ahead of them currently awaiting trains.

Her hands seem to glow as if embers writhed under the surface. Trickles of flames slid over her skin, as if she was coaxing them out. Clouds of smoke grew and billowed from her body and rolled forward. The air grew thicker and thicker with smoke.

Roan could see people in the tunnel as the smoke engulfed them. He told himself that they were all monsters, actively destroying the earth, poisoners who would kill him for his heritage. He told himself they deserved to die. He tried to recall every cruel thing that his childhood handler had taught him about humanity, to summon every reason why the queen's war was just and good.

Then people began yelling.

"We need to reach the other opening of the tunnel before they escape that way," Violet said, spurring him forward, reminding him that this was *planned* chaos.

"I know." Even opening his mouth to speak those two words made his throat burn. The fog-like air had the tinge of wood fires and ash, and Roan tried not to cough at the taste in his mouth. Minutes passed as they walked forward in silence. When they reached the other end of the platform, Violet sent a wave of fire to close off the mouth of the tunnel. No train could enter. No one could exit.

Then, the screams began in earnest.

Roan reached out with his affinity, not to pull droplets of water from the quickly drying air, but to find the pipes that he knew ran nearby.

People started running toward them, passing them as they tried to reach the wall of fire. Others tried to run toward the escalator. Both exits were sealed.

Reflexively, he started to warn them, "Wait, you can't—"

"Don't," Violet snapped, cutting him off, reminding him of his mission. Saving them wasn't it.

The heat from her body grew stronger, and sweat trickled down the back of his shirt.

"Focus, Roan," she said in a less harsh tone.

"I . . ."

He heard the yelling, the screams, grow louder, and he must've said something else because Violet started to glow brighter. She gripped his hand in hers tightly enough that he winced. He knew that if he didn't act that wall of fire would surge toward them. Everyone not being touched by Violet would be incinerated.

"I have this," he insisted, as he summoned the water, the force of his call breaking the pipes and driving the water toward the people on the platform, drowning them as they tried to flee the smoke and flames.

He didn't look at them. He didn't listen to them. He did his job.

Violet's fire retracted at some point when he was concentrating. All that was left was haze and ash. "We need to go," she said, her voice rough in that way that told him that the smoke was covering tears.

He nodded, but couldn't speak.

"Just don't look," she said.

And then her hand was in his, and they were walking toward the charred mouth of the tunnel.

five

EILIDH

Eilidh slipped back into the Hidden Lands. She'd been moving between worlds since she was old enough to walk. Back then, she didn't know that it was not authorized for the fae to travel. Back then, she didn't know that the queen had ordered an end to all contact between the worlds. She knew now, and it made her cautious.

. . . but obviously not cautious enough. Her only true friend among the fae sat on the branch of a dead tree. He was twice her age, but among the fae—whose lives lasted for centuries—that made them both children.

"You'll get caught one of these times, Patches," Torquil said. His tone wasn't quite lecturing, but it was close enough that she made a rude gesture.

He laughed and dropped to the ground in front of her, close enough that she felt the warmth radiating from his skin. Even though he was as dark as the night itself, Torquil still glimmered in the shadows of the Hidden Lands like a small star made flesh. Hair so pale it was merely a moment darker than white framed a face that sculptors could only dream of. Some fae could never walk among humans, could never hide their Otherness. Torquil was one of them. Sometimes Eilidh thought it was part of why he seemed so young, despite the years he'd lived before her birth.

She scanned the area, although she knew he undoubtedly had already done so. "I'm as careful as you."

"Careful isn't the same for you, now is it?" His voice felt like music to her after the harsh sounds of the mortal world.

"Because I'm so memorable?" Eilidh twisted her hair up to expose the myriad lines and fractures that earned her the nickname only Torquil and Lilywhite ever used.

"No." He traced a finger over her wrist, following one of the lines to her elbow. If she was any other fae, she'd think it was flirtatious, but Torquil was her childhood friend—despite the dreams she often had of him. "Because the queen worries about you."

Eilidh rolled her eyes. "Mother worries because I'm her heir. She worries that Father won't manage to gift her with a healthy child to replace me. She *worries* that she'll have to hand the throne over to a broken princess instead of the baby who was lost to the sea."

"So where were you?" He leaned close, sniffing the ashy scent that clung to her skin and hair.

She debated not telling him, knew that she shouldn't,

but Torquil already had enough of her secrets in his hands to have her locked inside the glass tower forever. One more was no extra risk. "I went to check on someone."

"You can't keep going to their world," Torquil continued. "They kill our kind."

She brushed the truth away with a sweep of her hands. "And *we* kill theirs. It doesn't have to be war between us. There has to be a way—"

"The queen asked me to watch you more closely," Torquil confessed suddenly. "If she knew that you were going over there, she'd see me punished. She'd see you locked away under guard. You know that."

"So tell her." Eilidh folded her arms and met his eyes. It was harder than when she was a child. Back then, she hadn't realized how ugly she was, how scarred, how pitiful to the beautiful ones. Even the least of the fae were stunning.

Once, many centuries before the war began, humans had thought the fae were gods. It was easy to understand why when she looked at Torquil. He was of one of the purest bloodlines, a family close to the regent of the Seelie Court.

Why the queen agreed to allow him to be her playmate, Eilidh would never know. Perhaps her father had insisted. Eilidh never asked outright, but it was common knowledge that Torquil's birth loyalty wasn't to the Unseelie Court. The unification of the courts didn't change history. His father was devoted to *her* father, the Seelie King, not to the Unseelie Queen. The regents' ruling together was new, only a few decades, but the rivalry between the courts stretched as far back as there had been fae courts.

"Eilidh?" He touched her shoulder, drawing her attention to him. "The humans would cage you. They cage anyone who has fae blood."

"And we *kill* them," she reiterated. "So much blood has already been shed. If Mother would—"

"Eilidh," he said, drawing her name out slowly. "You cannot keep going over there."

"She suspects something, then," Eilidh said, hearing the words he wasn't saying. She wasn't ready to deal with her mother. She needed time before she could utilize the secrets she'd collected. "She wants you to watch me because she has doubts about what I'm doing."

Torquil dropped his arm around her shoulders. "You know I've always tried to keep your secrets, but the queen knows *that* too."

Eilidh nodded and let him lead her deeper into the shadows of the Hidden Lands. The degree of purity in fae blood determined the ability to lie. Pure lines like his—and hers—felt extreme physical pain upon lying. The Sleepers were able to lie, to a degree at least. That was one of the reasons they'd been created. They could blend, and they could lie. She and Torquil couldn't have done what the Sleepers were sent to do.

"Just walk with me," she said. "I'm not asking you to suffer for me."

"I have. Willingly," he reminded her.

"But I've never *asked* you to."

He kept pace with her, shortening his stride so he was matching her much shorter one. Torquil wasn't unusually tall, just under six and a half feet. Like the light that radiated from his dark skin, his height marked him as belonging to one of the oldest, purest families.

When he finally decided on a bride, he would have his pick of them. Truth be told, even those who were promised already would probably say yes if he chose them. If he desired a man, no one would care—as long as he had a surrogate to carry his ancestry forward. Only someone who sought heartbreak would be foolish enough to seriously fantasize about him. Despite the embarrassing dreams she often had, Eilidh didn't seek to have her heart broken as her body once was.

Eilidh knew Torquil was as out of her reach as the stars are to the soil. She'd known it since she'd been old enough to realize that no other fae, Seelie or Unseelie, looked like her. The maze of scars that covered her body like a madman's map assured that no fae looked on her with longing. Only Torquil had ever looked at her with genuine pleasure. How was she to avoid caring for him? How could she *not* imagine that his friendship was the precursor to love?

"I'm sorry," she whispered.

"For?"

"You being in this position with the queen." They'd reached the caves where tunnels honeycombed out into routes that led either to disasters or to their homes. Only those who knew the way could safely navigate the tunnels. It was one of the many safety measures the king and queen had instituted to keep the fae safe should humans figure out how to access the Hidden Lands.

Torquil's luminous skin, as with most fae, lit their way as they stepped into the perpetual gloaming inside the passageways. Despite everything, she still took comfort in that—in their nature, in their very being. She didn't agree with the war, wouldn't ever believe that the death of one person legitimized the slaughter of millions. She did, however, understand her mother's need to save their people.

"The queen tells me you're to be looking for a bride soon," she said as they turned from one tunnel into the next. "She warned me that I'd need to find a new playmate once you're betrothed."

Torquil snorted, an indelicate sound she'd only ever heard when they were alone. "Playmate? Did you remind her that we're well past the edge of make-believe in the garden?"

"No." Eilidh smothered a smile.

"Afraid she'll put you on the market too?" he teased.

She was quiet long enough that he glanced her way, prompting her to answer, "That won't happen."

"Because?"

"Marriage would mean childbirth, and my mother would not risk my death that way." Eilidh paused, weighing out her words, rejecting and selecting the ones that would sound calmest before continuing, "The healers were shocked that I lived at all. None of the other children after me have. Our queen will order Father to have a daughter who will be raised to bed with Rhys before she agrees to risk me in that way."

Eilidh's voice was steady as she outlined the obvious. The king had two sons, Nacton and Calder; the queen had one son, Rhys. Since the queen couldn't carry another child, logically, the king would have to take Seelie women to his bed until he had a daughter, who—once old enough— would be given to Rhys. The child of *their* union would then be a child of both courts. Such a child would be able to take the Hidden Throne and rule.

When the two courts had set aside an eternity of conflict, they had agreed that either children of both courts *or* an heir with blood of both the Seelie and Unseelie would rule. There was no other option. It was the one inviolable term of the unification.

"Right now, Mother fears that something is wrong with me inside," Eilidh said softly. "She wouldn't want an even *more* broken child to take the throne, and she wouldn't want her only child with Leith to die. I will not have children unless Mother has no other options."

"Eilidh," he started.

"Hush." She looked up at him. "Lying hurts, Torquil. Don't do it to spare my feelings. I know what my mother thinks. I know what she fears. The broken daughter is only a stand-in until a new heir is born."

"I don't think you're broken."

Eilidh shook her head and pressed her lips tightly together.

"Are you considering anyone in particular for your bride?" she asked after a time. "I assume you're selecting a bride, not a groom?"

Torquil tensed. "I'm not considering *any*one."

"No one caught your eye yet, then?" she persisted, perversely needing to hear that there was someone, someone other than her, he truly looked upon with interest.

Coolly, Torquil said, "In exchange for my loyalty, the queen has given me free rein to choose anyone, no restrictions other than not taking a wife who still has young children."

That was the sort of open choice that was usually only reserved for royals or those to whom the queen felt indebted or deemed so pure as to need every incentive possible to wed. Marriage wasn't forever among the fae; even when the two courts were separate, the idea of permanent liaisons was odd. The first nearly permanent marriage between the Unseelie Queen and Seelie King would end when their heir took the Hidden Throne.

Eilidh couldn't say she was surprised. Torquil was among the purest of the fae, and he was trusted by both king and queen. She hoped that the king had given him other restrictions, but it was unlikely. Leith rarely disputed the queen's choices. Luckily, Torquil wasn't cruel. He wouldn't attempt to separate a couple in love.

"What generosity," Eilidh said mildly. "All of both courts

open to you for the low price of selling me out."

"It's not only for that, Eilidh. You know that as well as I do. She wants more strong fae, and I've not shown any interest in breeding. She's trying to bring me to heel." He tried to pull her near him, catching her hand in his and tugging.

She didn't resist. He spun her to face him, and slid his hand from her wrist to her elbow.

"I don't intend to tell her anything about your actions," he said, holding on to her with both hands now. "You can trust me to keep your secrets."

"I won't ask you to lie," Eilidh countered. If it came to it, she'd live in the human world. She had connections there who could shelter her. It would be horrible to leave the fae, to not see them, to be surrounded by the toxic environment humanity had created. It would be worse to be imprisoned in the tower. "You'll need to choose soon, I suspect."

He didn't meet her eyes. "Soon is relative when you live for centuries. Until she sets a deadline, I am ignoring it. If she sets one"—he shrugged one shoulder—"my father still has close ties to our king."

"The king would have to owe your family quite a favor to stand up to Endellion."

"True," Torquil admitted, as much as saying aloud that the favor was, indeed, worthy of such actions.

She pulled out of his grasp finally and resumed walking. It was pitiful that her greatest joy was in being held prisoner by him for a few scant moments. Sometimes she was so hungry for the touch of another person that she considered starting a quarrel just for the hope to be touched. Being the broken heir was a lonely state. It was part of why she'd cherished the years she played with Lilywhite. They'd hugged and laughed, played tag and fallen into a jumble of limbs. None of those were experiences she'd known here in the Hidden Lands.

Torquil walked with Eilidh in silence the rest of the way through the tunnels and into the land where all the fae now lived. Usually she enjoyed seeing the beauty of their home, but not today. Today, she stared at the glass tower that she shared with no one. It rose up into the sky like a beacon, glistening like a jewel in even the dimmest light.

The tower had been built for another child, a baby who was lost to the sea, a daughter whose absence started a war. Neither the king nor queen lived in it. In all of Eilidh's life, she didn't recall her mother even visiting. Her father had periodically, but he could barely stand the sight of her. The Seelie Court was the court of beauty and light, and his daughter was not beautiful.

Waves surged against the tower, leaving behind dried salt that only added to the glitter of the tall building. Torquil walked her to the door, as he had so many times. Now, though, it felt like there were stares heavy on her skin. There was no doubt that word of his orders from the queen had begun to spread, and prospective brides were watching. More eyes on Eilidh would make her secret tasks even harder.

"Maybe you should pick a bride now," she blurted. It wasn't what she wanted, but a distraction would decrease his attention to her comings and goings. An announced bride would mean that the prospects wouldn't be studying her, trying to decide if she was competition or a way to reach him.

Torquil opened the door to the winding stairwell that twisted halfway up the tower. This part of the tower was transparent, allowing any and all to see her approach so they could offer respect or flee her presence. The top, fortunately, was mostly opaque. The only other section of the tower that enabled watchers to see her was the uppermost floor. There, she moved like a wraith, not clearly visible, but a shape whose movement could be tracked through translucent glass.

On the outside of the tower was another staircase, this one minded by guards. The visitors' staircase was to be used by everyone other than the royal parents, any siblings, and her betrothed when there was one. Those few fae could walk on the spiral staircase inside the glass tower.

"I'll meet you at the—"

"No." She turned away and began ascending the steps as she added, "You shouldn't visit so much now that you're seeking a bride. It wouldn't be proper."

"Proper?" Torquil's voice was as cold as she'd ever heard it. "You're lecturing *me* on propriety?"

Eilidh's temper flared, not as brightly as her mother's did but enough that she was forcefully reminded of her parentage. She wasn't surprised. He *was* fae, after all, but he'd been her only true friend in this world. That earned him a fair warning. Softly but steadily, she told him, "I've been the queen's daughter, surrounded by machinations my whole life, while you were out being free. Don't try to challenge me."

"You sound very Unseelie right now, Patches," he charged.

He stared at her as she stood halfway between one step and the next. In that moment, she thought that this was good-bye, that her dearest friend was about to be lost to her forever. That would've hurt, but not as much as what he next did: Torquil started up the spiral staircase.

"I've decided not to wait, after all," he said. "I've made my choice."

He strode up after her, and she wanted to run—or perhaps shove him backward.

Behind her, behind him, there were gasps. No one could have heard his words, but his actions spoke like a declaration. Only the royal parents, siblings, or her intended could walk up those stairs.

He was *not* her family.

"Back up," Eilidh said desperately. She spun so she was facing him. "This isn't funny. Go back! Go back *now*."

"No." He continued up the stairs, stalking after her. "The queen said I could chose anyone. *Any*one."

"She didn't mean me! I'm not agreeing to this. Stop it this instant, Torquil."

He laughed. "And when has a princess been allowed to select her own groom?" He was on the step next to hers. There, in front of her, he kneeled and stared up at her. "Shall I tell the queen or would you like the honor of letting her know that we are betrothed?"

Eilidh swallowed hard. Words wouldn't come. She looked away from him, staring through the walls of her tower at the growing number of faeries clustering around the building. They stared at her, as they often did, but this time she saw surprise, envy, and anger in their expressions.

"What have you done to me? To us?" she whispered. "What have you *done*, Torquil?"

six

ZEPHYR

The semester was starting finally, and Zephyr's team would all be back on campus. When Zephyr arrived at his suite, he found a not surprising note that both his suitemate and his best friend had already left for a bar, so he dropped his bags and headed into town.

Belfoure was an overcrowded maze of streets and shops. It was one of the strongest cities on the Eastern seaboard. Crime there was at a record low, and the pollution levels were among the lowest in the country. Generous donations from the families of St. Columba's students no doubt kept it that way. The school was home to children from some of the wealthiest families in the world, those who graced the pages of magazines or screens because of their own talents . . . or, as in his case, because of a parent's talents.

"Waters! Hey, Zephyr!" a salesman called out as Zephyr

paused to wait for the traffic light.

This was it, the start of the future he'd been waiting for. He'd trained, and he'd readied himself, studying essays and treatises, paying attention to politics and laws of the Hidden Lands. All the while, he'd concealed those habits from all but his closest friends and become the person that best fit his role in the human world: spoiled, sardonic son of film legends.

Tonight he was going to see his friends, pretend to drink heavily, and flirt outrageously. He'd either leave with a girl whose name he didn't bother to learn or he'd cuddle up to his best friend, Alkamy. He would, in essence, be the person that he was assigned to embody as his cover—and he'd enjoy it. That was the trick to the game: enjoying the lie you lived, finding the pleasure in it. Zephyr enjoyed a lot of it.

The bouncer at the front of the Row House didn't even blink when Zephyr skipped the line. When school was in session, he was a fixture here. There were still a few regions where a drinking age was set, but the majority of the continent had eliminated that law well before Zephyr was born. That didn't mean that he *ingested* poison, but he'd learned young how to pretend. It was a part of the role he lived, part of how he hid his true genetics. The fae-blood, those with any portion of fae ancestry, couldn't drink alcohol without being weakened by it. Zephyr had never consumed more than the one glass of it he'd been ordered to drink to get a sense of the way it hurt. That was enough.

He couldn't understand why Creed drank—or how he endured it.

Shaking away thoughts that would lead to a fight once he saw Creed, Zephyr paused so a cute girl could snap a picture of him. It wouldn't be useful to go to the club without being *seen* doing it. The headmistress at St. Columba's didn't comment on the plethora of photos that cropped up online or in magazines *proving* that Zephyr routinely ignored the rules about leaving campus. Headmistress Cuthbert was a fan of minimal conflict and maximum donations. Neither Zephyr nor his teammates—Alkamy Adams, Creed Morrison, Violet Lamb, or Roan Kenrick—ever caught hell for flaunting the rules. Not surprisingly, the four of them were often in the same pictures with Zephyr. It was only their friend Will Parrish who stayed clear of the club and the cameras.

As he made his way toward the velvet rope, Zephyr scanned the crowd for interesting faces. Finding no one extraordinary, he reached his goal: the VIP section where he knew he'd find at least one of his friends.

The bouncer at the rope nodded at Zephyr, but no conversation was needed. Being the oft-photographed Zephyr Waters was a good thing.

Alkamy and Creed both lounged in plush chairs, seeming exceedingly polished and wholly jaded. If he didn't know better, he'd believe they were both nothing more than the budding addicts they appeared to be.

"Kamy." He leaned down to kiss Alkamy, but she turned

her head so his lips barely glanced off her cheek.

"Watch the face!" She pouted with the perfect mix of woe-is-me and aren't-I-lovely. She *was* actually stunning. Her hair was a shade of black that made everyone assume it was dyed. It wasn't. Nor did she wear colored contacts to get barely blue eyes. Her lips were naturally as ruby-red as they seemed, and her skin was so pale that she was luminescent in the dark. Alkamy was a living vision of a gloomier Snow White.

He straightened and murmured, "Yes, dear."

Her smile transformed briefly into something genuine, and he matched it with one of his own. She might look icy, but she was sweet to him. In another life, they might've ended up something more, but in this life, any feelings were steadfastly buried. Even if Lilywhite *wasn't* his future, Zephyr couldn't let his feelings for Alkamy go in *that* direction. She looked so similar to him that he'd wondered if they were siblings in truth. That fear was reason enough to keep her at a safe distance. If he allowed himself to fall in love with her, he wouldn't be able to let her go no matter what the queen decreed. More importantly, Alkamy wasn't the sort to accept being told she *couldn't* do something. Far wiser to stay friends, to keep a wall around those feelings, and plan for a future with Lilywhite.

Alkamy flashed another real smile at him as she took in his appearance. "You look perfect, as always."

Creed snorted.

Zephyr dropped into one of the plush chairs, intentionally drawing eyes to him. The Row House was all about being seen. The club made no apology for it. The VIP section was demarcated by a scarlet and gold rope, but it was in the center of the club. There was a back wall that was shadowed if one wanted privacy, but the front of the room was open, and the left and right sides were clear glass. Being here was being on display—and that meant strict admission rules. Unlike some places where anyone with a generous budget for the night could get access, the Row House was old-school: invitation or status were the only ways to cross the line.

Being in the VIP section required looking like you were meant to be watched. They acted like it, and they dressed for it. Alkamy was wearing some sort of dress that appeared to be mostly transparent. Wide red straps covered her body in strategic places, but the rest of the dress revealed skin. In the hazy blue lights of the club, she looked otherworldly—but safely so. Creed, on the other hand, seemed to have put zero effort into his appearance. Artfully faded jeans, a T-shirt for some band, and heavy boots marked him as just another teen boy—except everything he wore was designer label and the jewelry that he'd added was undoubtedly worth more than most cars on the streets of Belfoure.

Creed's shaved head, visible tattoos, and dark complexion made him far too likely to be hassled out in town, but by now, all of the lawkeepers were well aware of who he was and exactly how much of a fire storm they'd be in if he got wrongly arrested because of their overzealous racial profiling. Whether they thought he was African American or Seelie, he'd be a target because of his heritage. Of course, Zephyr had thought more than once that Creed *hoped* for a wrongful arrest. He thrived on conflict, far more than even Alkamy or Violet.

Pushing away thoughts that would lead to yet another argument, Zephyr motioned to one of the waitresses who usually looked after their needs.

When the girl came over, she already had the drink that Zephyr preferred—an alcohol- and caffeine-free concoction of fruit juices. He covered for his toxin-free drinks by paying the waitresses for their silence. He'd never once been drunk, and if he had his way, he never would.

"Yes, it's organic," the girl answered before he could ask.

Then she handed drinks to both Creed and Alkamy without comment. They didn't need to *pretend* to drink alcohol. Zephyr could smell it from across the table as they accepted their glasses.

"Don't start," Alkamy murmured. Her drink was as brightly colored as his, undoubtedly made of the same organic juice. Hers, however, had vodka in it too.

Creed said nothing. Even if Zephyr had commented, Creed wouldn't back down in arguments about his lifestyle. Someday soon, they'd have to have that fight. The alternative was letting the Unseelie Queen know that Creed was a liability. For now, Creed lifted his glass in a mocking toast to Zephyr and downed half of it in one go. He caught the waitress's hand and said, "Another. I'll be ready for it before you're back."

Once she was gone, the three friends resumed pretending that they weren't being watched like animals in a zoo. These sorts of clubs had perks, usually in the form of pretty, willing humans for a few moments of distraction.

"Which one caught your eye?" Alkamy asked drolly, making him realize he was staring.

Zephyr shrugged.

"Does it matter?" Creed asked, stretching his long legs out and slouching farther into his chair. "They're interchangeable." He started pointing at girls. "Ena, mena, mona, mite, which one will bite?"

Zephyr scowled. "Don't be crass."

Creed, as per usual, ignored him. He motioned a passing waitress over and said, "The girl in the aqua top. Tell her to meet me at the rope in"—he glanced at his watch—"*exactly* eighteen minutes."

The waitress verified that they were describing the same girl, and then she left with his message.

"Really?" Alkamy asked.

He shrugged.

"You could slow down. Pretend to be with Kamy for a while," Zephyr suggested.

"Is that an order?"

"No."

Creed nodded. "Then go ahead and update us. I have an appearance to keep."

"Lilywhite will be here tomorrow." Zephyr paused to

let them marvel at the pending change, but Creed simply nodded and Alkamy waited silently.

"This is *it*," Zephyr continued, trying to impress upon them the significance of her arrival. "The start of a new stage of our lives. She is the beginning of . . . everything."

"Right, then." Creed lifted his glass, drained it, and held it out to the waitress who'd returned with his drink. "Let's drink and be merry, for tomorrow we die."

Alkamy winced. "Creed—"

"Don't," he interrupted her. "Just fucking *don't*, Kam." He wrapped a hand around his new drink and walked away.

Zephyr watched him go. "Has something happened? He seems worse than usual."

Alkamy lifted one shoulder in a noncommittal shrug. She sipped her fruity drink and watched Creed, who was chatting up two girls at the bar. One of them shrieked in laughter, and the other pressed up against him. Typical. Even from here, though, anyone could see that there was something false in Creed's smiles.

"They were in some film Vi dragged me to see," Alkamy offered, as if Creed's choice of girls mattered at all.

When Zephyr didn't reply, she continued, "Flash in the pan, pretty things, no talent." She wasn't being vicious, merely echoing whatever Violet had told her. "They seem fun though."

"Creed could do with less fun."

"Not everyone is as sure as you," Alkamy said gently. "Lilywhite is *your* intended. We don't know if we mattered enough for *them* to even plan a future for us."

Zephyr turned his attention away from Creed and focused on his best friend. She didn't say "fae" ever if she could avoid it. It was what she was, what all the Sleepers were, but she never said it aloud, as if silence would change reality. She'd only been with him in the Hidden Lands once, but it hadn't erased her discomfort.

"Us. We are the same as *them*."

"No, we're not," she said.

"I'd never let anything happen to you," he promised her yet again. No one else understood him the way she did. Alkamy felt like his other half. He met her eyes. "*Ever.* I'd die before I'd let you get hurt."

Alkamy sighed. "You'll die for the queen's cause; you'll die for me . . . Maybe you should try finding something or someone to *live* for instead."

"Is it so wrong to have a purpose?"

She didn't answer. Instead she asked, "Did you see my new shoes?" She kicked her foot out so he was forced to catch her ankle in his hand or get a pointy-toed shoe in the face.

Silently, he slid the shoe off her foot, set it on the table, and gave her a foot rub. He was used to her not-so-subtle changes of subject, and it made for good pictures. No one needed to know that he and Alkamy were destined for a platonic relationship. That was one of the many secrets they hid—and most were far more deadly.

seven

EILIDH

Eilidh wasn't surprised to see her mother striding through the assembled fae like a warrior. The queen was undoubtedly notified the moment Torquil's foot touched the staircase. There were enchantments to protect Eilidh's virtue woven into the very building that was her home. Had she been beautiful those enchantments would've been more necessary. As it was, Eilidh had never considered them, never had reason to, until this moment.

"What have you done?" she repeated for the third time, hoping for some graceful way out of the mess Torquil had created. They needed an answer before the Queen of Blood and Rage reached them.

Torquil stood, keeping her hand clasped in his. Gently, he tugged, leading her to the ground. He said nothing as they descended the stairs.

The queen stood there, her armor absent for a change. They'd obviously interrupted her at a better time than most. For all meetings and affairs of state, she wore her war attire. Right now, though, she was dressed in what passed for casual with the queen—a heavy brocade dress in blood red with black accents. Her midnight dark hair fell unbound. To anyone who didn't look in her eyes, she might appear as a sister to Eilidh herself, but a brief glimpse of the queen's eyes would end that thought, as would the weight of her voice.

"Explain yourself, son of Aden." The queen regarded Torquil, one of the rare fae of Seelie origins who had earned her genuine favor, and her anger was thick in her every syllable. Right now, none of that esteem was in evidence.

"You directed that I take a bride," he said levelly. He didn't drop to his knees as he should, as he had every other time the queen had spoken to him, as *every* fae save the king, the three royal sons, and Eilidh did.

Eilidh tugged his hand, trying to remind him to kneel. He ignored her and watched the queen. He was declaring himself family to her in this action as well. If most fae attempted such a thing, Endellion was likely to kill them.

Behind Endellion stood Rhys, the queen's son, the fae who would've been heir to the Unseelie throne if the courts had remained divided. Eilidh met his gaze, but he barely acknowledged her as he stood waiting to act if their mother had need of his blade. He knew well that the queen was as capable of wielding every blade known to faeries, but his chosen duty in this life was to protect his mother and bloody his weapons at her word. The *king's* sons were frivolous things, but Rhys was devoted to the queen, and by extension, to her husband if necessary.

"You directed that I could wed anyone my heart chose," Torquil continued, as if he wasn't aware of the danger he faced from the queen and her son both. "There were no other rules spoken, no exclusions. By your word, I could select even those already wed."

"Do not think to outmaneuver me, son of Aden," the Queen of Blood and Rage said quietly. "Undo this."

"You know as well as I do, my queen, that if she was unwilling, I couldn't ascend the stair."

Eilidh's gaze shot to her mother. "Is that true?"

No one answered her. The queen prompted, "Would you take Torquil, son of Aden, to be your betrothed, daughter of mine?"

The real question was in there, but it wasn't as simple as what was spoken. Eilidh had been raised under the guidance of the queen. She was meant to rule both courts if no other heir was born. That meant knowing how to hear what was unspoken.

Eilidh met her mother's gaze unwaveringly. "If it pleases my queen, I will do so when and only when she decrees it wise."

The Queen of Blood and Rage smiled at her, pride in her eyes, before she turned her attention back to Torquil.

When she spoke this time, she raised her voice and said, "Then I will allow you my daughter's hand, and you will lay with no other."

"Of course! There will be no other in my arms." He bowed his head deeply and then said, "We will begin planning our ceremony today."

"There is no rush, son of Aden and soon to be my own." The queen waited until he looked up and met her gaze. "I am not ready for nuptials. It could be a great long time until I am. My daughter is young still."

Torquil's smile grew pinched, but he said nothing. Most fae were betrothed at birth; many others were already wed at Eilidh's age. The whispers around them grew loud enough that Eilidh knew that the assembled fae were thinking exactly that.

"Of course, my queen," was all he finally said.

The only rush would be in producing an heir, and that would require her to take him to her bed. Such things often happened when betrothed couples developed feelings, but Eilidh wasn't so foolish as to think that his selection of her as his wife was anything personal. All he had done was take himself off the marriage block—and sentence himself to celibacy. After a time, he would accept that the queen would only allow Eilidh to be wed if there were no other choices left to secure an heir for the Hidden Throne. He would, in the end, set her aside and take a wife who could carry a child.

"Mother, would you rather we were not betrothed? If you will it, we can end . . ."

Endellion paused imperceptibly. Eilidh doubted that anyone other than her and Rhys even noticed. They had learned to notice. The queen had never raised a hand to her, never would. Whether they were Seelie or Unseelie, children weren't struck in anger. That didn't mean that Eilidh had avoided the chill in her mother's voice or the refusal to give her the smiles she coveted like most fae coveted sweets.

"I offered Torquil his choice of partners. He chose you." The queen almost smiled at her. "He will cherish you as he should, or he will learn from his foolishness."

Eilidh curtsied before her mother and said, "I am yours to command."

The queen smiled, a real smile this time. It was the closest to laughter she ever came. "Of course you are," she said.

And, in that instant, Eilidh was certain then that her mother knew more than she'd admitted about her heir's trips to the human world . . . or one of the myriad other secrets Eilidh kept.

"Speak to your soon-to-be-brother, Rhys," Endellion added. "Be sure he is well aware of my expectations. I need to see the king."

Then, with as little notice as when she had arrived, the Queen of Blood and Rage turned to leave. The assembled faeries scattered as she turned. They might love and respect their queen, but that affection was tempered by fear. She was their greatest strength, but she was also the nightmare that they spoke of in whispers. All from the eldest to the youngest fae were raised to know that their queen was wrought of darkness.

Rhys gestured toward the glass tower.

Silently, Torquil took Eilidh's hand in his, and they led her half-brother into her home. Her unease increased further.

None of her siblings ever visited her. Her aesthetically inclined Seelie siblings were understandable. Nacton tolerated her, but averted his gaze when they spoke. Calder, however, despised her for more than her scarred appearance. Not even the king could order him to be polite to her. Her Unseelie brother was more complex. The Unseelie were not put off by scars, but they were perhaps even less at ease with emotions. Rhys had behaved as Unseelie did, typically seeming wholly indifferent, but he'd also comforted her more than once when she'd wept.

Their silence was unbroken until they reached the first floor of the tower. It was a sitting room designed to allow her the privacy of conversation without offering easy access to her bedchamber. The faeries milling around outside could see them all clearly. Awkwardly, Eilidh gestured to the uncomfortable but lovely guest chairs.

Rhys gave her a chastising look that spoke loudly and motioned toward her own divan. He was too court-familiar to sit before her. Torquil, likewise, had stayed standing. By right of rank, he and Rhys were equal now. Rhys was the queen's son, but Torquil was the heir's intended.

Eilidh blushed as she realized her faux pas. "Sorry."

Once she sat, Rhys and Torquil exchanged a tense look, neither willing to admit a lesser rank and sit last, but neither wanting to clamber into a chair gracelessly to insist on higher rank.

"Is this necessary?" she prompted after the two fae stood awkwardly for several moments. "We're in my home, not in front of the queen."

Reluctantly, both faeries simultaneously sat.

"May I speak freely?" Rhys asked.

"Always," Eilidh promised. She had wanted a closeness with her siblings for years. Only Rhys seemed remotely capable of that. If this horribly unplanned betrothal elicited sibling affection, she was ready to declare the whole thing a fine idea . . . even if she wasn't pleased at the idea of Torquil's unexpected political machinations.

"She'll have me slit his throat before she allows you to wed," Rhys announced bluntly.

Torquil said, "The king—"

"Does not control my mother, even a little," Rhys interrupted. "She is Unseelie, and angry, and has pinned every hope she has left on Eilidh and the halflings."

Torquil frowned at him. "The . . . ?"

"The Sleepers." Rhys spoke slowly, as if Torquil should've known that secret. When he realized that Torquil didn't, his gaze turned to Eilidh. "You didn't tell him?"

"If the queen or king wanted it spoken, it would be," she pointed out.

"You are more like her than I realized," Rhys said, and from his tone, she was fairly sure it wasn't a compliment.

Eilidh nodded. "I am their heir."

"Until she has another child or finds the missing daughter."

"The baby died at sea. Everyone says so," Eilidh said mildly.

"Can *you* say that she died?" Rhys prodded. "Tell me I'm wrong, *Patches*. Tell me you aren't aware of where our missing sister had been hidden. Tell me that I missed some of your machinations, and you actually planned this mess with"—Rhys gestured at Torquil—"him."

"You know I can't," she said.

He continued as if she hadn't spoken, "You are the heir, *my* replacement at the head of the Unseelie fae, as well as Nacton's replacement for *the other* court."

"There is only one court," Torquil started.

Rhys ignored him, speaking only to Eilidh. "I realized that I could serve you or hate you. Calder and Nacton chose hate. I think Mother was right to unify the courts. I will support that path, which means protecting the heir. To do that, I had to know your secrets—and the queen's secrets."

"Oh." She wasn't expecting this, not his support and certainly not his implied knowledge. Eilidh wasn't sure where to go or what to say. She glanced at Torquil again.

Through it all, he had sat silently, the slight widening

of his eyes the only true clue to how shocked he was. He'd maintained his calm facade well enough to convince Eilidh that he might make a fine consort after all.

"Eilidh?" he prompted.

She sighed. "Which disaster do you want to discuss first?"

eight

LILY

Choices matter. That was the greatest and the first of the Abernathy Commandments. Some families had the Ten Commandments hanging in their foyer; the Abernathy household had security cameras and a framed list of the first eleven Abernathy Commandments. There were more than eleven now, and the original ones had evolved a bit, but that framed list would never be replaced. Her mother had given it to her father before Lily was born. Daidí had said that it was how he knew that she was his soul mate.

Abernathy Commandments

#1: Choices matter.

#2: Be yourself.

#3: Never get caught.

#4: Weigh the consequences before beginning a course of action.

#5: Be bold.

#6: Never confess your vulnerabilities if you can avoid it.

#7: Secrets are valuable. Don't part with them for free.

#8: Make use of opportunities that arise.

#9: Be kind to those who deserve it.

#10: Know when to be assertive.

#11: Know when to walk away from trouble.

Lily had grown up in the shadows of those commandments—thinking that every family had a set of rules to avoid "complications," thinking security cameras and bodyguards were normal, thinking that all good fathers were opposed to sending their daughters to school.

In truth, Lily had been perfectly content with the way things were. She didn't want a change. Being around people her own age, especially people who weren't raised in a world where there were different kinds of "good," was far from appealing. Being around normal people would make it hard to hide her own peculiarities too. Learning at home meant not making many friends, but it had also meant not having to hide herself. It seemed like a fine trade-off.

Daidí had always said she was like her mother—drifting away on flights of fantasy. But unlike her mom, Lily had no desire to write. Sure, she wanted to read, maybe watch movies . . . and pretend that she was the girl smiling at Zephyr Waters or getting caught skinny dipping in a fountain in

Roma with Creed Morrison in the pages of a magazine.

But now, her isolation was being yanked away. Her bodyguard, Hector, was escorting her to the city of Belfoure in a black car with tinted windows, bulletproof glass, and heated leather seats. Lily stared out the window until the hum of the road and the soft patter of rain on the car roof lulled her into some semblance of calmness.

"This is a bad idea," she pointed out yet again as Hector made a left turn.

"It'll be fine. You'll meet kids like you."

Lily shook her head. The school was a haven for special people. All of the students were *somebody*: child prodigies; children of diplomats, politicians, and rock stars; glitterati; and of course, those whose wealth was inherited. Those like her—kids whose parents earned their money in less ethical ways—didn't attend fancy boarding schools.

"Your father is a smart man," Hector reminded her.

"Smart men make mistakes too. Being around others . . . like me . . . it's not a good idea," she said gently.

Hector wasn't going to overstep by arguing with her—or by siding with her against her father. He kept his mouth shut and drove through the streets toward the campus that sat on the hill above Belfoure like a medieval fortress.

As Hector started up that winding drive, Lily thought back to the night she'd met Creed. She wasn't going to lie to herself about what she thought about him. Creed was captivating, but that was precisely why she didn't want to see him.

He's probably forgotten all about me.

She'd done the right thing in not calling. She had. If not for her father's ridiculous urge to send her to St. Columba's, Lily would never see Creed again. That had been her plan, and it was a good one. As it was, the school should be big enough to avoid Creed to some degree.

As the car pulled up to the massive front gates at the school, Lily slipped her sunglasses on. It was a small comfort, like putting on a mask.

Stone walls surrounded the entire campus, but the front gates appeared to be iron or steel. They were made to resemble some sort of faux castle gate. It was modernized, of course, with a gatehouse and a guard. It also stretched across the road where she assumed the entrance to the inner walls of the fortress had once been.

Hector cracked his window and announced, "Abernathy."

After a minute, the guard found her name on the list and buzzed them in. The heavy metal gate slid open with a series of clangs and clacks. If the myths about fae sensitivity to iron were true, Lily would feel wretched right now, but she'd never felt any weakness from iron. Maybe full-blood fae did. The media claimed that was so, but Lily herself hadn't ever experienced any trouble with iron or its alloy, steel. Considering how often she wore a blade next to her skin, she was certain that she'd have known far before now if the metal was toxic to her.

As Hector drove onto the campus, Lily stared at the

main building. It was imposing and dark, unlike the bright front of her home. This felt more like visiting the courthouse on the rare occasions when she'd been allowed to accompany Daidí to one of the government's various attempts to convict him.

The central building of St. Columba's was a towering black structure with gargoyles at the top, spires straight up into the gray sky, and doors that looked like they were meant to let in some horrific beast rather than mere people. The many steps up to those doors spanned the width of the building.

"Home sweet home."

"Give it a chance," Hector said. He parked the car at the top of the circular drive.

"Why?"

Hector opened her door, and in an instant, he was at the trunk pulling out the luggage. There were only three bags. The rest would follow in the next day or so. These were just the essentials Shayla decided to send.

"Walk, Lilywhite." Hector looked behind them, glaring at the gate that wasn't shut yet before herding her up the steps with a terse one-word command: "Inside."

At the top, she could see that a smaller door was nested inside the vast one. Hector opened it, and Lily went inside.

She pulled off her sunglasses and surveyed the hall, looking for potential exits and hiding areas. *Abernathy Commandment #15: Always have a way out, more than one if possible.* There weren't any obvious egresses, unfortunately. It was a room designed for one way in and out, which made her nervous.

The foyer of the main hall was a vast high-ceilinged room. Sconces lined the walls, jutting out from the thick vines that covered the walls for as far as she could see. On either side of the room, staircases spiraled upward to the balconies that lined the second and third floors. In the center was a wide hallway. A small sign reading ADMINISTRATION was the only indication of direction.

They made it as far as the mouth of the hallway when a woman in a well-tailored suit walked toward them. "Miss Abernathy?"

Lily nodded.

The woman offered the sort of tight smile that didn't bode well. "We weren't expecting you until tomorrow. There are no suites presently available as a result, but if you give us an hour, we'll get it all sorted out."

Hector scowled, but Lily simply nodded and walked toward the plants clinging to the back wall of the massive room. Belatedly, she realized that she should've spoken, but there wasn't anything that the woman could tell her that would be as useful as the plants would reveal.

"I'll carry her bags to the office," Hector said, drawing the woman's gaze to him and away from her.

Lily's affinity for earth was sacrosanct. Every new hire was told without fail that any time she needed to pause to touch nature, they must facilitate it. To do otherwise was a firing offense. They were also told exactly how horrific their deaths would be if they revealed her fae-blood tendencies to anyone outside the house. At least one employee had vanished suddenly after he'd allowed a reporter to capture a picture of her with waves seemingly bending toward her. The picture vanished, and both the reporter and her then-guard had never been seen again. Daidí left nothing to chance—at least he hadn't until the night of her birthday when he'd invited Creed into their home.

Lily glanced down the darkened hallway. "Can I help in any way?"

The woman's stiff smile softened into something close to approval. "I'll get everything sorted out. You just take a look around your new home."

"I'll be right back," Hector told Lily. He glanced after the woman suspiciously for a moment before following her away, dragging Lily's bags with him like they weighed nothing.

"I'm in no rush," Lily said.

She watched him as he walked away. Her hands absently twined into the plants, and she was grateful for this bit of the natural world inside this unfamiliar place. The plants talked in whispers and rustles, telling her of students, of sounds from the underground, of the spiders that draped the leaves in webs.

It wasn't enough.

Once Hector turned the corner, Lily exited through the same door she'd just entered minutes prior. The woman had said Lily could look around. She hadn't specified that she'd only meant look around *inside*, and when Lily didn't have to stay inside, she didn't.

The water in the fountain outside wasn't pure, far from it in fact, but it was *there*. Lily could feel it tugging at her the way she suspected magnets drew metal. Soil and sea called to her; plants whispered to her. As she got older, she came to understand that most people didn't hear words in the wind or feel the weight of moonlight. It had taken years for her to learn to rest without her windows wide open—and longer still to hide her need to be barefoot.

Lily walked back out of the administration building and into the courtyard. Her intent had been simply to be in the sunlight, maybe sit near the large fountain that filled the center of the circular drive, but when she walked down the steps, she saw that the gate to the grounds still yawned open like an invitation. The guard was talking to someone on his phone, and the gates were unwatched.

It was a sign.

She slid her sunglasses on and walked through the open gate as calmly as if she were walking into the theater with Daidí. She didn't run or look around furtively. She didn't glance back at the administration building.

Abernathy Commandment #8: Make use of opportunities that arise.

nine

LILY

Lily slipped her shoes off for a few minutes, tilted her face to the sky, and let the sun and air calm her. Like a plant, she'd wither and sicken without the elements against her skin, so she walked toward the sea, under the sun, and with the wind. If she was to move out of the comfort of her home, she'd need to find a way to balance her need for nature with the illusion of being mundane. She'd do so. She was an Abernathy, and that meant knowing how to survive in a treacherous world. Being sent to school was, in some ways, a test of her readiness to be an adult. Lily wouldn't fail.

She followed the pull of the sea, and in no time at all, she was in downtown Belfoure. All told, it was about two miles from campus to the town, and in town there was a harbor. She could feel it tugging her close, as water always did.

Belfoure wasn't the sort of city where a girl walking alone drew awkward attention. It was overcrowded, and she suspected that there were talented pickpockets in the morass of people that wound their way through the streets. All things considered, it was cleaner than most cities. Even if it had been dangerous, it was no matter. Lily had been taught to defend herself. If she happened to be unarmed, she'd had some interesting teachers who'd taught her how to look at the environment around her to select weapons.

Ignoring the people who clustered the streets and milled in and out of stores, Lily walked to the end of the pier. She couldn't touch the water, but the wooden pier felt comforting under her feet and the air was relaxing on her skin.

Hector would come, but unlike her, he'd have to ask someone where the nearest body of water was—and ask it in a way that wouldn't reveal her secret. She didn't ever need words to find the water, so she had a few minutes of peace. The tightness in her chest that had started to seize her when she was in the St. Columba's administration hall released as she stood with toes just over the edge.

If she had her way, she'd live on the beach, near one of the clear water zones that Daidí took her to see every year. In a lot of places the pollution was horrible, but some countries had instituted plans to keep beaches open. They'd positioned massive turbines both above and below the water to keep the debris and stench out, and they'd installed huge purification systems. Belfoure wasn't as clean as a few of the places she'd visited, but it was better than most.

She had only been on this stretch of the harbor about ten minutes when she heard footfalls on the wooden pier.

"That was fast, Hec . . ." Her words faded when she glanced to her right and saw not Hector, but Zephyr Waters.

"Not really," he said.

Her shoulders tensed, and she hoped she was wrong about the identity of the boy who stood beside her. After almost a minute passed, she peered at him out of the corner of her eye.

It was definitely Zephyr. She felt like her body was humming again as she stood next to him—just like it had with Creed. Something in her had reverberated like a beacon when she'd first seen the two boys in the media. She'd wondered why, had suspicions, but then she'd met Creed. Now, she knew: they were both fae-bloods. It was the only logical answer . . . and *that* meant that she needed to get out of here. She didn't want to have a second stranger know her secret.

"I've been waiting for you," Zephyr said casually, as if they were friends catching up. "I wasn't sure when you'd get in, but I had a surprise planned. I thought you might come to the water."

Calmly, she glanced at Zephyr and said, "I think you must be looking for someone else. I don't know you."

He smiled.

The tension in her shoulders grew almost painful. Her hand went to the short knife she had concealed in her pocket. There was no way he could've been waiting for *her.* She wasn't in the magazines like him. Perhaps Creed had mentioned her. It was the only answer that wasn't completely troubling. The obvious alternative was that Zephyr could recognize her as fae-blood.

He held out a hand. "Zephyr Waters."

"I still don't *know* you," Lily said, but she accepted his hand briefly.

Being this close to him made her realize that his photos weren't touched up before they were published. Even more so than Creed, Zephyr really was flawless, so much so that she wondered how he'd escaped accusations of being a fae-blood. He had his mother's shockingly blue eyes and 1940s starlet lips, but those combined with his slash of cheekbones and raven-wing hair practically screamed "fae ancestry."

It wasn't Lily's business though. *Abernathy Commandment #13: Don't ask questions when you'd rather not know the answers.* She concentrated on watching a ship heading in toward the harbor. Being here at the pier should've been a moment of peace before she had to figure out how to live around several hundred people. It *had* been . . . up until Zephyr freaking Waters decided to stand at her side and act like they were old friends.

"Perhaps you should go look for whoever it was you intended to meet," Lily suggested. Unfortunately, the lilt at the end of her sentence made her words sound more like a question than she'd intended them to be.

"I've *been* looking . . . for years actually."

"You're making a mistake."

"No, I'm not," he said just as decisively.

Alarm bells sounded in her mind. Creed had said that he took the job at her party to meet her. Now Zephyr claimed he also had wanted to meet her.

"I don't know who you think I am, but I'm really *not* her."

"Oh, I know who you are, Lilywhite," he said softly. "I know exactly who and *what* you are."

She was about to argue, but an explosion rocked the pier. The hull of a cruise ship exploded into flame.

Zephyr's arm snaked around her waist, keeping her from tumbling to the pier or falling into the murky water.

Ships canted wildly as the waves from the explosion battered them. People yelled, both in the street and on other boats. The pier itself shuddered as Lily dragged her attention from the smoke pouring from the cruise liner to Zephyr.

"Welcome to the team," he whispered against her ear.

She tensed, her hand wrapped around the knife. She withdrew it and flicked it open.

But Zephyr spun her around to face him and leaned down. His lips pressed against hers.

Lily jerked away. She waved her hand around, trying to encapsulate the ship, the people running, the sirens, the chaos of it all. She couldn't even begin to deal with the kissing part. "*Seriously?* This? You . . . what are you doing? Are you *insane?*"

Zephyr's expression shifted. "You *are* Lilywhite Abernathy, aren't you?" He glanced at the knife in her hand, but it didn't deter him. He grabbed her again. This time, his hand was on her shoulder, turning her to face him. With his other hand, he gripped Lily's chin and tilted her head, staring at her intently the whole time. "You look like her."

"Of course I'm *me*!" She shoved him away with one hand and took a step backward. "But just because my father is an *accused* criminal doesn't mean I'm some sort of fan of random violence."

Zephyr looked pointedly at the weapon she still clutched in her hand. "Really?"

"Yes, *really*! You grabbed me. I'm defending myself." She was sick of the way everyone judged her. Daidí had often explained that he only engaged in violence for a *reason*. Lily agreed with that approach, although it had been a point of contention with Erik on several occasions.

Lily closed her knife with a *snick* and glared at Zephyr. "You can't go around blowing things up. There are people on those boats, and—"

"It was empty," he interrupted.

"But you . . . I . . . You can't just go around blowing things up and . . . and *kissing people*."

"It was a welcome gift," he said, staring at her in obvious confusion.

"Just stay away from me." She shivered, both from the intensity of his stare and her body's response to his kiss.

"You don't know," he whispered. His eyes widened, and his lips parted. "Holy Ninian! You don't even know."

His reference to the old Pictish saint, said to have been

fae, unnerved her further, but she still asked, "Know what?"

"Who you are," Zephyr said quietly. "You have no idea. That's why you didn't seek us out. That's why you . . ." He snagged her around the waist again, but this time his hold was so tight that she couldn't escape.

Lily tried to yank away. She knew what she was, knew that the blood of the fae was in her not-too-distant ancestry. That didn't mean she was admitting a thing.

"I thought you were just too Seelie for us," Zephyr murmured.

"Too *what*?" She took a step back. That was even more dangerous than invoking Ninian. Seelie was an illegal word, one not used casually in public. Lily needed to get the hell away from Zephyr. Blowing things up, kissing her, accusing her of being fae, he was frightening. He could get them killed . . . or worse.

"Seelie." He started walking, propelling Lily with him along the pier. "Come on. We need to talk."

"No, we don't." She pulled out of his hold. "I don't have *any*thing to say to you."

They were still. Then, after several moments, Zephyr nodded. "I'll see you around, Lilywhite."

He walked away. She returned to campus in hopes that her room was ready. She'd been here not even an hour, and she'd been accused of being fae, kissed, and witnessed a bombing. She wasn't entirely sure which was the most disturbing. Any of them were dangerous.

As she walked the couple of miles back to campus,

Lily debated what to do. Zephyr was clearly involved in something—either as a fae sympathizer or zealously anti-fae. Either option wasn't one she wanted any part of, but there were such similarities in what both Creed and Zephyr had said to her that she wasn't sure she could stay clear of it without more information. Both knew about her, her ancestry, and seemed to have been "waiting" for her. How that was possible, she didn't know.

However, what she *did* know was that it was better that Daidí not hear about her "welcome surprise" from Zephyr until she investigated. *Abernathy Commandment #4: Weigh the consequences before beginning a course of action.*

EILIDH

Eilidh was grateful that Rhys had decided to help her, to protect her and potentially Torquil. She knew that he was limited in what he could do, but knowing that she had an ally was a relief she hadn't expected. Of course, none of that made it easier to face him or Torquil. She'd admitted that the missing child had survived, been raised in the human world, and had a life there for years.

"Who are you?" a ten-year-old Eilidh asked the woman standing inside the Hidden Lands.

"Iana." The woman looked around the somewhat bleak land-scape. "Where am I?"

"Hidden Lands." Eilidh walked closer to her. "You look like Mother."

The woman squatted down in front of Eilidh. She didn't stare at her in horror the way some of the Seelie did, and she didn't ease away as if she couldn't see Eilidh the way a lot of the Unseelie did. They weren't technically *to use those terms any longer. The courts were one. They were simply . . . fae.*

"Who is your mother?" she asked.

"Endellion, Queen of Blood and Rage, once queen of only the Unseelie, but now . . . she protects all *of us." Eilidh was proud of her mother. The queen was their guardian, the warrior who would keep the humans from destroying them all. "She had no sisters. So how can you . . ."*

"Do you have sisters . . . ?"

"Eilidh. I'm Eilidh." She sounded her name out carefully— Ay-leigh—for the woman. "I had a sister. She died in the sea, and Mother had to kill the bad men."

"Oh." The woman brushed Eilidh's hair back. "I'm sorry."

"I didn't know *her. She was a baby, waaaay before I was born." Eilidh smiled at the woman.*

She looked like Mother would if she was happy sometimes. Her hair was night-dark, and when she moved, it looked like tiny stars glimmered in it. The woman's skin was more like the king's though. Leith looked like he'd been forever in the sun and was as dark as bog-soaked wood.

Quietly, Eilidh told her, "You look like Mother's face, but you have Father's skin."

Over the years, Iana and Eilidh had become close, and by the time that Iana confessed that she'd been plucked from the sea and raised by human parents, a fisherman and his wife, Eilidh had already figured it out. She kept that secret—and the secret that Iana had a daughter.

As Eilidh told the story to her brother and betrothed, Torquil interrupted, "The missing heir to the fae kingdom was raised *where*?"

"In a small village on one of the islands."

"How did she hide what she was?" Rhys asked.

"Her mother—"

"*Foster* mother," Rhys interjected with more anger than was typical of him.

"They found someone, a faery, who helped and taught her everything she needed to know. She learned it all, everything but who she *is*." Eilidh got up and paced to the edge of the room. Down below her, faeries stared up at the tower. They didn't usually watch her this closely, but then again, she didn't usually have the queen's son *or* one of the most sought-after pureblooded fae in her home. Having either of them in the tower was new; having *both* here was drawing a disturbing degree of attention.

"They'll think we're plotting against our queen," Rhys said.

"I know."

"She will ask questions of me," he continued.

"I know."

"And I will lie."

Eilidh looked over her shoulder at him.

"But we *aren't* plotting against the queen . . . are we?" Torquil asked.

Neither Eilidh nor Rhys answered.

After several moments passed, Eilidh looked back out

the window of the tower, staring at the dozens of fae who unabashedly gazed up at her. Quietly, she offered, "I will accept the withdrawal of your betrothal should you see fit to change your mind."

"And I will slide the knife across your throat if you go to Mother with what has been spoken here," Rhys added conversationally.

"Is your family always like this?" Torquil sighed. "No. To both of you, *no*."

He stood. Eilidh knew without looking that it was Torquil and not Rhys approaching her. Rhys was too silent to move so obviously through the sitting room. He had to make a conscious effort not to move like shadows.

She didn't turn around.

"I've held your secrets our whole life, Eilidh. Why would that change now that you're my betrothed?" His hands landed on her shoulders as they had often in their years as friends.

She felt his breath stir her hair as he stood behind her. Quietly, she told him, "We won't ever be wed. You can withdraw now or later, but we won't have a bonding ceremony."

"Endellion accepted my choice."

"No," Rhys said, drawing their attention back to him. "Endellion allowed you to be Eilidh's betrothed. There will be no wedding. She won't risk Eilidh's life that way. The heir is too important."

Eilidh slipped out of Torquil's hands and walked back over to her brother. "Is he in danger?" she asked Rhys.

Rhys was still as he thought. It was a look Eilidh had seen on their mother's face often as she weighed the consequences of various plans of action. After several moments, Rhys said, "Not from Nacton or Calder. They'd like you to die. If there were a living child, the infant would be at grave risk, but for their purposes, *you* must die and leave no young." Rhys glanced at Torquil. "You are not to bed the heir. Not now or ever . . . unless Iana's daughter comes home. Then you are no longer of any concern."

"Her life is worthless then?" Torquil came to stand at Eilidh's side. He didn't quite step in front of her, and no weapons were drawn, but the aggression in his posture was enough to make it clear that he wouldn't restrain if he thought his betrothed was threatened.

"Stop." Eilidh grabbed Torquil's wrist and stepped in front of him. She was facing him, her back to Rhys. "He's stating the truth. This is what it means to be the heir: always knowing that there are those who would have me dead, and . . . those who would use me."

If she'd revealed his motive for their betrothal, Torquil showed no sign of it. All he said was, "Then why not let Iana's child take her rightful place?"

"Because she's been raised away from this place. Because she's not meant for this life." Eilidh shook her head at how obvious it was that Torquil had never loved anyone. How could she wish *this* fate on someone she loved? How could he think that being bonded to a faery not of her choosing and living in a glass tower would be satisfying to a woman raised in the human world?

Eilidh turned to face her brother. "There is no risk of a child being born to me."

Rhys nodded. "Keep it so."

Torquil tensed behind her, and she squeezed the wrist she still held.

"I must go, and he can't stay here if you have no chaperone," Rhys announced with all the finality of a father.

Her own father never fussed overmuch about such things, not with her or with his sons. Nacton and Calder were both older than Rhys, and they'd been raised to believe that the world was theirs. Until the unification of the courts, it *had* been.

"I am immeasurably pleased to hear you speak of my safety, but the walls are transparent and our people watch," Eilidh reminded her brother. "If Torquil is to be my betrothed, he will visit me."

"Only in this room."

Torquil's voice was sharp as blades as he said, "You have no right to tell—"

"There are those who *would* kill him before they would see you with child." Rhys spoke over Torquil as if he wasn't there, speaking only to her, dismissing her betrothed pointedly. "And if Mother thinks he has bed you, I will be sent to remove him. There is no way to refuse that order once she has issued it. If you care for him at all, you will not allow him where the people cannot see him. They must know that you are inviolate."

Eilidh nodded. "He will only be here when in this room, but I'm not so young that I need a chaperone beyond"—she gestured to the glass wall—"our people's watchful gaze."

Rhys looked at her like he might consider some form of parting affection, but then he simply said, "Never forget that you will be watched constantly now—by her people, by mine, by Nacton's. Act accordingly."

She nodded again, and then Rhys left, and Eilidh was alone with her betrothed for the first time since his impulsivity had put them in this ridiculous position.

eleven

ZEPHYR

Indifferent expression firmly in place, Zephyr walked away from the pier. He'd let his facade slip when he met Lilywhite. Finally talking to her after all these years was exhilarating. She was to be the other person at the head of the Sleepers, his assigned work-partner. For years, he'd carried the weight without her. He'd done everything he needed, and she'd been hidden away. In his mind, she'd become more than his partner.

He'd imagined their first meeting, of course, pictured their eventual conversation in his mind. He'd pondered a variety of surprises to greet her, ultimately settling on a small explosion. He'd bribed one of the secretaries to let him know when she was arriving, set charges on ships every day in hopes that she'd be unable to resist the pier. It should have been perfect. It should have been a joyous moment.

Instead, she'd pulled a knife and pushed him away. It wasn't encouraging. If he hadn't been so shocked by her reaction, he'd have tried to ask her knife for any details it might have gathered. Lilywhite was aligned with water, so she couldn't ask it not to speak to him. He hadn't thought to ask the steel for information, however. He was too caught off guard by her response to him.

Obviously, he'd built up his expectations. He'd imagined this day for so many years that Lilywhite was almost mythical to him. She had become increasingly more so the longer she stayed away. He'd imagined that she was more like those he'd met in the Hidden Lands. He'd spent thousands of dollars to collect every scrap of intel he could so as to prep for today, for their first meeting, for the moment when he wasn't left alone with the responsibility for the others in their Sleeper cell, for the moment he met the faery he thought would one day be his mate. Despite everything he'd done, he was grievously unprepared for the reality.

"Roan," he called out as he walked into the surf shop.

Not surprisingly, Roan was the only customer in the surf shop. He stood in front of the bulletin board with sales and trip listings. Zephyr sometimes suspected Swell stayed in business solely on the purchases made by the St. Columba's students, most of whom weren't back to school until tomorrow. Of those students, Roan was easily the freest with his money. No trip was too dear for him. He would live in the water if he had his way.

"Zeph." Roan studied Zephyr with the kind of attentive

nonchalance that he excelled at. Like the seas that were his element, Roan was both calm and filled with energy simultaneously. If Roan hadn't admitted his affinity the moment they'd met, Zephyr would've still known it. The surf-crazed boy had eyes that could easily be mistaken for a seal's and his skin was dark enough that it seemed as elegant as the seal pelt he could don as comfortably as most people slipped into a winter coat. Only his unruly hair was unmatched to his water-dwelling appearance. Given a chance, Roan would let his hair form into the dreadlocks it so obviously wanted, but the future CEO of Reliance Pharmaceuticals wouldn't wear dreads.

They all wore their human personas. It was simply part of the task they'd been given by their queen. Sleepers could only succeed at their missions by being exactly what they were thought to be.

Zephyr turned and walked out of the shop.

"Well?" Roan prompted as he exited behind Zephyr.

Zephyr tried to find the calm he usually had, but he couldn't. Lilywhite was the last of the seven on his team, and now that she was with him, he had to report to the Unseelie Queen that all seven Black Diamonds were together. That was the protocol. What he didn't know was how much to reveal to the queen, and facing her for the first time with incomplete answers was more terrifying than he wanted to admit, even to himself. He couldn't let the others see how afraid he was.

The others relied on him. They had for years. He'd met

Alkamy, Creed, and Violet when he was still a kid, and he'd met Roan and Will when he started at St. Columba's several years ago. They'd always known that he was their leader. He'd worked hard to live up to that expectation, but today had thrown him for a loop.

"Lilywhite has no idea who she is," he told Roan finally.

"How did the handlers let *that* happen?"

"I have no idea," Zephyr admitted. The horrible shock of it had left him quieter than usual. Lilywhite was the seventh and final member of his unit, the missing piece, the one the queen wanted to meet—and she was clueless.

Roan fell into step with him, keeping pace and then little by little slowing so as to force Zephyr to walk at a more fitting rate. That was one of the things he valued most about Roan: he was a strategist. He was also the calmest of the group, trained to be so because he was the only son of the CEO and primary shareholder of Reliance Pharmaceuticals.

Roan turned onto a less crowded street and added, "Before I forget, Vi wanted me to let you know she might not be here for another few days. Whatever film she's in now is running behind schedule."

"When does Will get in?"

Roan gave him an are-you-serious look. "On schedule to the minute. He'll arrive in about eighteen hours, precisely at the stated move-in time. The mighty senator wouldn't have *her* son ask for any special consideration."

The senator was one of the few Native American

congress members, as well as being one of the rare single mothers who had attained and *held* a seat in the nation's New Congress. Perhaps because she was breaking boundaries, she focused an inordinate amount of attention on keeping up overall conservative appearances.

That meant that she didn't rage against her son's sexual orientation; she simply denied its existence—and insisted that Roan was merely a "good friend" to her son.

Roan's father was also strict, but in his case it was about staying away from "New Hollywood wastrels." On breaks from St. Columba's the unit functioned like two smaller groups. Zephyr saw Creed and Alkamy fairly regularly. Roan was able to stay in close contact with Will. Violet, of course, was able to do whatever she wanted. No one told her "no," or if they tried, she simply ignored them. So she was a liaison between the two groups.

The one missing piece had been Lilywhite. None of them had a way to reach the daughter of the acknowledged head of the country's most successful criminal organization. She'd been kept hidden from the media and the world.

Until now.

Until today.

Roan guided them to a pathway that cut through a small park a few blocks from the pier. After they passed the park, they'd be in a residential area, and from there they'd eventually come up to the side of campus. It would require scaling the wall to get into the grounds, but once they did, they'd be in the gardens.

"Creed is still communing?"

"In the back corner, by the yew trees," Roan directed.

They walked in silence for several minutes, which was precisely what Zephyr needed—no extra complications. He had enough to worry about with Alkamy's moods, Creed's drinking, and Violet's temper. He'd expected that Lilywhite would share his burden, be a voice of reason in their odd little group. Instead she added to his list of problems, although it was through no fault of her own. Someone had failed in their duty to let her know who she was, what she was, who *he* was.

"Did you ever think that maybe it's not an honor?" Roan's voice was low enough that Zephyr had to lean closer to hear. "Being chosen, I mean."

"No." Silently, Zephyr added, *because if I allowed myself to think it, the queen would kill us all.*

Roan looked away before almost guiltily adding, "I don't want to die . . . or hurt anyone again."

Zephyr *couldn't* be afraid, not to die and not to kill. There was no questioning, not of the regents, not of their handler, not of the missions they would be assigned. Questions could lead to answers he didn't like, to disobedience, and *that* would lead to death—and leaving his team, his friends, alone. He could die for his duty, for his friends, for their people, but he wasn't going to die because he questioned their regents. He certainly wasn't going to let *his friends* die if he could prevent it.

"You need to stay here when I go to see the queen," Zephyr told Roan.

"No argument here." Roan shuddered.

Zephyr gripped his friend's arm and repeated the words he'd been drilled on for years: "We owe the queen everything. She came up with a plan to save our lives, to save everyone. She's *bled* for us, Roan."

Roan said nothing as they reached the wall that stretched along the east side of campus.

Zephyr stroked the vines that covered the wall, asking them to part for him. The plants were meant to keep anyone from scaling the wall, but flora answered Zephyr. Once the vines shifted, Roan gripped the stone and began to climb. He reached the top of the rose-and-thorn-covered wall, and stepped over. Without seeing him, Zephyr knew the boy had landed in a graceful tumble. They'd been climbing this wall for going on four years.

He spoke to the plants again, thanking them as he climbed. Tendrils reached out, touching his skin, seeking contact with him as eagerly as he sought their touch. It was a terrifying gift in his childhood. He'd grown up in New Hollywood, where gardens were groomed meticulously. All Zephyr had to do was take a walk, and the plants rioted. They burst into bloom out of season; they snaked across paths and fountains. They tangled in his hair and shredded his clothes. Early on, his family had a fleet of gardeners and landscapers to keep their grounds from looking wild, to protect him from accusations of fae blood, but by the time he was twelve, his parents had simply erected a high fence with a gate and told their friends that they liked the "hedonism" of an unkept garden. Zephyr still wore the key to that gate like a talisman.

The gardens at St. Columba's didn't respond as vigorously as those of his childhood. Over time, the plants had taught him though, filled his mind with messages of patience and wisdom. If they hadn't, he'd still be at home, unable to be anywhere other than concrete and brick vistas. He'd wondered more than a few times if that was why Lilywhite had been hidden away all of these years.

Inside the gardens, Creed was stretched out in the sunlight. He looked listless, too limp to rise from the ground and greet them. He cracked one eye, saw that it was them, and closed it again. "No lectures, Zephyr. Kamy looks just as bad."

"I trust you to help keep her safe, but last night, you were *both* drinking before I even got there."

Creed flipped him off. "Alkamy doesn't listen to anyone but you."

"And *you* listen to no one." Zephyr dropped to the ground a few feet away from Creed. "Lilywhite arrived, so I need to go to the Hidden Lands tonight. What am I to do if the queen asks about any of you?"

Roan and Creed looked away.

The Queen of Blood and Rage held their lives in her hands, and she had done so since before they existed. It didn't matter if they agreed. She *owned* them. If she didn't find them worthy . . . He shook his head. Years ago, he'd asked his handler what would happen if they didn't want to be Sleepers.

"She'll have me kill you," Clara said as easily as if she were speaking about the weather. "Maybe another in the unit would be elevated, but the queen prefers seven members in your team. We'd need to import another Sleeper or eliminate the whole cell."

"All of us?"

"It wouldn't be the first time. There was an earlier version of the program. It wasn't successful." Clara met his gaze. "Do you want to be a Sleeper, Zephyr?"

"I do," he lied.

"Do you live and die to serve the Queen of Blood and Rage?"

"I will," he said. If it meant keeping his friends alive, he'd be the most devoted Sleeper there was.

"It's for the best if you keep this conversation to yourself," Clara added. "We wouldn't want the others to get the wrong idea about you or about their queen."

"I live for our queen, Clara." He straightened his shoulders. "That's exactly what the others will know: the truth. I live for her, and we do serve her will."

And that was that. He had to be devoted to the queen, or he'd die. His friends would die. *They* had to be faithful in order to live—and he would keep them that way.

Every one of them had been raised knowing about the Sleeper Program and why it mattered. Humanity had already had their chance to be the caretakers of the world.

They'd failed. Glaciers melted. Cities were lost to the sea. The whole of one continent was evacuated. After one chemical company went unpunished for toxic disposals, other companies began stealthily exporting their waste, and soon all of what was once called Africa had become too contaminated for people. Whole species of animals were wiped out; others were critically endangered, no longer existing anywhere aside from zoological parks. Africa had become a global trash dump. Its displaced citizens were integrated into other lands—most often Ausland and the South Continent. Humanity had *failed*.

And then, as if their pollution wasn't crime enough, they had assassinated the royal heir.

The Queen of Blood and Rage decided to strike back. At her order, the fae had bred and surrendered their young to be placed in the homes of people of influence across the globe. They'd allowed their children to be raised as humans, living in a world of disease and decay, because they *believed*. They'd sacrificed their own children because they'd believed. His real parents had believed enough to send him here, and Zephyr couldn't let them down.

Clara had explained repeatedly that their people were counting on him and the rest of the Sleeper Program. The humans had far outnumbered the fae, and the fae who had come forward openly were slaughtered. So the queen had turned to guerrilla warfare. The Sleepers were only one facet of her master plan. He saw the results on the news. There was a small city on the southern coast that was taken by the sea. Almost every casino in Vegas had been attacked by poison funneled into air ducts simultaneously; the death count there was high. Old Dublin had a siege of rats carrying the bubonic plague, and Chicago had been set to burn by over five hundred lightning strikes that were undoubtedly fae in origin.

The attacks weren't regular, and the media tried to explain them away, but the tabloids were filled with truth in this case. They cut through the government explanations and acknowledged that the Queen of Blood and Rage was steadily targeting humanity—and that humanity was defenseless.

The queen was merciless when angered, and Zephyr hoped that he wasn't going to anger her tonight.

"I'll let you know how it goes," he told his teammates. "Right now, you better concentrate on getting well. No more of this, Creed."

Creed didn't speak, neither agreeing nor refusing. He simply stretched in the sunlight, absorbing the nutrients it offered. Later, he'd do the same with the moon. Creed and Will were creatures of air, just as Zephyr and Alkamy were of the earth. Zephyr's second affinity, metal, was peculiar in that it was only recharged via fighting. Alkamy had also started to show a second affinity, but hers was air. Consequently, unlike Zephyr, she could find nutrients from the sun and the moon, as well as from the soil. Violet was fire, so she drew from the sun as well. Only Roan and Zephyr weren't able to be healed by sun alone. Roan needed water, and Zephyr needed soil.

Zephyr stroked the plants nearest him.

Creed drew his attention back to them by asking, "How was the explosion?"

Zephyr flopped down on the ground, shucked his shoes so he could feel the earth against his skin, and brought both Creed and Roan up to speed on the explosion, Lilywhite, and the difficulty of what to tell the queen.

He did not, however, tell them about the kiss. He didn't admit that he was more stunned by the way she'd kissed or that she looked momentarily terrified when he called her Seelie. He didn't tell them that she'd fled from him. Lily-white was a mystery to him, and until he figured out more about her, he'd be keeping that mystery to himself as much as he could.

twelve

LILY

Lily felt out of sorts as she walked through the administration building and down that over-wide, shadowed hallway. The stone murmured under her feet; the heavy bass voice of it felt like a monastic chant that soothed her nerves. Sometimes Lily felt bad for people who couldn't connect to one of the elements, but then again, *they* weren't breaking laws simply by existing.

After several minutes, she found Hector inside a surprisingly modern office. "The campus gates should have been closed after we entered. She could've been—"

"Hector," Lily cut him off.

The headmistress had a pinched look as she turned to face Lily. "We take security very seriously here at St. Columba's, Miss Abernathy. The gates are in place for a reason. They keep threats out, but you should know that wandering into Belfoure alone is not something we recommend."

"I understand," Lily said, tactfully avoiding any admissions.

Hector shot her a look that made quite clear that he knew what she was doing.

"Well then," the headmistress said. She cleared her throat delicately and told Hector, "Miss Abernathy seems to be safe after all."

"Maybe the school ought to consider guards," Hector suggested, his gaze fastened on Lily as he spoke. "I could help you set up a patrol route, Mistress Cuthbert."

Lily rolled her eyes even though Hector wasn't joking. Her father had guards inside the gate, as well as a security room to keep eyes on the whole estate at all times. Daidí took extra precautions because of his career choice. Nonetheless, she was fairly certain that such measures were a bit more draconian than those that St. Columba's employed, despite the affluence of their students.

"We are not a prison." Mistress Cuthbert pursed her lips again, and Lily thought she might like the woman a little bit after all. "As I was telling your driver, Miss Abernathy, students are free to explore the grounds within reason. It's simply the area outside the gate—the town of Belfoure, in particular—that is off-limits."

Lily nodded. None of this was actually surprising. It

wasn't pleasing, but it wasn't unexpected at all. Daidí held security second only to love of family in his pantheon of values.

"If you exit the rear of the hall, the grounds extend quite far," Mistress Cuthbert was saying. "You really have no need to go into town proper unless you need something from one of the shops, and there are sanctioned outings for that."

Her voice sounded almost sympathetic, and Lily suspected that she was far from the first student at St. Columba's who had an overzealously protective parent. In this, at least, Lily might be normal.

Abernathy Commandment #14: Blending in helps you seem less memorable should you need an alibi at some point.

The headmistress turned away to answer another student who had the look of a girl who was not used to any conflicts in her life. Lily felt a stab of sympathy, both for the girl's obvious emotions and for her inability to hide them.

"Don't leave the grounds again, Lilywhite," Hector ordered in a voice not to be refused.

"I don't intend to leave again," she told him, offering both an admission and a promise.

He nodded, having been trained to know that when she offered blunt promises, she could be trusted wholly. "I'll wait here with your things."

"I'm safe, Hector," she assured him, and then she went to find peace in the gardens.

She didn't need both the waves and the soil to keep

healthy. Either one would suffice. It was easier if she had both, but one was enough to sustain her. Daidí had undoubtedly already researched the matter. If they hadn't already had what she needed, he would've paid to add it.

The hall appeared empty so she slipped off her shoes again. The stone sang to her as she walked, speaking of a faraway quarry where men had carved the rock from the earth. The story was not told in words, not in the way that most people understood words. Stone spoke in thick slow images, like heavy syrup trailing across her mind. The news most stone could share was far from recent. Their words fell into her consciousness with a welcome surety though. Stone mightn't know the newest things, but what they did know was true.

On the other hand, sea was fickle, and sometimes the act of sorting through the sheer immensity of the words from the water was an exhausting task. Air, for her at least, was barely an affinity. It was there, but it came with difficulty thus far. Fire hadn't been an affinity that she'd felt as comfortable with. Mostly, she counted on the earth for knowledge. Earth had been her first, and of the earth options, the words of stone and soil were easiest for her to hear.

As soon as Lily left the hall, the hum of the roots seeped through the cobblestone path under her feet, beckoning her. She resisted stepping into the soil. It was one thing to walk barefoot on the old stone of the building; it was an entirely different matter to let the plants greet her, especially when her mind was so unsettled. Plants with so much human contact were chaotic in their words, more so than she could manage today.

"Soon," she promised.

The grounds behind the administration building were beautiful. Trees flourished as if they had never known dry seasons. Shrubs dotted healthy lawns, and flower beds offered bursts of reds, golds, and violet. Beyond them, however, was something far more exciting. A walled garden waited there, and the door was open. It looked seldom used, which was exactly what she needed. She wanted to step off the stone path and onto the living earth. She wanted to lose herself in it, fill the ache inside her with the surety of nature.

She pushed the door open farther, murmuring a soft greeting to the remnant of the spirit of the wood that still clung to the aged timber. Vines clung to the walls and exploded in every hue of green she could hope to see. Inside the garden, paths were clearly marked. At the far back of the curated part of the garden was the mouth of a labyrinth. To either side of it, the plants seemed to have been allowed to go wild. The juxtaposition of the sculpted maze and the chaotic expanse was perfection. People didn't enter the wild anymore. Fears of fae lurking in the shadows kept most of humanity to the fringes of nature.

Lily went into the maze and twisted through several passageways. Then, after a quick glance to make sure there were no witnesses, she asked, "May I pass?"

The plants rustled softly as they parted to allow her into the wilderness outside the labyrinth. She stepped through the opening in the hedge wall, expecting to be alone with the rarely visited plants of the wild, but there, dressed only in his tattoos and jeans, was Creed Morrison.

She was glad she hadn't arrived a few moments earlier. He was buttoning his jeans.

At her gasp, he looked up and saw her. "And here I'd begun to think you disliked me."

The anger in his voice was tempered by his apparent amusement at her discomfort. Lily looked down at her feet to keep from staring. She'd certainly seen pictures of him like this, bare-chested and barefoot. He'd been caught on a beach in Ibiza wearing nothing more than jewelry, ink, and a smile. He'd been photographed in the restored Trevi fountain in Roma. The journals had blurred just enough to keep from violating "privacy of minors" laws, but only just. She'd liked the pictures, as she suspected most anyone with functioning eyes would. Still, seeing the pictures of mostly naked Creed Morrison hadn't made her feel dizzy the way the real person was.

"I was just"—she gestured behind her—"taking a walk."

"And stepped through a hedge wall without a scratch? However did you manage that?"

She looked back at him as he buttoned the top button on his jeans. He didn't sound as friendly as he had at her party, and she had exactly *zero* experience in being challenged. She kept her lips pressed together.

"Is this the part where you injure yourself by lying again or admit that you're a fae-blood like me?"

She stared at him, consciously holding his gaze and not letting her attention drift to his bare skin.

Abernathy Commandment #6: Never confess your vulnerabilities if you can avoid it.

"Neither." She smiled then, letting a little of her temper into it. "I don't see the need to answer that question."

Creed laughed. He was dangerous in ways she didn't understand. Growing up with criminals had prepared her for a lot of things, but not *this*. She felt the urge to flee just as she had the first time she'd seen a mountain lion in the woods.

However, she knew enough to know how to protect herself a little. The fae were known to stand by their word—their literal word, but still, it was better than humanity, which could be treacherous for so many foolish, selfish reasons.

"Do you mean me harm, Creed Morrison?" she asked. It wasn't a perfect request, but she'd spoken his name as she knew it, and the intent was there. She'd never attempted to elicit a fae bargain before because of the risks of exposure, but he already knew what she was.

Creed's eyes glimmered in approval. "On my blood, I do not."

She opened her mouth to reply, but he spoke over her. "And do you, Lilywhite Abernathy, daughter of Iana, mean me harm?"

They were alone in the garden. There were no

witnesses, no one to hear her words or his. She sat down on the ground.

He matched her movements.

Slowly, not looking away from him, she spread her hands out over the ground. Tendrils of vines snapped to her like whips. They curled around her from wrists to biceps. It wasn't the extent of her relationship with the things that lived within the soil, but it was enough to point out that she wasn't defenseless even in their isolation. The knife in her pocket and the one strapped to her leg were a secret, and she opted to keep it that way. Her affinity with the earth she would admit, partly because her fae-blood nature wasn't a secret from him and partly because she needed the touch of earth.

"I mean you no harm on this day and until such time as you mean harm to me or mine," she vowed.

"Thorough," he said mildly.

"Contracts and negotiations are familiar territory. My father is a crime lord."

"*The* crime lord," he corrected.

Lily shrugged. She'd reached her limit of admissions for the moment. The vines on her wrists slithered away, and she stroked her fingers over the soil, not lingering long enough that the plants would share their most recent memories. Seeing the full image of a naked Creed Morrison was a tempting idea, but definitely not a good one. Her memory flashed back to the photos with the blurred sections.

After a moment when it felt like the air became perfectly still, he sang, "Deadly girl. All I've ever wanted was a girl like you, a girl who kills me a little more every day." His words touched her skin with each breath, despite how far apart they sat. "Sun-kissed skin and bloodstained heart. All I ever wanted was you."

She shivered.

"All I need is a deadly girl, a—"

"So air," she interrupted. "Your affinity is for the air."

"It is," he agreed.

Without meaning to, she lifted her hand to touch her skin where she'd felt his words. A small voice reminded her that Erik could never do what Creed just did, that choosing to be with a human would mean sacrificing parts of herself. Logic silenced that voice quickly. Her life was already going to be risky enough without adding the dangers of being with another fae-blood.

Creed watched her like he was counting the beats of her heart. Maybe he was. She wasn't as familiar with the aspects of working with the air. It didn't come to her easily so far.

He sang softly, "Knife-tipped fingers and rose-petal kisses. All I need is—"

"Stop." She pushed the air back toward him as forcefully as she could. Her eyes fell closed and she concentrated on not calling soil or stone to her defense.

After several moments, Creed asked, "I thought you liked my singing, Lily?"

She wasn't going to lie, but she wasn't going to listen to him as his voice brushed against the skin low on her throat either. Lily opened her eyes and said, "You know it wasn't your singing that I was stopping."

"I've never done that with anyone else," he said, his voice casual. "Not on purpose at least. Not until you."

She wasn't even sure she believed him. He'd already proven that he was capable of overcoming the fae aversion to lying. Everyone was very clear that fae-blood couldn't do so, and she'd always wondered if she was *less* fae-blood because she herself could lie. Then again, the fact that she had multiple affinities, strong ones, made her suspect that she was actually of purer lineage rather than being *less* fae.

She wasn't sure what to say, but before she could figure it out, Creed said, "No one knows I met you." He kept his voice emotionlcss.

Lily stared at him. He kept tossing her things that she didn't know how to catch. Sure, they'd had a spark when they met, and yes, she'd had a tabloid crush on him for years. That shouldn't mean that they dive headfirst into disaster. "Why are you telling me this?"

He sprawled out on the ground. "It will matter later. If it was about my reputation, I'd have found a way to get pictures out to the media. I didn't tell *anyone* though. And I'm glad I didn't. There are . . . others to consider."

It was easy to figure out who Creed meant. The welcome-to-Belfoure bombing was a pretty big clue. The kiss was another. And if there were any doubts, Zephyr's own admissions vanquished those.

"I met him today," she said, sinking to her knees on the ground to face Creed. "Zephyr. That's who you meant, right?"

She watched Creed as she said it, but he wasn't as easy to read as she'd like. For someone whose every emotion appeared to be on his face in the hundreds of pictures that cropped up everywhere, Creed's expressions one-to-one were implacable. She wondered how much of his media persona was cultivated. How much of the careless charm was *his*, and how much was a persona?

When he remained silent, Lily added, "I met him a couple hours ago in town."

All he said in reply to her announcement was, "I know."

She paused, hoping things weren't going to get *more* awkward. If Creed knew that she'd met Zephyr, that meant that Zephyr would've had to have seen Creed immediately after meeting her.

"So you know what happened? Between us?"

Creed nodded. "Why do I think there was more to the story than what Zephyr told me?"

"Claimed he was waiting for me. Explosion. No one hurt. I pulled a knife. He kissed me. Accused me of being Seelie," she summarized bluntly. It was a tactic she'd seen her father use to great effect: state the facts and move on.

"Zephyr left out the kiss," Creed said flatly. "And the knife."

"Oh." She shrugged. "I was taught never to be unarmed.

Using weapons helps me keep from drawing on an affinity and revealing myself."

"And the kiss?"

". . . is not the important point," she said.

They stared at each other, and she felt the bizarre urge to apologize. They weren't a couple. Creed had been hired by her father to sing to her. They'd talked. They weren't even *friends*. They'd flirted . . . and then he went on to be photographed with no less than four girls between that day and now.

Creed simply watched her.

The tension was growing thicker the longer the silence dragged on, so she steered the conversation back to his earlier remarks. "Zephyr is the other person, right? The one you're concerned about. You're friends, and obviously both fae-blood. How did either of you know about *me* though?"

Rather than answer, Creed closed his eyes and tilted his face up to the sky like he was asking some unseen being to give him strength. If she hadn't known he was a fae-blood, she would have suspected that's precisely what he was doing, but she'd felt the way he moved the air near her when he sang. He wasn't praying. Creed was *literally* drawing strength from the air above them, or more accurately, from the sun. In a voice so low Lily had to strain to hear it, he said, "I want to tell you everything, every secret, every good and bad thing I know, but I can't." His eyes were still closed. "I want to, but Zeph . . ."

"What?"

"It's complicated," Creed offered weakly, as if that was any kind of an answer.

"He blew up a ship. He's a terrorist, isn't he? That's the secret. You're not just fae-blood. You're *sympathizers*."

Creed laughed, a bitter, almost mean sound. "I'm not a sympathizer, not even a little."

"Have you bombed anything?"

"No."

His tone was hesitant enough that Lily prompted, "But?"

"I can't answer that." He stared at her, looking more lost than rock stars with bad attitudes ever should. "I wish things were simple. I wish no one could issue me orders. What I *can* tell you is that if people knew we were talking, if *Zephyr* knew we were talking, it would be bad. I broke a lot of rules coming to your house. I'm breaking more every moment we speak."

"I'm glad you're not opposed to breaking *those* rules," she admitted. Then, she nodded and sent the vines that had been tangled around her skin earlier out toward Creed. They slithered toward him like serpents, and he looked at them in wonder. It felt intimate to share her fae-blood traits with him. She'd never let even Daidí see the extent of what she could do.

She wanted to show Creed though, to confess her secrets to him. She wanted to have him look at her the way he was watching the leafy tendrils gliding toward his skin. Maybe all fae-blood could manipulate their affinity elements as she could, but from the way Creed watched the vines, she suspected yet again that she was more fae than even those who had been arrested and convicted. It wasn't the first time she'd thought it, but it wasn't a truth she liked to ponder.

As Creed stared at the vines that were twining their way over his body, Lily asked, "Does it always feel intense when another fae-blood touches you?"

"Zephyr's kiss?" he asked bitterly. "He's experienced."

"Not Zephyr," she interrupted.

Creed's attention snapped to her, but she refused to be embarrassed, not by the kiss, not by the question, and not by her next words.

She clarified, "When I met you . . . it felt different. Just having you stare at me . . . and then the kiss on my cheek."

As her words trailed off, Creed failed to completely hide a grin. "No. It's not usually like that."

Lily nodded. "But you're not supposed to know me?"

"No," he said. "I'm not sure I'm even allowed to speak to you once classes start. There are rules, Lily."

She felt like pieces of the secrets were clicking into place. He and Zephyr were tied into the same group, and for some reason Zephyr had a personal interest in her. "So you knew what I was before we met?"

"Yes."

"And that's *not* why you wanted to talk to me? Not that . . . or anything to do with my father?"

Creed made no attempt to hide his expression, making it clear that he wasn't lying as he said, "I've listened to stories about the missing Lilywhite for years, so maybe it was part of it, but when I met you? I wished you weren't fae-blood at all. Then you could be free of this."

She could hear things in the spaces between the words he was uttering aloud, and she knew that he was very carefully trying to adhere to the letter of the rules he was under. It was a very fae approach. Even so, what he did admit told her enough. Whatever secrets Creed had, whatever secrets they shared now, it centered around the fae and Zephyr. Coming to St. Columba's suddenly felt more than dangerous; it felt like a conspiracy, and getting tangled up in fae-blood conspiracies was both illegal and deadly.

"I don't run, and I don't let anyone decide my path but me." She let the vines retract, pulling them back from where they had begun to twist over his calves and knees, and stood.

Abernathy Commandment #5: Be bold.

With every bit of poise her father had taught her, Lily looked down at Creed. He hadn't stood.

"I've spent my life not getting mixed up in anything political. I haven't attended school, gone anywhere without a guard. I like my privacy." She let a little of her public facade down and smiled. "You're tempting, but temptation isn't enough reason for me to get mixed up in whatever mess you and Zephyr are in."

"It's not that easy," Creed started.

Lily laughed. "I'm Nick Abernathy's only child. It truly *is* that easy. To disappear. To eliminate anyone who tries to stop me from doing so. My father has taught me more about being ruthless than I ever want people to see."

And with that warning to the fae-blood, she walked away from him and realized that it was a reminder to herself as well. She wasn't going to be pushed around by a couple of tabloid darlings with penchants for drama. She was Lily-white Abernathy, and no one, fae or human, was going to control her.

thirteen

ZEPHYR

When Zephyr realized that Alkamy hadn't come outside all day, he went to check on her. He told himself it was because he had a duty to all of the cell members. He told himself it was because Alkamy wasn't good at being bored. It simply wasn't something she *did*. If there wasn't entertainment, she created some. If there wasn't anyone to amuse her, she found someone.

Zephyr wasn't jealous. He couldn't be. She wasn't *his*. She was his best friend though, and he had been responsible for her since the day they'd met. She never demanded it of him, never reminded him when he failed. She was patient and tolerant with him as she was with no one else. It was a rare gift to be cared for by Alkamy Adams, one he'd let lead them both astray a few times.

When Zephyr met her in one of her many, many classes,

he became an accessory. He didn't mind. She was amazing. Hapless instructors would tell her rock star daddy that she was a very talented young woman, but had trouble with authority. Zephyr was the perfect boyfriend for *that* girl.

By the time she was twelve, she could play everything from the lute to synthesizer, tribal drums to cello. Any instrument was a perfect fit in her hands. By sixteen, her father had her in studios performing like a trained monkey. Zephyr wanted to beat the man for not noticing how hard Alkamy tried to get his attention. He was clueless, never even suspecting that her inhuman gift for music was fae or questioning her unearthly beauty when she became a teen-ager. Alkamy's handler had noticed though and began to teach her how to feed lies to the media so she seemed that she had to *work* at looking like a doll. Without her handler, Alkamy would've been outed as fae before she was thirteen. Since then, Zephyr had helped, as had his handler, who was now their shared liaison with the courts.

He opened the door to her suite and looked around. Alkamy was stretched out inside the soil she stored inside her sofa. The sofa cushions were on the floor, revealing a bed of soil where Alkamy was currently half-submerged and mostly naked. She did, at least, have underwear on.

"No roommate yet then, Kamy?" he asked. It wasn't something she did in front of suitemates.

"Why don't you ever knock?" She flung a handful of soil at him. "What if I were naked? Or sleeping? Or naked *and* sleeping?"

He stepped into the soil and tilted his face upward like he was stepping under a water shower. Then, he leaned down and kissed her forehead. "You are naked, by the way."

"I am not. Underwear means not naked." She rolled over and wiggled her hips a little so she sank deeper.

Relieved that she had moved so he wasn't trying to talk to her without letting his gaze drop to her bare chest, Zephyr started scooping soil over her back. He didn't comment on the fact that she needed so much soil-time every single time she returned to campus. They'd fought about it enough to know all the lines already.

You need to tell him to keep his cigarettes and cigarette-smoking friends out of the house.

That's not my character.

You're not a character, *Kamy. You're a person.*

I'm a person whose father is a whisky-drinking, cigarette-smoking rock star. If I want him to be sympathetic to me, if I want to avoid being detained as fae, I need to be the daughter he wants. You know that.

What I know is that you need *to stop drinking.*

Zephyr didn't ask if she ever smoked too. Alkamy had enough self-induced sickening all on her own, and Zephyr didn't want to add to it.

"You could try being my public girlfriend again. Go vegan and organic because you're so into me." He rubbed the soil into her back, never once letting his hands even brush the top seam of her underwear. "Stop drinking, at least. Pretend like I do."

Even though Zephyr flirted, slept around like the spoiled New Hollywood child he was thought to be, and had publicly admitted to choosing dates to coordinate with his clothes, he'd always treated Alkamy with respect. Now that they were platonic, she nagged him that he didn't show that kind of respect to other girls.

Of course, there was Vi. Sometimes, he wasn't sure that he respected her as much as *feared* her. Her element was fire. In theory, an earth-aligned fae would balance her, but Zephyr wasn't sure there was a faery born who could balance her. She was volatility in motion. He respected her, but he gave her wide berth when possible. Now there was the third female member of their cell.

"I met Lilywhite."

Alkamy didn't budge. "Seelie?"

"I don't know," he said, not wanting to broach that topic. If Lily *was* Seelie, she'd obviously not be blood family. He could love her a little if he wanted . . . at least, he could if the queen allowed. Real love was a mistake though; it led to fighting, hurt, and desperation.

"Lilywhite could be Unseelie, I guess," Zephyr commented. "Or maybe her human upbringing confuses things. She was raised by Nicolas Abernathy, who makes monsters seem cuddly." His hands paused on Alkamy's shoulders for a moment. "Usually I have a pretty good guess. I couldn't tell with her."

There was a note in his voice that made Alkamy lift her head. No one else would've noticed. There were layers of things he'd need to confess in time. Today wasn't that day.

Alkamy looked back at him. "Guesses? Really? So you could be wrong about everyone in the cell."

"Maybe."

"*I* could be Seelie for all you know," she continued.

"Too pale," Zephyr pointed out, even though it wasn't *true* proof. The only sure way to tell was skin tone. The Unseelie, the more monstrous of the two, were pale like they'd only ever walked in moonlight. The Seelie, however, could vary in skin tone.

"*Any*how," Zephyr said, dragging out the word. "Lily-white had no idea who she was."

"*What?*" Alkamy jerked upright, flinging soil everywhere with her sudden movement. "How is that even possible?"

"I don't know." He brushed the loose dirt from her arms and shoulders. "She knows she has *some* fae blood, but she doesn't know about the Sleepers."

"But . . . her handler? How could she make it this long without knowing that she was one of us?"

"I don't know. All I can say is that she didn't greet me like she was expecting me. She was not pleased by the bombing I arranged to welcome her. It was strange . . . and troubling."

He lifted Alkamy to her feet, kissed her forehead, and grabbed her robe. Seeing her covered in soil only emphasized her otherworldly appearance. Of all of them, she'd always be the most likely to be outed—and if she was arrested, Zephyr wasn't sure he could restrain his vengeance. It was moments like this that made him more sympathetic to the Queen of Blood and Rage. There were people in life who were worth a storm of destruction and terror. He understood that . . . because of Alkamy.

"Go rinse," he said. "I'm going to swing by Cuthbert's office and see if I can find out where Lilywhite will be rooming. Do you want me to check on your latest suitemate?"

"Met her. Got rid of her." Alkamy grinned and shrugged on the robe he held out for her.

He kissed the tip of her nose. "You are so Unseelie. No doubts."

"We'll see some day, I guess." Alkamy grabbed her bag of oils and slipped her feet into sandals. "I'm going to the tubs."

Every dorm had a basic bathroom with showers, but there were also slipper tubs on every floor that were open for leisurely soaks. Zephyr had spent one very memorable night there with her. He smiled before he could help himself, and then shoved that memory back into the mental box where he kept it now.

He offered her his arm. "Escort?"

Alkamy rolled her eyes. "There's no one around to preen for, and everyone already thinks I'm a notch in your bedpost. Give it up until the masses arrive."

She wasn't like him: she wouldn't fight because the queen ordered it. One late night, she'd admitted that she was only going along with her role as a Sleeper because of him. He was her reason—which meant he had to keep her on target. If not, she'd likely die.

"I still miss you," he whispered.

"And I'm still right here. Always." She leaned her head against his shoulder.

Zephyr lapsed into silence as he escorted her to the door of the bathroom. That was the problem: she was here, but not really. She was in his arms, but not the way he wanted. She was at his side, but not his to keep.

"Don't do anything stupid," Alkamy urged as they stopped at the bathing room.

"Define stupid?"

Alkamy sighed and kissed his cheek. "Whatever you're thinking, most likely."

He grinned.

"I'm serious," she said. "She's not from our world—the fae one *or* the human one."

"She's the last of us, Kamy." Zephyr opened the door to the bathing room. "She needs to know. *We* need to tell her."

Alkamy ignored the opened door. "Can you at least not tell Endellion?"

He frowned at her and let the door fall shut. "Title only, Alkamy. No one speaks the old name casually. Not here or over there."

"And isn't *that* proof enough that we shouldn't let her know about Lilywhite yet? Should we obey someone we are *supposed* to fear?" Alkamy was clearly trying to keep her voice level, but failing.

Zephyr sighed softly, "I live to serve her. We *all* do."

Alkamy frowned. "I'm not saying you should *lie* to the queen . . . not really. Just omit what you can."

She stepped away from him, pushing the bathroom door open again.

Zephyr waited until she stepped into the room, but as soon as she let the door fall closed, he turned away. He didn't want to fight with her, but he couldn't listen to her treasonous words. Hearing them meant he'd have to tell Clara—or worse yet, Endellion herself. He couldn't even imagine what would happen if Alkamy were found guilty of treasonous thoughts or actions. The best-case scenario was that she'd be punished, and *that* would try Zephyr's loyalty the way nothing else had.

He'd fight the queen's war. He'd shed blood at her word. Those were decisions he'd made in order to protect his cell. But he wouldn't lose Alkamy. For her protection, he'd face the queen's wrath.

fourteen

WILL

Will curled up on the end of the sofa in Violet's hotel suite, watching her pack an astounding number of blouses, skirts, trousers, and shoes into an array of suitcases. It was bizarre to have *that much clothing*. "You really ought to have someone do that."

She leveled an unfriendly look at him. "No."

"I could hel—"

"No," she cut him off. "You read. I sort. I don't mess with your coping strategy. You don't mess with mine." She had one hand on her hip and the other upraised, pointing at him. "And don't think that provoking me is going to get any questions answered. I'm wise to your tricks now."

Unapologetically, Will shrugged. He didn't need a whole lot of tricks to guess what was wrong. Both Roan and Vi were being prickly. The news had a bit on a catastrophic tunnel fire, and the speculation that it was yet another attack by the Queen of Blood and Rage had been confirmed by one of her terse messages to a local news outlet.

"I'm sorry," he said.

Violet threw a boot at him. He caught it. Dealing with Violet's temperamental nature was more of a game than a challenge.

"Don't."

"Roan doesn't want to talk about it either," Will continued as if she hadn't spoken. He tossed the boot back toward her.

"It was horrible," she admitted, her tense expression fading away for a moment.

"Isn't it always?"

"Did you . . . were you given any work to do for *her* over the summer?" Very pointedly not looking at him, Violet tucked the boot into a bag with its match. "The movie has been . . . I should've checked in more."

Will sighed. "I'm not *actually* your little brother, Vi. I'm just as capable as the rest of you." He stared at her, looking for a sign that she understood. "I wear as many masks as you do. My mother's dutiful son, the team's quiet one, Roan's supportive boyfriend."

"But they're all real . . . aren't they?"

"They are, but I'm not just *one* of any of those things." Will shook his head. "Don't try to shelter me so much, okay? I know things are changing, but that doesn't mean

I'm not as capable—or as much under threat as you are. The same classes, the fighting, the requisite sword and gun and . . . all of it, Vi. I've been there too."

"But you haven't had to k—"

"I have," he interrupted. "Zeph knows. Kam too."

Violet's mouth gaped open, and Will wondered—not for the first time—if he should've told her when he'd had to do so. He knew her though. She would do as she had with Roan, as Zephyr had done for both Creed and Alkamy. She'd have taken his task as her own to protect him.

"If I'd have known . . ." Violet's eyes filled with tears.

Will shrugged. "That's why I didn't tell either of you."

"But . . ." Fierce moody Violet folded her arms over her chest as if to stop herself from shaking. It was, oddly, all the proof he needed that he'd made the right choice. She wanted to protect everyone around her, and as much as he loved her for it, he wasn't going to ask it of her—or allow her to do it on her own if he could help it.

Will was sick of everyone trying to shield him.

When he came home that night, hands still shaking but holding it together more than he'd expected when he'd received the orders from Clara, he thought he had managed it all well enough.

The door fell shut behind him with an almost inaudible snick. *It was the only sound in the townhouse, making it seem louder than it really was. He slipped his shoes off and was about to go up to his room, when a series of soft thuds drew his attention as someone stood and walked toward him.*

"I can't protect you," his mother said from the darkness of the

foyer. "If you get in trouble, you'll end up exposed for what you are. I can't protect you then."

"For what I am?"

"I know we don't talk about things," she continued on as if he hadn't spoken, "and I know that what I did in order to be your mother might not have been right, but I don't regret it and I wouldn't want to change it."

Her arms were folded tightly, and as she turned the light on, her fluffy yellow bathrobe looked oddly cheerful despite the conversation. They weren't talkers. They debated, and they discussed. That was different. It was mental exercise. This . . . this was bordering on emotional revelation, and Senator Parrish simply didn't do that.

"If you get exposed for whatever you sneak out to do, they'll test you. It's standard for arrests now."

"I was out late once and—"

"Don't," she cut him off. "I see your friends, Will. Do you honestly want to try to tell me that they aren't fae-blood? That you aren't aware of what they are?"

"So the anonymous donor . . ."

"There was no anonymous donor. There was an offer, a fae who offered me the one thing I wanted more than anything," she said softly. "I couldn't conceive, despite science. I didn't have a partner either. When I was offered a chance to be a mother . . . I accepted."

"You willingly slept with a fae-blood then."

"No," she corrected. "I slept with one of the true fae. The faery who fathered you was not able to pass as human. He had no desire to bed a woman—fae or human—but he wanted a child. We both wanted a child."

Will nodded. He wasn't sure what else to say. He had heard Zephyr explain that they were "modern changelings," that instead of leaving behind sick faery babies in exchange for stealing healthy human children as the fae once had, the fae had left strong fae children behind in order to be raised in this world to fight for their true families. There was no way, though, that Zephyr's explanation made sense. Will knew that his mother was truly his biological mother. That meant that it was likely that Zephyr was either lying to them or believing in a lie he'd been told. His mother had just given Will proof of his own suspicions about his heritage.

"Do you ever hear from him . . . my father, I mean . . ."

She shook her head, and then, in a very tentative tone, she asked, "Have you?"

Will shook his head.

"So you're not out . . . doing things for him?"

"Things?" Will prompted.

"If you are a fae sympathizer, if you are out working for t—"

"Do you love me?" he interrupted. "Even though I'm not all human, do you love me?"

"Of course I do! I chose to have you. I knew exactly what that meant." She scowled at him with the same ferocity he'd seen when she was arguing one of the causes she most loved. "You're why I support all those eco-acts. It's to give you a healthier world. That's what fae need. The cooks who are instructed about your 'allergies,' the house with purified air, the trips . . . It's not like there are books on 'How to Raise Your Not Quite Human Child.'" Her voice lowered at the end, as if even here there could be someone

listening. "I'm trying to do what I can to take care of you because I love you."

He nodded. It was good to hear.

"You made a bargain with a faery, Mom. That never comes without a price." He paused and looked at her. "I pay the price."

Her hand flew up to cover her mouth.

He sighed. His mother was tough, fierce, implacable . . . all things that she didn't appear to be tonight. He closed the distance between them and pulled her into a tight hug. "I love you too. Just . . . don't ask questions, okay?"

"Are you hur—"

"I'm as fine as I can be," he assured her. "Just stay you. Stay the way we've always been, and we will pretend that neither of us knows what was said here."

She nodded.

Will let go and stepped away. He was halfway up the steps when she added, "I'm not sorry. No matter what, I'm not sorry I said yes to him that night. I'm proud to be your mom."

And he wanted to say he understood, to say he forgave her, but the truth was that she wasn't the one paying the cost of the deal she'd made. She wasn't the one who had left bodies on the ground on the orders of the Queen of Blood and Rage. She wasn't the one with bloodied hands.

She wouldn't be the one to be imprisoned for life simply for existing.

He had to pay for simply being born. Murder, death, or imprisonment, those were the choices. As abhorrent as murder was, it was *the only option that let him have some semblance of a life.*

The phone in Violet's room trilled, pulling him out of his memories. The front desk called up to let them know that his ride to the airport was waiting.

"You know Creed talks to one of them," Will said quietly, his mind still on his own biological father. "The true fae, I mean."

"How?" Violet shoved her suitcase aside forcefully. "We're not to go there, have contact . . . what is he thinking?"

"Creed does what he wants, always has." Will shrugged.

"I'm guessing Zephyr has no idea, then?"

Will gave her a look. Zephyr was a good guy, so was Creed, but the two had been at odds for years. Will couldn't say he thought either of their approaches to dealing with the fae were exactly *wise*, but his answer—keep his own counsel and avoid the politics of any sort—wasn't necessarily better. It just worked for *him*.

"It's like they think we're animals, you know? Mangy dogs they train and put in pits to fight . . . except *we* fight humans who don't even know. It's . . . argh." Violet's temper simmered enough that her skin was throwing sparks.

Will walked over to her. "We all cope in our own ways, Vi. That's what you just said a few minutes ago, right? Creed does whatever it is that he's doing. Zeph follows orders. We all find ways to be okay with being Sleepers."

"Do you know what Creed's *doing* though? Who he's talk—"

"No. I just know that there is someone there that Creed meets, and if something happened to me . . . I wanted someone else to know too." Will wasn't sure why Creed spoke to them, or why he kept it from Zephyr, or anything beyond the simple truth: they might be a team, but every last one of them kept secrets from at least *some* of the others.

"You could tell Roan," Violet suggested.

"I told you instead." Will hugged Violet, kissed her cheek, and stepped back. "I'll see you at school, okay?"

She nodded. "Don't tell the others that I'm probably coming back early after all or—"

"Vi," he said, cutting her off. "I'll see you when you get there."

And then he left. She was okay, as okay as any of them were, and that's what he'd needed to know. They kept their secrets to protect themselves and to protect each other. One of these days, though, one of their secrets was going to be too much.

 fifteen

LILY

After Lily had left the garden, and Creed, she walked back to the office where the headmistress was. Hector said nothing when she walked in, but he did reach out and pluck the bit of hedge that was caught in her hair. She'd left it there on purpose, a statement verifying where she was. It was a lesson her father had taught her: provide clues to prove the theory you *want* people to believe. It helped hide the truth. She had been in the garden. No one needed to know that she'd met Creed there. No one needed to know that she'd revealed her heritage or that they'd made fae vows that they meant no harm to each other.

Hector held the tiny piece of greenery out to her. "I see you found the gardens."

She took the tiny branch. "They're perfect."

For all of his professional mannerisms when there were

witnesses, Hector did relax when they were alone. Lily watched as the tension in his shoulders eased, and he told her, "I'm glad for you."

"Two sixteen," the headmistress said, breaking into Lily's quiet moment with her guard. "Your suite is two sixteen. It's the end unit on the second floor of the East Tower. We are on the ground floor, so you'll need to ascend two levels. That is the lowest of the dormitory floors."

"Thank you," Lily said. Two floors of stairs was much nicer than it could've been. She'd requested a low floor, but the dorms went up to the twelfth level in both towers.

"When the dorms are not open or after curfew, all student access is through this building. An enclosed airwalk connects each dormitory to the main hall on the second floor." Mistress Cuthbert paused. "Your father mentioned an aversion to elevators."

This time, Lily only nodded. She'd known that admitting some of her quirks to the staff was necessary, but she still didn't like it.

Abernathy Commandment #6: Never confess your vulnerabilities if you can avoid it.

"I'm fine with the lifts when I must be," Lily demurred.

"Well, in any matter, to reach the second floor you can use the staircases." Mistress Cuthbert paused a heartbeat too long before adding, "I feel I should let you know that your suitemate is not representative of the majority of our student body. If you find that you need new accommodations, come see me, and we'll find somewhere else."

Having been dismissed with that mysterious statement, Lily walked out of the office.

Daidí had requested a single room, but for all of St. Columba's indulgences, this was their one sticking point: everyone was assigned a suitemate.

Lily could only hope that hers was bland enough not to bother her overmuch. Living with someone who trailed glitter everywhere, for example, would surely bring out her less charming side. When she'd answered the questionnaire, she'd been very clear: studious, quiet, no smokers. There were a lot of traits she could learn to accept, in theory, but she required good sleep and clear air. Those were non-negotiable.

When she reached the lift, which looked about as modern as the rest of the building, Hector folded his meaty arms over his chest. "I can walk up the stairs and carry your bags to your suite, Lilywhite."

"No. I can handle it."

He titled his head in disbelief. Everyone on Daidí's staff knew that she struggled with closed spaces. Lily had always had difficulty breathing if she wasn't surrounded by moving air. This, too, was a reason that Daidí had kept her home for so long—her fae traits were hard to hide when she was younger.

She drew several deep breaths in preparation for her few moments in the small space and insisted, "I *can* do this. I need to be able to pass as . . . not *me*, Hector."

Hector shook his head, but he didn't argue. He knew

that she had to work to blend in when she could. Silently, he put all three of the bags into the narrow car. Before he stepped back for her to get inside it, he said, "Mr. Abernathy doesn't want you to worry, but there were threats at home. You're safer here. Just . . . keep your *accessories* in reach and try to follow the rules, okay? He worries."

"I've been practicing with my *accessories* for years. Remind him . . . that I'm careful, okay?"

If she needed help, she'd tell Daidí, but right now, all she needed was space. Hopefully, she could tell Zephyr she wasn't interested in whatever madness he thought she'd be into joining, and that would be the end of it.

"Tell Daidí I'm going to be fine here. Tell him . . ." Lily paused when her voice shook, but she steadied herself and continued, "Tell him that *he* needs to stay safe too."

"I'll make sure of it," Hector promised as he gestured for her to get into the lift car.

She paused, thinking about Abernathy Commandment #9. *Be kind to those who deserve it.*

Briefly, she hugged Hector and nodded good-bye to him.

He watched her until the car started to ascend. It was only two floors, but she had to count her breathing in and out to cope with the narrow space.

When the lift stopped on the second floor, Lily all but leaped out. She shoved one suitcase forward with a foot and pulled another behind her. Once those were out, she yanked the third one clear of the doors.

Daidí had often said that trying the things that frighten us was how we got stronger. He'd also talked about how her mother was the strongest, bravest women he'd ever met. Iana Abernathy was a hard ideal to live up to.

Lily had tried. She did things that frightened her, strove to be like her mother, but that didn't stop her from having moments of weakness. Today, she was smack in the middle of a day-long "moment," so proving that she could handle the lifts was critical. Those were the tasks that stood out, the ones that were accomplished under duress, and now, she'd succeeded. She'd handled the enclosed space with no panic attacks. Earlier, she'd managed a conversation with the obscenely beautiful Zephyr Waters. All told, despite the downsides of both events, they were still victories of a sort.

With a brief smile, Lily lashed two of the suitcases together and then pulled the double bags with one hand and pushed the solo bag with the other. By the time she'd crossed the airwalk and reached the East Tower, Lily was ready to abandon one of the bags.

Not a snowflake! she reminded herself. That was the point she had to prove to herself. She could be just like other people, not a fragile thing to be safeguarded from the world. Lily had to become stronger and braver, like her mother.

That resolve was enough to make her push on with her luggage.

By the time Lily found the door to her suite, her arms hurt, and she missed home. The suite was an end unit as promised, and Lily suspected that it would have everything else Daidí had requested—a good view, wide windows, and as much space as allowed. Aside from the suitemate that waited inside the suite, it would be exactly as perfect as possible at St. Columba's.

Lily paused at the door.

Abernathy Commandment #5: Be bold.

Bracing herself for whatever nightmare waited in the suite, Lily opened the door and strode into the room.

"Forget to knock?"

The girl in the room glared. Much like earlier with Zephyr, Lily recognized her instantly. Alkamy Adams. Her father was some legendary, drugged-out guitar player, and she was amazingly talented on her own merit—at least that had been the public verdict after her one and only tour.

"It didn't occur to me since it's *my* suite." Lily shoved the first of her bags through the door to their common room, using it to prop the door open as she pulled the other two inside.

"You must have made a mistake," Alkamy started.

"Two sixteen." Lily pointed to the room number on the door. "East Tower. My suite as of now."

Lily realized that Alkamy was staring, but she'd been sized up by criminals since she was old enough to be around Daidí's colleagues. The mini diva was easy in comparison.

"Which room is mine?" she prompted.

"I've already dislodged my latest suitemate," Alkamy announced evenly. It was obviously intended to be a challenge.

"Congratulations. I guess that makes me your consolation prize." Lily gestured at the three closed doors. "Room?"

Alkamy pointed to the door on the right. "There. That's the second bedroom. You won't last though."

"Great. I'm Lily."

"Abernathy?" Alkamy blinked. It wasn't much of a reaction, but it was enough. Her new suitemate recognized her enough to fill in the surname Lily hadn't offered. She wondered whether that recognition was via her on-again, off-again boyfriend or through the sensational criminal allegations against Lily's father.

After nodding at her, Lily dragged her three bags into the room. Alkamy watched the whole time. Although Lily suspected that her new suitemate was trying to be intimidating, her whole routine was a lot less scary than she intended.

Alkamy was one of the host of girls who had been in the tabloids with Zephyr. Lily tried to remember if they were supposed to be an item currently. It would be just her luck to share a suite with the girlfriend of the boy who had just kissed her.

She started to hang her clothes in the closet, not bothering to look at Alkamy, who was leaning against the doorframe, arms folded, observing her.

"I'm Alkamy Adams," she announced after several minutes.

"I know. I've seen you in magazines." Lily withdrew a short blade that dangled in a holster and smiled. Shayla alternately sorted Lily's weapons as clothing or jewelry, depending on how she classified any particular item. This blade was one of the more functional ones, resembling a small scimitar, so Shayla steadfastly insisted that it was "not jewelry."

Behind Lily, Alkamy made herself at home on the over-stuffed chair in front of the window. "I don't think I've seen *you* in any magazines."

"That's probably true."

"So?" Alkamy prompted. "What's your story?"

"I'm new here this year."

"Obviously," Alkamy said, dragging the word out into more syllables than necessary. She stretched her legs out in front of her. It made her robe gape open, and based on how much skin she'd just exposed, Lily was fairly certain she wasn't wearing anything under the robe.

Lily arched her brow. "Are you aiming for intimidating or alluring?"

Abernathy Commandment #5: Be bold.

For several seconds, Alkamy stared at Lily incredulously, and then she laughed. For someone with the reputation of being a badass, she sounded like a little girl who'd been flying high on the park swings. When she stopped giggling, she said, "You're unexpected, Lilywhite."

"It's just Lily."

"Whatever."

Lily hung several more of Shayla's carefully labeled out-fits in the closet and lined up a few boxes of accessories on the shelf above them. The pretty wooden chests mostly contained daggers, but two held guns, one revolver and one semiautomatic, and ammunition. Some girls collected jewelry, and odds were that Shayla had packed that too, but these were the only items Lily had packed for herself. Every box was fingerprint pass-coded, so no one but Lily could access the weapons.

Without turning away from her closet, Lily said in a level voice, "Since you used my whole name, I'm guessing you've heard it before."

"I'd heard you were coming here, but I couldn't find any pictures of you."

"Daidí dislikes it when my image gets out."

Alkamy snorted. "My old man loves it. 'No press is bad press, Kamy Girl.' The paparazzi has always been . . . just *there*, you know? So what's your father's secret?"

"Hard to say. Maybe he kills photographers." Lily met her eyes, testing her reaction.

Alkamy smiled and then without missing a beat said, "Messy."

Lily nodded. Then she met Alkamy's gaze head-on and said, "I don't use. No drugs, no alcohol, no cigarettes. Nothing."

"Not a problem." Alkamy flashed her an odd look, but she didn't come right out and ask if Lily was fae-blood. She was more subtle than Creed and Zephyr. All she did was hint: "So no chemicals. Are you a nature girl then?"

"Eh. I like being outside." Lily shrugged.

Abernathy Commandment #6: Never confess your vulner-abilities if you can avoid it.

"Finish hanging your stuff, and I'll show you the grounds. St. Columba's bites sometimes, but the gardens are excellent." Alkamy hopped to her feet. "Oh, and since you're 'Just Lily,' you should call me 'Kamy.'"

Lily only wanted her solitude. "That's not . . . I've already . . ." She looked at her new suitemate, who was watching her and grinning. There was no graceful way to refuse Alkamy. Maybe her confrontational suitemate could be a potential friend . . . or at least an ally of sorts. Unlike Creed and Zephyr, Alkamy, at least, seemed to be offering friendship without strings.

sixteen

ZEPHYR

The moon was still in the sky when Zephyr slipped out of his suite. It was not yet morning, although his suitemate was only recently asleep. Creed had crept into their suite somewhere around midnight after another excursion to the garden. In a few days, his moonbathing and sunbathing would restore him to health, and as long as he abstained from the bad habits he seemed to cherish on holidays, he'd be as strong as ever.

It was one thing to occasionally behave like humans to avoid accusations of fae-blood, but Creed took it too far. He cycled between self-destruction and purification repeatedly throughout the year. Something in his life drove him toward self-destruction over and over. The whole group saw it, but so far, no one had gotten anywhere when they'd asked him about it. He'd been worse the past few months than ever before. If they were the sort of friends who talked, Zephyr would try harder to find out what had set Creed into such a spin, but Creed was as likely to throw a punch as to walk away.

So far, Zephyr had been able to let them do as they wanted. That was all about to change. Now that Lilywhite was with them, they'd start receiving regular orders from the queen. Whatever the queen demanded, they'd do. That was why he needed to get his team in order. They would obey, or they would be "retired."

But he was too far ahead of himself. First, he had to report to the Queen of Blood and Rage. There was a protocol that he'd been drilled on repeatedly. His handler, Clara, stressed the points at which he was required to visit the Hidden Lands. Lilywhite's arrival was uppermost on that list.

Silently, Zephyr walked up to the back wall of the West Tower. The old buildings that made up St. Columba's all retained a fairy-tale quality. The entire campus had once been a monastery, but time and traditions had changed and so the monastery was turned into a school for the wealthy.

From residents who took vows of poverty to those who lived lives of indulgence, the change was almost too great to ponder. Zephyr sometimes thought he would have preferred the former. He'd miss the comfort of money, but he wouldn't miss the attention it drew. There was a feeling of history, energy perhaps, that lingered from the long-gone monks, as if they'd left behind some sense of purpose that filled those who lived here then and now. He *needed* that—or maybe it just felt that way to Zephyr. Like the monks, he had a purpose; he never needed to guess about what he was meant to do. The queen would tell him, and he would serve her wishes. He'd been born to do this. Literally.

He stroked a hand over the leaves that crept and twined together across the dimly lit wall. Most students had no idea that the thick vines covered a section of stone that accessed a network of tunnels. Unless one could *ask* the vines to part, there was no way to tell the passage existed and still keep it secret—since a human hacking through the growth would've been detected.

Zephyr willed the plants to separate for him, thanking them for their kindness and asking if they would hide his exit. With a welcome rustle the plants divided, exposing the hidden door to the mouth of the main passageway. Zephyr pushed the stone that would expose the latch, lifted it, and shoved.

The door scraped open and Zephyr quickly stepped into a dark tunnel.

The air smelled of dampness and age, and he wondered—not for the first time—what the monks had feared. Escape tunnels weren't built by those without enemies. A fleeting thought of Lilywhite made him wonder if her homes had such hidden exits as well. When he'd first discovered his heritage, he wondered if that was why *his* parents had exit tunnels, but then Clara told him that he was a changeling and that his parents had no idea that he was fae. They, like the parents of all of the Sleepers, assumed that some latent fae DNA had surfaced in them. They protected him all the same.

After Zephyr pulled the door to the passages shut behind him, he flicked on the small light he carried in his pocket and followed one of the twisting routes to the other end. The tunnel curved and eventually this path came to narrow spiraling steps that descended two stories and dead-ended.

He'd figured out how to open it years ago, and he no longer had to look to find the stone that hid the giant key. He pried the stone out, retrieved the key, and opened the door. There were other passages. The one he typically followed led to the grounds outside campus. Tonight, however, although he *was* leaving campus, he was doing so via a route that was inaccessible to all but those who had the fae permission to enter the Hidden Lands—and the knowledge of tunnels at the very edge of the grounds of the campus, past the hedge maze, where only the Sleepers ever ventured.

Zephyr took his shoes off and set them on the floor at the end of the tunnel. Then, barefoot, he opened the door and closed it heavily behind him. The air tasted purer after the musty stone passageway.

He walked to the wall surrounding the private reflecting garden that was strictly off-limits even to the most indulged students. Here the walls were covered with roses. Again, he asked the plants to permit his access. Instead of parting, they shifted into a ladder of thorns and blossoms.

"As you will," Zephyr whispered to them.

He ascended the rose ladder, wincing as the thorns pierced his feet and hands. There was no use in trying to avoid grabbing the vine where the barbs jutted out. If he did, they shifted toward him.

Small cuts marked his palms and wrists. Tiny droplets of blood seeped from his feet as he walked, but the cuts weren't deep enough to do more than sting. They were hardly worth noticing.

Inside the garden, he began to pace, seeking one of the circles of toadstools that appeared when he needed to access the other realm. He walked and waited, calling out to the soil, asking for a doorway.

Finally, in between one heartbeat and the next, it appeared in the dew-wet grass. He wasn't sure how the circle worked. He didn't state a destination, simply went where it sent him. Once, he'd appeared on the shore of an island, seals rolling in the surf. Another time, he'd been at the edge of a forest where flickering lights seemed to beckon him nearer.

Quickly, before it vanished, he stepped into the circle, exhaled, and stepped out in the Hidden Lands. Today, he was at the edge of an expanse of slick black rock that glistened like ice. He let the feel of it, the weight and the age of it, speak to him until he knew what it was. *Obsidian*. It was a rock sharp as glass, made for sacrifices, carved into blades by both fae and mortals alike.

As he walked across a surface of the sacrificial rock, the small cuts on his feet continued to leave a trail. He wasn't sure where he was headed, only that these tests were inevitable. He faced a new one every time he came to the land of the fae. This time, no matter how long he walked, the path seemed no shorter.

Finally, Zephyr looked back, and when he did, he saw that his blood had hardened into dozens of sparkling gems. He wasn't sure what to do with them, but he understood that this was part of the test too.

"If I were a jeweler," he whispered, "I'd string them together for my queen."

At his words, the blood-drop gems skidded across the stone. He approached the pile as it coalesced into an ornate necklace on the ground in front of him. It was beautiful. Dark rubies fell into a jagged point as if they were strung on an invisible net, but at the center was a vacancy. The net was incomplete.

"Not yet worthy." He looked around until he saw a series of sharp spires of obsidian. "I *want* to be worthy."

Taking the necklace in hand, he walked over to the blade-like stones. He lowered the necklace to the ground, carefully spreading out the stones. Then, he stood and slid both palms over the dark blade, cutting gashes in his hands.

He knelt on the ground and squeezed his hands together over the center of the necklace. The blood ran from his skin into the void of the necklace, where it hardened into a large oval ruby.

"Well done," a voice pronounced.

And there she was at last, the Queen of Blood and Rage,

his savior and executioner. Her beauty was akin to terrors that left lands decimated and trembling. Her hair, so dark it appeared to be scattered with stars, flowed behind her like a cloak. Her eyes, so cold they made him want to run in terror, watched him intently. Her tiny feet were bare, and she wore armor the color of blood near hardened, neither red nor black but a hue that hovered between. Zephyr had the fleeting thought that the armor was dyed in blood. Stories of her cruelty had often been whispered, but he believed in her. She'd be the one to save them.

No one was with her. It was simply *her*, standing alone on the vast expanse of black rock.

Zephyr lowered himself farther. Clara had taught him the etiquette for this encounter by putting her boot on the back of his head and forcing his face into the dirt. There was no dirt here, only stone as sharp as knives.

"You made me a gift."

"I did, my queen." He held his arm up, the red jewels spilling over his fingers as he offered them to her. "It's not worthy, but I offer it . . . offer *myself* to you, to the Unseelie Court."

"The courts are united," she said.

"And as long as they are, I serve both. Should that change, I will still serve my queen."

"None of the Sleepers know which court birthed them, yet you call me *your* queen." She didn't lift her voice, but he was still fairly sure it was a question.

"It is my hope and desire that I belong to you," he admitted.

"So you want to be Unseelie, young Zephyr?" Her voice lightened, as if she were amused. She took the necklace, sliding it from his hand into hers.

"I do." He dared look up at her. "I exist to serve you."

For a moment, the queen's lips curved into a smile, and her beauty made him swallow nervously. Nothing he'd ever glimpsed in the world was as exquisite . . . or as terrifying.

"Tell me of the others."

And so he did. He stayed on his knees as he spoke about every member of his team, rapidly outlining their strengths and their courage. He spoke of Violet's ferocity, of Will's stealth, of Roan's cleverness. He spoke of Creed's courage and Alkamy's grace. He didn't mention their weaknesses; he only spoke of their abilities and of his own.

When he was done, the queen said, "And Lilywhite? You say nothing of her."

"We've only just met," he hedged. "I came to you as soon as she arrived, as I was instructed to do by Clara."

The Unseelie Queen stepped close enough that she could tuck one of her bare feet under his knee. It was an odd gesture, and he wasn't sure if she meant to injure him or merely get closer.

"I dislike secrets," she told him quietly. "Stand."

He obeyed.

She cupped his face in her hands. Despite the chill in

her eyes, her skin was hot enough that he wanted to cry out in pain. He didn't. The necklace of blood rubies dangled from her hand. It was pressed into his cheek and draped along his throat. He suspected it was burning marks on his flesh.

"Tell me," she said.

"She knows nothing of us," he admitted. "She didn't join us before now because she didn't know . . . anything."

The queen said nothing for almost a full minute. They stood with her hands on his face and the blood-wrought necklace searing his skin. He ground his teeth together to keep from asking for mercy.

"It is as I feared then." The queen released him and turned her back. The ruby necklace clattered to the stone between them. "You will bring her here before the next cycle of the moon."

And then she left without waiting for his reply.

"Yes, my queen," he whispered into the once-more empty air.

He wasn't sure whether to leave the necklace or take it. He had no use for it, but the queen had seemingly refused it. Silently, he scooped it up. They might look like rubies, but those stones were his blood. He wasn't entirely sure what they could be used for, but he was very certain that he shouldn't let his blood fall into just anyone's possession.

Zephyr turned away. He had his first direct order from the queen, and it wasn't a simple task like setting a bomb. Kidnapping the daughter of a criminal who had no desire to spill her secrets seemed unwise—but disobeying the Queen of Blood and Rage seemed even more foolhardy.

Somehow, he would have to gain Lilywhite's trust. He clutched the blood necklace in his hand and whispered a silent prayer to whatever deity listens to faeries. Then he headed back to the toadstool gate.

seventeen

LILY

Lily didn't expect the first night at St. Columba's to be so difficult. Alkamy showed her around and talked about a few of her friends.

"You've heard of Creed and Zephyr, I'm sure. You'd have to live under a rock to avoid their names." Alkamy paused. "Vi is in film, so you've seen her on the screen or in pictures with the boys or with me."

"I have," Lily agreed.

"Vi isn't back yet, but she's been the only other girl really until you got here." Alkamy shrugged as if her lack of female friends didn't bother her. "She's more of a friend than a sister. The boys, on the other hand, are like brothers . . . or maybe annoying cousins."

"Really? Even Zephyr?"

"That's the past," Alkamy said with a stiff expression.

"So, if you were interested—"

"I like Creed's music," Lily interjected, cutting off that topic before it could get any weirder.

"You'd never know that Zephyr has any skills other than looking pretty, but he does." Alkamy stared at Lily with a singular focus that was reminiscent of both of the boys. "Don't underestimate him."

"So you *aren't* over him . . ."

"We're not meant to be," Alkamy said.

Lily heard the omissions in her words as clearly as the words themselves. Alkamy *loved* Zephyr. Why they weren't "meant to be" was beyond her. She lapsed into silence for several moments before prompting, "So, you, Violet, Creed, and Zephyr, is that everyone?"

"There's Will and Roan too." Alkamy paused then and gestured at a closed door. "This is the dining hall. It's surprisingly good. Organic produce, grass-fed hormone-free beef, healthy stuff, you know? Plus, they meet every dietary restriction. Non-dairy? Non-meat? All meat? No carbs? Low-carbs? Raw food? Whatever it is, they can supply it."

Lily nodded. Her father had already told her all of this in one of his Columba's-is-good chats.

"So Will's mom is some politician. Roan's family is in pharmaceuticals"—Alkamy shot an uncomfortable look at Lily—"like *legal* ones."

Lily couldn't help it. She snickered.

Alkamy sputtered, "Look. I didn't want to be rude, and . . . Oh, *stop* it, Lily."

Lily had barely stopped when their eyes met, and then they both started giggling.

"I'm sorry. That was thoughtless of me," Alkamy said when their laughter abated. "I really *can* be tactful. Usually."

Lily waved her apology away. "My father has been in the public eye since well before I was born. I know what people say, *and* I know what he does. His associates are around like an extended family the way some people have uncles or cousins."

Alkamy looked very serious for a moment. "So until you got here today . . . did you know any *normal* people?"

"You mean rock divas like you?" Lily teased. "Or boys like Zephyr and Creed who have been on every gossip show? Or future CEOs like Roan? Or politicians' kids like Will?"

"Point taken." Alkamy leaned on the wall. "I've decided: I'm glad I met you, Just Lily."

Lily looked at her again and realized that Alkamy was exhausted. She looked like Lily did the few times she'd been exposed to toxins. For a moment, Lily wondered if all of the students at Columba's were fae-blood, but that was highly unlikely. Far more realistic was the idea that Alkamy's small group of friends were all fae-blood.

"Why don't we head back?" Lily suggested.

Alkamy flashed her a grateful smile. "I'll give you more of the tour this week. Most everyone gets back tomorrow, so you can meet the boys. Vi's delayed, but we should be able to help you get settled."

Lily shook her head. "Go to bed, Kamy. You can demonstrate your great skills at normalcy tomorrow."

Once they were back in the suite, Alkamy waved and wandered into her bedroom.

Lily closed her own door and curled up in her own bed. It wasn't late, but she'd had enough excitement to last her a while. The quiet and calm of her room were a welcome respite from the onslaught of surprises today.

She managed to sleep for a few hours, but she'd woken restless and bored. The sun wasn't yet up, but Lily wasn't tired enough to roll back over . . . which was why she found herself roaming empty hallways. Lily had no friends other than Erik. She had no one to call. Her closest confidante was Daidí, and he was out of the country. That left her with nothing to do but explore the buildings.

Lily had wandered to the other side of the administration building and into the walkway that connected it to the second dorm. That dorm was the not-very-originally-named West Tower. Like the East Tower, it was connected to the main offices via a walkway on the second floor. There was a doorway to the building, but as Lily understood it, all access to the dorms had to go through the administration hall after hours and on any of the holidays. Since campus wasn't technically open yet, that meant that all in and out traffic for both dorms went through the main hall.

A rustling sound drew her attention, and she pressed into the shadows as best she could. The greenery covering one wall parted, and when it did, a door was revealed.

Stepping out of that door was Zephyr Waters.

He hadn't seen her yet, and Lily couldn't decide if she was less likely to be caught by staying still or fleeing. He turned his back to her to pull the stone door shut. The door scraped across the floor with a rasp, and the plants fell closed with a swish of leaves. A flash of red dangled from Zephyr's hand. At first, she thought it was blood dripping, but a second look revealed it to be an ornate ruby necklace. Before she could wonder over the sight of Zephyr Waters creeping back onto campus with a priceless necklace in hand, he turned, saw her, and smiled.

"Lilywhite," he greeted. "I'm touched. There's usually no one to wait up for me."

"I wasn't . . ." She shook her head. Obviously, he knew she hadn't been waiting up for him. Stepping forward, Lily surrendered the brief cover of shadows and said, "You were sneaking out."

"*In*, actually. I went out a while ago." He sent her a smile that was far more endearing than she would have liked.

Lily turned and walked away. Whatever rules he broke were his business. *Abernathy Commandment #11: Know when to walk away from trouble.* Zephyr was trouble, and she had no need to get involved with it. So far, she'd seen him twice: once when he was smiling over an explosion he'd set and once when he was sneaking back into campus.

"Whoa!" He ran after her. "I was joking about you waiting."

"I know." Lily kept walking.

He kept pace with her. "I think we got off to a bad start."

Lily frowned. "Why are you following me?"

"Accompanying," he corrected. "I'm accompanying you because I thought we could talk."

His voice had a cajoling tone, and he smiled again. He was probably used to that smile working on people. If it didn't, his easy manner and his name undoubtedly would. In a low voice, Lily told him, "I have no intention of telling anyone that I saw you here *or* that I know what happened at the harbor."

"No one would believe you if you did." Zephyr reached for her hand, but she jerked away. "Do you want to go to breakfast?"

"It's still the middle of the night," she pointed out.

"So we go to a club first. They stay open all night here." He shrugged. "You liked the pier, right? We'll walk down there."

"I can't. I don't have permission to leave campus."

Zephyr glanced pointedly behind them at the vine-covered wall. "There are other exits."

Lily was tempted. There was no way to deny that. It wasn't *him* but the idea of going out that lured her. Being close to the water always made her feel better, and a walk wasn't the same as friendship.

More importantly, knowing about his secret exit would be useful. *Abernathy Commandment #15: Always have a way out, more than one if possible.* Even if she didn't use it, knowing she could was worth the tentative peace with Zephyr.

"Don't you need to do something with that?" She nodded toward the necklace.

"Do you want it?"

Lily's mouth opened in a gasp before she managed to say, "Are you mental? You can't just give that to the first girl you bump into."

"I wouldn't," he said levelly. "I'd only give it to a friend."

"Well, that's not me."

He shoved the necklace in his pocket like it was a cheap bit of trash and met her eyes. "So, breakfast?"

She nodded.

Wisely, he said nothing as they walked back toward the hidden door. He gestured at it, not looking her way, and the vines parted for him. She'd never met anyone else who could do that. Part of her wanted to ask him why he was showing her his secret. The more reasonable part knew to keep her mouth shut.

Abernathy Commandment #7: Secrets are valuable. Don't part with them for free.

Zephyr pushed open the door and stepped inside. For a moment, he was consumed by shadows, but then he reached out, extending one hand behind him. Silently, Lily took his hand and stepped into what appeared to be a hidden tunnel.

As soon as she was inside and the door was shut, she tried to pull her hand free of his grasp. Partly, she wanted to touch the wall, to ask the old stone for anything it could share, and partly, she didn't want to let Zephyr hold on to her.

He squeezed her hand in his. "I have a meager bit of light here, Lilywhite."

"Lily," she stressed.

"Lily," he repeated quietly. "The tunnel twists, and eventually, you'll need to descend a very narrow staircase." His breath brushed against her shoulder, stirring her hair. "I'd rather not have to explain just how the notorious Nicolas Abernathy's daughter broke a leg on her first night here."

Despite her issues with him, Lily laughed. "I'm not sure you'd want to explain to Daidí what I was doing off campus either."

She wouldn't call the silence that followed *comfortable*, but it was a lot more so than when she'd first met him. She had an opportunity here: she could understand what he meant when he said he was looking for her, and she could learn an escape route from campus. Lily noted the tricks she needed to remember in order to exit through the tunnels.

Zephyr appeared aware of her water affinity, and he clearly was aligned with soil. A part of her wanted to ask Zephyr what he knew about their shared heritage, but his fae blood and the explosion earlier combined to let her know that he was somehow involved with the war.

That alone was reason to stay silent, so she did.

They'd only been walking for a few minutes when a voice from the darkness drawled, "Odd time for a walk, isn't it?"

Zephyr sighed so softly that she wouldn't have heard him if she'd been a step farther away.

"Creed Morrison." He stepped forward, introducing himself as if they hadn't spent part of the afternoon talking. "And you are?"

She had already decided to play along when he'd confessed that he'd kept their first meeting secret, so she met his gaze now and said, "Lily Abernathy."

Creed looked at Zephyr, and his voice hardened as he asked, "Tell me, fair Lily, are you in need of a rescue?"

"No, actually." She nodded toward Zephyr. "He was breaking out and offering to show me how to get off campus."

"Ah. Strict parents?"

"Protective," she said. "If I read correctly, though, yours aren't?"

He wagged a finger at her. "Someone is a tabloid fan, I see."

Lily shrugged, unembarrassed, and a little amused at their game. "I've been home-schooled via private tutors since I was old enough for lessons. What can I say? I get bored."

"Oh, me too," Creed confessed. "That's how I end up in all of those rags."

She laughed.

"Maybe you should go back to campus," Zephyr suggested. "You couldn't have slept very long. I heard you stumble in before I left."

Creed shrugged. "I napped. I left."

"Go back to campus," Zephyr said.

"I'd rather he stay," Lily interjected.

There was a long silence, and a meaningful look passed between the two boys.

"Well then," Creed drawled. "You heard Lily. I'll be staying, but if *you* want to head back, feel free."

"I wouldn't want Lilywhite left stranded when you go off to get drunk again or meet up with some—"

"You might be my *boss*, Zeph, but that's only if I decide to stay in your little clubhouse."

Lily shivered at the tone of his voice. She'd spent enough time around her father's associates to know the difference between genuine threat and mere posturing. Creed wasn't posturing. Softly, she pointed out, "Maybe *I* should head back. I'd rather not be photographed with either of you, now that I think about it."

At that, Creed released her and shucked his hoodie. "Here. Just pull the hood up. We can protect your privacy. We do it all the time with Vi and sometimes with Will."

"Thank you," she whispered.

He was very obviously being warned off from her—by someone who had no right to make that decision for her. She might decide to only be friends with Creed, but Zephyr wasn't going to decide it for her. No one made rules for her life other than Daidí, and even that was often open for discussion. *Abernathy Commandment #1: Choices matter.*

Silently, she accepted Creed's shirt and tugged it on. It

fell past her hips, and the sleeves hung down over her hands. Creed reached out, took her wrist, and rolled the sleeve until her fingertips were exposed. Then he repeated the gesture on the other arm.

"Don't worry," he whispered loudly. "He's just grumpy a lot."

Zephyr sighed again. "Can we not play games tonight?"

"I think he's on his man-cycle," Creed whispered even louder.

Lily smothered a laugh. Even now, Creed made her feel safer and more nervous all at once. Zephyr's kiss hadn't given her the flurry of angry bees in her stomach that the mere brush of Creed's fingertips on her skin evoked. She stared at him as he reached out and pulled the hood of his shirt up so it fell around her face like a monk's cowl.

When Creed paused to tuck her hair around her face, Zephyr's voice shattered the tension that had been building in her again. "Step back," he ordered.

Lily froze.

"Creed," he clarified. "Step away from her."

"I don't think she minds, Zeph." Creed stared at her as he said it. "She's not afraid of me. Are you, Lily?"

She stared at him, at the tightening around his eyes, the way his jaw clenched, and she knew there was far more going on here than she could understand.

"I'm not afraid of either of you," she pointed out levelly.

Creed's already-tight expression grew even more tense.

He stepped back from her and said, "Come on. I need a drink."

"You're barely sober *now*—" Zephyr started.

"And yet you are already on my last fucking nerve," Creed drawled. "Lily doesn't need to watch us fight, so we can go where I can grab a drink or *you* can leave."

Lily didn't point out that she hated alcohol, or that Zephyr undoubtedly did too. Creed *should* hate it. She looked at him.

Abernathy Commandment #5: Be bold.

"So you're not fae-blood, Creed?"

Zephyr and Creed both paused mid-step. Zephyr looked stunned, but Creed started laughing.

"What did you say?" Zephyr asked.

"If he wants to drink and was already drunk, that should mean he's not fae-blood," Lily pointed out reasonably. "You, however, are admittedly fae-blood. So, it's only logical to ask what Creed's status is given the circumstances."

"No fear at all in you, is there?" Creed asked.

"Please. You know who my father is, and when I met *him*"—she gestured vaguely toward Zephyr—"he staged a bombing."

"It was a welcome present," Zephyr explained yet again.

"Right. For future reference, I prefer plants." She wasn't going to judge him for being a terrorist. Unless she was willing to condemn her father's activities, she had no business judging Zephyr.

"Plants?" Zephyr echoed.

Lily heard the real question he was asking: was she aligned with earth like he was? Hearing the question didn't mean answering it. She'd told Creed without hesitation. Telling Zephyr felt different.

Creed rolled his eyes. "Come on. None of this is stuff to discuss out here. Let's go to the Row House and grab a private room."

Resolutely, Lily looked from Zephyr to Creed. She could go along and get answers, or she could run. This was a case when she saw benefits of knowledge over the potential for trouble.

There had never once in her life been any fae-bloods she could talk to, and wasn't this what she'd always wanted? Wasn't it what Daidí wanted too?

Both boys watched her curiously.

She walked forward, so she was between them, and kept going. "So, Creed, my suitemate tells me that you'll be in most of my classes."

And just like that, she'd committed to a path.

eighteen

ZEPHYR

Zephyr was fairly certain that Lilywhite was going to be the biggest challenge he'd faced. He walked silently with her and Creed, wishing that Alkamy or Roan or, hell, even Violet was there. Lilywhite was his partner, his probable betrothed, *his*. Creed knew that, knew how Zephyr felt, but he was toying with her.

Maybe Creed was Unseelie after all. It was a game Zephyr played sometimes, sorting them all in his head, not that he told *them* that. Aside from Alkamy, he didn't share his suppositions with people. Some of them were clear: Violet was obviously Seelie. Her element was fire, like the Seelie King himself. Roan looked Seelie, but he was aligned with water, like the Unseelie Queen, and he was a strategist, always planning for contingencies. Will and Creed could go either way.

Lilywhite was a complete anomaly. She hadn't so much as blinked when he spoke to the plants. She'd also bared her feet as they walked, using the excuse of uncomfortable shoes. Earlier, she'd been drawn to the water. Her breathing had tensed in the tunnel, much like Creed's did when he used it.

Common knowledge was that fae-blood had more affinities the purer their blood was. True fae could have as many as four affinities. Of course, Clara had told him that the Sleepers were true *fae*, not just fae-blood, but so far only he and Alkamy had more than one affinity. Lilywhite appeared to have three.

"Are you claustrophobic?" he blurted out.

Both Creed and Lilywhite stared at him like he was speaking in tongues.

"Seriously?" Creed shook his head at Zephyr, turned to Lily, and told her, "He's usually not this way. It's been a stressful day."

The sheer truth of that careless statement made Zephyr laugh. He'd met the queen, bled for her, and been given an order he didn't know how to follow. He couldn't kidnap Lilywhite; even if she *wasn't* Nick Abernathy's daughter, she was someone he'd been raised to believe was his other half. Delivering her to the Queen of Blood and Rage was *wrong*—and unavoidable.

The walk through Belfoure was almost beautiful at this hour. He'd seen a lot of the world because of his human family, but there was something about Belfoure that he'd come to associate with the concept of home. Hollywood always felt too stifling. Sure, he had his garden, but outside of that walled space, there were eyes everywhere. Camera flashes were far more common than rain, and the whispers of strangers felt oppressive. The Hidden Lands, at least the part he'd seen, were unwelcoming. He hadn't expected that, but the harsh landscapes and glittering fae seemed alien to him. Even though he was a part of their world, was destined to kill or die for them, he felt like he didn't belong there. Belfoure was an oasis that he hadn't found thus far in either world.

In the slowly dawning day, the lingering shadows danced on the surfaces of dirty stone buildings, and the hum of humanity was reduced to only those strange souls who did their business—or were still out chasing their pleasure—in the darkest parts of the day. The glow of sunrise reflected and twisted in the water, as if the streetlights and the neon lights from the bars were meeting to share secrets.

Beside him, Creed was telling Lilywhite about a party at the Serpent's Den that ended with Violet setting every drink in the bar alight at once. "She was stressed, and when she exhaled, every glass with actual alcohol had a flame on its surface." Creed grinned, his teeth a flash of white in the darkness. "It completely ruined my 'oh, it's just juice, Zeph' lie. Kamy and I were totally busted."

No one commented on the fact that he'd all but told Lilywhite that Violet and Alkamy were fae too. The conversation had taken a turn toward blunt, but Zephyr decided that it was necessary to let it continue to be so. Lilywhite needed to know about the Black Diamonds. Although Creed's approach wasn't what Zephyr would've chosen, it was done now.

"Do you know any true fae, Lilywhite?" Zephyr interjected.

"No," she said flatly, her laughter of a moment ago totally vanishing. "No one does. Pure fae don't live in our world. *Everyone* knows that."

Creed raised both brows in an are-you-an-idiot expression when Lily looked away. Zephyr shrugged in reply. It wasn't the most graceful attempt at a segue from Creed's story, but it was a hard question to interject casually. The fear of the fae was an almost palpable thing after more than a half century of conflict.

Once the three of them were in a private room at the Row House, Creed flopped onto the love seat. Zephyr ignored both the other love seat and the empty space next to Creed. Instead, he took one of the two chairs.

Lilywhite didn't sit.

Creed patted the seat beside him, and Zephyr realized that they'd reversed their normal habits. Usually Zephyr took the love seat with Alkamy, and Creed sat alone.

"Let me grab a drink first," Lilywhite said.

"They will come to us," Zephyr explained. He didn't want to raise his hand to motion for one of the servers, preferring to keep his barely healing palms hidden. Showing them would mean questions, and any answer he could give wouldn't make Lilywhite eager to meet the queen. Instead, he said, "Just wait with us. It'll only take a moment."

After a slight pause, Lilywhite clarified, "I'm well aware of that, but I feel better if I see the layout and exits. I'll only be a moment." She tilted her head up a little farther, looking almost regal in the moment. "I came for answers, Zephyr, but I won't be able to concentrate until I sort a few routes. *Abernathy Commandment #15: Always have a way out, more than one if possible.*"

She walked away, and Zephyr wasn't sure what to think. There was clearly more to being Nicolas Abernathy's daughter than his research indicated. A lot of the data emphasized that her father was overprotective of her, and the implication was that she was sheltered and cosseted. Her most recent birthday party was by invitation that required fingerprinting, and the entrance to the gala was through a metal detector and full body scan like at public airports. Not one single photograph turned up anywhere after the event. Everything indicated that Lilywhite wasn't actively involved in her father's business, but she moved like she expected to be attacked or blindsided at any moment. She'd already pulled a knife on *him*. Was she more involved in her father's business than he'd expected?

Reluctantly, he caught Creed's eye. "I don't want to argue tonight," he said, keeping his hands folded together to hide his injuries.

"Then don't talk to me like I'm a child." Creed leaned back, arms draped on the back of the love seat. "I put up with a lot, Zeph, but we're all in this mess together."

"I know that. If you had any idea how—"

"Then fucking *tell* me." Creed's voice shoved into him like a physical touch. It stunned him.

"Did you . . ." He leaned forward. "You can solidify the air?"

Creed rubbed one hand over his face and sighed loudly. "Yeah. It's not reliable, but yeah."

"We can use this. Figuring out how to strengthen our weapons will take a little practice, but . . ."

"It's not a weapon, Zeph. It's *me*. It's my feelings, my voice."

Zephyr shook his head. "It felt like a weapon. You hit me with it."

"Well, you're a special case. Not everyone pisses me off the way you do," Creed drawled.

There was no reasoning with him when he got like this. Creed was exhausting, like a recalcitrant child in his best of moods. They'd decided years ago in silent but mutual agreement that they would always have a buffer with them. Often it was Alkamy, but sometimes Roan or Will drew the short straw. Tonight, they were unsupervised.

After a few silent moments, Creed asked, "Did you go?"

"Yes. I visited Endellion. I was coming back when Lily-white saw me. It was . . . harsh."

A muffled gasp behind him stopped any further words.

He turned. Lilywhite stood behind him, the door falling shut behind her. Her hand was curled around a glass of what looked like fruit juice.

"You were visiting *whom*?"

"Endellion," he repeated, after sparing a glare for Creed, who had obviously known Lilywhite was standing there when he asked the question.

Lilywhite stepped backward, not quite fleeing but on the brink of flight. "How do you know *that* name?"

Zephyr made a quick calculation and a decision.

"Because I serve her," he said, not looking away from Lilywhite's stricken expression. "The once Unseelie Queen, who holds the Hidden Throne. Endellion, the Queen of Blood—"

"And Rage," Lilywhite finished. She waved her hand like she'd brush his words away. She walked around the front of the love seat. "Hardly anyone knows her true name."

Zephyr shrugged. "You do," he pointed out.

Lilywhite settled onto the love seat next to Creed. His arm was stretched along the back, not touching her, but nearer than Zephyr liked.

He balled his fists until he thought his hands would bleed again. He hated the unfamiliar feeling inside him, a twist of rejection and envy. He couldn't expect her to know, not yet. She hadn't even known she was true fae, or a Sleeper. Still, it stung, no matter how much he could explain it to himself. Creed's expression was tense, as if he wasn't sure if Zephyr was going to lose his temper over the fact that she'd chosen to sit beside him or not. They'd had girls prefer one or the other of them, but Lilywhite wasn't *just* a girl. She was Zephyr's. They all knew it—all except her.

Both boys were still, not reacting, not speaking. Lily-white seemed oblivious to the tension between them. She was staring into her drink like there were answers hidden in her juice. After several moments, she said, "My mother left me a book. It tells a different story than the one in the textbooks and news reports. It calls her by *name*. The king as well . . ."

"You have a *book* about the *queen* herself?" Creed interjected.

"Yes." Lilywhite took a sip of the juice she'd carried back with her. Despite the revelations today, she seemed calm, but Zephyr wasn't sure if it was an act or not. She added, "About her, the war . . . a lot of things."

A waitress walked into the room with drinks. They were all silent as she approached them.

"She said you were here and asked that I bring you two of Zephyr's usuals," the girl said tentatively.

When Creed looked at Lilywhite and raised both brows, the waitress sent a nervous look at Creed. "But I could get you something else . . ."

Surprisingly, he said, "No. This is fine for now."

Once she was gone, Creed looked at Lilywhite. "Subtle."

"Rarely."

Envy blossomed again in Zephyr and threatened to rise up and choke him this time. "Sleepers can't have relationships without approval."

"Who?"

"Sleepers. There are seven of us. The three of us"—he gestured between them—"and Alkamy, Violet, Will, and Roan." Zephyr kept going, despite the angry look on Creed's face and the wide-eyed confusion on Lilywhite's. "We are a unit. For some reason, you weren't raised knowing like we all were, but you're here now."

"That doesn't make sense. You dated Kamy," Lilywhite pointed out.

"You know her?" Creed interjected.

"Met her tonight. Suitemate. Gave me a tour," she summarized.

Creed nodded, and Zephyr stared at them. They seemed to communicate so effortlessly.

"That was cover for both of us. I need to think about the good of the whole cell."

"And who gives permission?" Lilywhite asked.

"Me," Zephyr admitted.

"Right," she drawled, sounding too much like Creed already.

"None of us know for sure which court we belong to or if we're related. No one knows who our parents are."

"You're all adopted?"

"No, Lilywhite." The time for subtlety was long past. "*We* are all changelings. *You* are a changeling. Endellion, our queen, had a plan. Her loyal subjects placed their children in homes of humans who were powerful in some way. We would be safe that way, and our handlers taught us what we needed so when the time came we could be soldiers for our people."

Lilywhite said nothing.

Zephyr reached out and covered her hand with his, to offer her comfort, to let her know she was no longer alone. He'd always had true fae in his life. When he was trying to make sense of his affinities, so too was Alkamy. Creed was too. Lilywhite had only been alone.

Gently, Zephyr said, "I can't believe you made it this long without help, without anyone knowing that you were unguided. We're all together now. You have other true fae around you. We're a unit. We protect one another."

"No. You're wrong about me." She started to pull away from him, the gesture hurting as her knuckles jabbed the cut on his palm. "I'm human, and I know *exactly* who my parents are."

Zephyr's hold on her tightened. "No, you're not. You only know what they think they know. They don't know it, but *you're not human*."

When she didn't reply, Creed said, "Neither are we, Lily. Not fae-bloods, Lily, but *fae*. True fae. Full-blooded. Born of them, and placed here with a mission."

Zephyr was grateful for his presence for the first time that night. It wasn't enough though. Lily snatched her hand back from Zephyr's and crossed her arms over her chest. She didn't argue, didn't run, simply watched them like she was debating how best to make them suffer. She reminded him of the queen herself.

"You're not human, Lilywhite. Neither am I. Neither is

Creed . . . or the others." Zephyr watched her as he spoke. "There's so much you don't know, but—"

"I know everything I need to know." Lily met Zephyr's eyes and told him, "I am Iana and Nicolas Abernathy's daughter. I *am* fae-blood, but there's no way I'm true fae. This is ridiculous."

"You might be Seelie after all," he muttered.

"I can assure you that I'm not."

"I hope not," Zephyr said. "I'd rather you were Unseelie." He paused and looked at her before adding, "Like me."

"I need to leave."

"I'm sorry," Zephyr said quietly. "I don't know why you were left alone before or why you had no handler, but I'm sorry. I'm sorry that you had to go all of these years without the rest of us around to help you. I'm sorry we didn't realize that you were left to figure it out alone."

"I figured out that I had an ancestor that was other than human," Lilywhite said. "That's it. I have a father, a *good* father, who made sure I had everything."

Before Zephyr could try to figure out what to say, Creed shocked him. "What if I knew someone who could prove it?" he asked.

"Who?"

Creed shook his head. "That's the only catch, Zeph: you can't ask. I'm in no shape to endure lying right now."

"You could tell the truth," Zephyr said. "Novel idea, I know, but you could consider it."

Creed leaned back into the cushions and kicked his feet out in front of him. "I can help, but it has to be my way. It'll take a few days, but I can send a message." He turned to face Lily. "What do you say? Give us a week or so. I'll bring you proof. You're like us, Lily. Let me show you."

Lily studied him before countering, "Fine, but I don't want anyone else to know about this. Just the three of us."

"And the mystery guest," Zephyr snarked.

"Obviously."

"Outsiders? This isn't the way we handle things, Creed," Zephyr started.

"I agreed to it," Lilywhite said.

Creed remained silent.

"So . . . we have a week for this 'proof' to arrive," she said after a long pause. "Until then, you've both offered your friendship, and whatever else is going on, it would be nice to try that as long as we can."

Both boys glanced at her, exchanged a tense look with each other, but remained silent. Zephyr didn't want to table *anything*. He'd been waiting for her for years. This should've gone differently. For starters, Creed shouldn't have been there, and Lilywhite was supposed to look at *him* with appreciation, not Creed. Zephyr had given up Alkamy. He'd faced the queen. He'd looked after the cell on his own. When Lilywhite arrived, things were supposed to be better. She was to be his salvation.

"You can keep your secrets, and I'll keep mine," Lilywhite offered, drawing him out of his thoughts. "One week.

A truce between *all* of us."

"Done," Creed said with a nod. "Zeph?"

Zephyr looked at Creed. They'd been closer once, years ago. Creed had been his best friend. It would be nice to have that again, even for a little while. He nodded and said, "A holiday from fighting with you? It seems unlikely, but I'm willing to try."

nineteen

LILY

After a couple of hours, Lily returned to campus with the boys. Creed's hoodie was once again hiding her face. Lily stopped at the wall of the garden and the vines shifted for her. Neither boy commented, but she saw them smile. It was an admission of trust of sorts. She'd meant it when she had offered a truce. For the next week, they would be friends. Being friends with fae-bloods—because she refused to believe that they were actually true fae—meant being herself in a way she'd never been able to be. With Erik, she still hid that part of her. With most of the staff, she did too. Hiding in front of Creed and Zephyr, and by extension the rest of the Sleepers, would be unnecessary *and* a huge sign of mistrust considering what they'd shared with her.

Lily slipped into her suite as quietly as she could, but Alkamy was awake and in the main room. She was wrapped up in a blanket sitting on the sofa and looked worried. "Where were you?"

"The Row House."

"So do you know?" Alkamy asked softly.

"That you and all of your friends are fae-blood? Yes."

"We're true fae," Alkamy corrected. "And the rest?"

"I'm not sure how much of it, but enough." After a slight pause, Lily added, "So why weren't you already rooming with Violet?"

Alkamy laughed in that childlike peal of happiness. "Oh, you won't need to ask that after you spend a moment around Vi. I love her, but she's . . . chaotic. I'd need to meditate half the day to stay *close* to balanced. She's fire. I'm earth and air. We're friends, but we need space."

"Affinities matter that much?" Lily flopped down on the other end of the sofa from her suitemate, who shoved part of the blanket toward her. Wordlessly, Lily tucked her legs under it.

"Zephyr is earth, which you obviously know if you were off campus. Only the two of us can do that." Alkamy sounded much like she had earlier when she was explaining the ways around campus and extolling the virtues of the dining hall. She was a natural teacher. "Creed and Will are air," she continued. "Roan is water. Our only one of those."

"But only one affinity?"

Alkamy glanced at her hands. "I seem to be both air and earth."

"I have trouble with air," Lily confided.

"So earth or . . . ?"

"Earth and water." Lily had never admitted any of this, but regardless of what happened with Zephyr and Creed, she was hoping to keep Alkamy as a friend, so she added, "and a little air . . . sometimes."

Alkamy gaped. "*Three?* You have three affinities."

Lily didn't answer, both because she didn't want to lie and because Alkamy already had *this* reaction to three affinities. What would she think of four?

"That's incredible. We'll all be safer with you finally here." Alkamy folded her hands together beatifically, and Lily couldn't help thinking of statues she'd seen in the Uffizi Gallery. There *was* something greater than human about her. Even if Lily didn't want to believe that they were all changelings, she could almost believe it about Alkamy.

"Does Zephyr know?"

Lily shrugged. "I didn't say it. He and Creed know about the earth part. I think Zephyr knew about the water before we met. He was waiting for me at the pier when I arrived."

"Right. The pier." Alkamy drew the covers closer around her.

Lily took a deep breath before continuing, "I hadn't met you then. If I had, I'd—"

"Stop." Alkamy shook her head. "Zephyr and I aren't meant to be, Lily."

Lily let out a sigh. "I don't want him, Kamy. I just . . ."

Alkamy reached out and patted Lily's leg. "He's been waiting for you since we started at Columba's. You're the second head of our cell. To him, you're the grail."

"I'm *not*. I'm a person."

"Everyone loves Zephyr. Between him and Creed, I think they've stolen the hearts of most of the girls here. Roan and Will, the girls pine over them, but . . ." She looked down when she noticed Lily's expression. "We can't get attached, Lily. Not to any of the humans. There are rules, and now that you're here . . ."

"What?"

"I suspect we'll be called on to do more. For now, it's a few deliveries, the occasional escorting a fae or human somewhere they can't reach on their own. For Will, it's the passing of secrets. For Roan, access to chemicals. There are other things, but so far our tasks for *her* have been . . . small. Now that you're here, Zephyr thinks things will change."

"I don't serve her." Lily stood. "I like you. I like them too, but I don't serve *her*. Not now. Not ever."

Alkamy's eyes widened. "You can't say that. You didn't grow up knowing. You don't know what—"

"She kills people. I know that."

"And your father doesn't?" Alkamy challenged.

"Maybe he does. Maybe I will too, but not at some-one else's whim and not the innocent. If I'm to become a weapon, it's only ever going to be by my choice." Lily looked at her suitemate, who didn't look angry as much as worried. She sighed. "Look. I don't want to fight."

Alkamy nodded, but she didn't speak again until Lily was at the door to her room. "None of us want this, Lily.

Not even Zephyr. He thinks we don't know how he feels, but I see his doubts. We're trapped. None of us want the queen's guards to kill us in our sleep, either. They tell us we were born to do this, that we're special, and there is no choice."

Lily turned back. "There are always choices, Kamy. I don't know if they're *good* choices, but there are some. We can find them."

Alkamy was quiet for a long moment. Then she shook her head. "Not unless Zephyr agrees. I won't go against him."

Lily nodded. There was nothing to say to that, not really. It was the same sort of logic that she'd seen in some of Daidí's most trusted employees. It was loyalty at all costs, and she respected it. Quietly, she told Alkamy, "I'm going to catch a few hours before it's officially morning."

"Lily?"

She paused, and Alkamy added, "That's Creed's shirt. Please don't make things more complicated than they need to be."

And as much as Lily wanted to reply, she didn't know exactly what to say, whether she should point out that she didn't take orders or attempt to say that she didn't want Creed. The first was true, but saying it would be tantamount to admitting the latter, which despite her best efforts was quickly becoming a lie. So Lily opted for silence.

★ ★ ★

A few hours later, Lily woke to the sound of crying outside her bedroom door. The air smelled like someone had left a campfire burning, not the kind of smoky scent that worried her, but combined with the weeping, it was enough for Lily to investigate.

After stumbling to the common room, she found Alkamy sitting there with none other than Violet Lamb. The crying was coming from Violet, whose expression suddenly was anything but sad when she spied Lily in the doorway. In barely more time than it took to wipe the tears from her cheek, Violet was standing and glaring at Lily.

"So, *you're* the new roommate."

Like Alkamy, Violet was the sort of beautiful that made it difficult to deny her heritage. Even in the small bit of sunlight that came through the window, Violet's vivid red hair recalled living fire. Her skin was like twilight, and the contrast of the seemingly living flames of her hair and the shadowed hues of her skin made her every bit as stunning as Alkamy.

The words tumbled from Lily in her half-asleep state: "How does anyone believe that you're not fae-blood?"

Violet lifted one brow in an aristocratic query.

"Seriously, Zephyr and Creed might be able to pass, but you two?" Lily flopped on the empty chair, too emotionally drained to once again go through the whole do-I-admit-I-know game. She tucked her feet under her and said, "Lilywhite Abernathy. Missing member of your group, daughter of crime lord, exceedingly bad at social etiquette."

Violet turned her gaze on Alkamy. "Forget to mention something?"

Alkamy shrugged as if she was utterly nonplussed. "I said I had a new suitemate."

"You didn't say that it was *her*."

At that, Alkamy giggled. "Admit it, Vi. You wouldn't have let her sleep, and it was more fun to be surprised, wasn't it?" She nudged Violet with her foot. "If you'd stopped to see *any* of the boys, you'd know."

Violet shook her head and turned her attention back to Lily. "So, Zeph's imaginary girlfriend finally graces us with her presence."

"Vi!"

"It's fine, Kamy." Lily didn't look away from Violet as she spoke. Much like the daughters of Daidí's business associates had always done, Violet was assessing Lily, determining where she ranked, deciding if she was worthy or a threat or simply dismissible. "Violet is just embarrassed that I heard her weeping." Lily paused and met Violet's gaze. "Or is it a protective thing?"

"Protective. I don't *do* embarrassed." Violet stood. Flashes of fire seemed to hover like lightning in her dark brown eyes for a moment as she stepped in front of Alkamy, who sighed.

"Good." Lily nodded once. "So far, they all seem like they could use a bit of protecting. I haven't met Will or Roan, but these other three are all a little reckless."

Violet's entire posture shifted. Lily thought she might even see hints of a smile that was quickly dismissed before Violet asked, "What's your affinity?"

"I'm earth and water," Lily offered the half-truth with a yawn. Eventually she might need to let them all in on it, but not yet.

Alkamy glanced at her questioningly, but she didn't add "and air." That moment of silence told her a lot about Alkamy, and Lily was grateful.

"So are you okay then?" Lily risked. "The crying earlier . . ." She let her words trail off in an invitation.

Violet shifted. "Always. I am *always* okay."

"There was an incident," Alkamy said softly. "A shopping mall in York burned last night."

Violet's defensive posture told Lily more than she wanted to know, but she still asked, "You?"

She tilted her head, chin jutting out, eyes narrowed. "We all get orders, Lilywhite. Everyone must do things for the cause."

Before Lily could reply, Alkamy added, "It was either this or Roan. Vi took it on so he didn't have to."

"He would've," Violet said quickly. "We're obedient to our orders. Roan would—"

"I'm not judging either of you." Lily met her eyes. "I wasn't raised to obey the Queen of Blood and Rage, but I'm also not going to hate you for whatever you think you have to do."

"You'll have to do it too. Now that you're here—"

"No. I'm not hers," Lily interrupted.

Violet started to say something else, but at the touch of Alkamy's hand on her wrist, she closed her mouth.

The easy flow of words didn't resume. Violet had just committed murder, and from the looks of it she felt guilty. She'd done it to protect one of her friends from that very guilt. Like the rest of the Sleepers, Violet was someone Lily could respect.

Resolved, Lily stood and announced, "I still need to meet Will and Roan. Let's get breakfast and then you can take me to meet them."

"Perfect!" Alkamy clapped her hands together, once more seeming oddly childlike in her joy. She turned her eyes to Violet. "Can we go to the diner?"

"No."

"Come on, Vi!"

"No, no, no." Violet folded her arms. "Last time we were there, Creed passed out in his waffles, and Zephyr was all up on that waitress who, by the way, was *far* too old for him. I do not want drama."

Alkamy snorted and mock-whispered to Lily, "Get dressed. Her mood will shift in a minute anyhow."

"Piss off."

Lily left the two girls, and by the time she was in her room, she heard Violet's laughter. Sometimes she wished that she had a primary affinity to fire instead of earth. There was something impossibly attractive about being so fluid in mood, but Lily tended toward constancy. Her earth affinity was first and strongest. That meant that she pursued her course steadfastly.

"We're going to go to a café outside Belfoure," Violet called through the door. "I've called my driver."

"I'm not allowed off campus," Lily replied, even though she'd already broken that rule once.

"So wear a hat or a scarf. Zeph can take you out the back way, and we'll pick you up."

If Daidí or even Hector knew that Lily was ignoring the rules so regularly, they'd fit her with a tracking device. Somehow, though, the things that had seemed risky before didn't seem as much so now.

She was surrounded by fae-blood, who apparently thought themselves to be true fae *and* who were acting as— well, terrorists. Worse yet, they considered her to be one of them. The list of things that could go wrong was more than Lily wanted to contemplate, but rightly or not, Lily felt more at *home* with them than she ever had in her life. Being around these so-called Sleepers felt *right*.

She grabbed Creed's hoodie from the night before and pulled it on. In the midst of everything, he alone had made her feel better. He might unnerve her, but there was no way to deny that they had some kind of a connection. Sure, Zephyr had tempted her when he kissed her, but she suspected that would be true for any girl with eyes, a pulse, and an interest in the opposite sex. Creed . . . he was different. She felt drawn to him like fire to tinder, and her initial theory that it was purely a fae-blood reaction seemed disproven after meeting Violet and Alkamy. Lily felt right around the others, but it wasn't the same sort of irresistible demand she felt with Creed.

"I don't need Zephyr to open the back gate," Lily told Violet as she stepped into the room again.

A look between the two fae-blood made it very clear that Violet recognized the shirt too. All she said after Alkamy's nod was "Are you sure you want to wear *that*?"

"I am."

Alkamy pressed her lips tightly together, but she didn't say a word. At some point, they'd need to discuss the fact that there was no way in either world that Lily was getting tangled up in Zephyr. He was beautiful, but his zealousness about the queen and his perceived *mission* were major problems.

"And to think that the boys were so easy to handle before you arrived," Violet said, earning a frown from Alkamy.

Lily just laughed. Clearly the boys' drama had been going on for a while. "Food and fun, Kamy. That's the plan. No more talk of fae politics or any of it."

Alkamy pressed her lips together, but she nodded.

Now all that was left was convincing the boys to cooperate with her plan.

twenty

EILIDH

"Eilidh. Eilidh. Eilidh." The voice kept tugging at her, pulling her out of slumber. After blinking away the lingering tendrils of a very inappropriate dream about her betrothed, Eilidh looked around her room. The only people who could ascend the tower stair were those to whom she was related or betrothed. That left exactly two potential fae who wished her harm: her Seelie brothers, Nacton and Calder. However, she was fairly sure that either her mother or Rhys had some sort of system in place to notify them if either of the Seelie princes entered her home.

"Eilidh. Eilidh. *Eilidh*," the voice continued.

The words wafted in on the sliver-thin edge of a breeze.

"Eilidh, it's about Lilywhite," it added.

At that, she knew and came tumbling out of her bed. Hurriedly, she dressed and crept out of the tower. At this time of the night, there was no one standing below and staring at the glass tower. The moonlight made it shimmer a little, not as bright or glaring as the sunlight could. Instead it looked vaguely luminous as the softer light reflected from the salt-encrusted glass.

Unfortunately, that light was still enough to make Eilidh stand out clearly as she fled her home, so she walked slowly, trying to seem as if she only meant to take a night stroll. There were no visible watchers, but that didn't mean that no one waited in the shadows where she couldn't see them.

Once Eilidh was far enough from the glow of her home, she increased her speed, twisting quickly through the labyrinthine tunnels of the cave so quickly that a follower would need to either be close enough that she would see them or know these paths well enough to predict her destination. Few fae bothered with the gates to the known world, especially as the queen had banned them from return to the Hidden Lands if they left without her permission.

When Eilidh came out of the tunnels on the sea-edged side of the Hidden Lands, she saw her guest. He stood with his arms held loosely at his side, as if waiting for an attack. Unlike the fae, he had no safe place to hide. In the world where he lived, his blood was cause for imprisonment. In her world, he was an object, a tool created at the queen's order and deployed in secret. The Sleeper program wasn't common knowledge.

"Creed Morrison," she greeted.

He bowed deeply, the gesture far more courtly than she

expected from him. It did little to assuage her worries. Seeing him at the edge of the Hidden Lands was not the most surprising part of her week, but Eilidh had never been summoned by Creed before tonight. She'd sought him out a few years earlier, and she'd worked with him so he could send messages to her over air. At the time, she'd vacillated between him and the other air affinity in the group, but the other Sleeper, Will, was a touch too observant for Eilidh's comfort.

"Is Lily injured?"

"No." Creed glanced past her, as if his half-human sight would somehow be enough to see any threat that was clever enough to follow her this far. He moved closer to the sea, where the battering of waves against earth would make his words harder to hear.

Eilidh followed. If her betrothed or brother were here, there would be much lecturing on risks, but despite her mother's misuse of the Sleepers, Eilidh trusted this one. She was also standing on earth with sea in reach, so two of her affinities were easily called upon. So many of the fae acted as if Eilidh's physical differences made her weak, and in some ways, they were right. She wasn't *as* strong as some fae, but she was a daughter of the two regents. She was far from the fragile flower people thought her to be.

"Lily knows nothing of the fae," Creed said when Eilidh was at his side. His words were all but placed in her ears like tactile things. His control of his affinity was better than she'd ever seen from him.

"She knows she is, at least, fae-blood," Eilidh said.

Creed nodded. "She's *more* though, and she doesn't know about the Sleepers. She wants proof."

Eilidh smiled, causing Creed to frown at her. She had no urge to explain herself. She was too much her mother's daughter to be interested in unspoken questions, and even though she trusted Creed as much as she could trust any of the weapons her mother had wrought, she trusted no one completely. Telling Creed that she was well aware of what Lily did and did not know was unnecessary. "So you offered her proof."

"I told her there was someone I knew who could prove it," he hedged, obviously ill at ease now that he was faced with the audacity of offering her up. "I didn't say who. If you want to send someone else, you can . . ."

Eilidh's smile threatened to become a laugh. This was the thing that the queen would never see: the unpredictability of the humans, or in this case, the half-humans who had been told they were true fae. They believed the queen, and it didn't serve any purpose to reveal the truth—not yet at least. Eilidh opted to let them think they were changelings, to let them think the Queen of Blood and Rage might one day declare their service done. To the queen, they were disposable. To her, they were . . . a reminder of how far the queen would go. At least, most of them were nothing more than that. Lily, of course, was different, and for *her*, Eilidh would allow herself to be summoned.

Creed had said she "could" send someone else. She

found it oddly enchanting being told she *could* do anything. She was the heir of the Hidden Throne. That meant that there was little that she was denied. Certainly there were those things disallowed for her safety, but in all, she was . . . well, the *princess*, which meant that her whims could be laws if she saw fit. She didn't, but the possibility remained.

"I will come."

Creed nodded awkwardly. His gaze was fixed on far-away waves on the sea. "You won't hurt her," he said, the words sounding very little like a question.

"You care for her," Eilidh replied.

He shrugged.

"You want her to know not because I asked you to speak to her, but because you care," Eilidh pressed.

Creed's gaze darted to her. "I know the whole Sleeper thing isn't your plan, but it's . . . it's no good. The people who are dying aren't the ones who killed the queen's baby. They're just people. Me, and Lily, and the rest of us . . . and whatever other Sleepers are out there . . . we're being made to hurt people who are innocent."

Eilidh sighed. There was nothing she could say that wouldn't either be a lie or an admission she'd rather not make.

twenty-one

LILY

Walking into Zephyr and Creed's suite was a lot more difficult than Lily would've liked. Violet didn't even pause to knock. She opened the door and stepped inside. "Hey, pretty boys! I'm home early. Get your lazy arses out of bed."

Both boys came out of their rooms. Zephyr was topless, clad only in a pair of pajama pants. Creed was in the same clothes he'd had on the night before—aside from the shirt he'd given Lily. He looked like he hadn't slept at all.

"Hey!" He scooped Violet up as soon as he saw her and spun her around like she was a child. They looked like siblings as they cuddled close, the same dusky skin and striking eyes. He smiled at the tiny tempest still in his arms. "You said you weren't going to be here for days yet!"

"I explained to them that there was no way I could wait that long." Violet shrugged. "They adjusted."

Creed laughed. "Ninian forbid anyone tell *you* no."

"Hush." Violet kissed both of his cheeks. "I heard from a reliable source that you were a mess without my supervision."

Creed shrugged and said, "Broken heart. I'd met a girl."

"A girl? Well, then she's an idiot," Violet said loyally. "Do you want me to talk to her?"

Creed shook his head and glancing in Lily's direction. "I'm coping better now."

Thankfully, Violet let it go—although there was no doubt that she noticed Creed's look as much as Lily had. He was far too blunt, far too often for her comfort. The mere idea of making eye contact with him right now was enough to cause anxiety.

"Did you rest well?" Zephyr asked from Lily's side, startling her. The contrast between his quiet solicitousness and Creed's intensity seemed designed to make her crazy. She needed to keep her focus on the larger issues—the group of fae-bloods surrounding her and their theory that she was unavoidably meant to be involved in their terrorist activities.

Lily nodded in answer to Zephyr just as Creed released Violet.

"Well? Where's my hello?" Violet prompted Zephyr with the same tone Lily suspected dictators used.

"I can never guess what you want, Vi," he teased as he stepped forward and hugged her.

"I am subtle, oh, *never*." Violet stepped back from him.

"I hear you had to go see the q—"

"Breakfast," Creed interrupted, cutting off any reference to the Unseelie Queen. He glanced at Lily again, which Alkamy and Zephyr both noticed.

"No talk of *her*," Alkamy told Zephyr and Violet in a tone that allowed for no debate.

"We'll talk later," Zephyr said to Violet. "Let me grab clothes. Someone tell Will and Roan to meet us at the gate."

As he walked back to his room, Alkamy's gaze slid over Zephyr like she could physically touch him with it. She studied him like she was examining him for bruises. "Is he okay?"

"You know Zeph." Creed crossed his arms over his chest.

"That's why I asked."

"His feet were cut up, and his hands were too, but nothing needing treatment."

"I'm going to go talk to him," Alkamy said. She didn't wait for a reply, simply tapped lightly on the closed door before letting herself into his room.

"They're not together," Violet said.

Creed glared at her.

"Well, they obviously should be." Lily shook her head at the insistence that Alkamy wasn't with the boy she clearly loved. It was never easy joining an established group of friends, but these people had more baggage than she wanted to even begin to process. She glanced at Creed. "Meet you all outside the gate."

And then before they could stop her, she walked out of the room.

She only made it to the end of the hallway before Creed caught up with her. The feel of his presence was distinctive. She didn't need to turn her head to know it was him. Something about the way the world felt when he was near made her body hum, as if a light electric current pulsed just under her skin.

"Are you trying to fight with Zephyr?" she asked.

"No, but I'm not trying *not* to either." Creed draped his arm over her shoulder. "Zephyr isn't my priority."

Lily fought back the sigh that his words and touch elicited. "We agreed to be *friends* this week. Remember?"

"Yes. I'm being *friendly*." He walked with surety toward Zephyr's secret exit. "I want to see you though."

"Creed, Erik proposed," she said. "You were there that night."

"But you didn't say yes." Creed's fingers tangled in her hair with a familiarity he hadn't earned. "You wouldn't have danced so close to me if you were planning to be engaged to *Erik*."

Lily wanted to say he was wrong, but he obviously had seen through her attempt at a lie. It was harder with someone who was accustomed to the fae habit of verbal tricks. With most people, she could twist her words to seem like palatable truths. With the Sleepers, that habit wasn't a viable option.

She shrugged his arm off her shoulders. "I'm not a conquest."

"You're not," he agreed.

"Friends," Lily repeated weakly, speeding up to reach the passage.

"Tell me about the Abernathy Commandments."

At his question, Lily's steps faltered. "The what?"

"You mentioned one last night. Number fifteen maybe?"

"Always have a way out, more than one if possible," Lily said quietly. "There are commandments, rules for life that my father made."

"Tell me, please?" The words were more of an order, but she heard the lift in his voice that made the sentence a question too.

As they walked, she listed the primary ones:

#1: Choices matter.

#2: Be yourself.

#3: Never get caught.

#4: Weigh the consequences before beginning a course of action.

#5: Be bold.

#6: Never confess your vulnerabilities if you can avoid it.

After she was done with the first few commandments, she paused in her recitation. There were more, but those were the most critical ones. They sounded even more so as her voice had broken the silence of the dim passageway.

"And you live by these? All of them?"

Lily nodded, and then she realized he probably couldn't

see her in the low light of the tunnel. "As much as I am able," she said.

Creed's hand fell on her shoulder again, stopping her this time. "I could vow to live by these with you. As a sign of my . . . affection."

The pain in her heart was only equaled by the exhilaration in her body.

"I can't do this," she said after several tense moments. "We agreed to be friends, Creed. You admitted that Zephyr wouldn't approve of your interest in me. I don't want to cause you two trouble, especially as you seem to have enough trouble already. Be my *friend*, Creed."

"Don't say you aren't feeling the same things I am."

Lily exhaled roughly. "I never said that. It doesn't change anything though. All this talk of being fae, of a mission, it all sounds . . ."

"Crazy." Creed's arm snaked around her waist, holding her to him. "I think you're breaking your own commandments, Lily. Be bold. Be assertive." His words brushed against her skin, not because of his affinity but because he was standing that close. "You're *my* deadly girl, and I'm yours whether you want me or not."

Her one affinity that she'd not shared with him flared to life at his words, and she leaned back into his embrace and let him see that part of her too. Flickers of fire danced on her hands; sparks of blue and white flames slid across her flesh like prima ballerinas dancing across a stage. "I don't want to be drawn into the war."

Creed reached out like he'd touch the flames on her hands. "None of us do. We can't avoid it though, and if I'm going to die, I'm not interested in wasting time that should be spent *living*. Being with you, talking to you, touching you, that's living. If it comes with some risks . . ." He shrugged. "Feeling like I do around you is worth any risk."

"I don't want . . ." She tried to finish the lie and found herself unable to do so. She *did* want him to want her, did want to be his, even though it was a very bad idea.

Creed murmured against her ear, "I'm yours to command no matter whether you love me back or not."

"People can't love someone that fast," she objected, even though it took a lot of effort to say it.

"Really?" Creed whispered, and she couldn't tell whether it was his affinity or if he was now so close that his breath stroked her skin. "Maybe *people* can't, but that's not what we are. I may not like the lot we have in life because of our heritage, but I like this part of being fae. I like knowing that my heart has found its home. I wasn't sure it would happen before I died."

She couldn't speak, couldn't keep trying to lie. His words were playing havoc with her emotions. Lily knew she could trust him, felt it in her marrow, but that didn't mean she liked it—or that she could return his feelings.

"We should go," she said finally. "The others will think the wrong thing if we take too long."

"Not the wrong thing, Lily. The inevitable thing."

She chose to ignore him again, stepping out of his

embrace and walking into the dark. This time, though, she kept the fire in her hand. He knew now, and she liked having the light to help guide her.

When they reached the other side of the passageway and stepped out into the garden, the others were all waiting there. Two cars idled. As Lily and Creed came into view, doors opened in both cars. Violet sat in one with two boys Lily presumed to be Will and Roan, and Zephyr and Alkamy were in the other.

"Lilywhite." Violet beckoned as she stepped out of the car. She glanced at Creed and ordered, "You can ride with Kamy and Zephyr."

"Oh joy," Creed muttered. Still in a low voice, he added, "Better me than you, though, right? He needs to get it through his head that he has no claim on you."

Lily didn't acknowledge what Creed said, although she agreed with him. She walked out to the car where Violet was and slid in. Violet opened the front passenger door and climbed in there, leaving Lily in the back with Roan and Will.

"Hi," she said. "I'm Lily."

The boy immediately beside her peered at her from behind black-rimmed glasses that she was sure he didn't need, unless he was only barely fae. The sheer ugliness of his glasses did, however, help at drawing her attention away from his exquisite, delicate features. He had a soft mouth and the thickest eyelashes Lily had ever seen. He was dressed like he'd stepped out of an Ivy League university brochure, and his hair was cropped in a faux military style. His physique was anything but delicate; he looked like he exercised nonstop.

The other boy was the antithesis of the pretty conservative boy next to her. Floppy dark-brown hair fell into his face, partially hiding seal-dark eyes. His skin was also as dark as a seal's. He was obviously the other water affinity fae-blood.

"Roan, right?" Lily looked to the boy seated closer to her. "That makes you Will."

They nodded.

"I have water," she told them, selecting her words carefully since she didn't know the driver. "Not strong enough to *swim* though."

"I thought you were earth," Will said.

"I'm a mixed bag of tricks."

"No wonder those two are acting worse than usual." Roan draped an arm around Will possessively. "Luckily, we're already spoken for."

Lily smiled at the warning. "I don't poach." She met their eyes each in turn, looking from Roan to Will to Violet as she said, "And Zephyr is very obviously as much in love with Alkamy as she is with him, so he also . . ."

"Lily, the queen—"

"Doesn't rule me," Lily interrupted firmly. In a softer voice, she explained, "*Abernathy Commandment #16: Know how far you're willing to go for a belief.* I am willing to go all the way for freedom."

"I might like you after all." Violet reached back and patted Lily's knee. "You feel like chaos ready to erupt."

For a moment, Lily looked back at her, and much as she had earlier with Creed, Lily decided to take the risk. She lowered her hand to her side, and called a tongue of fire from her palm. The instant she knew that Violet saw it, Lily closed her fist around it, extinguishing the flames before the driver noticed them. "I suspect that we might both be a little prone to eruptions."

Violet laughed joyously. "Oh, I *definitely* like you, Lily-Dark."

"Lilywhite," Lily corrected.

For a moment, Violet simply smiled, and then she shook her head. "I don't think so." She glanced at the two boys, whose faces were practiced neutrality, and announced, "Things are definitely going to change with *her* around."

twenty-two

ZEPHYR

Zephyr couldn't deal with Creed, so he pretended not to even see the other boy. Instead he pulled Alkamy closer to him as he settled into the back of the car Violet had called for them. "Stay still for me."

Alkamy didn't argue, despite the question in her eyes when he pulled the necklace from his pocket. Her eyes widened. "Zeph?"

"Don't take it off. Don't lose it." He fastened it around her throat and looked at her. "Is it . . . okay? Does it feel okay I mean?"

"It's warm." Her fingertips touched the stones, sliding across them lightly.

"I brought it back from my meeting." He paused, debating how much to admit. "I made it."

Creed's gaze flickered their way briefly, but then he

studiously stared out the window.

Once she saw the cuts on Zephyr's palms, Alkamy took his hands in hers, holding them by the fingers. "Why didn't you come to me? Or ask Vi to cauterize these in case of infections or—"

"I'm fine, Kam." He pulled one hand free and used the other to hold her hand more securely in his. "It was only a little blood."

Creed looked back at them, gaze falling from the necklace at Alkamy's throat to Zephyr's hands. After a moment, he asked, "Was that all of it?"

Zephyr nodded. "I don't know if I should be relieved or wounded that she didn't want it."

"Oh." Alkamy gently traced the cut in his hand and then touched her fingers to the necklace again.

"Relieved. You should be relieved. Letting *anyone* have your blood like that is a risk. The humans could prove what you are. There are fae who could track you. Either way, it's scary shit."

Zephyr put his arm back around Alkamy. "Not with everyone." He watched Creed instead of looking at Alkamy. "I'd trust you with it. Even when we fight, I *do* trust you with my life."

The far-too-familiar scowl that often graced Creed's face vanished completely, and Zephyr wished he had the skill to *keep* his once-closest friend at peace.

Then, Creed's expression changed to an arrogant grin. "Don't want to wear your girly necklace. Best let Kam keep it. It matches her clothes anyhow."

Alkamy made a rude gesture, but she was still smiling and continued to stroke the necklace with her fingertips.

This was what he'd missed more than anything, the feeling of closeness among them all. Creed's anger and drunken binges had put them at odds so often the past year that he almost forgot what it used to be like. Until last year, Creed's steady presence and sense of humor had anchored him. Zephyr wished it could be like that again.

He pushed the button to raise the privacy screen and then, in a low voice, said, "She ordered me to bring Lilywhite to her within a month."

Alkamy took a shuddering breath.

"What? Start from the beginning," Creed ordered.

So Zephyr did, filling them in on every detail he could recall from his trip to the Hidden Lands. This was what he needed, all of them working together, thinking together, functioning as a proper unit again.

The next several days were odd. Zephyr was pleased at how well Lilywhite integrated into the cell. Alkamy seemed to adore her, and Roan and Will were instantly at ease with her. If anything, Roan had to be stopped from monopolizing her as they talked about contracts and conflict negotiation. The problem, unfortunately, was that Zephyr couldn't pretend not to see how Creed watched her. He'd never seen his friend so . . . love-struck. There was no way around it, no other way to explain it: Creed had feelings for Lilywhite.

He and Creed were getting along better than they had in years, but sometimes it took effort not to drag his long-time friend into a deserted classroom and punch him. It wasn't that Zephyr didn't understand Lilywhite's appeal. She was obviously clever and pretty. In more than a few ways, she reminded him of Violet, and he felt a growing fondness for her. Admittedly, there was no insistent need to be near her, but that didn't matter. Lilywhite was his partner, and Clara had all but said that if they both survived, they'd be wed.

Unions ordered by the queen were the sort of unions that were bound by fidelity charms. That meant that Creed's infatuation with Lilywhite could end badly—for all of them.

This afternoon, Creed's attitude seemed more grating than usual. He'd just opened the door to their suite and was already calling out, "Lily!"

He pulled her into a hug that made Zephyr clench his teeth. They'd known one another exactly as long as she'd know Zephyr, but with him, she was open. Maybe that was part of the problem. It wasn't just Creed who was making things more complicated. Lilywhite was relaxed with him in a way that she wasn't with Zephyr.

"Can you get Roan and Will to come out tonight?" Lily asked him, even though she'd been there for several minutes and hadn't said a word of her plan to Zephyr. She leaned on Creed and added, "Alkamy says I could go without your hoodie or that awful hat of Will's. She and Violet have a plan to make me up so—according to Vi—no one will be able to tell who I am even if they've seen one of the three pictures Daidí couldn't suppress."

Five, Zephyr corrected silently.

"You could come with," Creed started.

Lilywhite glanced at Zephyr. "No. Just ask them to come here," she said. "Kam and Vi were only a few minutes behind me."

Zephyr said nothing. He wanted to tell her that there were five pictures of her. Two he'd had expunged the same day they'd been released. The only remaining copies were in his possession. He didn't tell her that though; it made him seem . . . creepy instead of protective. He'd have done the same for any of the cell. He *had* done the same when a picture of Will dancing with another boy was snapped one night at what was supposed to be a paparazzi-free party. That time, he'd used fists rather than bribes. Will's mother was very much a conservative. Will, obviously, would have no protection in the human world if she shared the secret of his heritage, and Zephyr suspected she *would* share it if it got her votes. It would be a tidy way to explain away his other orientations if she needed to do so. Zephyr wasn't going to allow the crisis to reach that point. He'd beaten the photographer until Alkamy had stepped in.

"Anything for you," Creed said mildly, before he nodded at Zephyr, and then was gone in as quick a moment as he'd arrived.

Once he'd left to go drag Will and Roan back to the suite with him, Zephyr watched Lilywhite. She'd sent Creed on a mission specifically so that he'd be out of the room. He knew it, and he suspected Creed did too.

"I thought we were going to be fight-free," she started.

He closed his eyes for a moment, willing himself the strength he usually had. Zephyr opened his eyes and looked at her. "Endellion met with me in person, Lilywhite. She asked about *you* by name. You say that your mother wrote about the queen, about the war. Do you not realize yet that you are not simply someone with a dash of fae blood? Even if you don't want to believe me about your heritage, you have to accept that the queen of the joint throne doesn't know just anyone's name."

Lilywhite sighed. "Fine. Tell me what she said."

"She wants me to bring you to her."

"I see."

Zephyr stayed silent, waiting for something, anything, to tell him that she understood. He didn't cross the room, didn't go any nearer to her, but he couldn't help adding, "For three years, I've protected them alone."

"And if I don't go to her, she'll take it out on all of you, right?" Lilywhite's voice was soft, but he'd have to be thoroughly daft not to hear the threads of anger and reluctance twining into her words.

"It's not like you're the only one in this position." He paused, weighing the decision to tell her the truth. He'd not told anyone, not even Alkamy. Lilywhite had no loyalty to them, not now, possibly not ever. But she was the one selected to help guide and protect the cell. She was the last of the queen's seven Black Diamonds.

"What I say goes no further."

"Of course," she said without hesitation.

"I understand better than any of them realize. I obey her, no matter what, because if I don't she'll kill all seven of us. We do as we're told, as the queen demands, or we die. That's what it means to lead the cell, Lilywhite: you do what you have to so they don't die, and you never let them know because some of them are too stubborn to follow orders no matter the stakes."

"There has to be another way." She paced away from him, hand dropping to the pocket where he knew she carried one of her concealed knives. He had been trained; they all had. None of them touched a blade like it was a talisman. Only Lilywhite did that.

"You can't fight her." Zephyr followed Lilywhite until they reached the window overlooking a small copse of trees. If she were Alkamy or Violet, he'd know how to handle her. She was still a mystery to him. In a mild tone, he remarked, "I suspect you're capable with the various weapons you wear."

"I am my father's daughter," Lilywhite said softly, not looking back at him.

Zephyr shook his head, even though she couldn't see him, and said, "You sound very much like the queen herself. She's devoted to her family. She started this war for *our* people, Lilywhite. We were chosen, and whether we like it or not, that's the reality we have to face."

Lilywhite turned to look at him over her shoulder. "This is not *my* war. I won't kill for her."

"And I won't risk the people *I* love because you want to prove a point. Our queen has ordered me to bring you to the Hidden Lands, so you can either cooperate, or I will find another way." Zephyr hated that he had to admit these things, but she needed to understand how their world worked. "I'll not let *any* of them die because Creed has a crush and you think you're above the rest of us. She'll kill him if she thinks he's in the way of her plans. She'll kill your father if you don't comply. She'll kill Alkamy if I step out of line. Maybe Roan, or Vi first, but if she thinks I need more motivation, she'll slit Alkamy's throat. . . . It's her word that controls what blades are made wet."

Outside the room, he could hear Creed laughing at something Violet had said. He couldn't make out the words, but he knew the voices of those in the cell better than any others in this world or the other.

"If this proof of Creed's turns up and I decide that you're all telling me the truth—"

"Fae don't lie."

"I can lie. Creed can lie. I'm sure you can too."

"We aren't like that, Lilywhite. We keep our word, our vows. If humans did too, we wouldn't be in this situation."

They stared at each other in silence. There were things that were impossible, even for them. In this world, they lived lives of indulgence. In the Hidden Lands, they were special in a different way. They were tools, weapons fashioned by the queen's will. Weapons don't summon queens. That wasn't the way it worked.

"Do you understand?" he finally prompted.

"She's a monster."

"Maybe," Zephyr admitted. "That doesn't mean we can slay her like a storybook dragon . . . or even *dream* of it. The best we can do is protect those we love."

"There has to be more—"

"No," he interrupted firmly. "There isn't. Let Creed down easily or be harsh. Either way, do it. Only then do we go to see the queen—or you risk all of our lives."

"Fine. I'll come to meet her, but it won't change a thing between you and me *and* I won't go until I meet Creed's 'proof.'" Lily walked to the door and pulled it open, a smile once more on her lips as if everything was fine. Zephyr wasn't sure if anyone else heard the forced gaiety in her voice or if he noticed it because of what they had just discussed. Either way, he thought she sounded brittle as she told them, "Come on already, people! I want to go dancing."

And they were all coming into the room in a breathtaking blur. These few souls were his family, the people for whom he'd do anything. He served the queen, but he did it for *them* above all else. Fortunately, Lilywhite cared about them enough that she'd agreed to go to the Hidden Lands without his having to resort to force. It was fair progress.

twenty-three

LILY

Things with Zephyr were less tense after that night. Lily still felt more comfortable with Roan, Will, and Alkamy, but they weren't as painfully awkward as they had been before they talked. Violet was hard to resist, and they'd bonded over a collection of daggers that Violet had been forging by way of her own affinity to fire. She'd apparently started to do so as a child, and the earliest of her handmade blades was an ugly, crude thing. It was still impressive, and the tiny actress had started helping Lily practice with her own affinity to fire.

The issue, of course, was that as Lily thought about Zephyr's explanations, she realized that she needed to create more distance from Creed. Her ability to meet the Queen of Blood and Rage was not the same as agreeing to obey her. It did, however, highlight the fact that the queen was perfectly at ease with violence as incentive. She'd already called Daidí and Erik and asked them to be extra alert. With Erik, she was vague. With Daidí, she told him that she'd met some students "like her" and felt nervous. It wasn't a full truth, and he knew as much. It was the best she could do right now. She'd learned years ago that phone lines were never truly secure.

"Do you need to come home?" Daidí asked.

"Not right now."

"Later?"

She paused. "Maybe. I'm not in danger, and there's something . . . comforting about being around people like me." She laughed lightly then, knowing her father would understand what she meant after more than ten years of having multi-layered meanings in their conversations. "There are constantly people watching when you're like us though."

"Ah, paparazzi problems," he said.

"Some are worse than normal watchers," she agreed, letting him know that it was the "not normal" watchers that were an issue. For years, that had been a code word for those who watched the fae and fae-blood.

"I didn't think they came on campus."

"You know how it is," she admitted reluctantly, all but saying she'd been unable to stay on campus.

"Lilywhite!"

She sighed. "I know. I'm protected though."

"Do you need Cerise?" he prompted, using their code word for weapons.

Lilywhite laughed and clarified what sort of weapons she wanted. "Like *Hector* would separate from Cerise!"

"Right," he agreed, knowing that her emphasis on her father's largest guard was a request for a bigger gun. She already had a small one with her, but she felt the need for something with more stopping power.

"Oh, and if he's coming anyhow, could you send a few of my favorite pieces of jewelry too?"

At that, her father became very quiet. He knew she'd taken a small purse gun and several blades with her already. All she could hear was the steady rhythm of his breathing for several moments, and then he asked, "Are you sure you don't want to come home and get them yourself?"

"Not right now, but I'll tell you if it changes. Can you . . . can you talk to the Gavirias for me? I want Erik and his family to know that *they* matter to me."

"Should I tell them everything, Lily?"

"No," she all but whispered. "I'd rather that some things stay between us if possible, Daidí." She took a big gulping breath for courage and asked, "Do you remember Mom being pregnant?"

"You're my daughter, Lilywhite. No matter what else happens in this life, no matter what you ever hear . . . you are Lilywhite *Abernathy*."

"I have questions that doesn't answer," she admitted.

"When I get back from the Gavirias, I'll come see you and answer what I can." He took a breath of his own, exhaled in a sigh, and told her, "I expected you'd have questions. I hoped that Creed . . . that he could help."

"Don't let Señor Gaviria hear that you're matchmaking," she teased.

Like the rest of their conversation, her father heard what she was really asking and said, "At some point—"

"But not right now," she cut in firmly.

"Fine." Daidí paused, and she could hear people in the background now. Then he ordered, "You'll be careful."

"I *am* Nicolas Abernathy's daughter," she promised. "You be careful too."

"Always."

"Get back to work," she said in lieu of good-bye.

The week of their truce was almost up, and the closer that proof came, the more Lily worried. She had spent the past day and a half mostly alone in her room when possible.

She wasn't hiding. She simply needed space. *Abernathy Commandment #11: Know when to walk away from trouble.* The problem was that she wasn't sure this was trouble she could escape. Despite what she'd said to Zephyr and the assurances she'd given Daidí, Lily wasn't ready to meet the Queen of Blood and Rage, not now, possibly not ever. Even if Lily hadn't grown up reading and re-reading the tales her mother had written for her, seeing the news her whole life more than clarified exactly why Endellion was a living nightmare. Just in the past two weeks, the water supplies in ten mid-sized cities around the world had gone toxic. The media spin on the disaster ranged from environmental causes to governmental negligence. However, a few journalists, notably all independent media, suggested that this was yet another act of terrorism by either fae-blood sympathizers or by the fae themselves.

Lily could allow that they might be wrong, but ten coordinated attacks were unlikely to be an *accidental* disaster. Thousands of people sickened and died, many of them children or the elderly, whose immune systems weren't as strong, because their water supplies were tainted.

By Sleeper cells like the Black Diamonds.

Unfortunately, knowing that the queen was a terrorist wasn't news—or a legitimate excuse to refuse her *invitation* to the Hidden Lands. If Lily refused, she'd be taken against her will. If she went . . . honestly, Lily had no idea what would happen if she went. *Abernathy Commandment #13: Don't ask questions when you'd rather not know the answers.* The queen clearly had no compunction about killing. Would being a strong fae-blood be a strength or weakness in her eyes? The fae-bloods publicly claimed that being descended of the fae was a strength, a way to unify the two worlds if only humanity would stop polluting the earth. They were, in effect, radical environmentalists. Lily didn't agree with their theory that peace was that simple, but she did agree that humanity needed to stop being so careless with the earth.

"Your door was unlocked," Creed said softly.

She looked up to find him in the doorway to her bedroom. She hadn't even noticed that he was there until he spoke. Now she couldn't see anything else. She didn't want to cause more problems than necessary, so she had avoided any private conversations with Creed for several days now.

"If you're going to hide from me, at least admit you're doing it."

She shook her head and looked away from him. She had to. Whatever this pull was, it was strong and growing stronger. She couldn't afford to give in to it. As much as she didn't want to believe that she was anything other than who she'd always been—Nicolas and Iana Abernathy's daughter—the queen had summoned Lily by name. That meant that she needed to think about protecting the people already *known* to matter to her—and not invite more people close to her heart.

She stared out the window of her bedroom, not wanting to look at Creed. Lily had always known her mother was fae-blood. As Lily had gotten older and developed multiple affinities, she had considered the idea that her mother was wholly fae, so that wasn't that surprising either. But if she was one of the fae who had agreed to give over their children to be used as weapons, then why did she leave her stories for Lily? The answers Zephyr had offered simply didn't make sense. There was too much unknown, and Lily wasn't going to risk Creed's life by getting closer to him.

The boy in question walked farther into Lily's bedroom, and against her best intentions, she looked at him. His gaze was fastened on her like she would flee at any wrong move.

Admittedly, he wasn't far off. She was poised for escape, even though there was no exit save for the one he was currently blocking. "Does Zephyr know you're here?"

"I told him I was going to find Kamy."

"She told everyone she was going into Belfoure this afternoon. You were there."

"Oops." Creed shrugged. "Must've slipped my mind."

Lily shook her head. "You're making this more difficult than it needs to be."

He was directly in front of her now. "Really? I believe *you* are."

His hands didn't make direct contact with her skin, even though he raised them like he'd touch her. He didn't. He stayed perfectly still, his skin millimeters away from her. She could feel warmth radiating from him.

Then he shut his eyes, and she realized what he was about to do, but that meager second of knowledge wasn't enough to brace her for what followed. As he had in the gardens, he started to sing "Deadly Girl" using his affinity to reach out to touch her skin.

His voice was so low that she wanted to move forward to hear him.

She wouldn't, *couldn't* do that.

His breath was on her skin like a much firmer touch, like fingertips tracing her cheeks and jaw, like a caress on her lips.

She shivered.

"Run, my deadly girl," he sang. The words weren't

part of the song. They were only for her. "Run to a distant shore. Run from the monsters that lie in wait."

Creed's words fell like a kiss on the base of her throat and slid lower, stopping at the top seam of her blouse.

"Run before it's too late."

Lily stepped backward. It wouldn't change his ability to touch her with his voice, but it did give her the momentary illusion of control. "I'm not going to run from Endellion."

"But you'll run from me?" He gave her a sad smile. "Some would be flattered to be considered more terrifying than the Queen of Blood and Rage." The lightness in his tone did nothing to hide the darkness in him as his voice once more made the air take form. He caught her chin and forced her to look at him; at the same time, his next words held her wrist like a vise. "I am not one of them."

"What do you want from me?"

"Everything," he said baldly. "But I'll settle for honesty."

For a moment, she thought about telling him her fears and worries—her suspicion that she wasn't an Abernathy by blood—but she wasn't going to be so selfish as to put Creed in more danger than he already was.

Abernathy Commandment #19: If your loved one's life is in peril, break any commandment to protect her or him. She wasn't sure she could love anyone, but she felt something strong for Creed. That meant keeping him away from her.

"You're avoiding me," he charged. "You said we were friends. It's not what I want, but you offered me that crumb."

"We are."

"Why won't you talk to me alone then? I see you alone with everyone else." He inhaled, as if he needed to draw her scent in, reminding her that he was an air affinity and *only* air. The pain in his voice wasn't hidden at all as he added, "Even Zephyr, Lily. I see you walk with him and talk to Roan and Will. You are alone with Vi or Kamy every day. It's only me you reject."

Lily thought back to Zephyr's warnings, to the thought of the queen targeting Creed because of something Lily did, and she met Creed's eyes. "They aren't pursuing me like you are. None of them tell me that my friendship is a crumb."

"Are you trying to say that you don't want my attention? That you only want friendship?"

"That's what I'm trying to say," she told him. It wasn't a proper lie. She *was trying* to say she wasn't interested. If she had said she wasn't interested, that would be a lie, but her words as she'd uttered them were truth.

Creed laughed. "Oh, my beautiful liar." He traced her lips with one finger. "We'll talk about this tomorrow."

"Tomorrow?"

"I'll have your proof of what we are tomorrow," he clarified. "Then, we will discuss what happens next."

"We don't need to discuss it," she started, the words burning her tongue to even utter.

The way Creed watched her was frightening in its intensity. As much as she wanted his attention on her, it also made her want to run. If the queen asked for her by name, if Creed and Zephyr were right about what they all were, there were reasons aplenty to stay away from them all. It was Creed, though, who made her dare to believe that love could be true. It was Creed she already wanted to protect.

"You can refuse me, but don't try to lie to me," he chastised with a shake of his head. "I'm not some human boy who will be misled by your clever omissions. You feel this as much as I do, Lilywhite Abernathy, and I'm not giving up on the first girl who gave me reason to hope."

Lily was silent as he called her out by her full name as if they *were* true fae. As she knew it had been done for centuries before they'd either one drawn breath, the act of calling her out by her whole name made the words have a weight that was just shy of a vow. If he knew her secret name—one known only to her father, one that all acknowledged faeblood had—Creed could trap her with such words.

And for an awful too-honest moment, she wanted to tell him that secret, to let him bind her to him, to ask him *his* secret. She knew he'd tell her, but wanting a thing doesn't make it wise. Lily kept her lips tightly closed and dropped her gaze.

"We can't," she forced herself to say.

"You're wrong, Lily. You'll see," Creed said gently, and then he left her there with tears on her cheeks and a lie still burning on her lips.

twenty-four
EILIDH

Eilidh was in the courtyard outside the queen's quarters when she saw her brother watching her. She wondered how often he'd done so without her awareness, but she wasn't so foolish as to think Rhys would answer that question if she posed it. He kept rooms in the queen's section of the royal palace, as did the king. Eilidh technically had rooms there as well. While her father and brother used theirs, Eilidh hadn't ever lived there.

"Why do I need to stay in the tower, Mother?" eight-year-old Eilidh asked.

"You are their future."

"It's lonely."

The queen looked at her, and the usual chill in her eyes vanished for a moment. "You are a symbol, child. That means you must be above the emotions that weaken you."

"I don't understand."

"You need to prove that you are worthy, that you are the queen they need, that you exist to serve your people." Endellion held out an ivory-handled dagger. "You are not like any of them."

"Even my brothers?" Eilidh took the dagger in her hand.

"Rhys is a good example for you," the queen allowed. "There is no weakness in him. Your father's sons . . . do not count you as a sibling. You cannot trust them."

"Yes, Mother."

The queen nodded. "Keep that with you always, even after you master your affinities."

"Yes, Mother." Eilidh nodded and looked at the weapon in her hand. It was pretty for what it was, but it wasn't a doll. A lot of the fae had dolls. "Could I have a dolly too? Just one? I could practice being a mother, like you."

The queen cupped Eilidh's face in her palms. "There will not be talk of being a mother or of loneliness. You are above all of that. They will doubt your worth, and your duty is to prove that you are not weak . . . or your blood will soak into the sand."

At the time, Eilidh wasn't entirely sure if her mother was suggesting that she would kill Eilidh for weakness or if weakness would kill her. Either way, she didn't repeat her request to live near her mother. She did as she was expected to do: trained, studied politics, and watched her brothers— both her father's sons who wished her ill and the one sibling her mother loved.

And she started to study ways to reach a different future from the red-soaked one Endellion would have them lead.

Eilidh wasn't afraid to take a life if she needed to do so, but it wasn't something she wanted. She trained to kill, but hoped she would avoid that fate.

Silently, she walked to the wall of weapons and selected a bow she liked. Her hand fell on the quiver of arrows when Rhys spoke up. "Would you care to spar, sister?"

Eilidh looked over her shoulder and met his gaze. He'd never offered to cross blades with her. He'd spoken to her tutors, but he'd never unsheathed his own weapons to train with her.

Behind her she heard murmurs. In this, as in all he did, Rhys clearly had a reason. Joy rolled through her like a wave as he walked toward her. His hand was on the hilt of his sword, and he ambled across the courtyard as if they didn't have an audience.

"I'm not sure I'd be much challenge," she admitted, her voice loud enough to carry to the watchers. "I've watched you fight too often to think myself capable of offering you any sport."

He laughed. Her serious Unseelie brother *laughed*. "For your age, you would. For my age? Few other than our queen mother would be a genuine contest."

"And my father," Eilidh added quietly.

Rhys didn't reply to that assertion beyond saying, "The king is a skilled fighter. Mother declared that we do not duel though."

Eilidh gestured at the bow she held. "Best of three?"

Rhys took his hand from the hilt of one of the swords

at his side and walked over to grab a bow she'd seen him practice with in the past. "Not my weapon of choice, little sister."

"I know. That's why I selected it."

He laughed again and gestured toward the row of targets as he came to stand at her side. There was something more here than she realized, but she also knew that her brother was offering to fire arrows at her side. It was something he didn't do with anyone but the queen herself or the rare fae the queen sent to him for instruction. Training with Rhys was a boon not easily granted.

"You honor me, brother." She nocked an arrow, lifted her bow, and let loose. The shaft hit the first target mere millimeters from dead center. She glanced at him and added, "That doesn't mean I won't try to beat you."

He glanced at the target, flicked his eyes back toward her, and released an arrow while watching her. "Good."

They gathered a sizeable audience as they competed in marksmanship. She didn't best him, but no one expected her to do so. The queen's son and guard was the acknowledged champion with most all weapons in the Hidden Lands. He preferred sharp things, especially the longsword, but he was as happy with bashing as stabbing. Be it rapier or falchion, poignard or dirk, Rhys was always deadly. Eilidh understood, as few could, that he had no other choice. The queen was acknowledged as the best fighter in the Hidden Lands, and he was her only son. Her first daughter, Iana, was dead, and Eilidh was fragile. Rhys had to prove that the queen's get were not all worthless. Eilidh understood that urge, even though she'd never equal her brother's skill with so many weapons.

After another hour, they had gained the one watcher whose favor mattered most. The queen strode across the well-trod ground with barely a glance to her left or right. No one attempted to catch her attention. Seeing the queen at the courtyard was always a treat. For all of the doubts that the fae sometimes had in the silence of their homes, none among them ever doubted her prowess in a fight. Her daily armor was on, the leather appearing closer to ruby than midnight in the sunlight. Even here, she cut a figure that inspired awe.

"How is she?" Endellion asked.

"I would stand beside her on the field of battle," Rhys said. He bowed to their mother, even though he technically didn't have to do so.

Eilidh followed his example.

"Indeed?" Endellion murmured.

"She is not as fast as I am, but her arrows all fly true. Every one has been a kill shot." Rhys gestured to the targets. "She is your daughter."

"And with a blade?"

Eilidh's brief moment of pride faded. She didn't have the strength to fight her brother and fare as well as she needed to do in front of their people. She opened her mouth to apologize, but Rhys replied before she could, "I've not yet tried her. I have observed her often enough to know that for her age she is skilled."

Endellion nodded at her. Then she looked away from her daughter and announced, "I have need of exercise."

The queen was already drawing her sword. It was a thing of darkness, the blade etched with runes and symbols so ancient that no one understood all of them. It was blackened, as if fire had touched it often, and sometimes glints of red flickered in that strange metal. If there existed a blade that were strengthened by blood, this would be the one.

Eilidh didn't want to ask what truths hid in those softly spoken stories. There were questions best left unanswered, especially where the queen was concerned. All that truly mattered was that her mother was a warrior who had earned respect, and Eilidh was resolved not to fail her.

Although Eilidh wouldn't leave the courtyard, her time in practice was clearly at an end. She lowered her bow and walked to the wall to put it away. She would watch her mother demonstrate the skill that she herself couldn't master satisfactorily.

Before she was three steps away, Rhys said, "You do your family proud, sister."

The queen stilled. It was the first time she'd heard her son speak so to her heir. If Endellion were anyone else, she might ask what had transpired to have Rhys call her sister in such a tone. As it was, all she did was say, "She is my heir, Rhys. Of course she does us proud."

Eilidh looked back at Rhys as he bowed his head deeply and said, "I meant no slight."

Endellion attacked. Her sword was a two-handed one, made for larger warriors. The harsh black blade was heavy in the air, and Rhys barely had time to stop its swing. The clang of metal on metal was loud.

Rhys drew his second weapon, a shorter blade to stab as he blocked with his sword, and with a ferocity none save the king would even dream to dare, he attacked the queen.

The clash of steel and grunt of exertion continued as the two warriors crossed blades time and again. At several minutes in, Rhys lost his sword. It hit the ground with a *thunk*. He was left only with a poignard, and that shorter blade wouldn't do as much good against a weapon with long reach like the queen's claymore.

But within another ten minutes, the queen had a cut on her shoulder.

"Tired, Mother?" Rhys teased.

"Momentarily distracted by worry that you are only half armed," she countered with a wide smile.

"As if." Rhys angled so that he was moving closer to the wall of weapons. "Your reach is absurdly far with that beast."

"Some of us aren't worried about *pretty* fights," she returned, slashing at her only son with the kind of force that made the fight look far too real.

Rhys snorted. "Not all of us need a claymore to feel intimidating."

The queen laughed and lowered her sword. "Daggers? Hand to hand? Sickles?"

"Ladies' choice," Rhys said as he lowered his poignard.

He slid it into a scabbard and walked over to pick up the one she'd knocked out of his hand.

While his back was turned, the queen kicked out at his knee, drawing gasps from the crowd and Eilidh's exclamation of "Rhys!"

He turned and grabbed the queen's ankle.

Endellion dropped to the ground, pulling him off balance and swinging her other foot up and out to kick his forearm.

Rhys' muffled grunt of pain was all but lost under the queen's words. "You forget your childhood lessons," she said as she scrabbled back to her feet.

"Never turn your back on the enemy," Rhys recited as he pushed to his feet without use of his hands.

Eilidh couldn't tell if he'd fractured his wrist or simply bruised it. All she knew was that he had the implacable look she had seen so often on his face. He wouldn't cede defeat though. It wasn't Rhys' way, and their mother would be furious if he did so.

The sheer stupidity of what Eilidh was about to do should've stopped her, but if she was going to be regarded as the future queen, she needed to prove it. She felt like she was half-asleep as she reached out for a handful of throwing knives.

"Mother," she said, giving warning at least.

But Endellion didn't even glance at Eilidh.

The first blade flew through the air, sticking in the ground where Endellion's foot had just been.

The queen spun around, hand on her hilt and blade half-drawn around. "Who dares—" The words died as she saw Eilidh, another knife aloft to throw.

"I'm better with distance than close combat," Eilidh said. She shrugged and added, "My fragility of body made me learn to adapt."

The queen met her gaze. "Would you fight me, daughter?"

"I would dissuade you from pushing my brother further this day," Eilidh answered, cautiously avoiding any words that could elicit the queen's worst temper.

For a moment, Eilidh thought Rhys was going to step around their mother and strangle her. His eyes were warning her off this path, but there were times when a future queen needed to prove her mettle. This felt like such a time.

The queen bowed her head to Eilidh and then turned to Rhys and did the same. "You *both* do me proud," she announced. Then she strode over to Eilidh and in a rare show of maternal affection, the queen kissed her forehead. "Well done."

The Queen of Blood and Rage swept away in the hush that had come over the assembled crowd.

A few moments passed before Rhys looked at the fae who stood in a circle around them and said, "You are dismissed."

It was a polite way to tell them "be gone," but her brother wasn't known for mincing words. He played up his Unseelie traits, emphasizing his ferocity and candor both.

Once they were alone, Rhys turned to her. "Are you *trying* to get one of us killed?"

"You can protect yourself against anyone other than the queen," she reminded him. "We both know that, brother."

"And there are those who do not always heed our queen mother." Rhys folded his arms with an uncharacteristic slowness.

"It's broken, isn't it?"

"Maybe." He shrugged awkwardly. "I can fight with the one arm while it sets."

Hesitantly, Eilidh suggested, "Come to the tower. I can help."

Rhys lifted his brows in a silent question, but she wasn't going to answer him here in public.

Mutely, he followed her toward her glass tower. No one stopped them as they walked. It was growing common to see Eilidh walking with her brother, her betrothed—or both. The assumption was simply that Rhys was protecting the heir by determining if Torquil was worthy of her.

As they reached the tower, they found Torquil there waiting outside the glittering building. His lips were pressed tightly together, and she knew that both fae would be voicing displeasure once they were inside the privacy of her tower. They might be visible to the faeries who stood outside watching, but as long as they kept control of their gestures and actions, no one would know that she was being chastised.

The three silently ascended the tower. Once they were inside, Torquil was the first to speak. "What are you thinking? It's bad enough to be seen training with Rhys, but challenging the *queen*?"

"He is injured, and I offered aid."

Rhys held up a hand. "I could've continued fighting. Mother has broken far more than one of my bones in her darker moods."

Torquil raised a single brow.

"I know," Eilidh said quietly.

For a long tense moment, her brother stared at her. Finally, he said, "It was you. You've done this before . . . I would wake far less broken than made sense to me. When she cracked my spine . . . that was a worse injury than it seemed, wasn't it?"

Eilidh nodded. "I drugged your tea the first time and your wine the second."

"I knew someone had," Rhys grumbled. "I had poison testers after the wine incident."

"I know. It became more and more complicated to knock you out over time, but I didn't want you to know." Eilidh sat on the edge of the sofa, realizing that Torquil and Rhys were standing because she'd failed to sit. Having guests and remembering the propriety involved in doing so was still new to her. "I couldn't have you *see* me help you. I didn't know then if I could trust you."

"You can trust me, Eilidh. I swear on it. No one outside this room will know what you can do," Rhys vowed.

"I still don't know," Torquil pointed out. "Why did you drug Rhys?"

Silently, Eilidh patted the sofa.

Rhys sat.

Eilidh wrapped her hands around her brother's wrist, letting her sight and touch sink under his flesh until she found the imperfection in the bone. It was something she'd only done with a few people, but she'd healed Rhys often enough that she could see his bone quicker than she would have with someone she'd not healed in the past.

Vaguely, she heard Torquil say, "Is she . . . ?"

"Healing me," Rhys finished. "Yes."

Eilidh ignored them, concentrating on the surface of the bone. She drew the pieces together, knitting them steadily as she re-grew the pieces so they could fuse properly. It was akin to coaxing fire from tinder or a plant from soil.

Rhys drew a sharp breath.

"Sorry," she murmured as his body pulsed with pain. It wasn't an easy feeling, she suspected, to have bone meld together. She condensed the entire healing process into mere moments. There was no way to do it without pain.

When she released his arm, her usually imperturbable brother looked ill. He leaned back on the cushions and closed his eyes. "Perhaps being drugged first is wise."

"I doubt you'd have agreed to that willingly," Eilidh said.

Torquil was sitting across from her, staring at her with wide eyes. "Attenuation? That gift is all but a myth."

Eilidh offered him a weak smile. Healing made her tired.

For a brief few moments, she felt weakened. "It seems that the union of the two courts has had unexpected results."

"Do your parents both know?" Rhys prompted.

She didn't want to discuss that topic, but she couldn't refuse to answer him. She nodded. "They are aware."

While neither parent had overtly spoken to her about her affinity, they had both—in their ways—let her know that she was not to use it. Leith had said only, "My grandfather once spoke of a fae *his* grandfather had known who was cursed with an affinity for attenuation. Lessening the injuries of others weakened him until he was so frail that he died. It is not an affinity I would wish on any but those I despised."

At the time, Eilidh had bowed her head in silence.

It was one of the rare moments of affection that the king had shown her when he tucked his fingertips under her chin and said, "You are my child, Eilidh. I want you well and safe. If I or your mother ever were mortally injured, even *then* I would not wish that you had such an affinity. Do you understand me?"

And she had. She knew that she was not to use this affinity. Her mother had said similar things in less subtle terms: "If I were to find that you had used this affinity, Daughter, I would not be pleased."

None of those details changed the fact that she'd used it time and again to heal Rhys. There were others she'd healed—including both Torquil and Lilywhite—but it was something she did rarely. Rather than enter a conversation filled with unpleasant admissions, she told her brother and betrothed, "Tomorrow, I need one or both of you to come with me to the mortal lands. I will explain more, answer your questions then, but I *do* need at least one of you."

"I am yours," Torquil said.

"I will be with you," Rhys added.

Eilidh had expected lectures from both of them, but neither chastised her on anything, not about her secrets, not about standing up to the queen. They held their silence for several moments. Torquil sent a nervous look at Rhys that she didn't understand. Rhys still looked wan, but there was no danger in that.

When Rhys finally opened his eyes, he looked from one to the other, and then—in the sort of casual voice that made clear that what he was revealing was anything but casual—he said, "Tell me, Eilidh, what do you know of the king's affinities."

"Fire, compulsion, and air," she recited.

Torquil stood and glared at Rhys. His posture was such that Eilidh expected swords to be unsheathed. Clearly there was something here that was not known to her, something her betrothed knew and Rhys wanted her to know too.

"Do not do this," Torquil ordered.

The only son of the Queen of Blood and Rage wasn't known for taking orders other than the queen's. He met Torquil's gaze straight on and asked Eilidh, "Did you know that the king has a fourth gift, one not known to many?"

"As does the queen," Eilidh said quietly, drawing the

242

boys out of their stare.

Rhys rewarded her with a proud smile and said, "You have known and not spoken if it! You are better suited to the Hidden Throne than I realized, sister."

"Secrets are currency." She repeated their mother's words of wisdom.

"Indeed. One I would use to pay you now for your gift of health." Rhys glanced back at Eilidh's betrothed and said, "Dreams. The Seelie thought it a vanished gift. Very few have it. The king does, but there are whispers that the son of Aden is a rarity too."

Eilidh looked at Torquil, her dearest friend, her only confidant for many years. "Truly?"

"Eilidh . . ."

Slowly the import of this revelation began to settle on her. "So the dreams I had of you for all of these years, were they . . . *my* dreams or *your* manipulations?" Eilidh's voice shook with the effort of restraining her anger and hurt. "Do you give dreams or can you see others' dreams?"

"Both," Torquil admitted. He stepped toward her, took both hands in his, and held tight to her as if she would flee. "I saw one of your dreams by accident when you were younger, and when I realized that you dreamed of . . . what you dream, I didn't look again. It's why I couldn't stay near you sometimes. You were too young, Eilidh. The queen's daughter, the heir, I couldn't let myself see you that way."

"I fell asleep in your arms last winter," she pointed out, not asking, not sure she could stand to know.

"You were of age by then, and I needed to know if you still dreamed of me," he whispered. "The queen ordered that I would wed, and I couldn't do that, not while I was waiting on you."

"So you looked," Eilidh finished.

He nodded.

"And?" Rhys prompted.

Torquil glanced back at Rhys with a scowl. "That is not yours to know."

"She is my sister."

Instead of answering him, Torquil turned back to face her. "It was not until these past months that I've influenced your dreams. I swear. I would've waited, but if there was a chance, if there was a glimmer of a hope that you could be mine, I needed to know."

"Rhys, I need to speak with my betrothed in private," she announced.

"My debt is paid." Rhys looked at Torquil and then at her as he pronounced, "Your secrets are both safe with me. There is no one else who needs to know either of these affinities."

Then he bowed deeply and left them.

Once they were alone, or as alone as they could be with the watchers outside the tower, she asked, "And those dreams that . . . were unlike my old ones? The ones of us . . ." She couldn't say the words, didn't know how to go from thinking she was having dreams to realizing that they had *shared* those experiences. In a surprisingly steady voice, she admitted, "I don't know what to say here. Help me understand . . . why did you do that?"

"The first was an accident. I was weak because I knew that you were not uninterested in me, and my own dream projected to you," he admitted. "I did not mean to do so that first time, Eilidh. I swear it."

"And then?"

"And then . . . I looked at your dreams intentionally; I saw a dream not so unlike my own. The second time that I know that you dreamed of what we could be like together—that was *your* mind's creation, not mine. I simply saw it." Torquil stroked her hair tenderly, even as his eyes darkened with something more intense. "The rest were not a coincidence. Some were my doing, and others were yours. I watched them as often as I could. They were all that kept me from believing you found me repugnant. In our waking hours, you were so cold . . . so dismissive. If I hadn't known of the things you dreamed, I might've given up. But I *did* know. I couldn't touch another fae after that. All I could do was count the hours until we could dream together again."

"Oh," she said. There were so many things he was saying, so many revelations that she couldn't fathom how she'd been oblivious to each of them. In the midst of her shock was a not-insignificant measure of embarrassment. To know that she'd directed some of those dreams . . . it was hard not to feel awkward.

"Do you *feel* the dream, as I do?" she asked.

He didn't make her clarify further, fortunately.

"Every touch." He looked at her as she'd seen fae look upon one another, with so much fire in his eye that she could scarcely breathe. "Because of my affinity, it is as real as if we were awake."

"I see."

"As it is for you," he continued.

As he spoke, Eilidh realized that he was the safest possible spouse she could hope for. In dreams, there was no risk of a child. Part of her wished she could tell Endellion of his affinity. If the queen knew, perhaps she would allow a ceremony.

It was a matter to ponder. Not now. Possibly not even soon, but there would be a time to discuss the matter.

Then Torquil spoke again. "I wanted to give it time, to court you properly, but then you were walking away. You were telling me to find a wife as if you had no feelings, as if you didn't dream of me, of *us* with the sort of passion that I've never known. So I declared myself."

"Because we dream of mating?" Eilidh tried to dismiss it, to find a way to shelter her heart. "You don't have to marry for *that*, Torquil."

"I love you, Eilidh." He swallowed nervously. "I know you were trapped when I chose to marry you, but if you give me a chance maybe you'll feel differently in time."

"I won't." She felt tears in her eyes as emotions overwhelmed her.

"Oh," Torquil murmured. He turned away in defeat.

"I already love you," she clarified. "I have loved you for years."

And there, in her glass tower, with faeries of both courts watching them, she kissed her betrothed, not as a maiden kisses, but with the sort of passion she'd only known in dreams. Torquil's touch and taste were as familiar as if they'd done this a hundred thousand times.

"We can only be where the people can see us," Eilidh told him several moments later as she stepped back from him, resuming the proper distance to respect the queen's orders. Kissing wasn't forbidden, but the things that, in her dreams, came after that would be. She met her betrothed's eyes and asked, "Would you nap with me?"

Torquil laughed happily. "I've waited months, thinking of telling you, wanting to dream together a purpose."

Eilidh took his hand in hers and walked with him to the sofa. They sat, her leaning against his chest and him with an arm around her, until they fell asleep and dreamed together while the spies and fae staring into the glass tower had no idea of the joy that the betrothed fae in the tower were experiencing as they slept.

twenty-five

LILY

The next night, Lily met Creed and Zephyr at the same walled garden where she'd first thought she could be hidden. The fae-blood, because she refused to accept that they were true fae, apparently used it regularly for the same reasons she'd wanted it. There was a privacy in it that was precious to fae-blood trying to hide from the world. She couldn't begrudge them their need of it any more than she'd expect them to ban her from it. The problem, she expected, would be when she refused to go along with their madness about being soldiers for Endellion.

The day itself had been uneventful, which was a relief as she suspected they'd need their wits sharp shortly.

Silently, Lily walked up to them. "You told none of the others about tonight?"

"I agreed to your terms, Lilywhite." Zephyr pressed his

lips together like he'd bitten something unpleasant.

"So no one knows we're here?" she asked them both.

"I don't know who Creed has invited here"—he sent a surly look at Creed—"but that's the *only* person who knows where we are."

"Okay then," she said.

She walked into the labyrinth and looked at the hedge wall, willing it to part for her. When it did, she stroked a hand over the hedge in gratitude, and then glanced back at Creed and Zephyr.

"So you have affinities for water, fire, *and* earth, but you still insist that you're not fae."

Lily bit her lip to keep from adding, "and air." Getting away from them if they refused to let this whole soldiers-for-the-queen nonsense go would be hard enough. She needed to maintain some element of surprise. She'd meet the queen if it kept them safe, but after that, she might need to vanish.

A part of her had plotted ways to convince them to run with her. Surely her father could hide them! But even as she thought that, she wondered if she was being foolish to think there was a way to escape the fae.

She wasn't going to give up though. She'd spent hours imagining potential scenarios. Daidí had contingency plans, and those plans had contingency plans. Surviving when there were factions who wanted you dead or imprisoned taught a man to think beyond the obvious—and that man had taught her. Unfortunately, contingency plans were sometimes unappealing. Her best bet would be a move to the South Continent, and being there would be safest if she stayed with Erik's family. She might not want to become the next Señora Gaviria, but she trusted Erik and his father. Even if she outright told Señor Gaviria that she would never marry Erik, he would still take her in and keep her safe—and the Gavirias were even more intense about security than Daidí.

Inside the garden, Lily turned to Creed. "There's no one here."

"Wait," he said quietly. He looked around and led Lily toward a ring of stones and what appeared to be toadstools.

Lily's panic level shot up. There was only one reason to wait beside a ring, and that was because you were waiting for someone to come through from the Hidden Lands. She swallowed, the sound seeming loud in the dark garden.

Zephyr stepped up so he was on Lily's other side. He looked at Creed and muttered, "I hope you know what you're doing."

They stood in awkward silence for another three or four minutes before the ground seemed to shimmer off to the side of them. The gateway to the Hidden Lands was opening, and with it came a burst of sugar-scented air. Acrid tinges wove throughout the sweet notes, and Lily couldn't help but think of the single-malt that her father sometimes sipped. He'd told her once that the burnt scent was peat, and that it reminded him of her mother. As she stood here tonight inhaling that very aroma, she had to wonder if his late-night admission had meant more than she'd realized.

As the shimmer solidified, the scent faded, and there in front of them were three actual, true fae. They were obviously of the purest fae lines, as they were all preternaturally tall and terrifyingly gorgeous. Nothing in humanity could compare to them. It was why being beautiful was often the first reason people were accused of being fae-blood. If money or other excuses couldn't explain the beauty, it could earn a person the sort of attention that led to imprisonment.

Lily gasped, not because of their beauty, but because of the three faeries who stepped out of the circle, not all were unknown to her. Only two were strangers. Aside from being well over six feet in height, both boys were filled with light. Both bowed, to her specifically, and then they stepped backward one step.

There, between them and slightly in front of them, stood a third faery, someone Lily had thought existed only in her mind. She was older now, but there was no doubt that the faery in front of them was a grown-up version of Lily's childhood playmate—her *imaginary* friend.

"Patches?" Lily asked, even though it *had* to be her. No one else had the same strange weblike pattern over her skin. She looked like she'd been broken into tiny pieces and reassembled, her seams left visible in the process.

"Lily," she said softly.

Lily stared at her, and then looked at Creed. "You know my . . . You know her?"

"I do." He kneeled.

Zephyr was already on his knees, head bowed. He had been since the moment the faeries took shape. He glanced up at her and ordered, "Kneel, Lilywhite."

Before Lily could point out that she owed no loyalty to these three, Patches said, "No. Lily is not to kneel before me. Ever."

Lily folded her arms over her chest and glared at the girl she'd thought was imaginary. "*You* have some explaining to do."

Patches laughed, and for a fraction of a moment, Lily wanted to hug her. This was her oldest, her *only* female friend until meeting Alkamy and Violet. With Patches, Lily had felt free and safe and *normal*. With her, Lily had felt like she was invincible, despite the fear she had over the strange things she could do, things that Daidí and Patches both made her swear to hide.

But this wasn't the child who had played hide-and-seek in the garden at the Abernathy Estate. This was a *faery*. This was someone who had made her believe things that weren't true, who had lied to her and left her. Lily squeezed her arms tighter to her chest and frowned.

"Please rise," Patches said to Zephyr and Creed. Then she glanced at the taller of the two fae boys with her. "Are we safe here?"

He was as intensely alert in the way of all of the bodyguards that Lily had known over the years, and she knew for certain that he was a guard or militia of some sort. He was also frighteningly beautiful: eyes that could be mistaken for ice chips, a face more suited to gods than mortals, and muscles that spoke of hours of training every day. He looked at Patches and nodded. The movement made his pale-blond hair slide forward. It was so pale that, from a distance, Lily suspected that his hair would look like a halo.

"Would you sit with me?" Patches asked.

As she spoke, vines rose up, twisted and braided until flowering chairs were sprouting from the garden. Forming seats from earth was something Lily had managed, but not six chairs simultaneously.

At Lily's side, Zephyr was glaring at Creed like he was a stranger. Both boys came to their feet, standing on either side of Lily much as Patches' fae boys flanked her. It was all so very formal, reminding Lily of the sort of contract negotiations she'd attended with her father. When both houses wanted to establish their authority, every word mattered; every gesture spoke.

When she glanced at Zephyr, though, she saw that his eyes were full of accusations and betrayal. All he managed to say was, "Do you know who she *is*?"

"Eilidh. Rhymes with Kayley and Bailey. Apparently not a fan of her royal entity of vengeance." Creed shrugged, but Lily heard the tension in his voice that he was trying to hide.

Creed was nervous, but Zephyr obviously couldn't see it. He snapped, "How could you keep this from me?"

In the next heartbeat, Zephyr punched him hard enough

that Creed stumbled back.

Creed raised his hand to his jaw, winced slightly, and told Zephyr, "First one's free. After that . . ."

"You disrespected our queen. You have no right to speak to the—"

"She's not my queen," Creed interrupted.

"Or mine," Lily added.

"You're all wrong," Eilidh said. "But only as much as you're right." She sighed quietly. "Creed said you needed to see me, Lily, that you were ready for the answers I have."

Everyone had remained standing, even though there were braided chairs of vine and root there beside them. The two fae boys watched them all intently.

"Please." Patches gestured for Lily to sit first.

Zephyr tried to catch Lily's hand to stop her, but she jerked away. He explained, "In fae culture, the highest ranked sits first. Eilidh is the *heir* to both the Seelie and Unseelie courts. She was born to take the Hidden Throne."

But Patches offered her a small, sad smile and said, "Zephyr is correct. The highest ranking among us sits first. It is a court tradition that has resulted in many frivolous quarrels." Then she met Lily's gaze and said, "Take your seat, Lilywhite, so we can all sit as well."

Both of the fae boys gaped at Patches. The guard looked at Lily again and then at Patches. "Is this . . . ? This is our sister's *child*? You didn't think to share your knowledge of her?"

Lily lowered herself into the chair, not sure if shock

was settling in or if she was imagining the implications of the guard's words. "Your sister?" she echoed in a voice that cracked.

"You see why I protected her secrets, Rhys?" Eilidh said, taking her seat.

"Does Mother know?" the guard, Rhys, asked. He and the other fae boy sat in almost perfect synchronicity.

Lily was still trying to sort out a different explanation in the words that she was hearing. Patches *couldn't* be her aunt. For that to be true, her mother would have to be . . . *the* baby, the one whose death started the long years of attacks on humanity by order of the Queen of Blood and Rage.

"The queen's baby died," Lily said. "Everyone says as much. Even in the book my mother left . . ."

Patches shot her a sympathetic glance. "No, the book says that the queen believed the baby dead. She never found her daughter."

"My mother." Lily felt like her lungs couldn't fill. "My mother is the baby who started the war? *She* is the lost heir?"

"I'm sorry for keeping so much from you." Patches motioned to the guard, who sat on her left. "This is Rhys. My brother. Before my sister was born, Rhys would've been the King of Unseelie." She motioned to the fae on her right. "This is my betrothed, Torquil."

Lily swallowed, her mind racing to process everything she'd been told. "And what are *we*, Patches?"

"I am your aunt. My sister was your mother."

The thought that her childhood friend was her aunt was almost too much to process. This stern faery was her *uncle*, and the queen . . . Lily stopped herself, not willing to finish the thought. Being the granddaughter of the woman who had shed so much blood was something she couldn't begin to fathom.

While Lily sat silently, Eilidh glanced briefly at the boys. "I don't know who *your* parents were, so I cannot tell you which of you is of higher rank."

"That's not why we're . . ." Zephyr started, stopped, and sat. He looked over at Creed. "Did you know?"

He shook his head. "I just knew Eilidh because she came to me and asked that I attend Lily's birthday party. She'd brought me an invitation from Lily's dad."

"*You* sent him?" Lily asked her aunt. "I thought Daidí . . ." Her words drifted off as pieces clicked into place for her. "Daidí *knows* you. He knew you were real when I was a child, and . . ." She shook her head, as if the motion would help her sort the facts into the right order. "I don't understand."

Creed ignored the chairs entirely and stayed standing at Lily's side, despite Zephyr's glare and Torquil's slight tilt of head indicating that he found the action curious.

"Stand down, child. I mean my niece nothing but amity," Rhys said quietly. "There are those who will want to kill her. I am not one of them."

"Child?" Lily echoed. "How old are you?"

"Age is relative to the fae, niece." His lips curved in

a slight smile. "We'll simply say that I remember the day Mother decided to kill every human standing on the sand. I remember when your mother was a child new in my mother's womb and the queen had another name. I remember before that when I was her heir for many years, back when the thought of allying with the Seelie Court would have been called treason." He looked back at Creed. "Sit. Your point is made."

"His point?" Lily felt foolish repeating everything, but there were too many new truths to accept so quickly.

"He has just declared his loyalty," Eilidh said. "Not to the queen. Not to her named heir." She pointed at herself and then to Rhys as she added, "Or to the Unseelie prince. Creed has declared that his fealty is to *you*, Lilywhite. Should there be a drawing of sides, his is already stated."

"No! We're not familiar with fae customs, and—"

Creed cut her off, "I am quite familiar, Lily. You might not be, but every Sleeper was taught about fae customs and culture."

"I want no part of this," Lily told Eilidh and Rhys. "I want to be at home with my father. He *is* my father, isn't he?"

"Iana would never answer that," Eilidh said. "I asked."

"But if I am Daidí's, then I'm only half-fae . . . you're still the heir, right?" Lily reached out and took Creed's hand. Despite everything she'd decided, right now Lily needed his support.

At her touch, Creed sat on the empty chair beside her,

keeping her hand in his. "I didn't know about this, Lily," he whispered. "I promise. I didn't know you knew her or any of it."

She nodded. "Eilidh?"

"Creed does not lie," Rhys said.

"The Queen of Blood and Rage knew you by name, knew you were one of her Seven Black Diamonds. She summoned you, Lily. If there's anyone who has more answers, it's our queen," Zephyr said firmly.

"Not my queen," Lily and Creed said in unison.

Torquil finally spoke. "This will be fun."

"By fun, do you mean likely to result in bloodshed?" Rhys asked.

At that, Torquil scowled. "Yes."

"If I were fae, not fae-blood but true fae, wouldn't I be like you?" Lily asked all of them.

At first, there was only silence, but then Rhys turned his attention to her and asked, "How many affinities do you have, Lilywhite Abernathy?"

She could feel words being pulled to her lips as soon as he asked, as if he could summon the answer from her by sheer will. Her body wanted to answer, her lips were already opening to share truth she'd rather not offer. She clamped her mouth closed, teeth cutting into her tongue as she bit down to force herself not to reply.

Abernathy Commandment #7: Secrets are valuable. Don't part with them for free. Abernathy Commandment #6: Never confess your vulnerabilities if you can avoid it. She repeated the commands over and over in her mind to keep from answering Rhys, to keep the words from slipping from her against her will and wish.

It wasn't enough.

Without meaning to, her energy flung out in defense. The chair he was in became a prison, steadily enclosing him, but Rhys didn't resist the plants that were wrapping tighter and tighter around his body. They started at his feet and began lashing around him like living whips.

"Earth . . . ? And?" Rhys prompted. He glanced down at the vines and briefly smiled.

Lily kept her mouth closed with effort. She felt like the very words were being compelled from her body. Her hand went to her mouth to hold her jaw shut.

"Would I see a demonstration of all of your affinities if I attacked your lone subject, Lilywhite?" Rhys couldn't move from the vines holding him to the chair, but his words and compulsion continued.

Lily swallowed the copper tang of blood in her mouth. She stood. Her own chair stretched forward and re-formed as a wall in front of Creed, protecting him since he'd foolishly declared fealty to her in front of Rhys.

"I gave word of peace to *you*," Rhys said. "Those two? They are both disposable."

Her wall of vines extended the other direction to shield Zephyr. In her hazy mind, she thought she felt his strength adding to hers as she did so. He might not have declared anything, but he wasn't going to let them be attacked. The wall that she'd begun was dotted with thorny roses in front of him and were beginning to spread onto the section of wall that now blocked Creed almost entirely.

"He"—Rhys gestured to Zephyr, although his movements were sluggish as the vines had covered his legs and worked up to his chest and were now tightening around his arms—"would deliver you to Endellion. You would protect him as well? He's knelt before her. Bled for her. He serves the queen and only the queen."

Zephyr made a choked noise, drawing all gazes to him. Lily felt herself inhaling sharply and realized that she was drawing the air away from Zephyr.

Rhys looked at Lily and then at Creed. "Which of you stole his air?"

Even though he had to know that he wasn't responsible for stealing Zephyr's breath, Creed's voice came from behind the living wall she'd created in front of him. "My affinity is air."

"I hear the truth in those words, Creed Morrison, as well as the lie," Rhys commented. He looked at Lily with pride in his eyes. "You have two affinities. Are there more?"

She still wouldn't open her lips to speak, not to answer, not to deny her guilt. Her whole body was irritated like the touch of moth wings fluttering incessantly over her skin. When Rhys had said that the fae-blood boy would deliver her to Endellion, Lily couldn't stop her reaction—just as she couldn't stop the urge to protect both boys when Rhys uttered his threat.

"Stop," Eilidh ordered. "All of you. Please."

Lily and Rhys both released the other. The vines retracted from Rhys' body as the tugging sensation vanished from her body. Her attention was pulled to the boys on either side of her as the walls in front of them sank back into the ground.

When Zephyr was still unable to breathe, Lily realized that Creed *had* been afraid enough to strike out at one of his best friends. They'd *both* struck out at Zephyr.

"Creed," she said softly. "Release him."

As soon as Creed exhaled, Zephyr coughed. Her guilt at being the reason for this confrontation rose up, but this was not the time for contrition. There were three members of fae society in front of them, and Lily didn't truly trust any of them. She'd been raised to believe that fae—much like criminal associates—required careful handling. At the time, she'd thought Daidí's references to dealing with the fae were simply his nod at thoroughness, but he'd known about her, about her mother, about the future that she'd need to face. Being the granddaughter of the queen of all fae was a terrible thing. Humans would want her dead or captured. Fae would want to use or destroy her. The queen herself . . . Lily wasn't sure what *she* would want. She honestly didn't want to find out.

Simultaneously, she reached out to both Zephyr and Creed, taking a hand of each. "Peace between us, please."

As the air refilled Zephyr's lungs to the point that he no longer looked like he might faint, he glared at Creed. She debated telling him that Creed alone was not responsible, but she couldn't say it here in front of the fae observing them intently.

"Lily?" Eilidh prompted.

Lily looked up.

"There's blood on your face."

For a moment, Lily was confused, but then she realized that she'd bitten herself hard enough that blood was trickling from her mouth. She reached up to touch her lips and her fingers came away coated in red.

Rhys held out a small embroidered piece of cloth. "You are strong-willed, niece."

She took the cloth from his hand, looked at it, and said, "You can't have this back, not with my blood on it."

Torquil and Eilidh both smiled at her approvingly. Rhys laughed unexpectedly. It was an odd sound from someone so severe.

Then he said, "You are obviously my family, Lilywhite Abernathy. I would not take arms against Eilidh for you, but I would bloody my blade against Calder or Nacton or any other who meant you ill." He did not mention Endellion, but it was a comfort to know that she was not alone in the face of the others who might mean her harm. "It would be an honor to stand as your guard, niece, as long it does not harm my sister."

Rhys' voice was such that Lily couldn't help but think of truths from a pulpit, of pronouncements from her father's crime synods. Rhys spoke with the surety of a fae who knows that he cannot lie. He did not include the king or queen in his list of those he would not fight for her safety. That, too, spoke volumes.

"Accepted," Lily said quickly. "Your vow is accepted."

He smiled and said approvingly, "Definitely Mother's descendant." Then he grew more serious. "Some fae can compel truths of their relatives or those of lesser bloodlines. It is a rare trait, what humans call recessive, I believe. I am the only of the fae who can do so currently. Mother finds it useful."

"Does it work on humans?"

Rhys didn't flinch as he said, "It often leaves them unwell, sometimes comatose, but yes."

"And halflings?"

"The same."

Lily was the one to look away. Fae weren't known to be particularly gentle, but he'd just attempted something that *could* harm her. Something about it prodded at her memory. She stared at him as she thought back to fae vows. "Aren't you foresworn if you break your vow?"

"If it would hurt you, I wouldn't have been able to attempt it. Because of my vow, my gift would be ineffective. The vow allowed me to try it. That was the most efficient way to discover if you were fae or simply fae-blood." He gestured at Zephyr and Creed. "The Sleepers are all what the humans deem halflings. *You*, Lilywhite, are much more than that."

twenty-six

ZEPHYR

Zephyr stared at the fae in front of him, trying to make sense of the things he was saying. The facts of the situation didn't mesh. The fae couldn't lie without pain. The purer the fae bloodline, the worse the pain. Zephyr could hide the pain of lies when he'd had to do so. He *could* do it, but it wasn't easy. Somehow, though, either Zephyr had been lied to before or he was being lied to now. It had to be one or the other, but both were improbable.

"We are not halflings," he said.

"Lilywhite is obviously not," Rhys allowed. He was straight-spined on the vine-wrought chair Eilidh had created. Even after Lilywhite had lashed him to the chair, even after he'd tried to compel words from her, he was implacable. At his side, Eilidh was quietly speaking to Torquil.

"*None* of us are halflings." Zephyr stood, his anger

pushing him to move. It was a trick he'd learned as a child: movement helped him focus past the emotion. Creed and Lilywhite stood when he did. Even though there was conflict, they were still his friends. For a brief moment, he took comfort in that.

"*You* are, Zephyr. Lilywhite, as I have said, is more." Rhys leveled a stare at her that spoke volumes. It was abundantly clear to everyone present that she was far more like *him* than like them. Her gifts were stronger than anyone else's.

Because we are still young, and the gifts don't always manifest until later. Clara had explained it. All of their handlers had explained it that way when they were children. They'd had to hide some of their gifts, and their appearances were certainly fae enough to arouse unwanted attention. She'd said, "You were chosen because we could hide you more easily."

"The humans call it 'halfling.' You have one parent who is true fae."

"Okay, so we're born of one of the fae, maybe that's not so different than being fae-blood."

"Try saying so without 'maybe,' niece," Rhys challenged.

She couldn't, and they all knew it. They were less fae than Zephyr had believed, but they were also more fae than she'd thought.

"The Sleepers are not true fae, but not simply fae-blood." Rhys' voice had the sort of edges that made Zephyr's skin prickle. "You, however, are *more*. Your mother was the first child born to both fae courts. You are *her* sole child. Whether you were born of a fae father or not, yours is the union of the two strongest lines of all faeries. You are the child of the first, the strongest, and so you are *more*. It is that simple."

Again, Rhys gestured at Zephyr and Creed. "None of the Sleepers are what you are. *No one* is."

Zephyr's temper grew sharper and sharper. Geysers of soil and water erupted from the ground, showering all of them with mud. Leaves and blossoms clung to their bodies, stuck in the mud that was now covering all of them. If not for the fact that he'd all but attacked one of Endellion's children, it would be amusing. Jets of water continued to flow like a series of small fountains bubbling out of the earth around them.

Rhys wiped his hand across his face, revealing a studious expression. "Your fae parent was of a strong line." He tilted his head, looking similar to a household pet who'd been caught in a storm. "Earth and water. I have only the earth, but my mother . . ."

"Mother's primary gifts *are* sea and soil," Eilidh said as she looked at Zephyr again. "Creed said that you were the one she hand-selected for leading this cell. You've met her, as well. No other Sleepers have had a private audience with her."

What was Eilidh saying? Zephyr thought back to the terror of kneeling before the Queen of Blood and Rage. Was she telling him that Endellion was *his* mother? He wasn't sure if it was better or worse if she were to be his mother. It would mean that Lilywhite was his . . . *niece*, his family, not his intended.

"I'm sure the queen isn't the *only* one who has those affinities," Zephyr pointed out reasonably. "I've never summoned water. There's no saying *that*"—he gestured at the small geysers somewhat helplessly—"was me."

"You have hair that could be hers," Rhys said.

"And eyes that could be yours, Rhys," Eilidh offered.

The severe faery stiffened at her words. His attention swept over Zephyr. "I'd like to say Mother wouldn't do such a thing, but she has no lines she wouldn't cross for her plans."

"What human birthed you?"

Zephyr shook his head. "You *have* to be joking."

Torquil, who had remained silent for much of their meeting, spoke then. "He is not. You favor him, and the queen is thorough in her plans. She cannot carry young easily, not since the baby's death or . . . *disappearance* apparently." Torquil very carefully looked at Eilidh. "There was a time when some of us were invited to lay with mortals, to create young with them. She had hopes that we could breed with the humans, to have children—even halflings—to replace some of those we lost. Only those who were the strongest of the fae and those she herself trusted were invited to that night's party. It was an odd request, but we do not survive by disregarding our queen's requests. Even the king is not so foolish. He did as she bid. We *all* did. Rhys was there."

"It makes sense," Rhys mused. "She'd said the children weren't conceived, that the wine was bad and none of us had impregnated the women."

"She lied," Torquil suggested.

"She wouldn't want us to get attached to humans, but she *would* want to have strong halflings for the program. It would allow their fae traits to overcome the weaknesses of humanity." He reached out and caught Zephyr's jaw, holding him still and staring into his face like the truth was there if only he stared long enough. "I suppose you aren't disposable after all."

Zephyr jerked back.

"The human I bedded had eyes like spring skies, and her lips were berry red. She spoke of wanting a fae child, too. For a human, I thought she would've been a good choice to carry my young. The woman was called Arabella. She was a pretender in recorded plays for humans—"

"Actress," Zephyr corrected. "My mother is an actress."

There were a lot of people who could fit that description. Even his mother's name was not completely unusual, but after being called a miracle baby his whole life, Zephyr knew that Rhys was likely talking about her.

"So that is why Mother favored you," Rhys said musingly. "You are her grandson. My . . . son." The faery studied him much the way Zephyr had studied science experiments. There was no emotion there. "How is your swordsmanship?"

Zephyr said nothing. He turned to Eilidh, bowed deeply to her, and turned away from all of them. His father was fae. His mother . . . the woman he'd pitied for having no real child of her own, for thinking he was hers, was actually his true mother. She'd cheated on her husband to have him. She'd had no idea that he was being born to be used. Zephyr had always taken comfort in the fact that he was living the life his parents had chosen. They all had. Instead, his father, his *fae* father, had no idea he existed, and his mother apparently had only wanted to have a baby.

Was that the case for all of us? Were our human mothers all so desperate that they'd bedded with fae, knowing how hard it was to live as a fae-blood, knowing that their very existence was illegal? Zephyr felt his emotions getting increasingly out of control. The water he'd denied being responsible for surged higher.

He turned and ran. They could catch him if they wanted, stop him without even moving from where they were, but he didn't care. He needed out.

Everything is a lie.

Behind him, he could hear Lilywhite calling to him.

It didn't matter.

A lie.

Everything is a lie.

I am no one.

As he crossed the campus, he didn't slow to see if Lilywhite or Creed had followed him. Right now, he didn't know how he felt about seeing her—and he didn't want anything to do with Creed. Creed had brought them here, brought Zephyr's father here, and Zephyr knew that if he saw Creed, he'd want nothing more than to let his aggression out on him.

He made his way through the hedge, through the walled

garden, and to Belfoure, where he knew Alkamy would be. He could feel the pulse of his own blood warm at her throat, and he followed it unerringly. He'd hoped it would work as such when he gave it to her, and tonight he was grateful that the queen had allowed him to take the blood-wrought stones with him. He couldn't make sense of much in the world, but he knew this much at least: he needed Alkamy the way he needed earth.

The familiar thrum of the city did nothing to ease his mind tonight. Neither did the friendly voices as he crossed through the main part of the Row House. It wasn't until he reached the VIP section and Alkamy that he felt anything near calm. He didn't hesitate. He grabbed her by both hands and jerked her into his arms. He needed this, needed the peace that only she could offer him.

She yelped in surprise and started to ask, "What—"

He cut off her question with a kiss. Behind him, he could hear voices, and several flashes of light made it obvious that cameras were capturing it all. He knew on some level that he was being foolish. He should be stronger. He shouldn't care about the lies that were woven into his life.

He did care though. It was all fucked up. Everything felt wrong—except having Alkamy in his arms for this moment.

All of the need he'd been shoving away was in his kiss. It was the sort of starving embrace that they seemed to always share, as if there would never be another, as if this moment was the last. Every time they kissed, they both knew that one of them would say, "Not again. Remember? Not again."

Tonight, he wouldn't be the one to say it, and he hoped she wouldn't either.

When he finally released her, she was trembling. She didn't pull him closer, but she didn't run away either. He slid his hands to her hips, unable to let her escape, unable to do anything but hold on to the one person in both worlds who would never lie to him or use him.

In his peripheral vision, he could see Violet and Roan gaping at them. Beside Roan, Will's hat was drawn low enough to shade his face, and he was staring at the ground, further hiding himself.

As Alkamy leaned against his body, not even stepping out of his arms, she reached up and stroked his face. "Talk to me."

He shook his head, even as he reached out to touch the blood-ruby in the hollow of her throat. She was his only anchor in a sea of madness. He knew it, had known it for years, but that didn't mean he could say it aloud. He had to be responsible, to look after the Sleepers. It was his duty, and Zephyr Ryan Waters always fulfilled his duties. He'd been waiting for years for someone to help him do that, a partner, a love of his own—and the fae he'd been promised not only didn't seem to want him, she might be a blood relative.

Zephyr ignored everyone. He swept Alkamy into his arms and all but marched to the dance floor, carrying her like she was his bride. They passed the velvet rope. The camera flashes continued. The murmurs continued.

"You're scaring me," she whispered against his ear. Her

expression was light, making for good pictures, staying in the role she'd always held. Unlike him, she was still doing as she should.

"I need you. Help me." He lowered her feet to the ground, realizing as he did so that she was dressed up like a Gothic doll. Soft strips of gray silk hung in faux tatters from her waist to her calves. The winding cloth illusion was continued by the fact that some of the sections were slit high enough that decency was barely met. The top of the dress was lace with an overlay of silver—not material made to look like it, but actual silver that had been twisted into a corset. He stared at her as they stood in the middle of the dance floor, surrounded by gawkers and under the watch of three of their friends.

Violet was dragging Roan and Will to the dance floor. Despite the probability of being photographed, the boys weren't refusing. They might not know what was going on, but they were at his side.

"I just need to hold you. If we're on the dance floor, it's safe. If we're anywhere else, I don't think I can follow the rules tonight. I don't even want to try." Zephyr pulled Alkamy closer again. What he really wanted was the sort of silence he could only find when they'd been intertwined together. All of his reasons for not touching her were still valid. He knew that. Right now, he didn't care. "Tell me to stop or take me out of here or just let me hold you here."

"I'm right here with you." She rested her cheek against his chest. Her arms wrapped around him, keeping her as close to his body as they could be with clothes between them. She didn't reply to his admission that he wanted to go where they could be together as they once were, but she vowed, "I'm always here for you, Zeph. Always."

The tension that had held him like a coiled spring loosened slightly at her words and touch. He drew a deep breath, drawing in the soil and sunlight scent of her like it was the air he'd been denied. Alkamy was air and soil. She was every calming thing he needed.

In a voice so low that no one else would hear, he told her, "I met the joint court's heir tonight, and her betrothed, and the fae who might be my father."

Alkamy looked up at him. "Your father?"

"He has my eyes," Zephyr admitted aloud. "Or, I guess, I have his . . . and I have *his* mother's hair . . . and both of her affinities."

He must've sounded as overwhelmed as he felt because Alkamy didn't ask questions, didn't push or even offer foolish words of comfort. She simply asked, "What do you need?"

"You."

She stretched up to kiss him. Her kiss wasn't the desperate clash of teeth and tongue that his had been. It was the way they'd kissed before he'd been told that relationships among them were forbidden by order of the queen.

When their waitress came out to the floor with their usual drinks on a tray, Zephyr took Alkamy's and downed it in one go. The vile taste of alcohol burned down his throat, but as with any fae—or fae-blood, since that's what he apparently was—the effects were quick and intense. He felt the languor seeping over him, and tonight, he embraced it.

"That was hers," the waitress said as he put the now empty glass on her tray.

"Great," he said. "Bring me Creed's too."

The girl looked around. "Is he here?"

"No," Zephyr said. "But once you return with the drink, I'll take care of it for him."

Roan stepped forward like he was going to intervene, but Violet and Will both reached out and stopped him.

With the show that Zephyr and Alkamy were creating, it probably wouldn't have mattered if the boys finally *did* dance together in public, but they'd decided long ago to keep that much of their lives private. Violet danced with them, providing the same cover she usually did.

Zephyr's hands slid up Alkamy's spine, and cameras flashed. One of New Hollywood's darlings was news-worthy; two of them back together would earn even an amateur photographer a check.

By the fourth drink, Zephyr's face was buried against her throat when he wasn't kissing her.

They stayed on the dance floor for the next half hour, but when he attempted to grab another drink, Alkamy stepped back from him. "Me or it. You don't get both."

With a shaky hand he held it out to her. Instead of drinking it, she handed it back to the girl. "He's done. Take this to the back. Not the VIP section. We want a private room."

Then Alkamy nestled against Zephyr's side. "Come on, babe. We've put on enough of a spectacle. Let's go where it's quieter."

twenty-seven

LILY

After Zephyr left, Lily grabbed Creed's hand to follow him, but Creed shook his head. "He needs space."

Lily didn't know Zephyr as well as Creed did, but she wasn't sure that letting anyone as angry as Zephyr run out was a great idea. She wanted to follow him, but Creed squeezed her hand in his and kept her there with their three fae guests.

Torquil said to no one and everyone at once, "That one has the sort of temperament that would make me believe he's the queen's line even without proof."

Rhys scowled. "I thought he handled it well."

"Precisely. *You* thought that." Torquil folded his arms and waited.

Rhys' hand strayed to his sword hilt, seemingly without

conscious thought. The brush of his fingertips on the weapon appeared to bring him back to himself. "Point noted."

Softly, Eilidh told him, "Perhaps you ought to visit Zephyr's mother and see how she handles his moods."

Rhys nodded and stared in the direction that Zephyr had gone. "He's an attractive specimen, my son. With worthy fae strengths. I could see if the woman wants to mate again. She seems to be a good breeder."

Lily opened her mouth to point out that saying such things might get him a slap in the face, but Eilidh shook her head slightly, so Lily let it go. People's tastes were weird. Fae attitudes toward relationships were weirder still.

After a quick good-bye, and a stiff embrace from her newly found relatives, Lily and Creed headed to the dorms.

When it was just the two of them, Lily said, "This doesn't change a thing, you know. I'm no more willing to serve Endellion than before."

"I've never wanted that."

"And I don't want any part of politics or—"

Creed grabbed her hand again. "All I wanted tonight was for you to know. I don't want you to belong to Zephyr or Erik or . . ." He shook his head. "It's been a long time since I had a reason to do anything other than waste time or try to forget about the war. You give me a reason."

Lily shivered. "I don't want to be anyone's *reason*, Creed."

"Too late." His smile was sad. "I pledged myself. The queen's children know where my loyalty belongs. Even if you don't want me, I've already thrown my lot with you. I live or die to serve you and protect you now. No one else. Only you."

He started to drop to his knees, and Lily hurriedly grabbed him with both hands. She clutched his side with one hand and his opposite arm with the other. Her body jolted at the touch, and Creed's eyes flickered closed for a moment. Whatever the connection they'd had before, it was more so now. His pledge had enhanced it.

Lily's need to protect Creed vied with the power of their bond. "You could withdraw it. I'd . . . let you. That's what I'd need to do, right? I release you from—"

Creed silenced her words with a kiss. It was a kiss that told her she was special, that promised things she couldn't accept, that whispered words she didn't dare think. Her mind went silent, and her heart ceased being her own.

When she pulled away, he was staring at her with awe plain in his eyes. "There will be no other for me, Lilywhite Abernathy. I felt it when I met you, and I know it as truth when I'm near you." He cupped her face in his hands and looked into her eyes. "I cannot be released from this vow. I *will* not."

Lily felt tears streak down her cheeks. "How am I to resist Endellion now that I'm responsible for your life too?"

"The same way as you would've before this moment." Creed kissed her tear-wet cheeks. "I'd already decided to give up. I've been racing toward the abyss for years. I won't be a weapon used against the world that raised me. I see humanity's flaws, but I see the goodness too. In *both* the fae and humanity. The two can coexist and create something better than violence in this world. Meeting you"—he kissed her softly again when her lips opened to protest his words—"proves I was right. I'm still ready to die if necessary. Now, though, it would be for someone I believe in instead of simply to escape this fate."

She stared at him, not ready for what he was offering her, not sure if she *ever* would be ready for offers of love and devotion, but *wanting* to accept it all the same. "Tell me you'll stop drinking."

"Tell me you aren't going to say yes to Zephyr, and I will."

"On my vow, Creed Morrison. I will not accept Zephyr's misplaced attempt to court me."

The smile that came over him was enough to make her stretch up toward his lips again. Kissing Creed was both the stuff of fairy tales *and* the torrid romances that Shayla read. The stars could fall from the skies around her, and she wasn't sure she'd even notice.

A chime and a buzz finally drew her back to reality. Creed kept one arm securely around her, and she leaned into that steadying embrace.

"Messages. Both of us," he said, fumbling with his phone.

The only way they'd both receive the same message at the same time was if it was being sent from one of the Sleepers. No one else had contacts for both of them. Dread filled her.

Creed held his phone up so she could read it too.

Zeph crushed. Need answers. Come. NOW.

A flush of guilt came over her. She'd forgotten about Zephyr's upset for a moment.

"Do you want me to go?"

Lily shook her head. "Both of us."

Creed nodded, and in as short a time as possible, they were on the streets of Belfoure.

They walked several blocks in relative silence, and then a flash of a camera made her jump.

Creed released her hand and turned to go after the photographer.

"Leave it," she said, taking his hand in hers again. "Priorities."

"Nick Abernathy seeing me with you—and off campus too—seems like a priority."

"I'll handle Daidí. He's the one who brought you to meet me in the first place." Her picture was about to be in a magazine or up on an online site. Daidí would be livid, but it was too late to undo it, so she tugged Creed with her, and they went to the Row House.

Just inside the door stood Roan. His surfer attitude made it hard to tell how he felt, but then he pulled her into a hug. "Thank Ninian that you're here!"

"Kamy said Zephyr was upset."

"Drunk," Roan corrected. "Zeph is *drunk* and if not for Kam's ability to leash him, he'd have her naked on the dance floor right now."

"Zephyr doesn't drink." Creed scowled. "He's upset, but—"

"I watched him pound booze like you did the last few months. I know drunk, Creed. You've given us plenty of firsthand examples of what it looks like."

When Lily looked his way, Creed muttered, "I didn't take your rejection well."

"You're all mad. Every last one of you." Roan shook his head, stared at them a moment longer, and gestured to the back left corner of the club. "Come on. Vi and Will are over by the door. We didn't want to all go in there . . . yet."

"Yet you all think he's *mine*?" Lily laughed. "He and Alkamy are in love."

Creed caught her hand, and they twisted their way through the crowd on the floor. Unlike Lily, Will, and Roan, Creed's face was well known enough that cameras were flashing and girls were reaching out to touch him.

A sudden gust of wind nudged them back.

Roan glanced over his shoulder, past Lily to stare at Creed. "You?"

As she turned to see Creed, he shrugged. He didn't meet her eyes, but his action was clear enough: it was up to her whether or not she owned up to what she'd just done.

Creed, wisely, said nothing.

She hadn't thought to push the crowd away. She'd simply done so between one breath and the next, and she had no desire to explain it to anyone.

Behind her, Creed leaned closer to her. "There are no

others like you, Lilywhite. Not for me."

For a heartbeat too long, she stayed still, letting the heat of Creed's body press against her. If things were different, if she wasn't who and what she was, if he was just a boy, if neither of them were fae-born, she'd stay here on the dance floor. But Zephyr needed her. Whatever else he was, they were family, and she had a duty to her family. Her father had always insisted that she keep that belief foremost.

Now that she knew what she was, who her mother was, every lesson Daidí had taught her seemed more important.

Abernathy Commandment #4: Weigh the consequences before beginning a course of action.

Lily stepped away from Creed and said, "We need to talk to Zephyr. All of us."

Violet grabbed Lily's arm and leaned in to tell her, "I don't know what happened tonight, but our boy is totaled."

"Come on," Lily ordered. "All of you."

The look on Violet's face made it abundantly clear that following Lily into that room wasn't a plan she liked, but she did so nonetheless. They'd all been taught that Lily was their leader as much as Zephyr was, and Lily—despite not being told the full truth about *why*—had been taught to lead.

She pushed open the door, and the three boys and Violet followed her inside. Zephyr was stretched out on the floor. His head was cushioned in Alkamy's lap.

Alkamy herself was murmuring soothing words to the

blurry-eyed boy and stroking his hair. "It's not his fault! He was drunk and—"

"Stop. The next person that suggests there's a reason my *cousin* should be faithful to me is going to get smacked." Lily folded her arms over her chest. "Zephyr is not, and will not, be anything other than friend *and* family to me."

"Cousin?" Will prompted.

"Zephyr's father is the queen's son," Lily said. "My uncle."

"That's impossible. The heir has no children," Violet pointed out in a strained voice.

"True. Her older sister had one though."

For a moment, no one spoke. Their expressions were a mixture of confusion and thoughtfulness. Then, Roan whistled. "Holy Ninian . . . The queen's firstborn lived and . . ."

"And is my mother," Lily finished.

"So you're the . . . *heir*." Violet breathed the words. Her gaze dropped to Zephyr. "And you're . . ."

"The queen's grandson."

Violet whistled. "The queen can have more Unseelie than Seelie blood on the Hidden Throne if you mate. You might as well exchange vows now."

This time Lily was silent. She couldn't deny the fact that the queen—her *grandmother*—probably thought the same thing. However, Lily wasn't going to cooperate with that plan. She wasn't interested in Zephyr before she was aware that he was her cousin. She was even *less* interested now that they were family.

Her gaze shot to Creed, who was watching her. Silently, she shook her head. He stepped closer to her protectively, as if the threat were a physical one. It wasn't, but his action made her feel better all the same.

Then Zephyr looked up at her from his prone position and slurred, "Vi's right, *cousin*. We might as well start shopping for rings."

Then he closed his eyes and passed out in Alkamy's lap.

twenty-eight

EILIDH

By the time they'd left the Sleepers, Eilidh was ready to curl up in her tower and ignore both worlds temporarily. That, unfortunately, wasn't an option, so she did as the named heir to the two courts *should* do: she turned to her betrothed and her brother and said, "We should figure out the next step."

Rhys frowned. "Tonight changes nothing."

"You have a son, one Mother has been willing to sacrifice, one she has kept hidden from you," Eilidh said as they entered the Hidden Lands.

"Yes." Rhys slid his longsword free. The sibilant sound of fae-wrought steel against the scabbard was something that always felt like home to Eilidh. For as long as she could recall, there had been guards who stood at the ready when she was at any official functions. Both Rhys and Torquil had been among them. The elegant sound of drawing weapons was a sound that had always meant "safe" to her. Maybe it would be different if she'd ever been attacked, but up until now, weapons were drawn to practice or to guard her.

"Is that necessary?" Torquil asked.

Rhys glanced his way for a fraction of an instant, but said nothing. He obviously felt it was necessary, or he wouldn't have drawn the blade.

"Did you see someone?" Eilidh prompted in a voice that was a shade quieter than a whisper.

Again Rhys said nothing.

Eilidh had known him long enough to understand that his silence was because he was concentrating on whatever he'd seen or heard. Their journey to the tower wasn't going to be as direct or easy as she'd expected. "Where?" she asked her brother.

Torquil looked around them, tensing as he saw the threat that Rhys had heard. Both of the Seelie princes walked out of the darkness toward them. They were alone, without any friends or lackeys trailing in their wake, but that didn't mean that this was a friendly visit. More likely, it meant that the Seelie princes wanted no witnesses to whatever they did or said next. Like Torquil, Eilidh's Seelie brothers were beautiful in ways that defied words. Nacton was thin of build, dark of skin and eye, and taut of muscle. If every sunlit temptation were made into form, her brother would be the result. It was no wonder that fae of both courts had often vied for his attention. Calder, however, was a different kind of wonder. As a child, Eilidh had imagined him as a moving mountain, graceful despite his size, but intimidating all the same.

"Nacton," Torquil greeted his court-mates. "Calder."

"So you've thrown your lot in with her?" Nacton speared Eilidh with a disdainful stare, making it painfully clear that he found her beneath him in every way. "She's as hideous as most Unseelie, so it makes sense for the Unseelie dog to support her. But *you*? I'd expect more of you, Torquil."

"You speak of your *father*'s heir," Torquil said, his voice growing sharp.

"She might be the heir now, but that will change." Calder let his attention sweep Eilidh much the way he appraised a weapon or a meal. His next words made it very clear that she was found wanting. "Look at her, cousin. Broken chit that won't survive her childbed. She certainly won't keep the Hidden Throne long if she even dares take it."

Nacton touched his brother's arm, not in affection but as if he were halting an eager pet. The elder Seelie prince shook his head and said, "Bed her, and she'll die. That leaves you as father to her get, who will next take the Hidden Throne."

Calder shuddered exaggeratedly. "But the bedding . . . you go further than I'd be willing to."

Torquil didn't reply to either of Eilidh's Seelie brothers. He'd, undoubtedly, heard their hostility before this.

Rhys kept his blade tip pointed at the earth, but it did little to make him seem less threatening, especially if you knew anything about swordplay. The low-guard position

287

might be called the "fool," but it wasn't in reference to the fighter. It appeared as if Rhys wasn't prepared, but it was actually a difficult position to attack. Everyone there knew that. Rhys had crossed blades with both Seelie princes for longer than Eilidh had been alive. They never struck fatal blows, but they certainly drew blood often enough.

Rhys' next words only added to the menace emanating from him. "Do you think that the queen won't hear your treasonous words?"

Calder's smile was a flash of teeth and threat. "I don't care what *she* hears. My father won't let her have me killed or you'd have tried by now."

"Exile is not unheard of."

"When this one"—Nacton nodded toward Eilidh— "dies, there is no other heir. There will be no unified courts when she is dead." He met Rhys' eyes. "I may not like you, but I have no trouble with you taking the Unseelie throne. I will take *my* rightful throne. Things will be as they should: the two firstborn sons ruling two separate fae courts."

"And the *current* king and queen?" Rhys prompted levelly.

Calder shrugged. "It's not like they can have another heir." He nodded toward Eilidh. "This is their best effort. The others all died in the womb, aside from the one that died in the sea."

There was silence for a moment.

"And if I have a child?" Eilidh's voice fractured the hostile silence. "I would die for our people. If that means carrying a child who could be healthy enough to take the throne, I would do so. The regents know this."

"There are those who would have no trouble killing a child or stealing it and sending it to live with an unsuspecting human," Calder said with less emotion than he'd give to a fine meal.

Rhys' blade lifted, drawing all eyes to him. "I am charged with our sister's safety. Do not threaten her or her unborn."

"No sister to me," Calder spat.

Torquil drew his sword, moving into a position that had his blade raised high overhead like an oxen's horns. "I would willingly bleed out every drop of my blood for Eilidh."

"So be it." Calder's blade swung toward Torquil, whose own sword met it with a sharp ring of steel on steel.

Rhys was still in position awaiting this inevitable moment. It was far from the first time the two royal sons had crossed blades, but the sight of it always filled Eilidh with horror.

Nacton came in for a scalp cut, but Rhys knocked the sword away easily with his blade. The two eldest fae princes watched each other and feinted a few times. Rhys, in truth, was likely just toying with Nacton. That didn't make the fight any less traumatic for Eilidh.

They exchanged blows, each movement precise enough to make obvious that the two fighters anticipated the strikes as quickly as they were employed. The air was filled with the sharp clatters and sinuous slides as their swords met, pressed, and met again.

"Stop this foolishness!" Eilidh snarled at the four of them. Regardless of what she felt toward her Seelie brothers, having any of their blood flow would result in anger from one of her parents.

No one even deigned to reply.

Rhys was dominating the fight, and after several minutes, he hit Nacton with the flat of his blade—an insult that provoked an ugly word and sudden burst of attempted cuts from the Seelie prince.

Simultaneously, Calder swung his sword forcefully enough that only Torquil's agility spared him from genuine injury.

Louder, Eilidh repeated, "I said *stop.*"

Solid walls of earth surged up between Calder and Torquil.

Calder immediately tried to go around it, and Eilidh sighed in irritation as she bent the earth like a prison around him. "Do you truly want to challenge me? I am the *only* fae who could kill Father's son with impunity." With one brother imprisoned, she turned to her other Seelie brother. "I will not have you kill my betrothed *or* my brother because you hate *me.*"

Nacton lowered his sword and glared at her. Rhys and Torquil lowered their weapons as well, but they both kept their attention on the Seelie fae.

"Do not make this more unpleasant than it already has been," she managed to say in a falsely steady voice. The combination of her emotions and the forceful use of one of her affinities made her slightly shaky. It wouldn't do for any of them to know that, however, so she forced the tremor away.

Torquil and Rhys came to stand on either side of her, as if they were all at a formal gathering. They still had weapons at the ready. Although Seelie fae were thought by humans as more benevolent, the Seelie were just as untrustworthy as the Unseelie, and the princes were both particularly biased against Rhys.

Calder's earthen prison exploded outward, and if Torquil hadn't pulled air to him like a shield, they would all have been knocked to the ground by the force.

"Bitch!" Calder's blade swept upward into the *falcone* position, the sword raised high like a bird of prey waiting to strike. In the next moment, he swung on a downward diagonal that would very likely be a fatal strike.

Before he could touch her, Calder's sword was knocked away by Nacton. "Stop. We are done here. I have said my piece, and that one"—he nodded at Eilidh—"understands that her time is limited."

Rhys tensed at Eilidh's side, but he merely said, "The queen will not take this kindly when she hears of it."

"That matters little to me," Calder said. "She is no mother or queen to me, and the king won't let her strike us—else it would've happened the first time we attacked *you*."

"Stop," Nacton ordered his brother. He might not be reasonable, but he understood that there were limits to how far they could push the Queen of Blood and Rage.

Calder turned and stormed off, leaving Nacton alone with them.

Eilidh met her Seelie brother's gaze and vowed, "I have no need of enmity between us, but there will be if you harm or cause Torquil and Rhys to be harmed."

"I think you misunderstand the role of *guards*," Nacton said.

She shook her head. "Don't be droll, Nacton. I know their roles, but I am also my mother's daughter. Injuring those who are *mine*, those I love, would necessitate my showing you exactly how much of the queen's blood propels this broken body. I can be as calm as our father . . . until harm comes to my loved ones."

None of the three fae spoke for a moment. Eilidh kept her Seelie brother's gaze until Nacton nodded and said, "The warning is noted."

Once he left, Eilidh turned to Rhys and Torquil.

Rhys stared at her with something akin to hope on his face. If he were any other fae, she might even suggest there was fear in his eyes. When he realized she was staring at him, he straightened his features into their usual implacable mask, but his words belied his mien. "*Love*, sister? How did you form such an extreme lie without pain?"

"There was no lie, Rhys." Eilidh reached out and squeezed her brother's forearm. "You are my brother, and I love you—as I love Mother, and Lilywhite, and Father."

Rhys said nothing.

"Your son could love you too," she added. "He was unsettled tonight, but what else could he do? Your blood runs in him. *Mother's* blood. Ours is not a family known to respond gracefully to surprises."

Torquil coughed in what she was sure was an attempt to hide a laugh. Eilidh smiled softly at him. He knew her, and by extension, her brother better than most fae. Fortunately, that also meant that he wasn't going to call attention to the truths he noticed—mostly because none of the queen's descendants were receptive to such observations.

Instead of commenting, Torquil stayed silent at her side as they walked deeper into the Hidden Lands. The trees seemed to part as they walked, and Eilidh sent a whispered plea that they not do so. Her affinity with earth was strong enough that the plants often seemed to anticipate her needs, but she preferred to keep the extent of any of her affinities as private as she could. One never knew when unwanted witnesses were near.

"Perhaps we can discuss our plans tomorrow," Rhys suggested when they reached her tower.

"Of course."

Torquil stepped toward the tower, but when Eilidh moved to follow him, Rhys put a restraining hand on her shoulder.

"*Love* . . . No one has said that word to me before, sister. I will endeavor to be worthy."

Impulsively, Eilidh hugged him, wrapped her arms around his statue-still body and squeezed as if she were comforting a small child. "You are already worthy, Rhys."

He didn't enclose her in his arms or move in any way. For all of his affect, she might as well have been hugging a tree—although with her affinity, the tree was more likely to embrace her in return.

After a moment, Rhys patted her shoulder and said, "And I . . . you, sister."

Then he stepped away from her. He nodded at Torquil once and strode off toward the courtyard. She suspected her brother needed to vent anger from the ambush and hoped that there were participants aplenty willing to spar with him.

As they watched Rhys leave, Torquil wrapped his arms around her, and she leaned back against him. How much things had changed since the day he stepped onto the forbidden staircase! She felt less alone than ever in her life. She had her best friend as betrothed, her brother as friend, and her niece back in her life. If things didn't go poorly, she might come to know Zephyr too.

"You realize that you just threatened two of your brothers and earned the undying devotion of the third," Torquil said in a low voice. His arms stayed around her, and despite the attention they were drawing from the fae who always watched her and the tower, she felt no urge to move.

"I already had Rhys' devotion," she said just as quietly. "Now he knows he has mine as well."

"And your other brothers?"

Eilidh turned to look over her shoulder at Torquil.

"They deserved a fair warning. If they are so foolish as to strike out at us, I will kill them. I alone answer to no other fae. Would Father be pleased if his sons die? No, but I am the heir. I would not be sent to exile for it, and if I were"— she shrugged—"so be it."

Torquil shook his head.

"Come," she said, stepping out of his embrace. "I feel the need of a nap. Join me?"

Her betrothed gave her the sort of hungry look that she'd never thought to see directed at her.

"I always feel the need of sleep with you," Torquil murmured and then he kissed her in full view of the watching fae.

When he pulled away, she laughed in sheer joy and tugged him into the tower to dream with her.

twenty-nine

ZEPHYR

Zephyr wasn't entirely sure what happened after Lilywhite and Creed arrived at the Row House, but he woke up face-down inside the vat of soil in Alkamy's sofa. Someone had obviously removed everything but his shorts. Soil covered his entire body, and he was grateful for the healing nourishment it offered. Despite spending what he guessed was hours burrowed into the earth, his head felt like it weighed an extra twenty pounds, and his mouth felt like something had died in it.

He rolled to his side, blinked burning eyes, and looked up to find Violet watching him. In a voice that sounded almost as bad as he felt, he rasped, "What are you doing here?"

"Babysitting." She crossed her arms over her chest and leveled a disapproving stare at him. "We all took shifts, so

Lily and Kamy could sleep without worrying that you were going to die of alcohol poisoning."

"All?"

"Will, Roan, Creed, and me. Seriously, Zephyr, what were you *thinking*?"

She handed him a glass of water, which he gratefully accepted and sipped.

Voice less scratchy, he said, "I'm sorry you had to do that."

"But not sorry you got so drunk that we had to carry you? Or that you practically humped Kamy in public? Or that—"

"I get it, Vi. I fucked up. It's okay for you or Kam or Creed to get drunk, but I can't. I *get* it."

She stood and slapped him on the shoulder. "You're an idiot. Seriously. I don't care if you make mistakes. I *care* that you're going to be upset now, that you're hurting. You put yourself in danger. I care that you were in *pain*."

He started to sit up.

Violet's hand came down hard on his side. "Stay in the soil, Zeph. Let your body heal from all of the poison you swallowed."

Despite being embarrassed by his weakness, he obeyed her and burrowed his feet deeper into the soil. He'd only used Alkamy's soil once before when he was injured in an explosion. Doing so for excessive drinking seemed foolish, but he wasn't up to arguing with Violet—or ready to go back to his suite and deal with Creed.

"The girls made me promise to wake one of them when you woke," Violet said, her tone still disapproving. "After I do that, I'm going to see Roan and Will, so I can tell them you're okay. Then I'm going to snuggle up with whichever one of them is asleep, so *I* can get some sleep."

Zephyr grimaced. "I'm sorry."

Violet stopped, met his gaze, and told him, "You've done the same for most of us." In a flicker of a moment, she softened and added, "I'm sorry about your father being who he is, about your grandmother being . . ." She swallowed, unable to even say the words. "I'm sorry."

"Me too," Zephyr said again. Violet was terrifying sometimes, but under it all, she had nothing but love for the rest of the Sleepers. She would protect them if she could. He felt the same way, but he couldn't express it with the ferocity she embraced so openly.

"I need to wake them," Violet said in the silence that had filled the room as he thought about the things he'd learned.

"Not Kamy," Zephyr half ordered, half begged. "Just Lilywhite."

Violet said nothing, but a few moments later, Lilywhite was sitting in the chair beside him and Violet was leaving the suite.

"I'm not sure whether to yell or hug you," Lilywhite said quietly.

He looked at her. "I'm sorry I worried everyone. I've never done that." He winced as he tried to sit up so he could at least pretend not to be incapacitated. "I don't know how they do that repeatedly."

"Zephyr," Lily began, "what we learned—"

"Changes everything," he cut in. "You need to explain to Creed—"

"No." She shook her head. "It changes very little. I'm still not hers to command, or yours to have, Zephyr."

"Did you not hear everything I did last night?"

"I did actually."

"You're the *rightful heir.*"

"I am my father's daughter, and if I take any hereditary duty, it's to the Abernathy family businesses. I'll accept that I'm a little more fae than I thought, but that's it." Lilywhite folded her arms over her chest, and Zephyr couldn't help but think that she was painfully naive. She might be wise in the ways of drug dealers and money laundering, but when it came to the fae, she was almost pitiably clueless.

"No one tells Endellion no," he said. "You will be wed against your will if necessary. You will be threatened if necessary. She doesn't accept refusals."

"She'll have to. The queen may be our grandmother, but I am my own person."

"We're only half-cousins, Lilywhite. In the Hidden Lands, that's not so much. I don't like it either, but we just need to learn to—"

"*No,*" she said again, far more firmly this time.

"Am I that horrible?" He didn't mean to sound weak, but his pride stung. It hurt to be rejected so thoroughly.

"No, but you love Alkamy, Zephyr, and I . . . I *like* Creed." She blushed briefly, but she didn't look away. "Even if I didn't, I won't be commanded like that. You're a good person, but . . ."

Zephyr laughed bitterly, eliciting a frown from her.

"And I'm glad we're family," she continued. "I was raised to believe that family is everything."

"Endellion is your family too." Zephyr sat up. "We need to figure out what to do. We can talk to the queen and explain that—"

"I can't." She shook her head. "I won't serve her."

"The queen will make us both bleed or worse." Zephyr thought about the rest of the cell, about his friends, about Alkamy. "If you tell her about the true depth of my feelings for Kamy . . . You can't tell her." He reached out and grabbed Lilywhite's hand. "I can't swear fealty to you like Creed did, but ask anything else of me. I can't let you say anything that will cause Endellion to hurt Alkamy."

Lilywhite didn't pull away. "I don't need you to make any vows," she insisted. "I wouldn't do anything to risk Kamy either."

"I must obey the queen, Lilywhite. If she orders us to wed, you know that we will. Maybe we could at least forestall that if she saw that we were together." Zephyr tried to find words that were gentle, but he didn't know if gentle would get the point across. "You cannot disobey her, but maybe we could *compromise* for now."

"What are you saying?" Lilywhite's grip on his hand

tightened painfully.

"I'm saying that I don't want to see any of us killed, and I don't think that acquiescing to being mine would be a fate worth than death. Even if you don't mention Kamy, there are ways she can find out, or did you miss my father's truth extraction trick last night?"

"I'm sorry." Lilywhite looked up at him, staring into his eyes, and said, "I made a vow to Creed, Zephyr."

Zephyr felt like he was going to be sick, and he wasn't sure it was just the alcohol he'd nearly overdosed on last night. "Ninian help us all." He leaned back in the soil again. "Do you think you're the only ones who have feelings that aren't allowed? Will and Roan have been in love for years. I love Kamy more than I thought it possible to ever love anyone, but—"

"Then why not tell me that?" Alkamy said from behind him.

Any words he might have known vanished as he saw her standing there watching him with tears in her eyes. She didn't move from the doorway of her bedroom. Her robe was loosely tied, and her hair fell around her face like a dark veil framing perfection like no one else in this world or the other.

"Just once, Zephyr. Say it to me," Alkamy half ordered, half pleaded.

"I can't." He stood and went to her.

"Why?"

"Because I don't want you to get hurt," he whispered.

She shook her head. "I love you. Everyone knows. You think Endellion doesn't already know?" Alkamy crossed her arms over her chest. "I'll stand by your side, do whatever you ask. I always have. I always will. If that means you being with Lily, I can accept it. I *did* accept it years ago." Tears started to slide down her cheeks. "None of it means that I don't need the words. Say them."

"I love you," he swore. In that moment, he wished he could be more like Lilywhite and Creed, that he could ignore the consequences and do what he wanted, that he could take Alkamy and run far from their responsibilities. But standing there with Alkamy in his arms, with words of love on his lips, didn't change reality or duty.

A sound from Lilywhite's room made Zephyr look into the half-open doorway. Creed looked back at him from his seat on her bed. He was clothed, so perhaps they hadn't done anything to further complicate this mess.

He kissed the top of Alkamy's head, and then he turned so he could see Lilywhite instead of Creed. "I love Alkamy, but I won't sentence any of us to death at the queen's order. *That's* what it means to love someone: being willing to give them up to keep them safe."

Lilywhite held out the object she'd been carrying then. "I told you my mother had left me a book. The others all read it last night while you were . . . sleeping."

Zephyr looked down at it, read the title, and then glanced at her.

"Read the first bit," Lilywhite said. "Then we'll talk."

Silently, he walked over to the sofa. Alkamy sat next to him, her hand in his, while he read what he quickly realized was a story of the past written by the missing heir to the Hidden Throne.

The Book of Secrets

Iana Abernathy

It was almost dusk when the Unseelie Queen started to swim toward the shore. Today was the last swim until her daughter was born. Children weren't meant to be born into the churning sea—even children like hers. Although the babe wasn't due quite yet, Endellion was near enough to her birthing time that from here on out, she'd restrict herself to land.

Her daughter would be the beginning of a new era, the start of a treaty that had taken both Unseelie and Seelie decades to create. As part of that treaty, Endellion had lain down with the Seelie King, Leith. The Queen of Sea and Sky would bear the daughter of the King of Fire and Truth.

The two fae monarchs agreed that their daughter would one day rule the two courts as one.

Endellion took a deep breath and dove down again, enjoying the lightness the water gave her now heavy body. Her hair was still unbound after her visit to Leith, and her stress was temporarily set aside in the aftermath of his affection and the joy of the sea. It wasn't the sort of peace she'd known in past centuries, but she was closer to content than she'd been in more recent decades.

The burden of making decisions for her subjects had been heavy on her shoulders. Both the Unseelie and Seelie fae had been hidden away for several centuries, no longer meddling in the affairs of men. But faeries—as beings of nature—were left suffering from the consequences of the plague of humans that had spread over the world. The seas grew murky with poisons, and the soil had been exhausted from toxins that were discarded carelessly. To save their kind from the poisonous world, the two courts retreated to a series of islands hidden near the great whirlpool, the Coire Bhreacain.

With some subtle urging, the British queen had declared the Gulf of Corryvreckan "unnavigable," so Unseelie and Seelie Courts had hidden their islands near the Corryvreckan. The two fae courts were learning to find peace on the chain of islands they'd divided between them. They mostly kept to their own kind, but there were those who traveled between the isles.

Endellion herself had been diving into the twisting waters of even this whirlpool since before the mortals knew it existed. She was of the sea. In her long life, there was no ocean that she'd not visited. She drew her strength from the waters and from earth, much as Leith found his strength in air and fire. Their daughter would share the strengths of both courts, and so be able to safeguard both Unseelie and Seelie.

The queen surfaced on the far side of the gulf when a screech of metal drew her eyes to the left. An over-large vessel had sailed into waters too treacherous and too shallow. The rocks that marked the edge of the hidden islands shredded the underside of the ship.

Endellion dove to try to avoid the sinking heap of metal, but a piece from the hull of the ship smashed into her, sending her deeper than she would have gone with a babe growing inside her. As she kicked toward the surface, her skin grew tight from the oil that coated the water. The poison spilled into her sea, choking her, clinging to her skin.

Rage filled her as her body went into shock.

Blood mixed with oil as her daughter's birth began— too soon, in water too deep, in seas too poisonous.

Shock, blood loss, and birth proved too much. Endellion couldn't cling to consciousness.

When Endellion woke, she was on the shore of her island. The survivors of the crash were surrounding her.

"Where is she?"

"Who? There weren't any other women," a sailor near her said.

"My baby." Endellion's hands fell to her stomach, as if she could touch the skin and find that she was wrong.

The truth was in the blood and pain that she remembered. The truth was in her empty womb.

She pushed to her feet and looked around the beach. "Where is my daughter?"

Another sailor reached out to touch her, as if there was consolation to be found in his murderous hands. "There was no baby."

Endellion looked to the oil-slicked sea where her child had been born and ran until she could dive under the surface. She dove into those toxic waters, again and again. She cried out to the sea creatures, begging for help. She swam until her body screamed in pain. She searched until her lungs burned.

There was nothing. No sign of the life she'd carried and lost. Her child was gone.

When she reached the shore again, her subjects had arrived and stood behind the sailors. Every mortal and faery on the shore watched her as she stepped onto the land. Blood and oil streaked her skin. Her entire body shook.

Silently, the Unseelie Queen walked up to her son, Rhys, and held out a hand. Words seemed too heavy to speak.

Rhys frowned in confusion.

"Blade," Endellion managed to say. "I need your blade."

Once she had it in her hands, she turned to face the survivors of the wreck and her subjects and announced, "My daughter is dead." She paused to let her words settle on the assembled crowd. "You killed my daughter, my hope . . . my people's savior."

And then there were no more words. She turned her blade against the murderers and slaughtered every human

who'd dared to destroy her heart and her sea. Given time,
she would destroy every last one of them. She would erad-
icate the plague that had taken everything from her.

When Zephyr finished reading, he looked at Lilywhite. "As you told me when I woke, *this changes nothing.*
Not for me. I understand what the queen lost, and I understand her anger . . ."

"My mother wasn't killed," Lilywhite pointed out.

"It doesn't matter," Zephyr said. "We need to do as the
queen orders. Surely, you can understand that. Please, Lilywhite."

Lilywhite said nothing.

Creed walked out of her bedroom and said, "I prefer
Abernathy Commandment #17: Love is a risk, so if you embark
upon it, do it with no reservations. Never halfway." He clamped
a hand on Zephyr's shoulder. "No bargains. No compro-
mises. If we all stick together, maybe we can have a future
we *want.*"

"I'm not attacking humans, Zeph. I'm not giving up
Lily either. We just need a plan. Either we work to put Lily
on the throne or—"

"I don't want the throne," Lilywhite interjected.

"Fine," Creed continued with a shrug. "Then we try to
reason with the queen. Her granddaughter is *alive*. She has
a grandson." Creed nodded at him. "There are no reasons
to keep on this path of war with humanity. With Rhys and
Eilidh on our side, we stand a chance at being done with

the things she wants of us."

For a glimmer of a moment, Zephyr considered it. He wanted to believe the pretty fantasies Creed and Lilywhite spun. Reality was different.

"I won't be a part of any treason, Creed. Not even if my father is a part of it. I won't tell our queen, but that's the most I can offer you. If she orders me to wed Lilywhite, I will. If she orders me to die, I will."

"And if she orders you to kill?" Creed prompted.

"I obey our queen," Zephyr said.

"You'd kill us? The people you've been trying to protect?" Creed didn't sound angry. His voice was twisted with challenge and doubt as he pushed harder. "Can you truly say that? Without lying, Zephyr, can you say you'd kill us?"

Alkamy looked up at him with nothing but trust in her eyes, and both Lilywhite and Creed stared at him expectantly. Then Alkamy said in a clear, strong voice, "I wouldn't fight against the blade if you had to do it. I will stand at your side *no matter what*."

He swallowed against words he wanted to say, promises he couldn't make. Then he met Creed's eyes and said, "I will obey our queen."

thirty

LILY

Lily couldn't say that she was surprised by Zephyr's choices. She suspected he wasn't truly surprised by hers. They'd both been raised to believe certain truths. For him, that meant unerring loyalty to the faery queen; for her, it meant that she would fight for her *own* beliefs and choices.

The unavoidable fact, though, was that she and Zephr were still at odds. The queen had ordered Zephyr to bring Lily to the Hidden Lands. She could run, of course, but doing so was sentencing the rest of the Sleepers to punishment. Going, on the other hand, meant that maybe she would be able to convince the queen that there was no need for war. She'd started it over her daughter's death at sea, but Iana had survived. Lily was *proof* of that. Maybe the queen wasn't as terrifying as everyone thought. Maybe the stories Lily's mother had left behind were reason for hope.

"I'll meet her," Lily said. "I'll come willingly to see her. I can't make any promises beyond that, but . . . I will go with you to see her."

Zephyr nodded. "Thank you."

She said nothing. No matter how much Lily rationalized it, entering the Hidden Lands felt akin to entering a dragon's lair. The primary difference, of course, was that the Queen of Blood and Rage was real—and far more vindictive than the dragons of lore.

"Alkamy can't come," Zephyr pronounced.

When Lily still said nothing, he added, "Roan and Will should stay here too."

"So . . . just you, me, Creed, and Vi?" she asked.

"I'd rather leave Creed behind."

"Not happening," Creed said. "I wasn't joking when I gave her my fealty, Zeph."

"I didn't think you were," Zephyr said in a remarkably calm voice.

"Fealty to her outweighs any authority you might have over me." Creed strolled over to Lily and wrapped his arms around her.

"Lily could order you to stay."

"Nope," Creed said, popping the *p* loudly. "Not if she's walking into danger. You know better, Zephyr. She's the heir, the true heir to the joint throne of the Seelie and Unseelie Courts. A knight charged with the safety of his liege puts her safety above any order—including her own."

Lily stared at Creed, not sure she was ready—or ever

would be ready—to think in terms of lieges or knights or anything of the sort.

"I'm not going to be Endellion's heir," she said quietly.

This time both boys frowned.

"You *are* the heir. It's not an option to suddenly be something else," Creed said. He exchanged a look with Zephyr, before saying, "Even if I hadn't pledged myself to Lily, I'd be coming with you. She's going to get herself into more trouble than I can even imagine if she says these sorts of things to the queen."

"We'll see." Lily shrugged. *"'Abernathy Commandment #18: Better to die free than be controlled by anyone.'* I won't let Endellion—or anyone else—rule my life."

Neither boy commented. Instead, they went to Roan and Will's room where the others all were and filled the rest of the Black Diamonds in on Lily's plan to go to the Hidden Lands.

"I'm coming," Violet interrupted quickly. "Kam and the boys should stay here."

"I go where Zephyr says," Alkamy said levelly, her gaze sweeping them as if daring anyone to object.

"Here," Zephyr said. "I need you here where you're safer."

She nodded.

Roan and Will both shrugged. Will prompted, "Zeph? Lily?"

"I don't want all of us there," Lily started.

"But Vi can come," Zephyr finished. "The queen has

asked after her in the past. She stands a better chance of survival . . . I think."

"*I'm coming,*" Violet repeated.

"You are," Zephyr agreed. "The rest of you . . . stay here."

His gaze darted to Creed, who simply smiled and shook his head. He'd already made his argument. Zephyr sighed, but didn't press the issue.

No one else questioned the plan. Even though they'd seen Zephyr at his weakest now, they were still looking at him with the same faith Lily had seen since she'd met them. The difference was in how they watched her. Being the daughter of the missing heir made her even more special in their eyes. She saw it—and hated it—but she wasn't going to allocate time to it today.

Decision made, the three of them followed Zephyr to the entrance he used to access the Hidden Lands. Lily had resolved not to let fear reign over her, but resolve only went so far when she was entering another world, especially one where she was going to have to face the most feared being in either world.

"Are you okay?" Creed asked softly as they stepped through a toadstool ring.

"No."

"Anything I can do?"

"No." She reached out and took his hand. She needed the simple comfort of a touch, and Creed wouldn't reject her.

They were barely a breath inside the Hidden Lands

when Rhys' voice drew their attention. "Lilywhite."

"Uncle," she greeted after a pause.

Rhys nodded, and then looked at Zephyr. "Son of mine."

The four fae with Rhys all stilled, seeming not to breathe for a long moment. Then Zephyr nodded. He didn't speak, but he didn't deny the word that Rhys had spoken. It was apparently enough. Rhys smiled.

Then he returned to the same seemingly emotionless mien that he'd had for most of their initial encounter. He held out one hand. "Your weapons, if you would."

Creed and Violet silently shook their heads.

"We are unarmed." Zephyr held his arms to the sides as if inviting a search. "I would not approach the queen with threat."

"And you, niece?"

"Where's the trust?" Lily asked. She had only a few weapons: a dagger in her boot, a knife in her pocket, one single thin blade she'd given to Violet to jab into her hair twist, and, of course, a small gun she had hoped to hide under her jacket. The other fae girl wanted to secret a small arsenal on their bodies, but doing so could be interpreted as threatening the queen, so Violet agreed to carry only one weapon.

Rhys shook his head. "The trust is in *asking* rather than forcing you to give me the gun in your jacket."

She removed the gun and handed it to him, butt first.

"And the blade on your ankle," he said lightly.

Silently, she withdrew it and tossed it at him. The other fae all tensed, but Rhys snatched it out of the air with a grin.

He glanced briefly at Violet and said, "One more."

Mutely, Violet bent her head toward Lily. Once Lily withdrew the sliver-thin blade, she walked toward her uncle. The other three fae who stood behind him all watched her with myriad questions simmering in their eyes. Unlike Rhys, these fae didn't attempt to wear a mask of impenetrability.

Lily gently placed the blade in his outstretched hand. "I mean the queen no harm . . . as long as she means me none."

"Have you no sense of your own worth?" he asked in the same level tone.

She felt the compulsion to speak Truth so she admitted, "I do, else I wouldn't be here."

Either she could feel affinities more here, or her uncle seemed to use his gift more freely here in his homeland. Later, she hoped to be able to ask him which was the case. For now, she merely met his eyes and added, "Would you take me to see the queen, uncle?"

Rhys nodded and glanced at Zephyr once more before saying, "She is expecting you."

Zephyr, Creed, and Violet joined Lily. The other three fae let them all pass. Once they were at her side, Rhys led them forward. His fellow guards followed behind and to either side of the group, making quite clear that they were more *prisoners* than guests.

As they walked deeper into the Hidden Lands, the

landscape became lush, and Lily understood why the fae's home *was* hidden. There was a beauty here, a purity of earth and air that she'd never seen in the world she knew. If this was what the whole world had once been, it was a little easier to see why the fae were displeased by the decay of the current age. The trees here were green and thriving; the air was so pure that she felt guilty for exhaling into it.

"Being here is strengthening for anyone with our blood," Rhys remarked in a voice so quiet it was almost imperceptible.

She said nothing.

"Don't keep your hand so near the pocket with your remaining knife," he added in that whisper-silent voice. "It will draw attention."

This time she peered at him from the corner of her eye.

No further words were said as they reached the open courtyard where the queen waited. The courtyard looked like it belonged in a medieval town. A stone castle loomed behind it, and animals grazed untethered. Fae watched their approach, and although they were all remarkable, they were nothing compared to the queen herself. Endellion looked out-of-time. She had the same austere presence as Rhys, but hers was emphasized by both the aged wooden throne upon which she sat and the vaguely fearful glances that the fae shot her way.

Guards stepped in front of Creed, Zephyr, and Violet. Only Lily was allowed to move forward.

The queen watched her as she approached. Her

expression betrayed nothing, no rancor or joy, no malice or acceptance. Endellion was unreadable.

Lily couldn't look away. Aside from skin tone, the queen's face was so similar to the pictures Lily had seen of her mother that if photographs of the queen existed, she would've known Endellion was *family*. Since Lily didn't have her mother's dark skin, her look was even more akin to the queen's. Anyone who saw Lily here now had to know that she was of the queen's blood. There was no way to deny it.

"Lilywhite."

"Grandmother."

The queen paused briefly before saying, "So you *did* know."

"I've only just been told, but . . ." Lily paused, trying to measure her words while she figured out what to think of the faery queen. "My mother looked enough like you that if I hadn't heard, I'd be wondering now. She had Seelie skin; I look more like *you* than her."

When the queen didn't reply, Lily pulled out the picture she'd brought and walked the rest of the way to the queen. She held it out. "This is her . . . with me."

Endellion didn't move to take it. She didn't react at all, and for a moment, Lily was afraid. Perhaps boldness was the wrong tactic.

Lily started to lower her hand.

The queen moved serpent quick and caught Lily's wrist and took the photo. "Did she know? All of those years, did she know who she was?"

"She died when I was a child, and back then . . . *I* didn't know who she was or who you were."

"I've never seen her," the queen said in a voice that was thick with pain. "My own daughter, and I've never once seen her."

Lily met the queen's far-too-familiar eyes. "I don't know what to say. Until I met Zephyr and the others, I was just Lilywhite Abernathy, a girl whose dad protected her and whose mom died. The rest of this"—Lily resisted the urge to look around at the assembled fae who were listening to her every word—"is all new to me."

Endellion stared at the photo in her hand. She touched the image of Iana's face with one finger, the barest tip skimming the surface of the photo, and said, "For years, I thought she'd died. Everyone thought that. They killed her when their boat hit me. Human carelessness, and I lost my daughter. My people lost their next queen."

"But she *didn't* die that day."

The Queen of Blood and Rage looked up. "She was still lost to me."

"The humans did not kill her," Lily said in a firmer voice.

"And yet, my daughter, my heir, is not here ready to take the Hidden Throne." Endellion lowered the picture of Iana to her lap and peered at Lily. "Do you come seeking the throne, Lilywhite?"

There it was: the deadly question, the one Lily had no certainty how to answer without offending someone. So she opted for brutal honesty. "I have no need of a throne. I have a life in the other world."

The gasps and murmurs of the fae grew louder for several moments until Endellion spared her subjects a speaking look. At her glance, all noises stopped. It was clear that her subjects might revere her, but they were afraid of her as well.

"Would you rather kill? That is the job of the Black Diamonds, and it's what you were raised to be in *their* world, too. When I found out you existed, I was surprised at how groomed you already were for joining the mission." She looked past Lily to the other three fae-blood. "I had my grandson and the others born to do this task, to be my weapons in that toxic world, but you . . . you were a surprise."

This time, there were no gasps. The fae were silent, and the moment felt weightier than anything Lily had experienced. Here was their queen admitting private machinations as if they were nothing shocking.

Lily had to admire her grandmother. There was little doubt that word of Lily's birthright—and of Zephyr's—would spread quickly now. Lily hadn't realized what she'd set into motion by coming to stand before the queen, but she suspected that the queen's other two children did. More importantly, the queen's smile made quite clear that *she* knew.

"How did you find me?" Lily asked.

Endellion gifted her with a kind smile, as if that question was the right one, and then she replied, "I heard of a woman who had my look, who 'looked so like a darker version of the queen that she could be her sister.'" Endellion shook her head. "I had the reporter killed, of course, but I sent trusted fae to see the woman. She did favor me—not quite as much as you do, though."

"So you found my mother?" Lily prompted.

"I did, but she apparently died before she could be brought to me." The queen glanced to her left where Torquil and Eilidh now stood. "But . . . in my renewed grief, I learned that my youngest child visited Iana's house. I learned that Iana had a daughter—although Eilidh did not tell me of my daughter or granddaughter's existence."

Eilidh did not flinch away from her mother's stern gaze as she said, "I serve my people and my family first, as I was taught by my mother."

The queen said nothing, but her attention stayed fixed on Eilidh for several more moments. Finally, she simply looked back at Lily and said, "I've been kept apprised of you during the blink of time that has been your life. Now that you are here . . . you will know the things your mother did not. Welcome home, Lilywhite Abernathy, daughter of Iana, granddaughter of the Queen and King of the Hidden Court."

The queen's words were ominous, but before Lily could ponder what precisely she'd meant, she noticed that the whole of the fae assembly was sinking to their knees. Men and women, adults and children, every standing fae present other than Eilidh, Rhys, and Torquil kneeled—to *her*.

Lily glanced over her shoulder at Creed, Zephyr, and Violet. They were also kneeling.

"I don't want—"

"It is not your choice," Endellion interrupted.

Terror made Lily speechless. The queen had just declared Lily as family, formally acknowledging her as the direct descendant of her first heir. Lily wanted to ask what that *meant*. Was she now the heir to the Hidden Throne? Why wasn't she speaking the same way about Zephyr? Admittedly, he wasn't of both the king and queen's bloodlines, but he was still of royal lineage. Lily opened her mouth, but the words wouldn't come.

Endellion stood and stepped closer. In a slow, deliberate move, she kissed each of Lily's cheeks. "First, though, Granddaughter, you must visit your grandfather. The king knows of you, and he has been eager to meet you." She lowered her voice to a conspiratorial whisper and added, "The royal family feels it when someone enters the Hidden Lands. He is expecting you."

Then she stepped back and motioned the other Sleepers forward.

The guards stepped away from them so they could approach. Zephyr kneeled again and bowed his head. Violet curtsied. Creed, however, simply bowed his head.

"Do rock stars not kneel?" Endellion asked lightly.

Creed, in what was either arrogance or idiocy, met the eyes of the Queen of Blood and Rage with an almost casual glance. "I've offered my fealty to another, your highness. To kneel before you would dishonor that vow," he explained in a clear strong voice. "I thank you for your forgiveness in this."

Lily's mouth gaped open at both his formal words and the import of them.

"Pray tell, what other regent *is* there that would necessitate such a . . . *forgiveness* on my part?"

"Not a regent, your majesty." Creed stood closer to Lily. "Simply one for whom I would gladly die before disappointing. I live to serve your granddaughter."

Endellion stilled, glancing first at him and then at Lily and then at Violet. "And you, Seelie-blood, have you offered my granddaughter a vow as well?"

"I am—" Violet's voice broke. She swallowed visibly, and then she tried again, "I am undecided, my queen." She curtsied again. "I was born to be your weapon, but Lily is a fae worth following."

Zephyr's muffled gasp was soft enough that none standing farther from the throne heard it. Lily could see Rhys tense, however. Eilidh and Torquil did as well.

The queen merely told Lily, "My grandson will stay here"—Endellion spared a glance for Zephyr—"but you may keep the other two Black Diamonds at your side."

Lily nodded. She didn't know the queen's stance on the use of words of gratitude. According to the book Lily's mother had left for her, some of the older fae were uncomfortable with such words.

"Torquil will escort you to meet Leith," Endellion

continued in a slightly louder voice. "It is right that he should do so, to protect his own."

Lily had been long enough around Daidí and his associates to know that the queen was sharing another secret. Whether Violet or Creed caught the import of the queen's words, Lily didn't know. Several of the assembled fae undoubtedly did though, and she was *certain* Torquil did.

Lily already knew that Torquil had been present the night the fae-blood were conceived, and the queen's words intimated that he had family that would be present. Nothing about him seemed similar to Creed, but . . . Lily glanced at Violet. *They* didn't truly look alike either, but the queen had asked about Violet by name, according to Zephyr. Was Violet Torquil's daughter? There was something to the shape of their faces that made Lily suspect so now that the queen had hinted so boldly.

"Maybe Rhys could come?" Lily prompted.

Endellion's voice turned cold as she explained, "Although my spouse treats my son with respect, there are those within our joint court who aren't always embracing of the children the king and I had separately. He will stay here."

"As you wish," Rhys murmured.

There was nothing else for Lily to say, except . . . "Might I ask a small favor then?"

Endellion inclined her head.

"I'd like my things returned first," Lily said. "I'd feel safer entering unfamiliar places if I had my weapons."

The queen rewarded her with an undeniably genuine smile. "You are my blood, indeed." The queen raised her voice slightly as she added, "My granddaughter is neither prisoner, nor intruder, so there is no reason she cannot defend herself should the need arise."

Then, Endellion stood. She withdrew a sword from her own side and walked toward Lily. It suddenly felt so quiet that Lily could almost swear that they were alone.

The queen stopped in front of Lily and held out the sword that she had worn at her left side. She was still very visibly armed, but the act of handing her own sword to Lily was both generous and politic.

Lily accepted the blade.

Endellion spoke as if they were alone. "I trust that you can use it?"

"My father was insistent that I learn any manner of things that suddenly make far more sense than they used to," Lily said in a lower volume than the queen had used.

The queen's expression hardened briefly, and Lily opted not to stress her human upbringing just then. She wasn't about to deny that her father had been integral to preparing her for this moment though. Instead, Lily bowed her head and murmured, "I appreciate the use of your blade, Grandmother."

"You may not have a gun here, and I suspect you might find a sword more useful than daggers." Endellion's lips curved in a smile that was more frightening than comforting. Her hand lifted, and Lily wasn't sure if the gesture was intended to be threatening or the start of a caress. Suddenly, though, the queen extended her arm to the side instead. "Rhys? A replacement. I do not like to be unarmed."

Then, the queen turned and walked away. Rhys, Eilidh, and Zephyr trailed after her. The rest of the assembled fae dispersed as if a command had been uttered, and in mere moments, it was only Lily and her escorts who remained.

thirty-one

LILY

As they walked in silence, Lily wished she had the opportunity to admire the beauty of the Hidden Lands, but for now, she followed Torquil as he led the three of them away from the queen and her assembled fae. There was no planning, no discussion, simply a brusque, "Tarrying is unwise."

He remained silent but for the commands necessary to direct them to a tunnel system that would, apparently, spill them out in the part of the Hidden Lands where the king and the Seelie-born fae resided. His only revelation was when he said, "The queen used to swim across, but after the day of the incident"—he met Lily's eyes briefly—"tunnels were created. These are the only way to travel between the two courts or to travel from the Hidden Lands into the world where you have lived thus far."

Lily heard the things packed into that, the hint on how

to escape, the implication that returning home might be forbidden, the useful fact that there was a second route between the courts. She nodded her gratitude at her soon-to-be-uncle and left anything else unspoken.

"What is your affinity?" he asked Violet in a kind voice as they exited the tunnels into the Seelie's domain.

"Why?" Violet returned. She wasn't as prickly as she'd been when Lily had first met her, but she was far from friendly. She studied him with such a thorough assessment that Lily wanted to blurt out the truth of why he had asked.

Torquil met her gaze briefly. He made no gesture, but there was no need.

"Are you always so snappish, child?"

Violet barked a laugh that Lily now knew was a sort of self-defense. "*Child?* How old are you then?"

He smiled. "I stopped counting a few decades ago."

"Eilidh is far too young for you then," Violet snarked.

"We are fae, and she is of my age generation." Torquil shook his head. "Have you been taught nothing of your people?"

Violet shrugged, but didn't answer.

Creed, however, took pity on him. "She's trying to get your goat."

"My . . . goat?" Torquil scowled. "Why does she think I have a goat?"

Violet made a rude gesture at Creed, who blew a kiss to her.

"Lily?" Torquil prompted.

Before she could reply, she saw two faeries approaching. Torquil obviously saw them too as he stepped in front of her. Both were Seelie Court by birth, like Torquil, but in affect, they reminded her of Rhys. Their attitude was arrogant, and their gazes barely acknowledged the sword that Torquil had drawn.

"Please don't be foolish," he said by way of greeting as the two faeries walked up with swords already in hand.

"So this is the girl," the larger of the two said, studying her as most people would assess the mud on their shoes. "At least she's not as abhorrent as the *broken* one."

Torquil looked at the other faery, the one who stood silent. "Nacton, please remind Calder not to do something foolish. The queen has sent this girl to see your father, her grandfather, *our king*."

Nacton shrugged.

"Are you here then as an escort to take her to see Leith?" Torquil asked, although his tone made clear that he did not believe that to be the case.

In a low voice, Lily told Creed and Violet, "Stay back and let him do his job. They are undoubtedly far more adept at swords and affinities than we are."

The two Seelie princes were studying Torquil, as if he were the only threat. There was no way they could know that Lily and her companions were trained to kill—and she was hoping not to have to demonstrate that truth to them.

"Uncle?" Lily said, not caring which of the two acknowledged her.

The slighter one, Nacton, stepped away from Torquil and turned to face her. He studied her with a curiously pensive expression.

Violet started, "Lily—"

"No," she interrupted.

Behind Nacton, Lily could see Torquil assume the fool's guard, his sword tip pointed at the earth, as he attempted to bait Calder. It wasn't a particularly *bad* move, but she had thought it was an oddly transparent one when her coach had taught it to her. On the other hand, it might be perfect for woefully arrogant opponents.

Calder stepped in, his longsword lifted high and up in the *falcone* position.

Torquil's ploy wasn't a move that should've worked, but Calder's temper got in his way. He grew tired of waiting, stepped forward, and brought his sword downward from the right. The swords clanged together into the bind, and the fighters both tried to assess their opponent's next move.

Unfortunately, Calder had the strong position.

Nacton leisurely struck at Lily, testing her like this was a class.

Fine then, she thought. She raised her weapon and went through cuts she'd learned in the old medieval manuscripts—in both German and Italian—that her father had procured for her. Nothing she tried earned more than the occasional smile from Nacton.

"Not completely useless," Nacton acknowledged when she nicked his arm.

His strikes became aggressive, making her step back.

He drew blood on first her shoulder and then her leg. Neither was a deep cut. He was demonstrating that he *could* injure her.

When his sword tip grazed her hand, she stumbled.

Creed stepped toward them. "That's enough."

"Stay back," she ordered.

Behind her, Violet and Creed were silent. She'd seen them struggling—wanting to help, but not wanting to do something that ended up distracting her or Torquil.

As she defended against Nacton's cuts and swings, she turned round so that she could again see Torquil and Calder. They were both fighting aggressively. At the moment, Torquil seemed better poised. He transitioned into the ox—his sword jutting forward like the horn of a beast—and thrust forward.

But Calder leaned back, avoiding being impaled and allowing himself a moment's respite. He swung back and brought the sword down in a clockwise arc. In barely the next moment, the point of Calder's sword was plunging downward while simultaneously pushing Torquil's sword to the left.

As Lily's attention wavered from Nacton, he twisted his sword in such a way that her own blade was knocked out of her grasp. She met his eyes, and he smiled. "Foolish girl."

There was a brief moment before the tip of Calder's sword pierced Torquil's side. Then, the flicker of hesitation was gone, and steel vanished into flesh. The sword's tip pierced Torquil under his ribs on his left side.

"Are you going to *kill* me then? Kill us both? Kill us all?" She stepped back out of Nacton's range, gaze darting to Torquil and then to Creed and Violet.

Nacton laughed.

Was she a threat to them? More importantly, did they *think* she was?

Nacton kept his sword lifted, but didn't strike.

Lily wasn't sure whether she or Torquil was in more danger. She couldn't help Torquil. All she could do was watch as he stumbled to his knees.

Again Calder pulled his sword back, and she knew from the angle that this time it would be a killing blow.

"Stop!" she cried.

But Nacton said nothing.

Calder didn't even hesitate. His blade slashed down from the left.

Just as the sword was mid-arc over Calder's head, Creed charged. He caught Calder around the waist, using his mass and momentum to propel them forward. As they fell, the sword was caught between his shoulder and the ground.

Instinctively, Creed tried to stop their fall, reaching forward with his right arm. The combined weight was too much, and Creed cried out as his wrist snapped upon impact. A second, almost simultaneous, cry came when the sword—which had been trapped between Calder and the ground—sliced into Creed's leg.

"No!" Lily tried to run to him, heedless of Nacton's upraised sword.

In a blink, Nacton's blade flashed out and the tip rested at the hollow of her throat, not near enough to draw blood but so close that she couldn't move.

"Once we're wed, your behavior will need to be remedied."

Lily wanted to laugh. Unfortunately, there was no levity in the Seelie prince's words.

"Once you're what?" Violet asked in a tone Lily had come to realize meant trouble.

"Wed," he repeated. "She is the daughter of the true heir. Marrying her will allow me the throne that should've been mine all along."

Nacton spared Violet a glance. "Whose get are you?"

When Violet opened her mouth to reply, Lily spoke over her, "The *heir's* betrothed is injured, as is my friend." She refused to let her voice crack or her attention drift to either of the injured. "All of the queen's fae know where I am, and—"

"Calder," Nacton interrupted. "Contain them until I'm ready to wed my bride."

thirty-two

ZEPHYR

Zephyr had no great desire to speak to the Seelie King, but he wasn't keen on being left behind either. His only other meeting with the queen hadn't filled him with optimism, and his first meeting with his father had resulted in unpleasant truths and drunkenness.

Rhys had followed the queen silently when they left the rest of his friends, as if the queen's very glance told him all he needed to know. It struck Zephyr then that this was his lot in life: to live or die at her whim, to always be attentive to her will, to know that her attention would never waver. Short of death, there was no reprieve. Up until this day, he realized, he'd held some measure of hope, some glimmer of a dream that there was another future possible.

That hope had just died.

The queen led them to a small room inside a palace

that looked to be carved of the cliff itself. The floor inside the room was as white as bone. Swords and other weapons were mounted on the walls. The weapons and a diminutive throne of wood and vine were the only things inside the room.

Endellion settled on the throne as it seemed to reshape around her. Rhys walked to stand at her side, not quite behind her this time.

"So you know," she said.

It wasn't exactly a question, but Zephyr still answered, "That Rhys is my . . . biological father? Yes."

"No." She waved his words away and clarified, "That *I* am your grandmother."

"I do," Zephyr said as emotionlessly as he could. He walked closer to the queen and stopped directly in front of her. He wasn't as afraid as he'd been when he'd kneeled before her and offered her a necklace wrought of his own blood, but he wasn't so foolish as to assume that she was suddenly harmless.

"Do you no longer wish to be Unseelie then? You sound less thrilled than I would expect given our earlier meeting." Endellion's tone wasn't exactly mocking, but it was a near thing.

"You knew when I came here before," Zephyr half asked, half stated.

The queen looked not at him, but to her side where Rhys stood as she replied, "I've always known. Family matters more than anything in either world. My son, my once-heir, had a child. I knew that my grandson would be loyal to me." She turned her head to fix Zephyr in her gaze again. "I've always known who you were, Zephyr. I've known what you were doing, and I've done what was necessary to have you trained as best you could be while in that world."

Zephyr nodded. There wasn't much else to do. The most feared being in both worlds was the head of his *family*. A darkly ludicrous thought of confessing childhood misdeeds flitted through his mind. Somehow, he doubted that Endellion was as tolerant of his "boyish mistakes" as his mom had been. His mother was indulgent. The Queen of Blood and Rage wasn't known for being . . . tender.

"What would you have of him?" Rhys asked, interrupting the silence and drawing the queen's gaze back to him.

"I want him to do as he's always done, be my eyes, be an instrument of my will." Endellion smiled at Zephyr and prompted, "Are you my subject?"

He dropped to both knees without pause and bowed his head. "Without doubt or disobedience."

"No matter what tasks I order?" she continued.

A trickle of dread slid over Zephyr. He kept his head bowed, but lifted his eyes to his queen as he swore, "I am yours to command. That is unchanged."

For a long moment, no word was spoken. He stayed on his knees, and his eyes didn't waver. He'd wanted this, her approval, for years. He'd wanted to belong, to *matter*. The things he'd expected and prepared for had changed, but Zephyr was still filled with the longing he'd always felt.

"I would give you a boon," Endellion offered. "A token from the head of your family to show my pleasure in your service."

Zephyr shook his head slightly. "Serving you is enough."

She laughed, not mockingly but in what seemed to be honest amusement. "There will be tasks aplenty, and those who will test you for who you now are. My husband's sons often attempt to kill Rhys." Endellion gifted Rhys with a look of undeniable pride. "He is second only to me in his swordsmanship. He will train you."

"As you wish," Rhys murmured.

"I don't often bestow blessings, Zephyr. Speak," the queen asked.

"Alkamy," he blurted.

"Oh?" The queen tilted her head and studied him, and Zephyr knew that he'd said the wrong thing. After all of his efforts to keep Alkamy safe, he'd just put her too much in the queen's attention by asking for her.

"Her safety," he added quickly, trying to lessen the weight of his revelation. "She's my best friend and a trusted member of the team. She thinks clearly, and her ability to plan—"

"You are requesting that she is kept safer than the rest of my Sleepers," the queen prompted, her voice completely emotionless in the way that only true fae can manage.

Zephyr swallowed before he could reply. "Yes."

"You feel for her."

"She's my best friend," he hedged.

Endellion stood. "I will grant you this boon, Grandson." She stepped close to him, her feet almost touching his bent knees. "You may also mate with the girl for now. I have plans that will require your involvement, but . . . I will spare her from further missions if possible."

At her words, Zephyr was both terrified and relieved. Being told one was a part of Endellion's plans wasn't something that anyone could hear without feeling afraid. However, Alkamy was . . . if not safe, then safer. For now, that was more than a fine trade-off.

"May I ask who fathered her?"

Endellion cupped the side of his face. "You may not."

He wanted to bow his head again, but she held fast.

"I will treat you above those who are not my blood, but that requires that you earn my respect, Zephyr."

"I will do my best," he swore.

The Queen of Blood and Rage patted his cheek like he was a pet, and then she stepped past him and strode to the door.

Rhys followed in her wake again, grabbing Zephyr by the elbow and hauling him to his feet in a fluid movement. They reached the door to the room again, but as Endellion reached to open it, the door flung inward.

In a fraction of a moment, both Rhys and Endellion had drawn swords. Zephyr fumbled, having no weapon of his own.

Rhys shoved him toward the wall of weapons with a terse, "Arms."

Zephyr was only two steps away from his father, when the queen's voice snapped, "What were you thinking coming in here without notice? I could've stab—"

"I was thinking that time was crucial," the newcomer answered.

Zephyr glanced back at them. The queen still had her sword unsheathed, as did Rhys. His, however, was pointed at the floor. The queen kept hers upraised.

The newcomer gestured at Zephyr and said, "You won't need a sword, boy."

Zephyr looked—not to Rhys—but to the queen.

She rewarded him with a flicker of approval in her irritated expression before saying, "Get a weapon, Zephyr. You should always be armed."

He wanted to point out that *she* was why he was unarmed, but that served no purpose beyond easing his pride. Instead, he did as he was told, selecting a longsword from the wall and pulling it down. Then he went to stand on the opposite side of the queen, so he and Rhys flanked her.

Zephyr had a good suspicion as to the identity of the faery who'd entered the queen's throne room. He was a massive man, tall and striking, with skin so dark that he was clearly Seelie. Currently, he took them all in with a bemused expression and said, "I mean Endellion no harm . . . these

337

days. Isn't that right, dearest?"

The Queen of Blood and Rage was glaring at him.

He ignored her and added, "She's still not the easiest woman to be around, but she *is* my wife."

"Fool," the queen muttered. "Again, I say, what are you *doing* here?"

"My sons have vanished," Leith, the once-king of the Seelie and now co-ruler of the Hidden Lands with Endellion, said.

"And you think our granddaughter is with them, I assume," Endellion added.

Leith nodded once. "She is."

Zephyr wanted to ask why the king didn't go after his sons then, why he didn't rescue Lilywhite, but questioning either of the regents seemed foolhardy at best. Getting out without bloodshed was always the goal when it came to dealing with the fae.

"My patience is at an end with them." Endellion stepped around the king, her husband, and strode forward without another word to any of them.

Rhys followed her silently.

Zephyr paused. His queen hadn't ordered him to go or to stay, and truth be told, he would be of little use in a conflict with fighters of her caliber.

The king sighed. "Come on then. She's liable to kill them if I'm not there, and that son of hers isn't much on caution either."

"He's . . . my father," Zephyr said, not quite defending

Rhys but feeling like he should say *something*.

"Of course he is," Leith said cheerily. "My wife has particular plans for the offspring of that experiment. Why do you think all of you are together?"

Zephyr gaped at him.

"The get of those she hand-selected were all put in *your* team, Zephyr. She made sure that you commanded the highest born—the very best."

Then the king sauntered off, whistling cheerily as if they weren't headed toward violence, as if he hadn't dropped a giant revelation on Zephyr, as if all of this was somehow mundane.

Dazedly, Zephyr followed. He wasn't sure if the Seelie King was any less frightening than the Unseelie Queen. At least with Endellion, there was no confusion as to whether or not she was livid. Zephyr couldn't honestly tell if the king was happy or insane.

thirty-three

LILY

Lily paced around the damp cave where they'd been imprisoned, assessing the situation as best she could. Both Torquil and Creed were injured, but she and Violet were fine. It was as if the two Seelie fae outside the cave had forgotten that the most ruthless faery in history was a woman. Lily might not aspire to the ferocity of her grandmother, but she had Endellion's blood in her veins and Daidí's teaching in her mind.

Although she wasn't sure what she was going to do, Lily knew there wasn't long to figure it out. Torquil's wound wouldn't stop oozing blood, and he was drifting in and out of consciousness. Creed appeared to have no permanent damage, but she'd learned many years ago that internal bleeding wasn't always obvious. Violet was uninjured so far, and Lily was . . . being threatened with marriage. *That* wasn't going to happen, not as long as she had any breath left in her.

In the world Lily had known until now, marriages could be dissolved. Divorces were possible, and if that was a problem for some reason, she knew that Daidí would happily remove any unwanted husband in a more permanent way. Unfortunately, Lily suspected that marriage to a Seelie prince, one who lived for a virtual eternity and presumably couldn't be killed without massive consequences, was a bit more complicated. She simply could not, *would* not, allow herself to be forcibly wed—especially to Nacton.

Her only fae advisor was not of much use currently, and Violet and Creed looked to her for answers. So that left Lily to figure out what to do. *First problems first.* She needed everyone alive.

Torquil was flat on his back with a handful of moss clutched to his wound. Violet squatted at his side with a pile of moss that she'd collected. There had been precious little of it, but Lily had coaxed it into growing larger for their purposes.

"Well?"

Violet looked up at her and shook her head. "It's not slowing at all. If he keeps bleeding—"

"So stop the bleeding," Torquil interrupted in a broken voice. "You're *fire*. You can stop it for me."

"You want me to . . . *burn* you?"

"To cauterize the wound. It makes sense," Lily told her gently.

Violet gaped at her. "So I can burn the *good* faery, but not the ones who attacked us? What kind of plan is—"

"The only one we have." Torquil opened his eyes and looked at her. "I know you mean me no harm, Violet Lamb, and I need your help."

He pressed the moss tighter to his side. It was already thick with blood; the dirt turned to red mud and dripped down to pool on the ground beside Torquil.

"Will you help me?" he asked her softly.

Lily considered telling Violet what she suspected of their true relationship, but she wasn't sure if that would help Violet or make her more hesitant to do what he was asking.

Torquil looked at her and shook his head once. Did he somehow know what she was contemplating?

"What?" Violet said. "I *saw* that. What was it? What aren't you telling me?"

"Can you do it or do I need to try to grow the moss again?" Lily snapped.

Violet didn't reply. She looked over at Creed, who was trying to push to his feet. He stumbled toward them.

"Please, Vi. I need you to do this," Lily said.

"I'm so sorry," Violet whispered. Then she brought both hands down on Torquil's bloodied side. With one hand, she jerked the moss away, and with the other, she cupped fire onto his flesh.

Torquil screamed, a horrible raw sound that was more animal than Lily had thought a voice could be, and then he passed out. Violet turned away and vomited as soon as she

342

pulled her hand away.

Creed lifted her with his good arm and pulled her to his side.

Lily couldn't look at them though, couldn't stand seeing Creed hobble away on his broken leg or Violet sobbing after searing a wound. Torquil's skin was sizzling like meat on a grill, and Lily had to pull moisture from the air to cool and wash it. She couldn't draw as much as she wanted because they would need water to drink if they were left here too long, but she washed the blood away so that she could see that the gash was closed, and then she covered it with clean moss and earth to sooth the ache.

Once she'd done all she could, she walked over to Violet and said, "Thank you."

Violet wiped her mouth. "What didn't he want you to say?"

"It's not my—"

"I did as you and *he* asked," Violet cut her off harshly. "Tell me, LilyDark."

"Look at him carefully, Vi," Creed interjected, as he leaned against the wall. "He was there on the night we were all *made*."

Violet stared at him and then glanced at the fae she'd just burned. It didn't take but a heartbeat for her to see it, but she still objected. "He's not . . ." She pursed her lips, not able to utter the lie now that she saw it. "What affinity?"

"Fire," Lily said quietly.

"That doesn't necessarily mean anything," Violet said,

but her gaze was fixed on Torquil. It wouldn't take long for her to admit the truth.

Lily looked at Creed. He shook his head.

"She'll be fine," Creed murmured as Violet walked back over to Torquil and sat at his side.

"Assuming we walk away from this."

"Yes. Assuming that." Creed stroked her cheek with his fingertips.

Lily exhaled loudly. "You seem fine with this . . . Honestly, between you and Zeph, I'm starting to feel like it's odd *not* to be okay with dying." She scowled at Creed. "We're getting out of here."

"Yes, ma'am," Creed said lightly. "What do we do then?"

At that, Lily's burst of confidence fled. "I don't know. We're unarmed. Torquil is . . . I just don't know." She met Creed's eyes and confessed, "I don't know what to do."

Creed reached out for her hand and squeezed it. He didn't offer empty words. He simply held on to her hand.

After a moment, Lily squeezed back and said, "Come on."

They walked over to Violet, who was still staring at the seemingly unconscious fae. She glanced up at them briefly. "He looks our age. It's weird to think of my mom and—"

"As I understand it, children aren't to think of their parents mating," Torquil said, eyes still closed.

Lily let out a relieved sigh that he was alert. She crouched down and checked the bright red wound. The burned skin was warm, but there was no new blood.

"So, you're my father?" Violet prompted.

Torquil opened his eyes. "I believe so. The queen . . . gave me reason to think that I am. I thought it best not to mention it before you—"

"Burned you?" Violet shrugged. "If you don't die, we can fight about it. Then you can buy me a pony or something."

"A pony?" Torquil glanced at Lily and Creed. "Is this a human custom? Like the goat?"

Before they could answer, Violet said, "So since *Dad* isn't bleeding out, what do you say we get out of here?"

"Nacton and Calder are full fae who have trained longer than you've lived, and I am . . . unwell," Torquil objected. "You are not a match for them on your own."

Violet simply stared at Lily and waited. They needed a plan. Unfortunately, Lily hadn't come up with one—and she had no idea how long they had before their captors came back.

"Vi's right. If we stay, you'll die. All of you." Lily pulled her hair back into a twist. "Our options are escape, die trying, or die by *not* trying."

"Easy choices, as far as I'm concerned." Creed looked at her. "I pledged myself to you once, Lily. I can say it again if you need, but the reality is that if you need me to buy you time to escape, I'll gladly do so." He gestured to Torquil. "I won't have him or Vi doing it."

"Back up, boy." Violet's temper finally sparked, setting off a mini light show in the dark cavern. "One of us can set fires to idiots, and one of us sings pretty songs. Guess which is more useful?"

"He can do a bit more than that," Lily pointed out. "Part of working with air means stopping it too."

For a second, Violet stared at him as she processed what that meant practically. "Suffocation. That's good. We can use that."

Creed winced. While he was apparently fine with being injured, he seemed less so with injuring anyone. That, more than anything, told her that he was Seelie. Despite the evidence given by the Seelie princes, the Seelie as a whole were the more gentle court—not by huge measures, but enough to draw the distinction.

"He could feed your fire," Torquil suggested to Violet. "If he's adept enough to suffocate with his affinity, he's good enough to be your aid as you attack."

The smile that came over Violet's face was enough to make Lily shiver.

"I think we're onto a plan then. What do you say, Lily-Dark?" Violet prompted with a grim tone.

"I don't know that *plan* is the correct word, but it's something," Lily agreed. "I think . . . what we need is to fight like *us*, not like fae. You were both raised as guerrilla fighters, and I was raised to be ruthless. Proper swordplay isn't us."

Violet nodded and began twisting her own hair into some sort of knot. "I'm guessing Lily's grandmother isn't going to be very pleased about those two . . . *jerks*. I can't wait to tell her."

"We just need to survive long enough to do that," Creed said.

"True," Lily said.

She looked at Torquil and Creed, assessing their injuries. They weren't anywhere near in fighting shape, but Creed only had to use his affinity.

Torquil extended a hand to Violet. "Hold on to me until I release you. If you're mine, I can lend you my fire."

"What if I'm not?" Violet asked, even as she took his hand in hers.

"Then this will hurt," Torquil murmured.

For several long moments, there was no sound. Then a roar filled the cave, as if a wall of flames surged toward them. Lily looked around. There was no visible fire.

Torquil jerked his hand away, and Violet sighed. Her eyes were solid flame, eerily flickering like she was far from human. When she opened her mouth to speak, her very exhalation was a tongue of flame.

"Don't," Torquil ordered hastily.

Violet turned her gaze on him.

"Not to us," he amended. "Go talk to our captors, Violet."

She stalked out of the cave.

"I may have given her more than I meant to," Torquil said half-apologetically. He stumbled as he stepped forward, and if not for Creed grabbing him, he would've fallen.

"I have him," Creed assured her. "Go."

But Lily was already running after Violet. She caught

up with her as Violet stepped outside the cave. The stones, usually so slow to speak, were all but yelling to Lily. *Go. Go. Go. Hot.*

A long whip of fire snapped out from Violet's hand and grabbed the sword the queen had given Lily. As the sword surged toward Lily, she thought she might be stabbed by it, but the fire retracted as if it had all been inhaled into Violet's body. The sword clattered to the ground a few feet from Lily.

The two Seelie princes, who had been arguing, stumbled toward them. Nacton already had a sword in hand. Calder scrambled toward his.

Lily lunged for her sword, grabbing it and coming back to her feet in as quick of a move as she could manage.

"Are you really this foolhardy?" Nacton stalked toward her.

Lily lifted her sword into position. "I didn't ask for any of this."

She studied him as he moved into a defensive guard. For several minutes, they circled, moving in response to one another. No blows were exchanged. He'd been fighting for longer than she'd lived, longer than her mother had lived.

Lily, however, had been taught to use any resource available to survive. She wasn't fae-born and raised. She was an Abernathy, daughter to *the* crime lord. As Nacton watched her, she moved through various positions, silently answering his every guard with her own. All the while, though, she summoned earth and water.

A scream from behind her almost drew her attention, but she didn't look away from Nacton, not this time.

"The girl is adept," he continued. "That scream was my brother. It's a shame we must fight. Perhaps we could talk instead, Lilywhite."

Nacton's voice grew melodic, and Lily felt herself wanting to smile, to nod, to agree.

"Lower your sword," Nacton suggested.

This time, she did nod.

However, simultaneously, she summoned every root she could call, wrapped them around Nacton, and held him fast.

"How very lacking in honor," Nacton murmured. "Is this how the child of the missing heir acts?"

Another scream, louder this time, drew her attention.

Lily glanced past him to see Calder crab-walking away from Violet. The fiery whip had reshaped into a sword, and Violet was stabbing it into Calder.

"Vi!"

The fury-ridden girl glanced at Lily.

"No *killing*," Lily stressed.

Then she turned back to Nacton. A thorn-covered vine darted out at her will and snatched his sword away. He was pinned and unarmed.

She lifted her sword to his throat, released the vines holding him fast, and asked, "You wanted to talk about honor then?"

thirty-four

LILY

Nacton glared at her, and she pushed the tip of the sword a little tighter to his throat. Maybe it was unnecessary, but Daidí had always stressed that you needed your enemies to know that you were willing to shed their blood. The trickle of blood slipping down the center of Nacton's throat wasn't an accident. From the look on his face, they *both* knew that.

"You shouldn't have crossed me," he said in a voice so low that no one else could've heard him.

"I didn't."

He tilted his head, cutting his own skin further on the sword tip in the process. "You are holding a blade on me. *My* blade."

"True," she allowed. "But this is a response to your crossing me. I didn't seek you out." She slid the tip farther down his throat, trailing it in a line down the center of his chest, and stopped when it was at his sternum. "I could push this in. Puncture a lung."

Instead of looking cowed by her threat, he smiled. "You will be a wonderful bride."

Her hand shook. "I'm not flirting, you idiot. I'm *threatening* you."

Nacton shrugged.

"You threatened me," Lily reminded him. "You held your blade to my throat."

"I did."

Suddenly, the entirety of the vines containing Nacton erupted in fire. Her sword faltered as she jumped backward.

At first Lily thought it was Torquil or Violet, but as the flames retracted into Nacton's body with barely a blink, she realized what *his* primary affinity was. "You could've done that before I disarmed you."

"I have honor."

Lily lifted her sword and slashed at him. "Honor? Seriously? You are trying to *marry me.*"

Nacton's fire extended toward his fallen sword, much as Violet's had done earlier. "The girl is from a strong bloodline," he said calmly as his sword returned to his hand.

When his gaze drifted to Violet, who had pinned Calder to the ground with a net of fire, Lily pulled water from the ground in a giant gush. She soaked all of them in the process, dowsing the fire on Calder, dowsing the remaining flickers in Nacton's hands.

He aimed his hands toward the ground, and fire raced

down his sword to touch the earth. It ran along the ground until it had encircled them.

"Earth and water. A good pair." Nacton inclined his head toward his brother, who was motionless on the ground. "He's air. I taught him years ago that it was useless against fire, but"—he raised his voice—"added to fire, air can be quite . . . useful."

Calder might be injured but he still heeded his brother's order. The flames that Nacton had used to create a circle around them, entrapping her with him, rushed toward the sky.

Lily clutched her sword. Fire was the least of her affinities. She couldn't draw it to her as Violet and Nacton had both done. The earth roiled around her feet as she tried to call both earth and water again. Maybe she could smother the flames.

She tried, pushing mud toward the wall.

Nacton merely smiled and reinforced the fire as he knocked her sword through the wall of flames.

Once again, Nacton was setting the rules. That wasn't going to work, not if Lily had any chance of winning. *Abernathy Commandment #5: Be bold.* She didn't want to kill, but she wasn't willing to be taken captive again.

Lily drew what water she could to herself, letting mud coat her legs, drawing it up her body like a cloak. Then she threw herself across the fire and rolled to grab her sword.

As Nacton dropped the fire and stepped toward her,

she lunged forward and started to sink her blade into his stomach.

"Please do not kill my son, Lilywhite," a man's voice said from behind her. "I have two, but I would rather they both live."

Lily faltered slightly.

Nacton was motionless. The tip of her blade was still in his stomach. He didn't withdraw or move.

"And you, young lady," Leith said to Violet. "You might want to return that fire to your father. He looks weaker than I would like."

Violet stared at Leith, not reacting.

Creed hobbled over to her. "Vi?"

She looked away from Calder, but said nothing.

"Come with me," Creed urged gently. "We're safe now."

For several tense moments, Violet was motionless, flames danced over her entire body. She glanced at Lily, asking questions Lily wasn't entirely sure how to answer. Unlike Creed, she couldn't force her lips to say that they were *safe* yet.

"Lily?" Creed prompted. "Let him go. Tell Vi to do the same."

Slowly, Lily drew her sword out of Nacton's stomach. She didn't lower it, but she pulled back until it was no longer piercing him.

"Vi, go with Creed," Lily said levelly.

Then she moved to the side so she could keep her eyes on Nacton but still see Violet and Creed.

Violet walked away from Calder. With Creed at her side—but not touching her—she went to Torquil and kneeled beside him.

Lily watched Violet's hand shake as she took Torquil's limp hand in her grasp, and for a moment they were both illuminated by fire. Then, it blinked out, and Violet swayed to the side. Creed caught her with a loud grunt of pain, and they both stood beside Torquil's prone body.

"Your sons really need to be leashed, husband," Endellion remarked in a deceptively casual tone, drawing Lily's attention to the queen. "My granddaughter—"

"*Our* granddaughter, Dell," he corrected Endellion. "The child is as much my family as yours, and you would be wise to remember it."

"Don't think I am soft suddenly, husband," Endellion said warningly. "I won't see her treated as *your* sons just did."

"She handled herself admirably." The king graced Lily with an approving smile.

"No thanks to you!" Endellion dropped her hand to her sword. "She isn't trained for—"

"But look how well she did," Leith interrupted. "Look at both of them."

Lily wasn't sure what they were on about, but she didn't particularly like it. Worse still, behind the King and Queen of the Hidden Throne were *throngs* of faeries. Rhys and Eilidh were there. He was holding Eilidh by her arm, as if preventing her from movement, and she was clearly arguing about it.

Violet walked back over to join Lily. "Now what?"

Lily frowned. She had no idea. "Excuse me?" she called.

There was a bleeding Seelie prince in front of her, and another Seelie prince burned and lying on the ground. A third Seelie—one injured in Lily's defense—was motionless beside the cave.

And the regents were speaking together in low tones. Everyone else simply waited on what they would say next.

Surprisingly, Zephyr ignored everyone and everything. He walked past the regents, past the Seelie princes, past Violet and Lily, to reach Creed—who stood like a guard at Torquil's side. The fae-blood boy who had been completely focused on the queen's will ignored everyone to check on his friend and a fae he didn't seem to like much when they'd met.

"He's alive," Zephyr called out.

Seemingly shocked by his son's words, Rhys released Eilidh. As he followed his sister, he paused for a fraction of a moment beside Lily and asked, "Are you well and whole?"

"I am."

"Good," Rhys pronounced. "I would be troubled by Eilidh if I had to discipline Torquil for failing you."

Lily smothered a smile at his grumbling. Now that she knew that he was Zephyr's father, she could see it more fully. Both of them did what they thought best, even if it wasn't always *technically* what was ordered.

"Father?" Nacton said levelly. "Would you ask the girl to lower her blade?"

Lily lifted her sword to his throat again. "*Grandfather*, would you tell your son that it's rude to try to marry a girl without her consent?"

Leith laughed. "You appear to have my wife's temper, Lilywhite."

Violet moved closer to Lily's side.

Endellion's voice was clear and loud enough for every faery there to hear her as she pronounced, "I see no harm in stabbing him again. In fact"—she lifted her own sword—"I think it's a grand idea."

Leith grabbed her sword in his bare hand. "Endellion."

"Then get them out of here before my good mood vanishes," she ordered.

The King of Fire and Truth walked up to Lily and grabbed Nacton. With a nod toward Calder, he told several armed guards, "Take them. We'll discuss this when I'm done here."

The two Seelie sons glared at her, appearing more like petulant children than like adult fae, but they didn't speak as they were escorted away. No one offered them aid or checked their injuries. Of course, no one did anything about the fact that they'd kidnapped her and Violet and injured both Creed and Torquil. The two Seelie princes were simply taken away.

There were no Abernathy commandments that seemed particularly fitting for this situation. She thought idly that she might need to start adding to the list after her encounters with the fae. *Abernathy Commandments for Dealing with Fae: #1—If they try to marry you, a sharp sword is a fine reply.* She smiled at the thought of the list, but then she realized that her grandparents were looking at her expectantly.

"What?" she asked.

Endellion's brows both raised, either at Lily's tone or question. Lily looked beyond her grandmother and saw myriad fae watching as if the entire situation—one that started with threats to her life and was resolved with a sword to Nacton's throat—was a bit of entertainment.

"Show respect, niece," Rhys warned, and then he returned his attention to the injured. "Zephyr, go with the guards who are escorting Torquil and my sister."

Creed hobbled over to join Violet at Lily's side, as two of the armed fae stepped forward to flank Zephyr, Eilidh, and Torquil.

"The king and I are willing to make you our heir," Endellion said, again in a clear voice that everyone there heard.

"I'd rather not," Lily said, just as loudly.

Innumerable gasps filled the air.

The king continued as if Lily hadn't spoken. "I was concerned about the taint of your humanity, but you handle yourself better than most true fae. The queen suggests that perhaps this Nicolas person was not your actual father."

At that, the hold Lily had on her manners slipped away. "I can assure you that Daidí is my father."

She didn't mean to tighten her grip on the hilt of her sword, but she realized she was doing so when Violet whispered, "Stop that."

Endellion smiled and looked pointedly at Lily's hand and then at her face again, obviously quite aware of the reaction Lily was having. "You'll make a fine queen."

"Again, *no*," Lily stressed. "I won't."

The Queen of Blood and Rage stepped away from the king and walked up to Lily. Violet, for reasons of fear or foolishness, did not move back. Neither did Creed. They stayed at her sides.

"No one refuses me," Endellion said. "Not my daughter, not my spouse, not my son . . . and not you, Granddaughter."

"I'm sorry, but I'm not interested in being a queen."

"What if we offer you a trade?" Leith asked, staying where he was. "If Endellion and I were to call a cease-fire against the humans, would you be willing to accept your rightful place?"

Endellion glanced back at the king in barely concealed shock. "How dare you suggest—"

"Our daughter *lived*, Dell, and we have a strong healthy heir right here in front of us," Leith said gently. "That was what we wanted, what *you* planned. Do you still remember? You marched into my court and announced that I would give you a child and share your throne or you'd kill me once and for all."

"Of course, I remember! My baby died. They took her from me—"

358

"But she didn't. *They* didn't." Leith walked over and took Endellion's free hand. "Look at her daughter. We have what you wanted *right here*. We can end the war and the bloodshed. Bring the Sleepers in if they want, and we all stay here where we are meant to be—no more a part of that world. That was what we planned."

For a moment, Endellion tensed, and then she looked past her husband to take in the faces of the fae. Lily could already see the hope on their faces, and she knew her grandmother could too.

"We could discuss it," Lily said cautiously. "If you'd end the war and spare the rest of the Sleepers . . ." Her words faded as the Queen of Blood and Rage met her gaze.

But Endellion gestured for her to continue. "What else is it that you want?"

"I will not be married against my wishes *or* live here full-time," Lily bartered.

"Royal marriages, as with any marriage of high-ranking fae, require my approval," Endellion said levelly, glancing pointedly at Creed. "It is not a decision you can make without my approval."

"*Our* approval," Leith added.

Endellion ignored him.

"Fine," Lily said. "But it cannot be decided without *my* approval either—and you can't gain that through coercion. No blackmail, no threats, no tricks. What they just tried—"

"Was not something I authorized or will authorize." Endellion met Lily's gaze. "Those two . . . wretches will never be approved to marry *my* granddaughter."

At that, Lily smiled. "Thank you."

The queen nodded once. "Queens, however, live with their subjects."

"The Hidden Lands still have a queen *and* a king on the throne." Lily didn't look away from the queen's face as she spoke. "I have a father, duties in the other world, and school."

"Divided time then," Leith said, loud enough to be heard by all assembled. "You would split your time between the worlds, Lilywhite."

"LilyDark," Lily corrected, deciding in that moment that Violet's renaming of her was fitting. She met first her grandfather and then her grandmother's gaze and said firmly, "I am neither Seelie nor Unseelie. We might as well be very clear that I am of *neither* court solely. I am of the light *and* the dark."

Both of her grandparents smiled—Leith widely, and Endellion slightly.

Leith nodded. "Agreed, LilyDark."

She added, "And I belong to neither *world* solely while there is no need to assume the throne."

Leith looked at Endellion, who gave a curt nod.

"Are those *all* of your terms, LilyDark?" Leith asked.

She hesitated. There were more than a few reasons not to make deals with the fae, but the idea of stopping the war was too tempting to ignore. Her friends would be safe. The reality was that now there was nowhere she could truly hide forever, not since she was being claimed as the heir to the Hidden Throne. She hadn't meant to be declared heir, or to impress the regents, or to fight the Seelie princes. She'd simply hoped that talking to the queen, telling her that Iana wasn't killed by the humans that day long ago, might appease her. She'd had a vague hope that the queen would see reason to end her attacks. She'd hoped to spare Zephyr and the rest of the Black Diamonds from the queen's wrath.

Abernathy Commandment #4: Weigh the consequences before beginning a course of action.

She had weighed them, but even being raised as the daughter of Nick Abernathy hadn't prepared her for this situation. There was manipulation and machination, and then there was *fae* manipulation and machination.

"I won't be wed without my consent. I will not be engaged to someone not of my choosing. I will not favor one court over the other or reside solely in the Hidden Lands, nor will I stop being Nicolas Abernathy's daughter," Lily said, reviewing the terms. She paused, thinking over any other terms she might be forgetting.

Abernathy Commandment #15: Always have a way out, more than one if possible.

"And," she added quickly, "if a more suiting heir to the Hidden Throne can be agreed upon by Endellion, Queen of Blood and Rage, and Leith, King of Fire and Truth, I will have the right to return to a normal life."

"But you will not cut your family out of your life," Endellion inserted firmly.

"Agreed," Lily said, feeling—despite everything—touched that her grandmother wanted to know her. The queen was far from an embracing woman, but she obviously cared for her family in her way.

"I accept your offer," she vowed.

"Your terms are accepted, LilyDark, daughter of Iana and the Abernathy, granddaughter of Endellion and Leith," both regents said.

Endellion took Lily's hand in hers and gazed around at the assembled fae. "I present to you your future queen, LilyDark."

Every fae knelt, including Creed and Violet. Her grandparents were the only ones still standing, and Lily felt the weight of the vow settle on her skin. She had stopped the war that her mother's birth had started, but at what cost?

thirty-five

LILY

Returning from the Hidden Lands to a world where the air was thick with pollution shouldn't have felt soothing, but right now it did.

"How are we going to explain this?" Violet gestured at Creed.

He shrugged, still leaning on Zephyr heavily as they walked. "Bar fight."

Zephyr sighed, as if the idea was ludicrous, but he didn't object.

"I'll be fine within a week," Creed reminded them. The queen herself had given him strength that would speed his healing—"to protect my granddaughter," she'd said—so he was already beginning to look as though the fight had been weeks ago.

"A fight? Then how do we explain the way you look

363

healed so fast?" Zephyr shook his head. "We don't want attention. Until we know what the queen decides about coming out to the world, our job is to stay out of the papers—and to keep Lily safe."

Violet let out a laugh. "Hell-*o*, darlings, you have a makeup pro right here. Either we say I've been hiding the proof of the boy's nitwittery while it heals *or* I simply hide it now." She linked her arm with Lily's. "Ninian help us. It's like they need to bicker, you know? If they weren't so tediously *straight*, I'd swear they needed to kiss it out."

Lily laughed, despite the scowls that both boys gave Violet.

"I'm not 'tediously straight,' Vi." Creed flashed her the sort of smile he typically reserved for cameras, and Lily wondered if they had an audience she hadn't yet seen. When he grabbed her arm and pulled her in front of him so she was facing him, Lily knew they must.

"Look down," he whispered.

Laughing, she tugged a little, keeping her face hidden as she did so.

"Zeph's just not the one for me," Creed continued, glancing at Zephyr and grinning.

Violet was at Lily's back then, and she was all but surrounded. A large part of her wanted to object, but Violet and Creed were authorized to guard her. That was one of the terms of her return to the human world. Endellion had wanted to send fae to live at Columba's, as if there was any way that true fae could hide there. Only Leith's intervention had forestalled that plan.

So Lily had agreed to being protected. For now, she'd tolerate it, but if she was going to be the heir to the Hidden Throne, she was going to set some rules of her own. Surely, that was something a princess could do.

"They've gone," Zephyr said suddenly.

"Fae? Humans?" Lily scanned the area as soon as Creed released her.

"All I know was that I heard voices in the air, ones that spoke your name." Creed hobbled toward her. "Let's get to the dorms, yeah?"

"Okay." She squeezed his hand. "But I'm not defense-less. You didn't miss that whole fight with my uncles, did you?"

Zephyr and Violet said nothing. In fact, Zephyr had been unsettlingly quiet since they'd reunited in the Hidden Lands. She hoped he'd be forthcoming about whatever he'd discussed or done with the queen, but if he wasn't . . . well, she wasn't eager to experiment with her affinity for compulsion. It felt wrong to even consider, but she was the heir to the throne now. She had no idea who she could or could not trust—aside from Creed and Violet. They alone were the people she knew she could trust without reservation. She had a general degree of trust for Eilidh, Rhys, and Torquil. She had a strong degree of trust in Zephyr for many things, but he had secrets, and he had loyalties that predated her. If she needed to compel answers from him, she would.

"Alkamy, Roan, and Will are probably worried sick," Lily said. "We can figure everything else out later.

Zephyr did his duty, walking with the others until they reached the dorms. He felt divided from them now, more than ever before. The queen had separated him from them before sending them to meet Leith. He could choose to believe it was for the same reason that she kept Rhys at her side—that her Unseelie descendants weren't welcome there. He wanted to believe that.

He also knew that the Queen of Blood and Rage had machinations inside her plots inside her maneuverings. She had sent Creed and Violet with Lily into what he suspected she knew might be a battle. She'd sent the former heir's betrothed with them. There were more than a few explanations for this that Zephyr could guess. Perhaps the queen wanted Torquil injured or dead. Perhaps she wanted Lily to feel closer to Violet and Creed. If Zephyr thought long on it, he realized that he'd *known* which of the Sleepers to bring. But how? Had the queen known that Creed visited Eilidh? Was anything that had happened to them *not* orchestrated?

He sighed.

"Are you okay?" Lily asked gently. "I don't know what happened when we were away but—"

"I saw a bit of the palace, talked to the queen." Zephyr shrugged. "She explained that I would need to be trained by my . . . by *Rhys*, so I can earn her respect. Then the king arrived."

"Uh-huh." Violet stared at him, not quite calling him a liar, but the statement was there whether she said it aloud or not. "She just kept you back to tell you to be a good boy?"

"Vi," Lily said warningly.

Zephyr opened the door to the tunnels. "It's okay, Lily. Maybe Violet's adopting *her* court's dislike for mine. Her father is Seelie after all."

Violet made a rude gesture, a well-illuminated one as her hand glowed with fire to light their way in the tunnel.

"There is only one court, Zephyr," Lily corrected him. "Unless both Eilidh and I are killed, there is a united court. One throne. One court."

He nodded. There might be, but it didn't feel that way— not to him and not to a lot of the fae he had seen. They divided themselves among their kind even as they watched both their king and queen. There were still rifts.

"You heard the princess," Creed said in a cheerier voice than Zephyr was used to. "One court. One throne . . ."

He started humming to himself, slipping into some sort of space in his head where he went when he was writing music. That alone was proof that he was feeling better than he had in well over a year and a half. Creed hadn't been writing, just drinking between concerts. Violet looked at Creed and smiled. She knew as well as everyone on their team, other than Lily, that Creed had been very near the edge until she arrived.

Zephyr opened the door to the dorms.

"Do you think they're in your room or—"

"I know where Kam is," Zephyr interrupted. He walked away, toward his room. The others could do whatever they wanted. Tonight, he was abdicating all responsibility for them. Honestly, probably for more than just tonight. Everything had changed. They were no longer the queen's seven Black Diamonds. He was no longer in charge.

Now, he answered only to the Queen of Blood and Rage.

Creed and Violet answered to Lily.

He wasn't at all sure what that would mean for Will and Roan, but he knew—he'd always known—what Alkamy would do.

Zephyr didn't quite run to his suite, but it was a close thing.

He slowed when he reached the door, schooling his face, trying to seem like everything was okay. Then he opened the door.

"Kam?"

She was in his arms, flinging across the room like a blur. "Thank Ninian," she whispered as her arms tightened around him. "I was so worried and . . . Is everyone else okay?"

"They are. Lily's burned, but . . . not that bad. And Creed was stabbed, and his wrist is broken but . . ."

Alkamy leaned back, looking at him. "That's not what I'd call *okay*, Zeph."

"No one died. Lily was declared heir. I was openly announced as the queen's grandson . . . oh, and Violet met her father."

At first, Alkamy's mouth opened silently. Then she closed it and shook her head. Finally, she said, "Come sit with me. Tell me the rest . . . unless you want to join the others?"

"No. I really don't." He took her hand in his. "I need to tell you something else though."

"Bad?"

"No." He took a breath, trying to find the words. He didn't want her to misunderstand, to think it was only about physical things. It wasn't. Even before he admitted to himself that he loved her, it had never been only the physical between them.

"You're scaring me," she said, even though her voice sounded steady.

"The queen offered me a boon . . . a gift for serving her so well," he started.

"And?"

"And I asked for you, your safety above the rest of the team—"

"Oh, Zeph," she interrupted. "That's not fair to—"

"I don't care," he cut her off. "I'm Unseelie-born; my father is *her* son. Do you honestly think I'm going to be a fair person? I've tried, but . . . I *love* you, and if the queen is going to let me have anything, it's your safety I'll take."

Alkamy smiled a little. "So that's it? I'm . . . safe?"

Slowly, he walked toward his bedroom, holding her hand in his. "That's what I *asked* for. What she offered me was permission to be with you."

"No strings?"

Zephyr laughed. "I'm sure there were, and I'll agree to whatever they are. That's how negotiations with the fae work."

Alkamy stopped and stepped closer to him. "So are you asking me to stay here then? Here in this room with you?"

"We don't have to do anyth—"

His words were lost under her bubble of laughter. "You can be awfully dense, Zephyr Waters. I'd have stayed in your bed *against* the queen's orders. You are the one who was all about her rules . . . or are you forgetting that?"

He wasn't. He wouldn't. He'd follow every rule he had to for her safety. She didn't get that, but it didn't matter now. Zephyr scooped her up into his arms and carried her the rest of the way to his bed.

"Tell me again," he asked.

"I love you, Zephyr."

He sank down beside her and kissed her. There was no telling what would come next. Zephyr wasn't so foolish as to believe that things were going to be peaceful simply because Lily had accepted her role as heir, or that he was going to be absolved of duties to the queen. Everyone else seemed to think they had a victory, but their trip to the Hidden Lands had put them more fully under the queen's control than they'd ever been. He had no idea what that would mean in the coming days, but right now, he'd enjoy the one good thing that had happened. He had permission to be with Alkamy, and he fully intended to enjoy every possible second of time with her.

LILY

Days turned into weeks, and the only contact Lily had with the Hidden Lands was a strange leaf-wrapped package. It was hand-delivered to her door by a courier that was obviously more fae than not.

Everyone but Creed was out. These days, she was never truly alone. Sometimes she thought it was worse than being with the guards Daidí assigned.

Daidí. Soon, she'd need to tell him what had happened. Today, though, she had to figure out whether a fae-blood courier making it all the way to her suite door should terrify her or comfort her. Her instinct was not toward comfort.

"How did he get that close? Did you know—" Creed's words stopped suddenly when the leaves unfurled to reveal a crown of black diamonds.

At least, it had looked like a crown at first, but as Lily

lifted it, the seemingly solid metal appeared to melt into a serpentine rope. At a second touch, it reshaped into an ornate crown.

Creed lifted a letter from the package and held it out so they could both read it.

LilyDark,

There will be need of something official in the coming weeks. Until such time, your crown can be worn as a necklace to protect your privacy. Do not remove it until it is required for ceremony and revelation. You'll know when. Until such time, you should wear it as a sign to any fae-blood or fae that to mean ill to you is tantamount to treason.

Endellion & Leith

The thought of "something official" filled her with terror, but a cease-fire was apparently the sort of thing one announced.

"I *really* need to talk to Daidí before this 'official thing' actually happens." She held her crown, not wanting to ever wear it, not wanting to do anything that made the world know that she was the heir to the Hidden Throne.

Being fae-blood was still illegal, and she was fairly sure that the laws didn't vanish simply because her blood happened to be the same as the blood of the Queen of Blood and Rage. If anything, being the queen's granddaughter was more likely to get her arrested.

And if Lily was arrested, the cease-fire would end. That

wouldn't undo her vow to her grandparents ... but it would give them a new reason to attack.

"Do you want me to come with you to see your father?" Creed offered. He was rubbing his hands up and down her arms soothingly. "I can. We *all* can if you want."

Lily nodded. As much as she didn't want them there when she asked questions of her father, questions about her mother and about him, she *did* want them with her. They were a part of her life now, and until her life ended, they would be.

Creed took the crown from her hands and stepped behind her. Once it became pliant and lengthened, he lowered it over her head. The weight of it felt heavier than it should.

As Lily reached up to touch it, she wondered how she was to walk around with such grossly expensive jewelry on her every day. There had to be a way to hide it. Her fingers traced the stone and metal, and whatever it was wrought of seemed to be sinking into her skin. Within a fraction of a moment, it was nothing more than skin under her fingers.

"You have a tattoo," Creed said, staring at her throat. "Can you undo it?"

Cautiously, she traced her fingertips over the warm skin where she knew the crown was hidden, thinking that she wanted to see it, and it became solid in the instant the thought was finished. Just as quickly, she returned it to ink on her flesh.

"Well then." Creed kissed her tattoo. "That's certainly

easier than the way I got mine."

They were snuggled up in one chair, her nestled in his arms, when the door burst open, and three of the five other Black Diamonds trouped into the suite.

"The boys are studying for some test or something," Violet announced with a huff as she dropped onto the sofa.

At Lily's questioning look, Zephyr added, "They kicked her out."

"Ah."

"It isn't as if it matters," Violet said with the sort of pet-ulant grace that made all of them bite back smiles. "This whole school thing doesn't matter."

"I dare you to say that to Will," Creed teased.

Lily was so amused by Violet's dedicated pouting that she startled when Alkamy asked, "What is *that?*"

Every eye turned to Lily.

"Crown? Necklace? Tattoo? It sort of depends." Lily ran her fingers over the hollow of her throat. "My grandparents sent it. I guess there will be some sort of 'great reveal' about the end of the war, and I'll need a crown for it."

"So they're *outing* you?" Alkamy all but breathed the question. "As not just fae, but *the fae heir?*"

"Looks like it," Lily said in a voice not nearly as casual as she would've liked.

Creed wrapped both arms around her. "You won't be alone. If you're out, so am I."

"Ditto," Violet said.

"If they tell us to do so, we will." Zephyr had his

I'm-in-charge voice. "I'm sure the queen has a plan, and until then—"

A loud knock on the door interrupted him.

"Lily?" The knock resumed. "I'm looking for Lilywhite Abernathy."

It felt like both parts of her world were colliding as Lily stood and walked to the door. None of the others spoke, although Creed stood. She glanced back at him and said, "I'm sorry, but I need to . . . just wait . . . let me talk to him."

Then she opened the door and said, "Erik?"

"Lily."

She stepped aside, and Erik walked into the sitting room of her suite.

The only person there whom Erik had met before was Creed, but that didn't matter. Erik was as confident here as he was anywhere. He might not have his guards nearby. He might even not be carrying a weapon. The lines of his suit were clean enough that if he did have a gun, it was under his arm in a concealed holster.

He surveyed them briefly, and she recognized the wary way he responded when he realized that even armed, he might be out-powered here. "Is there somewhere we can speak, *querida*?"

"Here." She gestured at the rest of the group. "They are my friends, Erik. We can speak freely."

He surveyed them, gaze lingering a touch longer on both Creed and Zephyr. He shook his head. "It would be best—"

"We're not leaving," Violet said. She came to her feet, which made her eye level with his chest.

Still, Erik recognized her as a person worth treating with caution. He nodded at her before turning to Lily and pulling her into his arms. "Fine. I've come to take you home."

Lily stared at him.

Before she could reply, Creed stood and walked out of the room.

After a significant look at Alkamy, Zephyr followed him.

"We have this," Alkamy promised. "We'll be *right* back." She shot a glare at Erik before she followed the boys.

Only Violet remained. She was making no move to give Lily any privacy with Erik. Instead she folded her arms over her chest, crossed her legs, and said, "You're not getting out of my sight, especially with Mr. Tall, Dark, and Pushy, so don't even think about it."

Lily smiled. Despite everything, Violet was unflappable. She didn't seem to grasp that she could be wrong or unwelcome. *Ever.* Right now, though, she was exceptionally welcome.

"You're that actress," Erik said suddenly.

"And you're that criminal," Violet said drolly. "Now, on to the part where you explain yourself to Miss Lily-Dark."

"Lilywhite," he corrected.

Violet laughed. "Oh, sweetie, you couldn't be further from warm on that one. You just don't know it yet."

"Vi," Lily started.

377

"Shutting up now."

Erik looked at Lily. "Can you *please* lead me to your room so we can pack?" He gestured toward the three closed doors. "Which one?"

"I'm not going anywhere, Erik."

"I saw the pictures, Lily. You were *bruised*, and he had you restrained by the arm. He's just lucky I didn't address his mistake today."

"No! You don't understand—" She stopped herself before she tried to explain. She couldn't say that she'd been injured trying to keep secrets from the former heir of the Unseelie Court, who was her uncle. There was nothing she could say truthfully. Telling Erik her secrets was one thing; revealing everyone's was something else entirely. She settled on, "There's been a misunderstanding. Creed wasn't restraining me, and he certainly hadn't *hurt* me. I swear it, Erik. He would *never* hurt me—any more than you would."

Erik scowled. "*Someone* did though. I'm here to bring you home."

"But Daidí said the house wasn't safe enough. I do need to talk to him tho—"

"No. To *my* home. I can protect you from the law *and* from the monsters." Erik pulled her stiff body into his arms so he could whisper in her ear. "I know what you are, Lily. I've known for years. I'll keep you safe and hidden. Just come with me. You don't even need to pack."

She pulled away. "Oh, Erik . . . I can't run. Not now. I just . . . I can't. I'll explain. I promise, but I need to go get Creed first." She turned to Violet and asked, "Keep him here?"

Violet nodded.

"And Vi? *Don't hurt him,*" Lily added.

The petite girl smiled broadly. "Oh, ye of little faith . . ."

Lily rolled her eyes. Maybe the fae *were* the monsters, and maybe in the end she'd still be unable to be with Creed. After the bargain she'd made with her grandparents, she had less control over her future than she'd ever thought possible, but unless Endellion and Leith *ordered* her to stop seeing Creed and move to the Hidden Lands, she was going to spend as much time as she had with him.

Without another word to Erik or Violet, Lily yanked the door open and ran out into the hallway to catch Creed before he was too far out of reach.

When she found him headed toward the exit of the building, she yelled, "Creed Morrison! Stop. Right. There." It was the first time she'd used her affinity for air so forcefully. Her words grabbed his body and held like an anchor. He could shake it off if he wanted, but he didn't.

Zephyr and Alkamy, who were trying to talk to him, both looked at her with curious looks, but Lily's attention was on Creed. He folded his uninjured arm over his chest and stared at her. He didn't move to shove away the air that gripped his arms.

"Why?"

Ignoring the stares they were all getting now, Lily walked across the stone floor almost fast enough to be called a run.

The stones sang out to her, *heir, little queen, danger,* but she didn't have time to hear any of it. Her sole priority was the beautiful boy who was obviously trying to hide the hope and worry in his eyes.

"You're an idiot," she breathed.

"You made a vow to me," he said.

"And I kept it." She poked him in the chest. "Which you would've known if you hadn't stormed out. I'm not going anywhere. My heart is already taken."

Creed caught her hand and kissed it. "Truly?"

Lily shrugged. "I have a thing for moody, impulsive singers."

"So you're not leaving?"

She put both hands on his chest. "Is that enough for right now? Are you willing to settle? To put up with Daidí *and* my grandparents?"

He said nothing, just pulled her closer and kissed her until Lily thought that the only reason they hadn't run out of breath was that they were both air affinities. If not for the sudden applause that she could hear, Lily wasn't sure she'd have ever been able to stop kissing Creed.

When he pulled back and smiled at her, he slung an arm around her shoulders and said, "So, I know a place we can sunbathe in private."

Alkamy giggled, and Zephyr muttered, "Just walk, you two. This is far more of an audience than Lily needs."

Creed rolled his eyes. "Garden?"

"Umm, I need to check on Erik first. I left him with

Vi." Lily shot a guilty look over her shoulder. "Erik was my friend before he tried to be anything else. I owe him more of an explanation, and I obviously need to talk to Daidí, and I still need to figure out where I factor in the queen's decision to call a cease-fire in the war and—"

"*We* need to do that, Lily," Zephyr said. "We're still a team."

"One thing at a time." Alkamy reached out and squeezed Lily's hand. "Smile pretty, princess. Everyone's staring at you since that kiss. It'll be in the papers *despite* the no-photos-at-Columba's rule."

"Black Diamonds Commandment #1," Creed whispered. "We're in this together."

With the practiced calm that all four of them had mastered by now, the group headed back toward the dorms. They'd figure it out.

Together.

Acknowledgments

Some of the usual suspects need thanks:

Jeaniene Frost, Kelley Armstrong, and Jeanette Battista read and kept me sane(ish) while writing. I'd hide a body for all/any of you.

Neil provided shelter and space where the words are many and the peace is endless. Sending much love to you, as always.

Merrilee gave me the mad enthusiasm and faith that makes me think she might be a wee bit crazier than me. I'm grateful for having you in my corner.

Susan Katz, Kate Jackson, Jean McGinley, Alison Donalty, and Colleen O'Connell have been with me at Harper for eight (?!) novels before this one. Having a team like you has made all the difference over the years. Thank you.

Additional thanks must go to:

Laura Kalnajs read, reread, reread this book again—and scrawled margin notes every time . . . all while reminding me of the things I need to do, sign, or attend. You are a gift.

Diana Santillán double-checked my Spanish. (Who knew that a friendship from seventh grade would lead to such an odd request, umm, a *few* years later?) Thank you, Di.

Youval Kuipers walked me through various sword-fighting scenarios (and convinced me that I needed to have a sword in my hand in order to do so). You've been completely unexpected.

Kristen Pettit (my new YA editor) thought a three-word pitch ("faery sleeper cells") was *actually* the start of a new book and patiently listened when I went on folklore digressions in conversations. Thank you for being hard-core in slashing my prose.

Extra gratitude needs to be sent to:

Cynthia Omololu, who listened and laughed when I was writing this. I love you (enough to constantly try foods you hold out, even *eel* because your son gave me puppy eyes, too!).

My son Dylan, who doesn't hold my frequent travel or bad cooking skills against me.

My spouse, who has marginally better cooking skills and excellent toddler-wrangling skills.

My toddler, who thinks that my job is either "go *avion*"

(plane) or "drink cat pee" (coffee) and is sure I need kisses to do so. (He's right.)

My readers and reviewers, who have been buying my books and/or borrowing them from the library for ten years now. Thank you for a decade of support. XO.

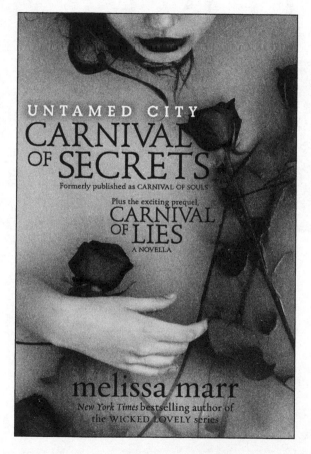

JOIN THE

Epic Reads
COMMUNITY

THE ULTIMATE YA DESTINATION

◀ **DISCOVER** ▶
your next favorite read

◀ **MEET** ▶
new authors to love

◀ **WIN** ▶
free books

◀ **SHARE** ▶
infographics, playlists, quizzes, and more

◀ **WATCH** ▶
the latest videos

◀ **TUNE IN** ▶
to Tea Time with Team Epic Reads